ELOISA JAMES

Four Nights
with the
DUKE

AVON

An Imprint of HarperCollinsPublishers

AVON BOOKS
An Imprint of HarperCollins*Publishers*
195 Broadway
New York, New York 10007

Copyright © 2015 by Eloisa James
ISBN 978-0-06-222391-3
www.avonromance.com

First Avon Books mass market printing: April 2015

Avon Trademark Reg. U.S. Pat. Off. and in Other Countries, Marca Registrada, Hecho en U.S.A.
HarperCollins® is a registered trademark of HarperCollins Publishers.

Printed in the U.S.A.

10 9 8 7 6 5 4 3 2 1

Four Nights with the Duke

With one swift movement, Vander dropped both his and Mia's reins, caught her around the waist, lifted her from her sidesaddle, and pulled her up and over until she was seated in front of him.

Mia gasped. "What do you think you're doing?"

He looked at her silently, and then his mouth came to hers, the kiss open-mouthed, as if they were speaking to each other. Her right side was plastered against Vander's chest and he had one of his hands tangled in her hair, and his tongue . . .

Feeling swept through her body, crashing into her like a thunderstorm.

The way two tongues met . . . it was carnal. She had clutched his coat, certain she was about to fall; now her fingers curled into thick, soft hair.

Another moment and parts of her body were hotter than others. A sound like a growl came from Vander's throat. Mia responded as if a piece of silk were being drawn across her naked body.

She pressed even closer and Vander's grasp tightened. Mia melted against him as if she had no bones. As if he could do whatever he wished to her.

Then he stopped. "Any interest in requesting one of those allotted nights?" he asked, his eyes impenetrable.

It took her a moment but she croaked, "Request? Don't you mean that I should beg for a night? Never!"

With one swift movement, he deposited her back in her saddle.

By Eloisa James

FOUR NIGHTS WITH THE DUKE
THREE WEEKS WITH LADY X
ONCE UPON A TOWER
AS YOU WISH
WITH THIS KISS (a novella in three parts)
SEDUCED BY A PIRATE (a novella)
THE UGLY DUCHESS
THE DUKE IS MINE
WINNING THE WALLFLOWER (a novella)
A FOOL AGAIN (a novella)
WHEN BEAUTY TAMED THE BEAST
STORMING THE CASTLE (a novella)
A KISS AT MIDNIGHT
A DUKE OF HER OWN
THIS DUCHESS OF MINE
WHEN THE DUKE RETURNS
DUCHESS BY NIGHT
AN AFFAIR BEFORE CHRISTMAS
DESPERATE DUCHESSES
PLEASURE FOR PLEASURE
THE TAMING OF THE DUKE
KISS ME, ANNABEL
MUCH ADO ABOUT YOU
YOUR WICKED WAYS
A WILD PURSUIT
FOOL FOR LOVE
DUCHESS IN LOVE

Coming Soon

SEVEN MINUTES IN HEAVEN

For the wonderful writer Cathy Maxwell,
who told me tales of passionate Arabian horses
grieving for their loved ones,
and then sent me a photo of herself
on a gorgeous steed that became
the model for Jafeer.

And for my husband, Alessandro,
who gives me the joy I share with readers.

Acknowledgments

My books are like small children; they take a whole village to get them to a literate state. I want to offer my deep gratitude to my village: my editor, Carrie Feron; my agent, Kim Witherspoon; my writing partner, Linda Francis Lee; my website designers, Wax Creative; and my personal team: Kim Castillo, Anne Connell, Franzeca Drouin, and Sharlene Martin Moore. Jody Gayle lent her expertise with regard to magazines in the period, as did Carola Dunn with the etiquette and appointments of private boxes at Regency racecourses. In addition, people in many departments of HarperCollins, from Art to Marketing to PR, have done a wonderful job of getting this book into readers' hands: my heartfelt thanks goes to each of you.

Prologue

Spring, 1787
A Music Recital
The Duke of Villiers's townhouse

At fifteen, Emilia Gwendolyn Carrington already had a pretty good idea of what hell was like. Mia's governess had taught her all about Dante's nine infernal circles.

Mia's first circle had required her to make her debut at fifteen, under the aegis of a hired chaperone, because her mother was dead. Her second circle had added a far worse indignity: her charming, widowed father was conducting a flagrant *affaire* with a married duchess that everyone in the fashionable world knew about.

She had entered the third circle over the last year or so, when against all reason, she had fallen desperately in love with the same duchess' son, Vander. He was the most sensitive, intelligent boy in the world (or so Mia thought). And he was beautiful too, with a face that resembled the stone angels that guarded babies' graves.

The remaining circles of hell? All six?

They were revealing themselves in rapid succession. Mia had begged her father to attend the Villiers's musicale on the chance that the object of her adoration, Evander Septimus Brody, future Duke of Pindar, would be present. It seemed probable since the Duke of Villiers's eldest son, Tobias, was best mates with Vander.

As it turned out, the house was indeed overrun with boys on holiday from Eton and among the horde was Vander, who roundly ignored her. Mia didn't mind that: she was happy worshipping him from afar. He was too godlike for someone like her.

Besides, it wasn't as if he danced attendance on any other girl. He and the other Etonians spent their time swigging brandy although it was not yet noon, cursing loudly, and generally pretending to be far older than their fifteen years. Mia finally retreated to the library, a tranquil room with book-lined walls.

She was searching the shelves for anything resembling her favorite novel, Eliza Heywood's *Love in Excess*, when she heard, to her horror, the sound of boys approaching. Even worse, she quickly recognized the voices as those of Vander and his friend Tobias, who seemed to be calling himself Thorn these days.

The library was at the end of the corridor, so there was no escape. Panicked, Mia dashed behind the sofa and slid down until she was entirely concealed.

It was only then that she truly understood that she had entered that final, innermost circle of hell.

The boys were discussing a love poem.

Not just any love poem, either.

They were puzzling over *The Love Song of E. Septimus Brody*—in other words, a poem addressed explicitly to Vander—that Mia herself had written. That she had poured her heart, her love, and her tears into.

It wasn't very good; none of her poems were very good.

Still, it was her poem, and it was supposed to be safely in her desk back home. Not being bandied about at a musicale. And definitely not in the hands of the very boy she'd written it about.

Even in the midst of a wave of nausea, Mia guessed what had happened. Her father had found the poem and thought it would be amusing to share with his mistress, and his mistress had in turn shared it with her son. Mia had been such a fool to give it that title.

At least Vander wasn't howling with laughter, probably because he couldn't understand it. He and Thorn were hardly literary types, if a fifteen-year-old boy could be such a thing.

"Do you suppose the part about how *moonbeams kiss the sea* is some sort of innuendo?" Thorn asked.

Mia rolled her eyes. What an absurd suggestion. He probably still moved his lips when he read.

"I don't think so," Vander answered, rather uncertainly. "Let's toss it in the fire. I don't want anyone to see it."

She had scarcely breathed a sigh of relief when there was a clatter of boots and a boy shouted, "I've been looking all over for you fellows. One of the Villiers twins just threw up from nerves. It *stinks* down there!"

"I can't imagine why you were looking for us, Rotter," Vander stated, sounding all of a sudden like a future duke. "We told you last week that we wanted nothing more to do with you."

"Bloody hell, no need to be nasty," the boy retorted, entirely unmoved by this set-down. "What have you got there?" To Mia's horror, the question was followed by the sound of a scuffle and tearing paper.

If Dante had conceived of a tenth circle of hell, this was it. Francis Oakenrott was a boy as rotten as his name implied. She had met him twice, at house parties her father dragged her along to. It was a case of mutual loathing-at-first-sight.

"A love poem," he shouted, clearly delighted. "Don't tell me that you've taken up with an opera dancer with a literary bent. The headmaster will have your guts for garters."

"Give me that," Vander snarled.

But Oakenrott apparently evaded capture. "Blazing hell, this is utter rubbish!" He broke into an escalating, barking laugh. Another thump followed. "Oh, for God's sake, back off and let me read it. It's too late to keep your little secret now. You'd think you were ashamed."

Mia pulled a sofa pillow over her face with a silent groan. She wanted to die, to fall into a crack in the floor.

"*I am mad with love,*" Oakenrott recited, in a squeaky falsetto. "You know, I could see this on the stage. Have you been hanging about the back door of Drury Lane?"

"She's definitely cracked," Thorn said. "Who could fancy a smelly, sweaty bloke like you?"

"You're just jealous," Vander retorted. "She'd have to be barmy to look in your direction. Or Rotter's."

"So who's the madwoman?" Oakenrott said, paper rustling as he turned it over. "Emilia *Carrington*? You mean the daughter of your mother's—"

"Don't," Vander warned, his voice suddenly dangerous.

There was a telling moment of silence. "Right. I'll just go back to this literary masterpiece. *No one understands my plight,*" he read, his voice squealing even higher. "I like this part about the *moonbeam kissing the sea.* Obviously, you have the moonbeam, and she's the sea." He went into another barking cascade of guffaws. A sob rose up Mia's chest, pressing so hard that pain shot through her breastbone.

"You're such an ass," Thorn said. "How old is that girl, anyway?"

"The same as me," Vander replied. "Fifteen."

"*In my dreams, you married me,*" Oakenrott said, reading from the beginning of the next stanza. A tear slid down Mia's neck. "*Your beauty makes me drunk.*"

Oakenrott hooted. Vander groaned.

She heard a hearty slap and then Thorn said, "Look at it this way, at least you've managed to charm a girl who knows a thing or two about brandy."

"Not as much as you do, after last night!" Vander retorted.

Likely they were all drunken sots. Mia's governess had told her that boys pretending to be men drank far too much.

Oakenrott was relentless; he just wouldn't shut up. "*My room is full of moonlight, and your eyes are like pearls.* Do you suppose you're being invited to take your pearly eyes into her moonlit room?"

"I'd have to grope my way," Vander said, and Mia could hear the laughter in his voice. "Nobody could see through pearly eyes."

Mia's lips involuntarily shaped a curse word that she would never dare say aloud.

Oakenrott whistled. "Pearls? You know what kind of pearls she's really talking about, right? Pearl drops! Pearly potions, like we used to call it back in first form. No—wasn't it pearly passion potions?

Something like that. Anyway, this is the first poem I've ever read that talked about love custard!"

Suddenly all three boys were laughing hysterically.

"Love custard"? Mia hadn't the faintest idea what that meant, but she knew instinctively that it was something disgusting. Boys were disgusting by nature; she'd temporarily forgotten that while pining for Vander. When she thought he was god-like.

In reality he was a heartless pig.

"You haven't gotten under her skirts, have you?" Oakenrott sounded gleeful at the prospect. "Her father could take this line about being *lost in your sweetness* and pressure you to make an offer."

"Never!" Vander sounded so appalled that the word slid over Mia's skin like a snake. "It's a little odd to think that she's been lusting after me. What sort of fifteen-year-old girl thinks in these terms? Though I suppose she is her father's daughter."

Mia could hardly breathe because she was trying to sob without noise. He made her sound repulsive, saying that she was lusting after him. It wasn't like that. She wasn't like that.

"Have you ever noticed her staring at you from the side of the room?" Thorn asked. "Because here it says, *Like the bird that gazes all night at the moon, I gaze at you.*"

"Like a bird, or a Bird of Paradise?" Oakenrott put in. "Maybe she can set herself up as a literary light-skirt. One sovereign for a poem and two for a you-know-what."

"All I can say is she's a God-awful poet," Vander said. "Even I know that poems are supposed to rhyme."

What an idiot. Mia took a shuddering breath. She

had to escape. She simply could not stand any more of this.

"I think you should frame it," Thorn said, "because I can tell you right now that no one else will think you're pretty enough to rhapsodize about. Especially given the size of your moonbeam."

That brought on a scuffle and more laughter. At her expense. Mia could feel the air rattling in her throat. Likely it was the death rattle. Maybe she would die, and they'd find her body in this very spot.

"You know, I have to warn the fellows," Oakenrott said. "Some bloke might be chatting with her right now, having no idea what a jam tart she is."

Mia stiffened.

"If she's like that at fifteen, what'll she be like at twenty?"

"Don't even jest about it. You'd ruin her," Thorn said sharply. "You mustn't say a word."

"The poetry is evidence for the obvious," Oakenrott protested. "She's got a sluttish look about her. It's all there. Most girls that age have apple dumplings in front, but hers are more like cabbages than cherries!"

Cabbages? *Cabbages?*

Mia stifled another sob. There was silence for a second, just long enough so that Mia could imagine Vander standing up for her, like a knight in shining armor. Growling, *Shut your mouth, Oakenrott. She does not look sluttish.*

That didn't happen.

"There's no need to issue warnings," Vander said flatly. "There isn't a fellow in this house who would bother speaking to that dumpy little thing. The only reason she was invited was that my mother brought along her lover, who dragged along his daughter. She's a charity case, that's what she is."

A charity case. A dumpy one, at that.

She loathed him even more because he was right: she *was* dumpy. Other girls were tall and willowy, but she was "petite," which was just a pretentious way of saying that she was short.

And round. He meant she was fat.

He was a beast, a horrid beast.

Rage is a useful emotion. Rage burns away sorrow and disgrace. Rage propelled Mia to her feet, and she came out from around the sofa with her fists clenched.

Even knowing what he thought of her poem, despite her rage, the sight of Vander slammed into her. She had loved him too long to be unaffected by seeing him this close.

He was already tall and broad-shouldered. You could see the man he would someday be in the lineaments of his body and the strength of his jaw.

She looked at him up and down, curling her lip, and then gave his friends the same inspection.

Thorn looked horrified, and Oakenrott surprised, but Vander was utterly expressionless. All the things she'd thought she'd seen in him, every good characteristic that she had believed he had, the gentlemanly nature that seemed an antidote to her father's indiscretions . . . well, she must have made those traits up. There was nothing readable in his face, and clearly she had seen whatever she longed to find.

"So," she said, thankfully discovering that her voice was steady. "Three boys whose imaginations are so disgusting that they can read lechery into a silly love poem." She snatched the crumpled page from Thorn's hand and tore it in half. The sound seemed very loud in the otherwise silent room. She tore it again, and again, and dropped the pieces on the floor.

"I may have made a fool of myself by falling in love," she told Vander, "but you have no right to ridicule me for it. Do you know that I was foolish enough to think you a gentleman, unlike—" She caught herself. Her father was her father, no matter his sins. "I should have known better," she added. "You say I am my father's daughter. Well, *you*, Lord Brody, are obviously your mother's son."

To her left, Thorn made a protesting movement but she swept him a glance and he shut his mouth.

Vander only stared at her. Why had she never noticed his beautiful eyes were hard and cold?

"I shall now take myself and my *cabbages* into the drawing room," she said, head high, though it took every ounce of willpower she could summon to hold it there. "If you would do me the courtesy to remain here for fifteen minutes, I shall find my father and be gone."

None of them said a word, the pestilent cowards.

One more thing occurred to her. "Moreover, I wouldn't marry a single one of you," she said, making her voice as scathing as she could, "even if I were desperate! Even if you were the only men left in all England!"

Chapter One

Thirteen years later

From the offices of Brandy, Bucknell & Bendal, Publishers
August 27, 1800

Dear Miss Carrington,

I am writing to inquire about the prospect of receiving your new novel. As you know, we had hoped to receive the manuscript some six months ago. We are all most sympathetic as regards the tragic death of your father and brother a year ago. But I would be remiss not to tell you that letters begging for Miss Lucibella Delicosa's next novel are piling up in our offices. Your title, <u>An Angel's Form and a Devil's Heart</u>, has proved so enticing that subscriptions already exceed sales of your last two novels added together.

With deep respect, and anticipating a favorable reply,
I remain,

William Bucknell, Esq.

P.S. I am including Miss Julia Quiplet's latest novel. I believe
you said that you had not yet read her work, and we are
persuaded that you will find it pleasurable.

September 4, 1800
Rutherford Park
The Duke of Pindar's country estate

Mia hated to admit it, but she was trembling like
one of her own heroines. She generally put her poor
ladies in Mortal Danger, standing at the brink of icy
waters, for example, pursued by a lustful landlord,
knees knocking pitiably and delicate hands shaking.

Her readers expected Mortal Danger. In capital
letters.

She'd happily choose a plunge over a waterfall to
the humiliation that lay ahead of her.

Her own less-than-delicate hands were trembling,
so she curled them into fists, watching as her groom
announced her name. Vander's butler—or, to be
exact, the Duke of Pindar's butler—glanced down at
her, patently surprised that a young lady had arrived
without a chaperone.

Did intense humiliation count as Mortal Danger?

No, because if it were possible to die of humiliation,
she would surely be dead by now. After all, she had
survived the mortifying poetry incident in Villiers's
library all those years ago, then she'd failed on the
marriage market, only to go through an even worse
humiliation: being jilted at the altar a month ago.

The truth was that as an author she was always kind to her characters. Mortal Danger never included jiltings. What's more, thanks to her heroines' thin, wispy bodies, they always floated safely downstream, too light to sink. Another author she knew had caused a character to die after an eagle dropped a tortoise on his head. Murder by tortoise?

Not in a Lucibella novel!

Her readers knew that there would be no blood-thirsty birds, no one left at the altar. She had never forced any of her heroines to propose marriage, let alone to a duke.

Gentlemen fell at her heroines' feet, not the other way around. It was a strict requirement of the genre. Lord knows, Lucibella Delicosa disappointed her readers at her own peril: a torrent of indignant letters would pour through her publisher's door if she were to shame one of her heroines the way Mia was about to be shamed.

But at least, Mia reminded herself, she was not, in reality, falling at Vander's feet.

She was in charge.

In control.

Before she could think better of it, she took a deep breath, handed her pelisse to the butler, and marched past him into the morning room. Mia had spent a good deal of time in the ducal country estate as a young girl, given the late duchess' decades-long *affaire* with her father, and she knew where she was headed.

Even though the principal players in that drama—her father and Vander's mother—had passed away, it seemed nothing had changed in the manor house. Every horizontal surface was still crowded with animal figurines, evidence of the late duchess' fascination with small creatures.

She turned to the butler. "Please let His Grace know that my call shall be quite brief."

"I shall ascertain whether His Grace is receiving," he said, and left.

Surely Vander would see her? How could he deny her, given their parents' relationship? Commonsense reminded her that he might well deny her for that precise reason.

She wandered over to look at the glass menagerie that resided on the mantelpiece. The unicorn had lost his horn, but all the animals were still there, silently poised with a paw up or a tail waving—some with little animal families, as though they had paired off and multiplied while the house slept.

But she couldn't concentrate on the little curl of glass, a tadpole, she picked up. The thought of what lay ahead of her—the marriage proposal—made her feel dizzy, as if her corset was constricting her chest and making it hard to breathe. Years before, when she'd vowed to Vander's face never to marry him, a gleam of amusement had sprung to his eyes.

What if he burst out laughing now?

She was not exquisitely beautiful, refined, intelligent . . . and she didn't even have a fortune. Who ever heard of a wallflower asking a duke for his hand in marriage?

Mia took another deep breath. She wasn't precisely *asking* the duke to marry her. That would be pitiful. She was *blackmailing* him, which was altogether different.

More swashbuckling. More perilous.

More criminal.

She should pretend this wasn't happening to her, but to one of her heroines, the way she did with almost everything else. She already had plenty of practice observing her life as if from outside. She regularly chatted with patently bored gentlemen, simultaneously rewriting the conversation in such a way that a fantastically idealized version of herself left them dumbstruck with desire.

Back home she would jot down the scene precisely as she had reimagined it—giving herself violet eyes and a slim waist. Sometimes she stayed up all night describing the adventures of one of her heroines, a girl so well-mannered, biddable, and pure of heart that only the most discerning readers noticed she was quite intelligent.

In contrast, men noticed that Mia was intelligent, but it seemed to put them off.

If life imitated one of her novels, Vander would stride into the room and after one glance begin wooing her with such passion that the distasteful question of blackmail would never need be mentioned.

His blue eyes would flare with possessive fervor. For the rest of his life, His Grace would regret the thirteen years he might have spent with her, but had lost due to his callow and callous blindness as a boy. He would bitterly reproach himself for his cruel insults.

Unfortunately, that was more than unlikely. In Mia's experience, people never regretted clever insults, no matter how much they might sting the recipient.

She hated cabbage to this day. As well as Oakenrott.

A queer numbness came over her. She, Emilia Gwendolyn Carrington, was about to coerce a duke into marrying her. An old maid in her twenties, possessed of neither violet-colored eyes nor a slender waist, was—

This was not a helpful train of thought.

She had to stop trembling. The proposal wasn't for

her benefit. Nor was it for an extended period of time. She simply needed Vander to marry her in name only, for a year at most. It was the only way she could take guardianship of her nephew, Charles Wallace.

Nephew? In all the ways that counted, Charlie was her son. Her own child.

She took a deep breath. Women dove from the decks of tall ships to save children fallen overboard. They fought tigers and wild boars.

What was a mere duke compared to a man-eating carnivore? She'd heard some creatures had such large teeth that they could be hollowed out and used as soup ladles.

Right.

The tricky part was that Mr. Plummer, her solicitor, had been adamant that the duke could not be informed of the reasons for her proposal, or His Grace would almost certainly say no.

By marrying her, the duke not only took on guardianship of a small boy; he gained control of an extremely large estate running adjacent to his, which would look highly suspicious to his peers. Their marriage would be a *cause célèbre* without even taking into account the scandals caused by their parents: Vander would undoubtedly face a lawsuit charging him with theft of the estate from Charlie's uncle on his mother's side, Sir Richard Magruder.

Vander—His Grace, the Duke of Pindar—was just another supercilious, privileged, silly *man*, she reminded herself. He wasn't a tiger with soup ladles for teeth.

She could do this.

She must do this.

Chapter Two

NOTES ON *An Angel's Form and a Devil's Heart:*
a Novel

Heroine is slender, ethereal, willowy . . . another way to say thin? Strangely light for someone who actually eats breakfast.

So desirable that the hero is struck dumb at the very sight of her. Blue eyes, yellow hair, dainty everything.

Lace coming into fashion? Lace-maker. Research how lace is made. Bobbins?

First sight, hero on his knees. In the rain.

Mud.

Definitely mud.

"Your Grace, a Miss Carrington is requesting to speak to you."

For a moment Vander had no idea who she was. Then he realized it had to be Mia, the hapless poet. His complete avoidance of polite society in favor of the stables meant that he hadn't seen her in years.

"Did she give any indication of the reason for her visit?"

"No, Your Grace. She is in the morning room, should you wish to speak to her, or I can inform her that you are busy at this time. I might add that she is unaccompanied. Furthermore, your solicitor is in the library. He has been waiting some time and is becoming impatient."

The last time he could remember having seen Mia was that bloody embarrassing thing that happened when they were fifteen.

What in the hell was she thinking, calling on him early in the morning, without a chaperone? Why call on him at all?

"I'll go to Miss Carrington," he decided, heading from his bedchamber. He owed the poet an audience, if only because he should have handled that situation better. The very memory made him shudder a little. He had been stupid and young, but even so, he'd behaved like an ass.

Vander strode down the stairs adjusting his cuffs. Mia's name must have been as besmirched as his by their parents' deaths a year ago. There was no covering up the fact that the Duchess of Pindar had died in bed with Lord Carrington. All of England knew about the damaged stove flue that had led to their deaths: that flare of scandal had eclipsed the deaths of eight other unfortunates sleeping in the same inn—a list that had included Mia's brother and sister-in-law, if he remembered correctly. It must have been a terrible year for her.

Just as he reached the final step, his solicitor,

Grieg, erupted from the library and accosted him. Vander almost groaned aloud as he listened. Apparently, Sir Cuthbert had made a rash promise to finance an archaeological expedition to the Andes Mountains.

Insofar as his uncle's sole source of income was the allowance Vander gave him, which Chuffy promptly spent on velvet coats and bottles of sack, he wasn't in a position to make good on the promise. It seemed that Chuffy had got around that little problem by scrawling a note promising that the Duke of Pindar would back the expedition.

He would have to tell Chuffy that his funds were tied up in his stables and he could not finance an expedition to the Andes at this time. Or, for that matter, ever.

The primary thing he remembered about Mia Carrington was that she had a chubby face and magnificent breasts.

All these years later, her face was thinner. Presumably her breasts were still there, but she was wearing a drab gown of homespun that concealed everything below her chin. She looked like a missionary. Perhaps she'd become one?

He felt a flash of sympathy. Her religious leanings, if she had them, were likely a response to their parents' blatant disregard for the sanctity of marriage. Though if she had come to try to proselytize—

"Your Grace," she said, dropping a curtsy. "How very wonderful to see you again."

Was that a drop of sarcasm in her voice? Surely not. After all, she was the one who had come, uninvited, to his house, not the other way around.

He bowed. When he straightened, he found that she was observing him, gloved hands folded, with the air of someone watching a play.

Peculiar.

"Miss Carrington, what can I do for you?" he inquired.

"I have come to request a favor."

Vander's shoulders relaxed. This missionary woman had likely joined a mission in an effort to atone for her licentious father's sins. She wanted a contribution. He was accustomed to solicitations: virtually everyone in his life except his friend Thorn had asked him for money at some point. It was part and parcel of being a duke.

A donation was a perfect way to assuage the last of that inconvenient guilt he felt due to hurting her feelings years ago.

"I would be most happy to help," he said. "Would you care to be seated? I could ring for tea if you wish."

She stood as still as a tree, only her hands twisting together. "You might not feel inclined to be generous after you've heard my request."

"If only on the basis of having known you since childhood, I assure you that I will agree to whatever sort of help you wish." He gave her a measured smile, wondering how quickly he could bundle her out of the room. His secretary could hand over the actual sovereigns. "How much would you like?"

She had a quite delicate jaw. He noticed because it visibly tightened, as if she were grinding her teeth. As a child, she used to be shaped like a stout pigeon, with a little potbelly and legs that whirled across the lawn as she tried to keep up with him.

Not that she ever could.

"Miss Carrington," he prompted, when she didn't answer, "I gather that you are collecting for a charity, and I assure you that I will contribute."

"No," she said, her jaw tightening again. "I came to ask for something quite different."

"I am happy to assist you," he said, allowing a trace of impatience to leak into his voice.

"Marriage," she blurted out, and took a gulp of air.

He stared at her for one perfectly silent moment.

"I should like you to marry me." She said it fast and the words ran together.

He frowned. "I beg your pardon?"

"I am proposing marriage," she stated. Then she closed her mouth.

Vander had to curb an impulse to shake his head to make sure he had heard correctly. The woman must be touched, though madness ran in his family, not in hers.

But mad she must be, because she was looking at him expectantly, for all the world as if she thought there was a possibility he took her seriously.

He cleared his throat. "Well, how kind of you to offer." Surely this was some sort of ruse? "However, I regret to inform you that I have no intention to marry at this time."

Something crossed her face—disappointment? Was that possible?

"I suppose you think I'm mad. I'm afraid that I am, a bit."

"I see." Vander was, against all expectations, starting to enjoy himself. After all, her family had ruined his. Her father's seduction of his mother had made the Duchess of Pindar the laughingstock of the ton.

And now Carrington's daughter had the temerity to think that he would consider marrying *her*? Truly, the family had balls.

Even the women.

"So you are looking for a husband," he said agreeably. "And you thought, hey ho, I'll have a go at a duke?"

"That is not kind of you," she said, her eyes narrowing.

Her eyes were a remarkable green, with thick eyelashes. Not that their color made her in the least attractive; rather the opposite. He preferred women with melting blue eyes. Eyes like the sky in summer.

"I must insist that you be seated," he said. "Wooing is such an arduous business, don't you think?"

After a long second she moved to a chair opposite his, and damned if she didn't try again. "Will you marry me, Your Grace?"

"Absolutely not." The words shot out like a bullet. "Given our family history, you are the last woman in the world I'd marry. In fact, I believe that you expressed the same sentiment to me some years ago, and I cannot imagine what has changed your mind."

She was unbalanced. There was no other explanation for a woman's proposing to a duke, let alone imagining that he would accept. She suffered from delusions.

"I can hardly imagine the scandal that a marriage between us would cause," he added.

"I am aware that our union would be a subject of speculation," she said, for all the world as if they were discussing the weather. "I try not to let gossip bother me. Besides, I have come to view our parents' relationship as something of a star-crossed tragedy."

"It's a tragedy, all right," he drawled. "Your bastard of a father seduced my mother, made her into a whore, and ruined my family name."

Her grip tightened on the arms of her chair, but she showed no other sign of being intimidated. "Our parents loved each other, Your Grace. Their union was not sanctioned by society, but to the best of my observation, it was positively tedious in its domesticity. If not for the accident that took their lives, I am certain that they would have spent the next forty years together."

Vander suppressed a shudder. He had loathed Carrington as no other man. He'd worn his hatred for so long it had become comfortable, and he had no interest in reappraising the way it fit.

For years, he had made damned sure that he and Carrington were never found in the same residence, even if he had to bed down in the stables.

Which meant that he hadn't seen his mother for months before her death.

A stab of guilt made his tone harsher than he intended. "Miss Carrington, I cannot imagine why you believe I would consider your request, let alone agree to it. When—*if*—I decide to marry, I will both choose the woman, and propose to her myself."

Damn it—this was absurd. He had no mistress at the moment, but if he had, anyone in England would guess that she wouldn't be a short, round woman dressed like a missionary.

"Why in the hell do you come to me, of all people, with this request?" he asked, with genuine curiosity. "There are a million men in England whom you could marry, if you have determined to go against custom and do your own wooing. Though, to be perfectly candid, I don't think it's a good idea."

Under her dreadful gown, he'd guess that she was as lush as she had been at fifteen. Voluptuous, even. If she put her assets on display, she could probably marry almost anyone she wanted. He might prefer the tall, willowy type, but he knew plenty of men who preferred a pocket Venus.

Beyond which, it wasn't *her* mother who had been an adulteress. Far less shame attached to a man who made a duchess his mistress.

"You have a dowry, don't you?" he asked, since she hadn't responded to his previous question. Her family's lands ran adjacent to his ducal seat, so he would have heard if there were obvious problems. Last he heard, Sir Richard Magruder was running the estate because the Carrington heir was underage. Sir Richard was not a man he admired, but he'd probably do an adequate job.

"I have a dowry." She hesitated for a moment, then took a deep breath and pulled a sheet of yellowed paper, folded many times into a small square, out of her reticule. "I also have this."

"Bloody hell," Vander said with a groan. "Not another poem. I'm not a literary fellow, Miss Carrington. You can't change my mind with a lyric."

Her cheeks flamed a surprisingly lovely shade of red. "I would never—" She caught herself and started over. "No, it is not a poem. It's a letter."

He narrowed his eyes, a drop of ice sliding down his spine as a realization hit him. "You intend to blackmail me? I suppose that is some revolting piece of tripe that my mother addressed to your father."

He stood up and took one stride forward, leaning over and bracing his hands on the armchair. "Publish and be damned, Miss Carrington. Publish, and go to hell while you do it."

She was staring at her hands and didn't look at him, even though he was leaning so close to her that he almost touched her forehead. He caught a delicate whiff of honeysuckle—an unexpected scent for someone thoroughly swathed in thick wool.

"I gather you planned to force me to marry you?" He spoke through clenched teeth, enraged by his body's disturbing response to being close to her. "To hell with that. Take care you get a premium from whatever Grub Street hack buys your letter, because I give you fair warning: I shall ruin you."

"Don't you wish to read the document first?" She finally met his eyes.

"My mother's fulsome nature practically guarantees that the letter is full of drivel. Moonbeams and pearls, I expect?"

She flinched and her face grew even paler. But she was as brave as he remembered. She cleared her throat and looked him full in the face again. "The letter was not written by your mother, but by your father," she corrected him.

This was a surprise, but he said, "My father spent most of his adult life confined to a private asylum, a fact you know as well as I do. I doubt you'll get more than five pounds for publishing one of his rants."

There was a moment of silence.

"Your Grace," she said. "I implore you to read the letter."

Vander stared at her for one second longer, before he took it from her and straightened, falling back a step. The letter was definitely from the late duke; Vander could recognize his hand anywhere. It was dated long before his father had been declared insane, but his handwriting belied that fact.

When his father was suffering from a mad fit, his writing reflected his state of mind. The script hurtled across the page, the letters slanted as if blown by a stiff wind. There had been weeks when twenty- or thirty-page letters arrived from the asylum, each page urgent, demanding . . . incoherent.

He read the letter.

He read it three more times, then carefully folded it back up.

"They'll take my title and estate if you publish this."

Her eyes were grave, not at all triumphant. "I believe you are correct."

Vander felt light-headed. "So my father was a traitor to the Crown." He'd believed his family had hit rock bottom when his mother died in Carrington's arms; it turned out that there was a further drop. Madness, adultery—and now treason.

"So it seems."

"I doubt he could have assassinated the king, even if he had mailed this offer. My father had no entrée to the court. As I understand it, everyone avoided him even during his schooldays; his feelings were too extreme and unpredictable to make him easy company."

His mind was reeling from the blow. His dukedom was the key to everything that mattered to him: his stables, his estate, his cottagers. Everything would be forfeit to the Crown. After the debacle of his childhood, and the scandals his parents caused, his horses were his life.

Words shot from his mouth without conscious volition. Swear words, rough oaths that he had never used in the presence of a lady.

But was she a lady?

No. She was a damned blackmailer.

Her mouth tightened, though she was pretending not to hear him.

"Despite this letter, you can't possibly think that I will agree to marry you." For a second control eluded him, but he reined it back in. He'd be damned if he threatened a woman, even one who was trying to bend him to her will.

Not that she showed the faintest sign of fright.

No, Mia Carrington looked like an Amazon, if that race of female warriors had a corps of petite archers. It was oddly provocative.

But he felt like a footman being called to a bedchamber, summoned for her lady's pleasure, which
was intolerable.

"Years ago, you vowed not to marry me if I were
the last man on earth. What in the hell has changed,
Miss Carrington? Besides the fact that our reputa-
tions are even more notorious than they were when
we were young? Why in God's name would you em-
barrass yourself like this?"

Chapter Three

NOTES ON HERO

Angel's Form: Hero is elegant to a fault—wears coat made by Weston, silver-topped cane. ~~Tumbling black hair.~~ Hair—flaxseed in the sun. Brown eyes.

Titled. A count? Last 4 Lucibella heroes all dukes.

But why does he have a devil's heart?

Draw from real life? Heroine jilted? REASON>>> Not bec. change of heart—hero too enamored. Bring in evil count? Twin?

Is 'Count' an English title? Never met one (check Debrett's). Or: ~~French~~ Bavarian comte. More perifidious. (Will readers understand perifidious? Comte, for that matter? Spelling?) stay with Count.

Count Frederic!
Leaves her at the altar in St. Paul's Cathedral ... Why?
Good question.

"*E*mbarrass myself?" Mia had never heard a voice that angry. And cold.

If she was gorgeous and dewy-eyed, it wouldn't be quite so humiliating to propose marriage. But as it was ... some part of her was writhing with humiliation. Some part? The whole of her.

"I do not consider a proposal of marriage to be an embarrassment," she said untruthfully, fighting to keep her voice from rising into a squeak. "I am in possession of a special license, and I would like to marry quite soon."

Instead of thunder, she got another crack of laughter, sharpened by rage. "You have to be joking. You think I would marry *you*?" His eyes raked her from head to toe.

She fell silent, swallowing hard. She tried not to think about her attractiveness—or lack thereof—and most of the time she was successful.

"You are not joking." He didn't move a finger, but she felt danger in the very air, as if he might turn and smash his fist straight through the window if he lost control of his temper. He had already uttered some words she'd never heard before.

She forced herself to speak. "My solicitor obtained the license. I hoped we could marry in a few days. At the least, within the week, Your Grace."

"Unbelievable. I've asked you repeatedly, and I'll ask again. Why do you want to marry me, Miss Carrington? Is it a matter of ambition?

"Oh my God," Vander continued, not waiting for a

response. "You're getting revenge for the poetry episode all those years ago?"

"Of course not! The subject is irrelevant." Mia pulled another folded sheet from her reticule. "You may keep the letter written by your father, Your Grace. I took the liberty of putting into writing my specifications as regards our marriage."

" 'Specifications?' " Vander echoed.

He felt as if he had fallen into another world. Ladies did not propose marriage. They did not issue "specifications" for male behavior, within marriage or without.

"The terms of our marriage." She put the document on a side table. "Here they are."

Vander took a step forward and caught her wrist. It was shockingly small. "This makes no sense."

She tried to pull free, but it was no use; he had restrained horses that were far taller than she was and weighed ten times as much. "Are you ambitious for social status? Or did your father put you up to this before he died?"

Her eyes skittered away, and he realized the truth with a sickening thud. "That's it. I didn't even ask how you got that damned letter. He stole it, didn't he? Or my mother gave it to him. It wasn't enough to drag my mother into the gutter and shame my father—Carrington made sure that he would befoul the Pindar line."

"Befoul?" She stopped struggling to free herself and stared up at him with an absurd air of innocence.

"Taint my blood," he said, wanting to hurt her. "I think anyone would agree that children of your family will sully the ducal line. My father expected me to marry into the best of families, Miss Carrington. *Your* father was not ennobled by his association with my mother. Quite the opposite."

She glared at him. "May I remind you that you're talking about sullying a ducal line headed by a madman and—" She stopped.

"A what?" he said, his voice dangerously low. "By what word would you characterize my mother?"

"We should not be having this discussion, Your Grace."

This time he snatched both of her hands and reeled her close to him before she could do more than gasp. "I think the word you were looking for is *whore*."

"I wasn't, and you should not speak about your mother that way," she cried. "What's more, you shouldn't even speak that word in my presence!"

Vander's grip tightened. "You don't make an outcry when I curse, yet I say the word 'whore' and you squeal like an insulted nun? Who are you, really, Mia Carrington?"

"I'm all those things you've called me, Your Grace," she said steadily. "A wallflower, an old maid, a charity case. A desperate woman in need of a husband."

"A husband?" He looked her up and down. "In your bed? Is that what this is about?"

Red flashed through her cheeks. So that was it. She still lusted after him, which should make him laugh. But this close, he could feel the warmth coming from her lush little body.

He didn't want to look at her eyes; they made him feel odd, unbalanced. With one swift movement, he turned her about so that she was snug against his front, his arms crossed over her chest.

She fit in the circle of his arms perfectly, so perfectly that he pulled her even closer, before he realized what he was doing.

"Do you imagine that you and I will have the sort

of relationship that our parents had?" he asked. He spread his right hand over her stomach, pulling her tightly against him so that she could not mistake the reaction of his body to hers. He was still hard as a rock and had been since he loomed over her in the chair.

She was no lady, and he refused to do her the courtesy of treating her like one. What he wanted to do was act like a man who had never heard of civilized society: bend her over that chair and take her.

"Let me go!" she demanded. He heard no fear in her voice, so he ignored her protest.

"If I want a whore, I pay for her," he said, thrusting forward with his hips in a rough motion that she could not mistake. "I don't marry the woman. Your father didn't bother with such formalities, so why should you?"

She didn't respond other than continuing to struggle to pull away, her head bent forward and her hair falling from its pins. Vander had a discomforting feeling that perhaps *he* was the one more affected by their position. For some damn reason, her body was practically burning him, and he felt as if he were surrounded by her soft elusive scent.

He had never felt like this: dizzy with raw lust, hungry to take her and prove—

With an oath, he released her and backed away, as if that would save him from the hunger that had him wanting to throw her on a bed, any bed, and tuck her body beneath his own.

She turned around slowly. Pale gold ribbons of hair fell around her neck and curled against the drab fabric of her gown. It sent another shock through him.

"Your mother was not a whore," she repeated, as fierce as ever. "She was in love with my father. It's not fair to brand her that way!"

"She may not have been, but her son will be. After all, you're buying my services, are you not? The market price for one duke, in fairly good physical condition, seems to be an incriminatory letter. Perhaps you should search your father's belongings. Just think what you could do with two such letters. Two noblemen, in the same bed, at the same time."

"That is a loathsome thing to say," she said, her voice shaking for the first time.

He plowed his hands through his hair, frustration mixing with his lust. "I'll give you a dowry, if that's the problem." He was grasping at straws, he knew. "I can make you rich enough that you can attract a man by conventional means. You needn't do this, Miss Carrington. We can forget it ever happened."

Her eyes narrowed at him, her chin back up in the air. "You think I couldn't possibly attract a husband without a large dowry?"

Vander eyed her truly awful gown. "If you bought some reasonably fashionable frocks, I'm sure that you could find someone," he offered. "Hell, I could help there too. I know several gentlemen who—"

"Who are desperate enough to marry someone like me if a duke paid them enough?" she cut in.

He eyed her, then shrugged.

She went stiff all over, like a Greek statue sculpted by the hand of a master. But she likely had a lushly feminine grace when unclothed, a figure that those stalk-thin Greek goddesses would envy. Put it together with lips of deep rose, and those eyes . . . she could certainly have a man at her feet. Maybe a whole crowd.

He wouldn't be one of them.

"Unfortunately for your scheme, I already have a dowry," she said. "It is sufficiently large. Moreover, I have . . . I have money of my own."

He narrowed his eyes. "In that case, why in the bloody hell are you forcing this? You say it isn't revenge. Or lust. God knows our marriage would be a disaster." And then it sank in, well and truly seeping in like a stinging poison. "Miss Carrington, you have to trust that there's someone out there who would fall in love with you in return. You don't really love me. You don't even know me."

"I don't—"

"Look, my closest friend Thorn—Tobias Dautry— never thought to marry. He fell in love just this last year, as unexpectedly as if he'd been hit on the head by a cannon ball."

"Love is like being hit in the head?"

He nodded, warming to the subject. "What if that were to happen to you? *When* it happens to you," he amended. "When you meet the man of your dreams, you will be desolate if you and I are already married."

The sensual, plump curve of her lips tightened into a thin line, suggesting he was making an impression. "There's no possible way that our marriage will thrive," he continued. "Not under any circumstances. Hell, I courted Lady Xenobia last year. One of the most beautiful women in all London, perhaps in all Britain. And the daughter of a marquess."

She didn't say anything.

"India is tall and willowy," he said, forcing the issue. "Exquisitely beautiful, with the bearing of a goddess." Never mind the fact that he'd decided India was a bit too tall for him.

"We are both already aware of what you think of me, Your Grace," Mia replied, her chin held high and shoulders back, for all the world as if she were facing a judge. "You labeled me a dumpy charity case years ago, before I emerged from behind Villiers's sofa."

Actually, what he remembered was her bravery.

There had been more than one time when he might have turned away from a challenge, but he remembered little Mia charging around the sofa.

"Your waxing on about love has not changed my mind, nor have your insults." She picked up her reticule and headed for the door. "Please excuse me."

With two long strides he was past her, blocking the door. Her green eyes were dark and misty: she wasn't as unmoved as she had sounded.

"You must give up this mad idea," he ordered.

Mia took a deep breath. She was trying desperately to think how to respond. Her solicitor had made blackmail sound easy. *Wave the letter, and the duke will realize that he has no option, and must meet your requirements.*

It was all different now, in the event, when she was actually faced by Vander. She hated doing this. She felt miserable and low, battered by his rage and distaste. But rather than give in, she made herself think of sweet little Charlie. And his uncle, the horrendous Sir Richard.

The thought steadied her, and she managed to hold back her tears. "I'm sorry," she repeated. "But I must marry you."

A muscle worked in Vander's cheek.

"My expectations for the marriage are enumerated on the document I left on the table," she stated, keeping her voice steady through some miracle. "I ask for very little," she added. "Please, Your Grace, just . . . just do me this favor."

Vander wasn't listening; she could tell. The flare in his eyes would have burned her, if such a thing was possible.

He reached out for her and like any silly rabbit, she froze.

"If you're to be my wife, I might as well have a taste of you," he said, raw and low.

But before she could say anything else, his mouth came down on hers and he forced her lips to open.

It was an angry kiss, a vengeful kiss.

When Mia had been betrothed to Edward Reeve, son of the Earl of Gryffyn, she had enjoyed his kisses. Edward had been respectful and never strayed beyond the bounds of propriety . . . or not far.

During the months of their betrothal, while they waited for her mourning period to end, there were times when he kissed her until she was flushed and giggling.

That was before he'd jilted her, of course.

This kiss of Vander's had nothing in common with Edward's. When Vander slanted his mouth over hers, Mia felt a shock of heat so acute that her scalp prickled.

His tongue slid into her mouth and his big body shoved against hers with none of the gentlemanly restraint that her fiancé had shown. Mia felt as if she'd been thrown into a river without the ability to swim.

Every point at which he touched her felt a glaze of fire, a small ache. Her mouth opened wider, inviting him in, and she tipped her head to give him greater access. Her mind went blank and her hands stopped pushing at his chest and encircled his neck. The brush of silky hair against her fingers set a fever blazing in her stomach.

Trembling, her eyes closed, she didn't notice at first when Vander pulled away. Not until the arm holding her against the door dropped, and she landed with a jolt that rattled her teeth.

If only she'd kept her eyes closed.

The contempt in his eyes was warring with pity, and she didn't know which was worse.

Vander reached out and tilted her chin up. "You can't force a man to love you, Mia." The words were rough but there was softness there too, pity for the old maid who had no way to get a husband except by blackmailing him. And he used her personal name, as if he were her big brother offering counsel.

Mia drew in a breath of air that scorched her lungs, as if it burned from the inside out. Could this be any more humiliating? Once they married, she would take Charlie and go live in Scotland.

"I know it's a difficult lesson. You simply have to trust that in time you'll love someone else," Vander added, looking sorry.

Sorry for her.

Scotland wasn't far enough.

Bavaria. She and Charlie would go to Bavaria, where no one knew them. Charlie could return to England at age eighteen and reclaim the Carrington estate from Vander.

At least she knew that he would have an estate to inherit, if Vander was in charge. Sir Richard would waste it all in frivolous lawsuits, with no regard for Charlie's patrimony.

Mr. Plummer could help Vander petition the House of Lords for a divorce in her absence; he would take care of everything. She herself need never return to England.

Vander's eyes were intent on hers. "Tell me to destroy the letter, Mia. Keep your dignity and your self-respect. Don't make me hate you."

He had no idea how much she wanted to keep her self-respect. Her dignity was gone . . . but her decency? She shuddered, knowing what she would think of a woman who had acted as she had. Villainesses in her books always came to a bad end.

"I'm sorry," she whispered. "But I can't."

Mia looked regretful . . . but Vander could tell that she didn't have the faintest intention of freeing him. She was determined to tie him to her apron strings. Or perhaps bedpost was more accurate.

She couldn't have the faintest idea what a man needed, what a man would demand of his wife. To put it bluntly, she was an old maid without the faintest understanding of what really went on between men and women: the sweaty, grunting, pleasurable truth of it. Anger filled him again, like water coming to a boil.

"You think you're getting my moonbeam, Mia? Whatever you want to call it, I can assure you that it will not perform under these circumstances. Not when you've commanded the act. We men are odd that way. We like to *choose* our bed partners. And if you'll forgive my bluntness, I would not choose you."

Her cheeks flooded with color again. "My poem had nothing to do with that—with, with intimate matters!"

"I disagree." Vander tore off his coat and tossed it behind him.

"What are you doing?"

He started on his waistcoat, her eyes going wide as he tossed that aside too. This time he heard a tinkle of broken glass.

She gasped. "You just—"

"Don't you think you should see what blackmailing a man does to his cock? Excuse me: to his *moonbeam*?"

His hands moved to his waistband and undid the first button. At the same moment, the combination of Mia's wide eyes, luscious bosom, and that kiss wrapped around him. He felt his body grow hard.

In fact, his cock was about as stiff as it had ever been.

"Hell," he muttered. That ruined his initial plan. Never mind: he could shock her into realizing that marriage wasn't poetic, but sweaty and real.

"What do you think you're doing?" she demanded.

Vander ran a hand slowly down the front of his breeches and sure enough, her eyes followed the movement. Mia likely believed that wedding vows had some sort of romantic power to them. Hell, she had spun a fairy tale around the dissolute relationship their parents had shared.

She had probably read too many of those novels, the ones full of tripe about gentlemen who behaved as no man ever would, falling on their knees from one moment to the next. Begging for a woman the way a spaniel would a bone.

"What I'm doing is showing you every inch of what you wrote about in that damned poem," he said, baring his teeth in an approximation of a smile. He undid another button, his breeches straining in front.

He expected her to squeak like a mouse and dash from the room. Ladies did that sort of thing to avoid reality.

But Mia surprised him. Again. "Is there something I am supposed to be noticing?" she inquired.

For a moment he almost admired her. He wasn't boastful, but he knew he was large—all over. Seasoned courtesans had looked shocked at the size of his rod.

Not her.

For someone who was going to all the trouble of threatening his dukedom in order to climb into his bed, Mia seemed astonishingly nonchalant.

Button number three.

"You stop what you're doing this instant!" she

Four Nights with the Duke 39

said, finally looking a bit unnerved. Her voice had taken on a husky lisp that only made him harder.

"Do you mean that you don't want to assess the merchandise? Really, Mia, you must learn to conduct yourself in the marketplace. Vendors always want to display their wares."

At that, her back stiffened. "There's a reason gentlemen keep such details to themselves," she flashed. "You, for example, seem to have delusions of . . . of adequacy!"

"Actually, I have a conviction," he drawled. "Of grandeur." With every button he undid, with every sign of her determination, he felt anger swelling in his throat, threatening to strangle him, making him behave more and more outrageously.

He courted danger, not women. He had sometimes talked vaguely about a wife but now he realized with abrupt clarity that he didn't want one.

Every ounce of his being resisted the idea, screaming at him to fight in the only way he could fathom in this insane circumstance. He undid the final button and his tool sprang free, shielded from her eyes only by the thin silk of his smalls.

"So, Miss Carrington, does the moonbeam live up to expectations?"

For a second, he could have sworn her green eyes darkened, but in the next, she folded her arms over her chest. "As I recall, when you were merely fifteen, your closest friends were already expressing some concern about your size."

Surprise ripped through him, and he gave a bark of laughter.

"What I see, Your Grace, is a man who has the good sense to celebrate what Nature gave him, overlooking Her stinginess!"

Vander grinned, the surprising thought that few people were capable of verbally sparring with him flashing through his brain. He was about to respond, but he realized that Mia was feeling behind her for the latch. Instantly he dragged her to him, bucking his hips against her body. Then he slid his hands down her back and splayed his fingers over her bottom, holding her tight against him.

She didn't say anything, but a sound escaped her lips, a little puff of air that sent an answering shudder through his body.

He had made another mistake. He had just played into her hands. What was he thinking? This woman had been writing sensual poems at fifteen. She wanted him for bedding and probably didn't give a damn about his title.

She was her father's daughter, after all.

Before he could speak, Mia shoved at his chest and he let her go. Color was burning in her cheeks; she didn't meet his eyes, staring somewhere to the left of one shoulder. "I shall—I shall leave you now," she said, her voice huskier than it had been. "Please let me know your response to my requirements."

Vander was so dumbfounded that he didn't stop her.

He stood there, staring at the closed door, the flap of his breeches hanging open, cock throbbing.

What the hell was he going to do now?

Chapter Four

NOTES ON PLOT

First chapter opens with Flora walking to . . . work as a lace-maker. (Add humble background, orphan, etc.)

A respectable, elderly gentleman, Mr. Mortimer, glimpses her crossing the street in her clean and patched gown. A girl this lovely, gentle, and deserving cannot be left Impoverished, at the mercy of the Cruel World. (I like this!)

He dies the very night after he changes his will to leave her one hundred thousand pounds (too much?), with a single proviso: that she not spend even a ha'penny on someone other than herself. If, e.g., she buys her aged nanny a cottage—or a lettuce leaf—she loses the entire estate.

Interesting. Large dowry on marriage.

So why would Frederic jilt her?
Who gets the money afterward?
Angry relatives!

$\mathcal{V}$ander stared at the fire, a half-empty bottle of brandy on the side table next to him. It was one of the few times in his life that he cursed his ability to hold liquor.

He wanted to be drunk.

After Mia had left, he had had a grim conversation with his solicitor, who made it clear that he had no choice. Whatever it was Mia was demanding in that bloody letter—which he hadn't yet opened—he would have to comply.

Or lose his dukedom.

When Thorn walked into the room, Vander didn't even look up, though he could feel his closest friend's eyes on him. "What the hell's going on?" Thorn reached over and took the bottle of brandy from the table, dropping into a chair. "Did you lose a race?"

Vander was silent for a moment. "Do you remember when I told you that I planned to marry for love? One of my more idiotic ideas, I might add." What the hell had he been thinking? It wasn't for men, all this passion.

"I don't consider myself idiotic," Thorn said, holding up the bottle. "You're drinking brandy that was laid down in '78. This calls for a glass." He got up and returned a moment later with a glass cut with the Duke of Pindar's coat of arms.

"Your marriage is not the topic at hand," Vander said, taking a healthy swig of the brandy. "Mine is. You're here in time to congratulate me."

Thorn put down his glass without drinking from it. "What the hell? What's happened?"

"My father was mad," Vander said, observing how the golden liquid made little streams on the side of the glass as he tilted it. "But it turns out he was also treasonous. Not just ordinary treason, either: My father offered—in writing—to kill the king, thereby enabling Bonnie Prince Charlie to sit on the throne."

"*What?*"

Vander was still following his own train of thought. "He was a lunatic. And a cuckold. But I'll be damned if I let him be blasted as a traitor as well."

"What does that have to do with marriage?" Thorn asked, looking confused.

"The treasonous letter is in the hands of a woman. And she is demanding marriage."

"Bloody hell."

"My thoughts exactly."

"How can they take away your dukedom? *You* didn't commit treason."

Vander shrugged. "My solicitor is confident that the dukedom would be confiscated. Apparently, dukedoms to hand out to favorites are in short supply, and I've never been a toady to the Crown." He wasn't the type who had bothered to ingratiate himself with George and his court. Or with society in general, for that matter.

Witness the fact that his only friend was a bastard, albeit a duke's bastard.

"Hell," Thorn muttered again. "Who is the woman?"

"You've met her."

"I have? What's her name?"

"The poet."

Thorn frowned. "Poet? I don't remember any . . . not Carrington's daughter!"

"That's the one." Vander poured more brandy into his glass.

"The daughter of your mother's lover is forcing you into marriage?" Thorn sounded genuinely shocked, which was amusing. After growing up on the streets, he was rarely surprised by evidence of criminality.

"That's an accurate title for her," Vander agreed. "You could also call her the Lyricist. Or Imminent Duchess of Pindar. If I wasn't furious, I'd be impressed at her ingenuity. Not to mention tenacity."

"Let me make sure I have it right: you are being blackmailed with the threat of a charge of treason and loss of your dukedom into marrying the daughter of your mother's paramour."

"It sounds like Greek drama when you put it that way."

"The hell with that," Thorn said flatly, his voice ringing with distaste. "She wrote that excruciatingly bad poem about you. Her father was a debauched philanderer. Your marriage will be a subject of gossip for your entire life. It's not worth it. Let the dukedom go."

"I thought about it."

"Well?"

"My father's madness tarnished the name—but it's still my name. One of my ancestors lost his head defending King Charles against the Puritans. Another fought a battle for King Henry II. A castle—my family's castle—stood here three hundred years before this house was built. I would just let them go, the history of my family go, because a women wants me so badly that she'd resort to blackmail?"

"Let me put it this way: Your mother married a madman, and you're about to marry a madwoman."

Thorn's voice was troubled, and Vander paused for a moment. But he *knew* madness. He had been around it his entire life. He had only to come within earshot of a person with a touch of mania and his scalp began to prickle.

He didn't feel that from Mia. "She's not mad," he said finally. "I'll be damned if I know how to describe her, but she's not mad. Obsessed, maybe."

"We'll put the best solicitors in the country on the case," Thorn said. "They'll discredit her. Mad or not, we'll have *her* put in Bedlam. Or—we'll steal the letter! Give me her direction and I'll put a lad on it immediately."

"No need for that," Vander said, smiling faintly. "She gave it to me."

"Burn it," Thorn snapped.

"Can't," Vander said. "Code of a gentleman and all that."

"That's utter rot. In any case, I'm no gentleman. Hand it over."

"No."

"It was a stroke of brilliance to hand you the letter," Thorn acknowledged. "She must have known you'd find yourself constrained by your own standards. I would have had her house tossed or just burned down the whole place and have done with it."

"It's a question of name and lineage," Vander explained. "It's bigger than I am. The whole mess has made me think about what I really want. My mother was desperately in love with Carrington, willing to risk everything to be with him. Even though the man was an empty-headed, light-fingered fool."

"No argument there."

Vander looked over at Thorn, knowing his face was rueful. "I used to talk vaguely about falling in love— because it was an excellent excuse for avoiding society events where I might find a bride. Frankly, I would be horrified if I was trapped by that sort of passion."

"I used to think that as well," Thorn observed.

"What's more, I would loathe it if my name became a byword because my wife took lovers. I might well go mad," Vander said dispassionately.

"Well, there is that. Given the persistence of her adoration, Miss Carrington likely won't ever think of another man."

Vander's smile was probably a bit feral. "There you have it. Perfect marriage for me."

"You'll have to get an heir on her—which means you'll have to bed her. I couldn't perform, not with a woman who was blackmailing me. Unless she only wants your name?"

"Don't you remember that poem? If I'm not mistaken, my title is coming in a distant second to my moonbeam."

Thorn swore again. "That's intolerable."

"Not necessarily. I've often thought it would be hell to have a frigid wife. I seem to have the opposite. But I do mean to set some restrictions in that regard."

"Such as?"

"I'm allotting her four nights."

"Per month or per week?"

"Neither," Vander said, enjoying himself. "Four days per year."

He looked up to find Thorn's face alive with laughter.

"I might give her an extra night now and then," he added. "On her birthday."

Thorn rarely laughed; it just wasn't in his nature. But he guffawed now.

"Four nights should be enough to produce an heir," Vander noted. It wasn't the end of the world to have an adoring wife. Particularly because the terms of their arrangement meant that he need not dance attendance on her.

"India will hate her no matter what." Thorn got up from his chair. "She had plans for you."

"That girl you pushed off on me the last time we went to the theater bleated at me like a goat all night. And her face was beaky."

"Those are cheekbones, you ass."

"I didn't like them." The girl had been all angular bones and hard edges. He preferred . . .

He preferred a woman who fit under his arm like a sheltering bird. Even Thorn's gorgeous wife, India, was too tall for him, if the truth be told.

Thorn stared down at him. "Just tell me this: Does Miss Carrington agree with your limit of four nights?"

"I haven't told her yet, but she will. She's *mad with love*, if I recall the phrasing correctly from that poem. She'll take any scraps I throw in her direction. I think she repeated her proposal three or four times. To be succinct: she begged me."

"Damn it," his friend said, obviously disgusted. "This marriage is going to give you a wildly inflated idea of your own importance."

Vander grinned at him.

Chapter Five

NOTES ON FLORA & LONDON

- Mr. Mortimer's solicitor buys her jewelry, coach, servants
  . . . what else?
- Modiste ecstatic to provide wardrobe for young lady so
  exquisite. Slender, coltish legs, doelike eyes (watch for too
  many animal metaphors)
- in wks, all London at Flora's feet.
- Virtuous, ~~farmer~~ impoverished squire, Mr. Wolfington.
  "My heart is the only gold I offer!"
- Count Frederic—side of the ballroom—longs for her hand.
- Frederic and Flora dance once, twice. Ballroom sighs at
  sight of his celestial beauty, dark locks next to yellow,
  & etc.

*~ Yet even in the scene of mirthful festivity, Flora aware of an
unaccountable feeling of Apprehension . . .*

Vander had ignored the question of marriage all day, working in his stables from five in the morning to evening. A stallion that he'd bought from Africa, chosen due to his bloodlines, had been delivered that morning. The young horse, Jafeer, had turned out to be both ferocious and completely unnerved by his new residence, and Vander had spent most of the afternoon trying to settle him.

His stable master was convinced that a good night's sleep would make all the difference to Jafeer's temperament. Vander wasn't quite as certain. There was a wild tone to the Arabian's whinny that suggested true distress.

Marvelous. He'd had the stallion shipped all the way to England . . . and now it was showing every sign of being difficult, if not impossible, to train.

He walked into his study and caught sight of an untouched letter: Mia's supposed requirements for marriage. Rage ran up his spine like a flame. The woman actually thought that *she* could dictate the terms of their marriage?

She was blackmailing him into making her a duchess, and on top of that, insisting on her own terms as well? The hell with that. A man is the master of his wife. Once Mia and he married, he would be in control.

She might be able to buy his title, but nothing else. With a sudden jerky movement, he crumpled the sheet and hurled it into the fire. It fell against the logs and within seconds was consumed by flames.

He had never deluded himself about his intimidating size and rough demeanor. He knew he was the least sophisticated duke in the land. But Mia hadn't shown any fear in response to his explosion of anger, though grown men had trembled in his presence.

Her infatuation was that powerful.

She must have made up her mind as a girl, biding her time until precisely a year after the death of his mother. He balled his fist and tapped it against the mantelpiece, thinking. There was something deeply unsettling about the idea that she wanted him so much, even after all this time, that she was willing to blackmail him.

By all rights, he should feel revolted at the idea of bedding her. But fool that he was, despite his outrage, he still liked her voluptuous figure.

He dropped his hand and turned away, walking back to his desk. She would probably attempt to use his desire to tame him. Every fiber of his being rejected that notion.

It might be time to let the dukedom go.

But . . . he *was* the duke. It was everything he was, and everything he had. The bones of the house were his. The portraits of his ancestors which lined the walls, the crypt full of those ancestors' bones . . . the coffin where his mother was interred, his father's beside her, an ironic pairing, under the circumstances.

No.

He couldn't let all that history fall into a stranger's hands over something as trivial as marriage. He wanted to keep the title for his own children, even if those children came from Mia Carrington's womb.

Something barbaric stirred in him. Her curves, plump mouth, golden hair: it would all be his. He hardened even more at the thought.

Revulsion followed that wave of lust. She was incredibly short-sighted. What if he locked her in the garret? Starved her? Killed her? He had the feeling that a jury of his noble peers would refuse to convict him of murder, if it came to trial and the sordid facts of their marriage emerged.

Not that he would actually harm her; thoughts were one thing, actions entirely another. But she could damn well accept *his* terms for this marriage, and the hell with whatever demands she'd made on that sheet he'd consigned to the fire.

He dropped into his chair, took up a sheet of engraved stationery, scrawled a letter, and signed it with his full name.

Miss Carrington:

> *You will find below the parameters of this marriage. Without your express consent to my terms, I will not marry you and the dukedom can go to hell.*

> > *Evander Septimus Brody*
> > *4th Duke of Pindar*
> > *Viscount Brody*
> > *Baron Drummond*

He folded it, took out the sealing wax he never used, and busied himself with lighting a candle, melting the wax, and all the rest of the rigmarole involved in stamping the letter with the ducal seal in dark crimson.

A grim smile curled the edges of his mouth as he rang the bell.

When a footman arrived, he handed over the letter. "Send that to the Carrington estate in the morning. Inform Miss Carrington that the groom will wait for her reply."

Chapter Six

From Miss Emilia Carrington to William Bucknell, Esq.
Mssrs. Brandy, Bucknell & Bendal, Publishers
September 6, 1800

Dear Mr. Bucknell,

I assure you that I am writing as quickly as I possibly can, given the fact that I am scarcely out of my blacks. ~~And I was jilted~~

I have been making excellent progress on <u>An Angel's Form and a Devil's Heart</u> and indeed, I have nearly ~~fifty~~ one hundred pages written.

I have made some salutary adjustments to the plot, and I believe this will be a most original and fresh novel. My heroine, Flora, is jilted at the altar by the hero, much to her consternation. However, this indignity will not go ~~unrevenged~~. unavenged.

She also nearly dies of hunger, and barely escapes the evil Lord Plum with her virtue intact, until she is finally reunited with Count Frederic, ~~who saves her from a runaway horse~~.

I believe my readers will find the plot quite enjoyable.

With all respect,

Miss Carrington

P.S. Please send me all of Miss Julia Quiplet's novels by return post. I very much enjoyed reading the book you sent. For many reasons, it has been a vexing few days, but I was much comforted by the novel. In fact, I was unable to sleep last night until I turned the last page of The Lost Duke of Windhower.

Carrington House,
Estate of Master Charles Wallace Carrington
Residence of Miss Emilia Carrington
(And, for that matter, Miss Lucibella Delicosa)

Mia had been at her desk since five that morning, agonizing over her impossibly late manuscript, which translated to trying—with little to show for it—to write the first chapter. If she and Charlie had to escape to Bavaria, they would need her writing income.

She had only reached the stage of writing notes about the plot and trying out scraps of dialogue, which she was capable of doing for weeks before actually sitting down to write a novel.

Perhaps Flora could knock down the devilish

scoundrel, Count Frederic, with her mother's prayer book (a nice touch), after which he would bleat pitifully, "But I love you . . ."

Flora would snap back, "I don't know why you're crying, Count. I lost closer friends than you when I was deloused!"

Mia had read that insult somewhere.

Alas, there was no point in even considering a heroine who had been inflicted with lice. A Lucibella heroine would never find herself infested by vermin. Her heroines were always being chased into ravines or threatened with ravishment. But they knew nothing of lice, menstruation, or even rotten teeth. Boils. Smallpox. Syphilis.

A Lucibella heroine would faint or possibly even die if she was diagnosed with a disfiguring infection.

What's more, every gentleman who met a Lucibella heroine instinctively genuflected. It hardly needed to be said that no man would ever whip open his breeches and display his private parts.

That just brought Mia around to thinking about Vander again, though to be honest, she hadn't stopped thinking of him.

She had a fair understanding of the mechanics of the marital act. But that—that part of a man was much larger and more vital than she had imagined.

Because she had imagined it. Roughly the size of a quill, she had thought. Or a pencil.

She had been badly mistaken, clearly.

Unless it was just Vander who was outsized.

After all, everything about him seemed bigger than other men. His chest was wider, his shoulders were wider. It stood to reason that the other parts of him were congruous.

He probably had a huge big toe. Enormous kneecaps.

Humiliation was warring with . . . with mortification. She swallowed hard. It was one thing to deduce that most men's dismissive attitudes meant that they found her unattractive. But it was another to have heard it all confirmed. Vander found her fat and short and embarrassing. And tarred her with her father's brush, obviously.

Mia had been horrified when she first realized Lord Carrington's adulterous activities . . . but at the heart she was a romantic. Her father had loved the duchess so much that he never re-married. Whenever the duke was released from the asylum and returned to Rutherford Park, her father would worry himself ill.

He would walk around and around his library, muttering to himself. In a week or two, something would happen at the duchy—Mia was never quite certain what—and a note would arrive, summoning Lord Carrington.

The duke would be locked up again; her father would resume his place at the duchess' side. Mia had learned from her father that love was more important than wedding vows. Love was everything.

Not that any of her characters were adulterous, because Mia had a clear understanding of her readers' requirements. At the mere mention of adultery, Flora would have fainted. "Orgy" would have made her squeak and run from the room, though Mia couldn't stop finding new and finding interesting uses for it—an orgy of crows, for example, or an orgy of sweets.

An orgy of Vander.

The memory of Vander caressing himself made her heart quicken again. Lucibella heroes weren't lustful. They were principled and sincere in their declarations of love, without a grain of lust. What's more, they maintained calm even in the face of Mortal Peril.

Vander was not calm. He burned with passion and fury. When he lost his temper, it was as if a lion were raging around the room.

Perhaps the reason she was having trouble with this novel was that her hero felt so ineffectual and insipid by comparison to Vander.

Mia gave herself a mental shake. It was time to stop shilly-shallying and determine the broad outlines of the plot. After writing six novels, she knew that once she had the plot, she could write the book fairly quickly.

She picked up her quill again: Frederic plans to humiliate Flora at the altar, but Flora detects his nefarious plan. Finally understanding where his true emotions lie (but too late), he abases himself at Flora's feet.

The count waited on his knees, his elegant head bent, his eyes searching the dust for the answer he sought.

But unfortunately for the arrogant, supercilious nobleman, Flora saw through the Trappings of Title, and mere Circumstances of Birth. The count was not a good man.

Mr. Wolfington, was a far, far better man, though he wasn't a peer.

Life in a hovel with him would be preferable to life in a palazzo with the despicable count.

Mia paused. Her readers would be surprised by this sentiment, since Lucibella's previous novels had concluded with heroines in command of many servants, not to mention diamond necklaces. In fact, she had a strong feeling that many of her readers would not share Flora's ideas about the pleasures of life in a hovel.

She shrugged. The hero could dig up the floor of his hut and find a bag of gold.

The door opened. "Yes?" Her eyes fell to the silver salver in her butler's hand. On it lay a letter: rich creamy paper folded and sealed with red wax as if it had been sent by the Emperor Charlemagne.

Her estimation of Vander's character was diminishing by the hour. Not that she was in a position to cast stones. But he appeared to have grown into someone with an overweening sense of his own consequence.

Commonsense prodded her. What had she expected?

He was a *duke,* for goodness' sake. People probably fawned over him day and night.

Thank goodness, Vander had no idea that he was marrying someone with an undignified alter ego, to wit, Lucibella. He'd probably give up his dukedom rather than endure the shame. Not only was he marrying a dumpy charity case, but one who had turned her talent for maudlin poetry into a career fashioning disreputable fiction.

She took the letter and broke the seals. So he'd allow his dukedom to "go to hell" if she didn't agree with his demands? It didn't matter what his terms were; she had no choice but accept them. What would be, would be.

She read the lines below his signature twice and, against all odds, started laughing. She was marrying a madman, so arrogant that he truly believed she was desperately in love with him and would implore him to bed her.

And he was going to ration her. He would give her four nights.

Implore him?

Her smile disappeared. Vander could wait until all

of Dante's hellish circles froze over before she'd beg for a night from him.

The duke was extraordinarily handsome, no doubt about that, but he was also the most conceited man she'd ever met. By far. She thought back to the moment when he'd unbuttoned his breeches. Was she supposed to be overcome by his magnificence and quiver with fright?

Presumably, she wasn't supposed to be gripped by curiosity. (Which she was, shameful and unladylike though it was.)

Obviously, Vander had thought that she would size him up and flee in the other direction. Her previous knowledge of the male anatomy had been limited to a few marble statues and whatever she could imagine lay behind a largish fig leaf.

The size of those leaves did suggest he had a point about his grandeur.

Still, women must have flattered him dreadfully, if he believed one glimpse would terrify her.

Whatever else one might conclude about Vander's letter, it was clear that he had ignored *her* letter, in which she had explained the short span of their marriage. Fine. She merely had to get him to the altar, and Mr. Plummer could take over thereafter.

She kept her answer brief.

I agree to your terms for our marriage; to wit, that you and I will be intimate only in the event that I beg you for that privilege, and on no account more than four nights in a year.

The very idea of intimacy made her fingers shake, leaving a blot after her signature. Vander . . . naked. In bed.

She would leave Rutherford Park directly after the wedding, making the question irrelevant. The marriage could not be consummated, as that would threaten its annulment, though not, according to Mr. Plummer, Vander's guardianship of Charlie.

This marriage wasn't about pleasure.

Not four nights . . . not *any* nights.

She sealed the letter and sent it back with Vander's waiting groom. Then she wrote two more sentences and crossed them out, until she decided that what she ought to do was sit down and reread Miss Julia Quiplet's novel. That would convince her that there were decent gentlemen in the world.

But first she should see how Charlie was doing. She got up and headed for the nursery. Charlie was far more important than all trivialities such as dukes. Marriage. Wedding nights.

Her nephew was sitting at the small desk in the corner of the nursery. His eyes brightened the moment she entered. "Aunt Mia! Would you like to read my essay on Aristophanes?"

"Certainly," she said, smiling at him. In the year since her brother had died, Sir Richard had dismissed Charlie's tutor, after which she convinced the vicar to take over her nephew's education.

Her brother John would have been appalled. He had been disappointed by his only son's condition, but he never shirked on his son's instruction, understanding that Charles Wallace would manage the Carrington estate someday.

Charlie swung across the room on his pipestem legs, stopping next to the sofa and leaning on his crutch. "What's the matter?"

She reached out, pulled him onto her lap, and

hugged him. Soon he would be nine years old. Then ten, then twenty . . .

If she had to marry the devil himself to keep this child happy and secure, she would do it. John's will required that she be married; luckily it did not specify how long.

"Nothing's the matter!" she said, trying to sound cheerful. "I'm fine. In fact, I want you to be the first to know that I just accepted a proposal of marriage from a duke." She pushed from her mind the fact that she was the one doing the proposing. Charlie didn't need to know that. He had far too much worry in his young life as it was. "Just think, darling, I shall be a duchess. That's much better than marrying Mr. Reeve."

"No!" Charlie scowled. "Mr. Reeve will come back; I know he'll come back! He promised to make me another crutch. He wouldn't leave without doing that. He *promised*."

Mia sighed. Charlie refused to accept that she had been left at the altar. "Mr. Reeve left a note saying he meant to travel to India, remember?"

Her former fiancé, Edward, hadn't bothered to save her the humiliation of waiting for him in church, for which she would never forgive him. Why couldn't he have made up his mind to flee the night before the wedding?

That would have been humiliating, but bearable. She would have grieved in private. As it was, the letter was delivered to Sir Richard, who had read it aloud as she was waiting in the vestibule of St. Ninian's.

Edward hadn't even informed his parents of his decision to flee the country; the Earl of Gryffyn and his wife had been in the sanctuary awaiting the ceremony. When she'd seen them later that morning, they'd looked as shocked and distraught as she felt.

In a small, secret part of her heart, she wanted to

believe Charlie was right. Someday Edward would return. He had loved her. He had looked at her . . . well, he had looked at her the way she used to look at Vander.

One day Edward would wake from the terror of marriage that had sent him running from the altar, but it would be too late.

"I cannot wait, Charlie," she said, swallowing hard. "Only two weeks remain before the guardianship clause in your father's will takes effect." Her brother had named her Charlie's guardian—but specified that she had to be married to a man of substance and worth within a twelvemonth of his death.

It would not have occurred to her brother that she, Mia, could undertake the repetitive and boring work of estate management. He and her father had always dismissed her airily, calling her books "scribbles."

Her scribbles earned more than the Carrington estate did last year, but she hadn't shared that fact with her father, not since her first book came out and he magnanimously granted her the right to keep her pennies to herself.

In his words.

"I wish he hadn't left," Charlie said, voicing the obvious. "Mr. Reeve promised to buy a sleigh next winter and pull me over the snow, and he was going to teach me how to invent things."

Mia's arm tightened around him. When her brother died, Sir Richard had promptly tried to retain guardianship of his nephew, on the grounds that Mia's betrothed was illegitimate and consequently not a man of "substance and worth." That had come to nothing, mercifully.

Sir Richard often won his lawsuits—which were legion—but he lost this one. Instead, Edward's solicitors had promptly launched a counter-suit for slander. Edward may be illegitimate, but he was the son of an earl. What's more, he was an Oxford professor who had made a fortune perfecting various machines, including a new type of paper-making machine that was used by printers.

Mia had actually met him in the office of her publisher, when Lucibella Delicosa was visiting London. For a moment she thought wistfully about the heady first days of their romance, when her father and brother were still alive, and she had believed she'd finally met a man she admired.

Then she shook herself. Ironically, Sir Richard had been proven right: Edward was not a man of "substance and worth," or he never would have jilted her.

"You will learn how to invent things on your own," she told Charlie. "I have to marry someone other than Mr. Reeve. Luckily for us, the duke has offered to step in." She pressed a kiss on his forehead. "I will not let you go to Sir Richard, Charlie O'Mine."

He leaned his head against her shoulder and she wrapped her other arm around him as well. She could feel his bones, thin and birdlike, against her body. He may be on his way to becoming a man, but for now he was still a child, and a frail one.

"I don't like being Sir Richard's ward. He looks at me as if I had three fingers, or two noses."

"We needn't worry about your uncle ever again. You'll be a duke's ward. What do you think of that?"

Charlie looked heartbreakingly uncertain. "I've never met a duke. Do you know him well?"

"Of course I do," Mia said. "I've known His Grace since we were children, which is why he is being generous enough to do us this favor, on the basis of our old friendship."

If only that were the truth. "After this marriage

business is over, I thought we might take a trip, the two of us. What do you say about making a tour of Bavaria?" Bavaria had always struck her as a most romantic place with castles that she could use as the setting to future heroines' adventures.

The sooner she left England after the marriage contract was signed, the sooner Vander could file for divorce on grounds of desertion or annulment on the grounds of non-consummation, whichever he pleased. As she'd explained to him in the letter he hadn't bothered to read.

It was rather sad to realize that although she would miss her horse, Lancelot, there was no one and nothing else to keep her in England—not if Charlie was with her. Just at the moment, her life seemed oddly thin.

"Yes, please!" His voice rose with excitement. "I should like that above all things."

"Then that is what we shall do."

"I might have trouble walking on board ship."

Mia shuddered at the very thought of Charlie on a slippery deck. "We'll stay in the cabin and find ourselves across the Channel before you know it," she said, trying to sound gay.

And failing.

His slight arms wound around her neck. "It will be all right, Auntie," he said, putting his tousled dark head, so like her brother's, against her shoulder.

"I love you," she whispered.

Charlie's voice was only a thread of sound. "I love you too."

Chapter Seven

NOTES ON PLOT

- All London at Flora's feet.
- Flora unsure of Count Frederic: Could it be that the count, so assiduous in his intentions, was in reality naught but a Cruel Betrayer?

Frederic: "Who could behold such a picture of Feminine Grace and Sweetness, and not recognize one of Heaven's Perfect Works?"

- should he declare himself immediately, at the first ball?

"My heart is madly devoted to you," the count cried. (Ugh. Exclaimed? Protested?)

"*By all that is most sacred to my soul, I swear that my heart is ~~madly~~ eternally devoted to you,*" *exclaimed the count, his heart beating with ~~love~~ the agony of his emotion ~~he felt~~.*

Not bad.

Rutherford Park
Three days later

The morning of Mia's wedding was clear with the promise of unexpectedly sultry late summer sunshine. She woke, disoriented, at five, thinking that it was almost time to see if Charlie was awake.

But as she blinked at unfamiliar wallpaper, she remembered that she had kissed her nephew goodnight the day before and traveled to Vander's estate. It was only a matter of an hour between their houses, but the duke had ordered that she spend the night at Rutherford Park, and she didn't think it politic to bicker over such a trivial matter.

Her rebellion was to arrive very late at night, whereupon she was ushered—without a welcome from her husband-to-be—straight to a bedchamber, one she presumed had belonged to the late duchess.

Mia looked around with a twitch of distaste at the lustrous gold tassels hanging from the bedposts, the Lyonnaise silk hangings along the dressing table, the silver urn engraved with the ducal seal poised on the mantel.

The urn was surrounded by a clutter of small animals made of china and lacquer and jade, a collection that was beginning to feel desperate to her. Could it be that her father had given his lover china animals because he could not give her children?

It was a morose thought. The duchess had had a

sad smile, like a woman with a secret. Perhaps the secret wasn't her adultery but something sadder. More intimate.

Mia shrugged and hopped out of bed. She would be gone by midday. There was no need to antagonize Vander with her presence more than absolutely necessary. He would be overjoyed to hear that she had no intention of remaining under his roof, and that the marriage was in name only.

Her maid, Susan, popped her head in the door with a smile. "Good morning, miss!" She ushered in footmen carrying cans of steaming water that they took into the adjoining bathing chamber.

For the life of her, Mia couldn't stop thinking about the late duchess. Why, for example, would Her Grace have wanted a bathtub surrounded entirely by mirrors?

She herself always did her best to not look at her own figure or, indeed, any part of herself. It was impossible not to catch sight of distressing expanses of pink flesh when the walls were adorned with silvered glass wherever one looked.

She refused to soak but washed, climbed out, and wrapped herself in a length of toweling as quickly as she could. Really, she wanted everything about this trip to be got through as quickly as possible.

"What does the household think of this marriage?" she asked Susan.

Her maid's eyes met hers in the glass and then moved back down to the comb she was drawing through Mia's long hair. "They daren't say aught to my face."

They'd been together for three years, and Susan knew almost everything about her, even the story of that benighted poem. Susan being Susan, she had hooted with laughter over the "pearly potion," though she agreed that it was fiendish of Oakenrott to tell the world about her infatuation for Vander.

"You'd think they'd be glad to see their master married," she continued. "But they seem to think that His Grace is making an enormous mistake. It was all I could do not to give Mr. Nottle a piece of my mind last night." Her cheeks turned pink and she started combing a bit faster.

"The butler?"

"It's that formal downstairs, my lady, you wouldn't believe it. Mr. Gaunt would fall about laughing if we bowed and scraped to him the way that Mr. Nottle demands. And yet he didn't stop the servants from chattering about the upstairs in a way that Mr. Gaunt would never allow."

"I doubt that my father was very popular in this establishment," Mia pointed out. "I made myself notorious with the love poem, and after my father and the duchess died together, the scandal flared up again."

"His Grace is lucky to have you!" Susan insisted. "From what everyone says, he's never shown the slightest interest in ladies, only in horses. He doesn't go to balls or even to London for the season; he just spends all his time in the stables. He's never even made a pretense of wooing a lady." She lowered her voice. "Some folk think he's not interested in women, if you know what I mean."

Mia felt her cheeks grow warm. Those people were wrong. Vander was interested in women. "You can't blame the household for being dismayed by this hasty marriage, Susan. They would likely wish him to find someone elegant, like his mother. Someone to match all this." She waved her hand at the furnishings.

Susan wrinkled her nose. "Her Grace wasn't from the peerage," she said, "and you can see it in this room. It says everything about her."

"We mustn't say such things," Mia said. "It isn't polite."

"This is an anxious room," Susan pronounced. She wasn't wrong about that; there wasn't a single place in the bedchamber where a person could restfully gaze without being reminded either of the duchess' status or her passion for miniatures.

"What I'm saying is that the servants likely wish that I were a different woman, Susan."

"All you need is a new wardrobe," her maid said, not for the first time. Susan was a dear, and always claimed that her mistress underestimated her own charms, whereas Mia insisted she was merely being practical. Tall women could wear gowns that swirled elegantly down from their breasts, but she was so short that her legs looked stubby no matter the style.

She had the vague idea that it would take three or four fittings to achieve a gown that would actually be flattering. She had never had time for that, and the local seamstress definitely wasn't up to the challenge.

What's more, Sir Richard had been in charge of the estate monies for the last year. As he wasn't allowed to withdraw funds himself until he came into full guardianship, he had contented himself with restricting every expenditure—and had ended her allowance on the pretense that, because she was in mourning, she had no need for new garments.

Her Lucibella money was reserved for possible flight with Charlie. Consequently, she would be wearing an ill-fitting muslin gown to her wedding. Vander would probably be in sackcloth and ashes, so it hardly mattered.

Edward wouldn't have cared. He was a man of

intellect, uninterested in the superficial aspects of a person's appearance. She was a little surprised to discover that she didn't feel utterly heartbroken at the idea of marrying a man other than her fiancé.

According to the novels she loved (and wrote), she should still be prostrate on the floor, sobbing. It had been only a month since the jilting, after all. She intended to describe Flora as turning white as parchment, with haunted eyes and newly slender limbs resulting from a vanished appetite.

Mia, on the other hand, was as hungry as ever. In fact, after the first shock of the jilting, she primarily felt irritated rather than grief-stricken, and a temper always made her crave buttered crumpets.

The larger problem was that Mia was petrified by the idea of descending the stairs for her wedding. How could she face Vander again? She had engaged in such unethical conduct toward him. He must loathe her.

Of course he loathed her.

Finally, she made herself leave the room. There was nothing to be done about it: She had to face the irascible duke and say her vows as quickly as possible, after which she could go home and pretend none of this happened.

It was horrifying to reach the bottom of the stairs and hear voices coming from the drawing room. Surely Vander wouldn't have gathered a wedding party?

Her heroine in *Love Conquers All*, Petronella—or was it Giuliana?—had had to face the guillotine. Petronella lifted her chin and walked bravely to her doom (though, of course, no doom awaited her, because a duke was overcome by her exquisite beauty and risked his life to save her).

Mia lifted her chin and tried to walk bravely

toward the drawing room. It wasn't exactly the same as moving toward a guillotine, but her heart was certainly thumping as if she faced death. Vander's butler, Nottle, didn't make it easier; he looked condescendingly down his long nose before he opened the drawing room door and announced, "Miss Carrington."

To her enormous shock, the Duke of Villiers stood directly before her. The gentleman—a distant acquaintance of her father, as she recalled—was renowned for his sartorial splendor and true to his reputation, he was dressed like a peacock, in a coat of blue-and-green striped silk taffeta over a waistcoat embroidered all over with flowers.

Mia looked rather wildly for his duchess, but the only other person in the room was Vander, also dressed splendidly, in a coat of dark amethyst silk with embroidery around the cuffs.

So much for the sackcloth.

She was underdressed for her own wedding.

Vander stepped forward and bowed. "Miss Carrington." Her stomach clenched. He had that kind of voice, a truly masculine voice. "I apologize for not greeting you last evening."

"Your Grace." She dipped a curtsy. A deep one because it gave her a moment. She turned and curtsied before the Duke of Villiers. "Your Grace," she murmured.

"I trust you are well?" Vander inquired, his face utterly expressionless.

She could feel rosy blotches spreading up her neck. "Of course. I am surprised. I did not expect that we would have a wedding party under the circumstances."

"What'ya saying?" a voice broke in, coming from nowhere. Startled, Mia jumped sideways, straight into Vander.

His big hands came around her shoulders to steady her and he held her there, against his warm body. "Uncle, I had no idea you were in the room. Miss Carrington, may I present my uncle, Sir Cuthbert Brody?"

Sir Cuthbert had just risen from a high-backed chair positioned before the window. He was a short man, about her height, though a great deal rounder. His nose was red, and his cheeks were red, and what hair he had left had once been combed over his bald head but was now standing up like a flag at the prow of a ship. He wore an extraordinary, if crumpled, coat of sage-green paisley silk and carried a matching green cane with a brass top.

"I prefer Chuffy," he said, with just the faintest slur to his words. "Good morning to you, my dear." He was drunk. No, he was not just drunk: he was utterly bosky, actually swaying slightly.

Vander groaned. "When I saw you last, at two in the morning, you said you were going to bed, Uncle."

"Oh, by then it was too late to go to bed. Besides, I would have missed this glorious occasion, this nuptial . . . this marital meeting."

"Were you planning to change your coat?" Vander asked.

"This coat is good enough to drink in," his uncle said cheerily. "So it's good enough to walk *you* to the altar. Besides, it ain't as if this is the kind of wedding that'll involve wiggle-wagging our way up the aisle of Paul's, is it?"

There was something endearing about his brown eyes, muzzy or not. Mia stepped away from Vander's hands and the first genuine smile of the day came to her lips. "It's a pleasure to meet you, Sir Cuthbert." She curtsied.

"You can call me Chuffy," he said, listing a bit as he

bowed. "You'll be my—my—my *niece*, after all. I must have met you before, haven't I? I mean, back when your father was diddling around with my sister-in-law?"

"Uncle," Vander said from behind her, his tone flinty.

Chuffy squinted at him. "What? Are we pretending that we've never met the gal before? Though I don't know as I did meet you, m'dear. Vander's father was my brother, though his brain was all higgledy-piggledy."

"She knows that," Vander stated.

"Don't mean that we should just stand about and stare at her as if she were a potboy dressed up in a vicar's cassock," Chuffy said. He managed to get himself upright and made a wobbly swipe at his head that made his hair fly into the air again. "How's every little thing, Villiers? Didn't expect to see *you* here, I must say."

It was interesting to discover that the most discriminating peer in London apparently counted a drunkard among his friends. "I had no idea you were in the room, Chuffy," Villiers said, with a bow and a warm smile.

"Well, I ain't going to lie," Chuffy said. "I took a little nap once I realized that the two of you were standing around nattering about the bride-to-be."

Mia bit her lip. It was one thing to imagine she was facing the guillotine and another to have it confirmed that people were muttering 'Off with her head.' So her future husband had been standing around and making fun of her. What had she expected?

Surprisingly, Chuffy came to her defense. "You should be ashamed of yerself, Leo," he told the duke. "You were not exactly the catch of the season yourself, you know. I never did figure out how you talked that lovely lady into accepting you, what with all those bastards of yours. Nearly a dozen of 'em, wasn't it?"

Villiers's countenance had eased. "Only half a dozen. And now I have one legitimate son as well."

"Am I supposed to congratulate you on sowing seed in your own field?" Chuffy demanded. "You're not one to call the kettle black, or however that goes." He took a step closer to Mia, like an unsteady knight in tarnished armor. "Now I ain't going to stand for any more gibble-gabbling around like a bunch of old women."

The Duke of Villiers nodded and said, "Chuffy, you've made me feel ashamed of myself." He looked at Mia and said, "I'm sorry that you were made uncomfortable, Miss Carrington. I have known His Grace since he was a small boy, and the circumstances of his betrothal are not what I hoped for him."

Mia took a breath. "I apologize for those circumstances," she said, and she meant it.

The duke waited, as if for Mia to change her mind, simply because a duke—another duke—didn't approve of blackmail. But she couldn't. Charlie's welfare was paramount, and far more important than the Duke of Villiers's opinion.

"*I* understand why this gal wants my nephew," Chuffy announced. "She has good taste. The boy speaks any number of languages word for word without so much as a book in the room—"

"No, I don't," Vander said quietly.

"He's not the best looking," Chuffy said, ignoring his nephew entirely. "But he is a duke, and comes with a title. The problem is that he's a great quarreler."

Mia could see that Vander was growing angry.

"Not like his father, though. My brother—God rest his soul—couldn't keep his temper. But that was the fault of his brains and not he. He was a great eater of beef, and I believe it did harm to his wit." He paused and looked expectantly at Mia.

She nodded. Was she supposed to play name-that-quotation? She recognized the text, but it wasn't an appropriate moment to be bandying about Shakespeare.

"The lad has an excellent head of hair, though," Chuffy said.

That wasn't Shakespeare; it was simply a statement of fact. Vander had a wonderfully thick head of hair.

"I think that we might as well sit down," Vander said, impatience darkening his voice. "Miss Carrington and I are to marry within the hour, but the vicar seems to have gone missing. He left to prepare the chapel. It has seen little use in recent years," he explained to Mia.

She was just grateful not to find herself in the local church, St. Ninian's, reliving the Great Jilting. She felt distinctly nauseated. She could hardly believe that she was blackmailing a man into marriage. She didn't want to meet the eyes of his uncle, or think seriously about what it meant for Vander.

The door opened and Nottle reappeared. "Mr. Tobias and Lady Xenobia India Dautry," he announced.

Mia's heart sank. Apparently, Vander had invited his friend Thorn, one of the witnesses to the horrible poetry reading years ago.

"Why not invite the whole countryside?" Chuffy demanded. "Here, you, Nottle: this is all hugger-mugger. Where's the champagne? Your master is getting leg-shackled!"

The butler's mouth tightened to a thin line. Vander's

chin jerked, and Nottle withdrew, Chuffy trotting after him with a wave in the direction of Dautry and his wife.

Mia felt dizzy watching the Duke of Villiers greet his son and daughter-in-law. What on earth was she doing standing in a room with people this distinguished and beautiful?

Thorn Dautry and Lady Xenobia were remarkably well suited. It hardly needed to be said that they were as decorated as a pair of maypoles, and as tall, too. The kind of people who made her feel like a grubby mushroom.

"Have you invited any other guests?" Mia asked Vander in a low voice.

"Why do you ask?" It was astonishing how clearly his eyes expressed anger, while his words were perfectly civil. "Don't you wish to celebrate this happy occasion, my dear?"

Of course he was angry. She knew that, and acknowledged that he had a right to be. She just hadn't realized what it would be like to stand next to a huge man practically vibrating with rage.

"I had imagined that we would have a private ceremony," she said, not entirely in command of her voice.

"Private? Why on earth would we do that?" Vander turned and gave Thorn one of those brusque clasps that men give each other. "Thank you for coming."

"I wouldn't have missed it for the world," Dautry said, his voice clipped.

At least her heroine in *Love Conquers All* was saved from the guillotine before she was actually threatened by the blade. Mia had the wild sensation that the blade was flashing down toward her neck.

Too late she realized that she should have insisted Vander read the letter detailing the short term of their marriage.

Vander's hand slipped under her arm. "Miss Carrington, you will remember Mr. Dautry, though you may not have met his wife, Lady Xenobia India. They are close friends of mine."

Thorn Dautry was homicidal. With one glance she realized that his wife felt the same way.

When she had made the desperate decision to blackmail Vander into marrying her, she hadn't envisioned the clear-eyed contempt she now saw in Lady Xenobia's eyes. After the briefest possible greeting, the lady turned away as if Mia were no more than an impudent scullery maid.

Mia had heard that Lady Xenobia could reorganize a household within two days, and now she knew how she did it; the lady probably just glanced at the servants who were pilfering the brandy, and they confessed on the spot.

Dautry was escorting his wife over to the sofa with the kind of solicitude that suggested she was carrying a child. Vander followed, leading Mia over to sit beside Lady Xenobia, even though anyone could guess that she would prefer to sit anywhere else. In the corner, for example.

At that moment, Chuffy barged back through the door, followed by Nottle, who carried a tray laden with champagne glasses and a bottle. His lordship held two more bottles, one in each fist. "Here we are," he bawled. "This party is so gloomy I expect to be measuring my poor nevvy for a grave, not a marriage bed!"

Vander headed over to his uncle, probably hoping to prop him up before he and the champagne smashed to the ground.

"He's drowned in drink," Lady Xenobia observed, not bothering to whisper.

Chuffy was the only person who'd demonstrated

any kindness, so Mia felt she should defend him. She cleared her throat. "Sir Cuthbert seems to be making excellent sense to me."

Lady Xenobia turned and looked down at her, as a queen might look at an errant chambermaid. "Only a fool finds a drunken man sensible," she said.

"I wish you wouldn't," Mia said haltingly.

Her ladyship raised an eyebrow. "I wouldn't?"

"There's no need to be angry."

That was a mistake. She knew it the moment that Lady Xenobia's smile deepened rather than slipped, which was a most disconcerting skill. "I am watching a dear friend caught in the coils of a shamming woman waving a letter that she likely had made up in a back alley," the lady said with ferocious, if quiet, eloquence. "We need not discuss the ethics of blackmail. But who's to say that Vander's father actually wrote that letter?"

"He did indeed write it." Honesty compelled Mia to add, "although he was likely already mad. I am sorry for causing you distress."

Lady Xenobia paused for a second, reached forward and put her hand over Mia's. "Please don't do this," she whispered.

Vander was on his way back to them, but Lady Xenobia waved him away. Perversely, Mia felt as if he were deserting her.

"I lose my temper far too easily," the lady was saying. "But you see, Vander is a true friend to me. We cherish him deeply. He deserves to choose his own wife, Miss Carrington. A wife who is suitable for him. *Please.*"

"I well understand your concern for His Grace," she said, trying not to think about her unsuitability, "and I respect your good wishes for him. I assure you that there will still be time for the duke to find a lady who is deserving of him. We shan't be married long, and he's still quite a young man."

"*What?*"

Before Mia could answer, Chuffy swooped down and sat himself between them. He had a glass of champagne that he handed to Mia, and a bottle that he was drinking from.

"I thought I'd better rescue you," he whispered loudly, and turning to the group at large, "There's no music at this party."

"That's because it's not a party," Vander said, coming around the settee. Lady Xenobia hopped up and swept her husband away to the other side of the room. Maybe she would be more polite now she knew the temporary nature of the union she and her husband were supposed to witness.

"Well, my boy, you are in luck: I can provide the music. *What is love? 'tis not hereafter,*" Chuffy caroled, or perhaps warbled was a better word for it. "*Come kiss me, sweet and twenty, Youth's a stuff will not endure.*"

He leaned toward Mia, lips puckered.

Vander's hand shot out. He pulled her to her feet and back against his chest before she could stop him. "Miss Carrington is not for kissing, Uncle."

Chuffy blinked up at them. "Are you older than sweet-and-twenty?" he asked Mia.

"Yes," she said, feeling very old-maid-ish.

"Well, then, I wasn't offering to kiss you," he pointed out.

"Shall we join the vicar in the chapel?" Mia asked desperately. She longed to have this ghastly morning behind her so she could head back to her own house. Charlie might be anxious. She had never left him overnight; she was always there to greet him in the morning.

"Are you in a hurry?" Vander asked.

She stepped back, away from him. "Yes," she said baldly. She wanted to get away from these people, all of whom loved Vander—which was nice for him— but reminded her that she had no one who cared for her, other than Charlie. "Your Grace, surely you don't want to make this occasion more emotional that it already is?"

"*O, stay and hear, your true love's coming,*" Chuffy sang. "'Coming'? Did you hear that? People think ol' Shakespeare was stodgy but we know different, aye?" He staggered to his feet and upended his bottle over Mia's glass, but nothing came out.

He swiveled and glared at Vander. "It's a poor house that doesn't have a drop of champagne for a bride on her wedding day."

"Someone must have drunk it," Vander said.

"*Coming* after *wedding*, you see," Chuffy cooed.

"Miss Carrington, you're biting your lip again." Vander bent closer. "It turns your lips a very appealing color. Some women would do it for that very reason."

She scowled at him.

"I gather you weren't trying to entice your soon-to-be spouse," he said wryly, turning to his guests. "Shall we adjourn to the chapel? The bride is eager to be married."

Eager to be married? That did it. It topped the humiliation of her poetry, of being jilted, of being disdained by Vander's friends.

Welcome, Mia thought grimly, to the Twelfth Circle of Hell.

Chapter Eight

NOTES ON BEQUEST

Count Frederic wealthy beyond wildest dreams—begs Flora to give up Mr. Mortimer's bequest. "Buy a nosegay for my buttonhole, my darling. No man except myself shall give you aught. Not even from beyond the grave!"

- Flora fears to trust him. (avoid 'Flora fears')

"If you have no confidence in me, we are not destined to wed," Frederic exclaimed, his blue eyes bright with betrayal. "How can I take a woman as my countess who ~~trusts~~ loves me not?"

Then he jilts her—after making her give up her inheritance. (Perfidious! Devilish! I like it!)

The vicar was clearly unhappy, likely for any number of reasons. "Who stands for this woman?" he demanded.

Vander was proud to see that Mia didn't flinch. She regarded the vicar steadily, folded her hands, and said, "My closest living relative is eight years old."

Chuffy tottered forward. "She has me. I'm it. I mean, I'll be her kinsman and walk her where she has to go. Up the aisle, is it?"

The vicar regarded him with distaste. "Sir Cuthbert, how come you with this lethargy so early in the day?"

"Is it early?" Chuffy asked, with perfect surprise.

"I believe we should begin the ceremony," Vander stated.

They waited while the vicar fussed about with his missal, and Vander started thinking about the way his father used to rant. His mother would listen, or pretend to, but then she turned to another man whenever she could.

Thinking about his parents' wretched union, he looked down at Mia with a genuine smile. Her head was bent, and morning sunlight streaming through the chapel's east window turned her hair to honey and gold.

A few days earlier he never would have imagined it, but he was coming to understand that this marriage really was the best of all worlds: *She* was desperately in love and wouldn't turn aside from him. *He* was emotionally untouched and need not be concerned about becoming besotted by a woman.

As if sensing his gaze, Mia looked up at him. True, he had promised her only four nights a year together. But he might not mind giving her more.

His eyes drifted lower, to the way her breasts swelled against the tired fabric of her gown. She needed better clothing; she had to dress like a duchess, rather than a governess.

Then India's gown caught his attention. Her breasts were on display, albeit in a fashionable manner, and he wouldn't care for Mia's to be exposed.

"Why are you smiling?" his wife-to-be whispered.

Surprised, he dropped the smile. "Perhaps I'm happy to be getting married."

"There's no need to mock me!"

Chuffy bustled up. "You stand over there, Vander." He gestured toward the altar. "I'll bring my girl into the chapel from the courtyard, and you pretend that you haven't seen her this morning. That's important, you know. Not seeing the bride before getting married."

Without waiting for an answer, he grabbed Mia's arm and dragged her straight out of the chapel.

Thorn broke into a crack of laughter. "Shall I stand beside you?" he asked Vander.

A sudden memory of Thorn's wedding shot into Vander's head. They had married in St. Paul's. The cathedral was filled to the dome with members of polite society, eager to witness a marquess' daughter marry a bastard, albeit a duke's bastard.

He had stood beside Thorn at the front of the church, watching as India walked toward them, her happiness shining from her face. She didn't take her eyes from Thorn, even for a moment.

"Yes," he said abruptly. He turned to the Duke of Villiers. "If you would join me as well, I should be honored."

"You're like a son to me," the duke said, touching Vander's arm. "Between us, Thorn and I will work out this mess. I promise you."

"I will stand next to Miss Carrington," India said grimly.

Vander nodded. "Thank you."

Chuffy poked his head into the chapel and shouted, "Shall I bring in the bride now?"

The vicar sniffed and turned to face the back of the church. Vander moved to the side, Thorn's presence warm at his shoulder.

Chuffy started down the aisle with his arm through Mia's. He was stepping high, apparently aiming for a ceremonial effect. Halfway up the aisle he missed his step and lurched sideways, pulling Mia with him.

India gasped. Luckily Chuffy managed to catch himself on a pew and proceed.

"By God and all the saints at the back door of Purgatory, there was a moment when I thought I might shipwreck us both," he said cheerfully, when they arrived at the chancel railing and he handed Mia over to Vander. "Losing my balance as I grow older."

"I would remind you, Sir Cuthbert, not to take the Lord's name in vain in his own house!" the vicar snapped.

Chuffy gave him a magnificent scowl. "Does thou think that because thou art virtuous, there shall be no more cakes and ale?"

At this pronouncement, Mia gave a charming giggle. Vander was still trying to untangle his uncle's speech—what had cakes and ale to do with anything?—and India was frowning in confusion. But Chuffy and Mia were smiling at each other, and he was patting her arm.

"That one worked, didn't it, my dear?" he said. "Hit that one on the nail head."

Vander raised an eyebrow.

"Sir Cuthbert is quoting from *Twelfth Night*," Mia explained. "He's been doing it on and off all morning."

"He has?" That was from India, apparently as surprised by this information as Vander.

The vicar cleared his throat. Even he seemed amused, if reluctantly. "I could take that reference in offense, Sir Cuthbert. But you must cease your 'disorders,' so that I can get on to the business of marrying His Grace to Miss Carrington."

"Right!" Chuffy agreed. "Time to tie the knot."

The vicar launched into the text. Clearly, he had grasped that the marriage he was solemnizing had little to do with love or, for that matter, sanctity.

Vander allowed the words to flow over him while he thought about his wife-to-be. Mia knew her Shakespeare. Chuffy liked her. His uncle was an old drunkard, but of everyone in Vander's family, he'd been most like a parent. Vander had loved him when he was a boy, and he still did.

When it came time for Vander to say his vows, he felt an unanticipated peacefulness. He'd been coerced into this marriage, and likely he'd never be able to entirely forgive Mia.

But he was gaining a wife who would always be true to him. That thought raised a primitive feeling in his chest, a possessive streak that he'd probably developed the moment his mother had first brought another man into the house.

Mia repeated her vows in a clear, calm voice. It was surprising, actually. He would have supposed she'd be in tears, having achieved a goal she'd yearned for since childhood.

She never met his eyes during the ceremony, just looked at her hands. Even so, he enjoyed sliding a ring that had belonged to his great-grandmother onto her finger.

The vicar pronounced them man and wife, snapped his prayer book closed and said, "You may kiss the bride."

Vander hadn't considered this part of the rite. His first thought was that he shouldn't indulge in casual intimacies of that nature—his new duchess might assume that he would regularly engage in affection-ate gestures. Mia looked up. Her gaze seared into him, even though there was no reproach there.

Before he could move, Chuffy bellowed, "Well, lad, if you ain't going to do it, *I* will!" With that he rounded Mia into his arms and gave her a smack on the lips, making her laugh.

Vander forced himself to relax. For God's sake, he didn't give a damn if his uncle kissed his bride.

Thorn, India, and Villiers gathered around, offer-ing measured good wishes. He watched Mia blink when she was addressed as "Your Grace" for the first time. She looked endearingly uncertain.

"Right," Chuffy said, clearly having taken on the role of master of ceremonies. "I instructed Nottle to lay on the champagne and a decent wedding break-fast, so let's get ourselves out of here. You can accom-pany your wife from the chapel, I trust?" he said, giving Vander a narrow-eyed glare that appeared surprisingly sober.

Vander didn't answer, but simply held out his arm to his wife.

His *wife*.

Mia walked down the aisle next to Vander, in the grip of a tremendous sense of relief. It was done. No one—not even the despicable Sir Richard—could gainsay her marriage to a duke. It tied her to a man who loathed her, and to a lonely life after the mar-riage was formally dissolved, but Charlie's safety was assured.

No more Sir Richard and his litigious, fault-finding ways. She would hire a tutor immediately and pay him double to accompany them to Bavaria. She would arrange to have the cottages in the village re-thatched; they had leaked last winter, but Sir Richard was of the conviction that cottagers should repair their own roofs, even if owners of those roofs had grown old in service to the Carringtons.

Furthermore, she would dismiss any servant who looked at Charlie as if he had two noses. Thinking of Charlie calmed the feelings cascading through her. She had promised him she would return by late afternoon.

Life would soon settle down to its usual quiet rhythm. She would get back to writing; perhaps she could finish the novel in a month or so. She would pretend this painful episode never happened. She had practice forgetting humiliations . . . this was just another one, albeit acute.

Throughout the wedding breakfast, the party discussed *Twelfth Night*, which kept them away from stickier topics.

"I didn't like the play," Lady Xenobia confessed. "I thought it absurd that the countess vows to remain in mourning for her entire life merely because her brother just died. But I have no siblings, and perhaps I underestimate the bond."

"Siblings grow on you in insidious ways," her husband said. "I count myself lucky to be related to every one of mine."

"But would you go into mourning and declare yourself unable to marry if one of your siblings passed away?" Lady Xenobia demanded. "The whole premise of the play is absurd. Shakespeare created an improbability and hung the whole story on it."

"*Come away, come away, death,*" Chuffy sang.

"The play is about the way grief can overwhelm

reason," Mia said. "Viola is a little mad with grief. When my—" She stopped short, wondering what on earth she was doing. She never talked about her feelings. It must be the champagne.

"I gather you lost your brother, which would explain why I was the one who walked you down the aisle," Chuffy said. "Older or younger? Can't say I've spent much time poring over Debrett's."

"My brother John was older than me. He actually died in the same inn fire that killed my father and the late duchess," Mia told him, managing a weak smile.

"That was dashed bad luck," Chuffy said, patting her hand. "I suppose that's why you went a bit cracked."

"Oh, did you crack?" Thorn Dautry asked, his eyes innocent, as if the question wasn't astonishingly discourteous.

"Of course she did," Chuffy said. "Look, she's in this house, ain't she? Marrying the son of her father's mistress. If that ain't mad, I don't know what is. Like to like, they always say, and madness runs rampant in this family."

After that charming observation, Mia glanced around and realized that everyone's plates were empty. She and Vander needed to have the last conversation of their married life. Given that he couldn't even bring himself to kiss her after the ceremony, he would surely rejoice at the news his wife planned to desert him before the wedding night. She might as well give him that pleasure now.

She rose, perhaps with a bit more eagerness than was truly courteous.

The Duke of Villiers's eyes were wryly amused as he kissed Mia's hand goodbye. "This has been a remarkably literary morning. I confess I find myself far more interested in you, my dear, than I was earlier. My wife will be truly regretful that she was unable to join us."

Mia shook her head. "I assure you that there is nothing interesting about me, Your Grace." She mentally crossed her fingers; some people might consider a secret identity as a writer to be fairly interesting.

"Just a minute," Villiers replied, laughter running through his voice. "Literature is not my forte. And my memory is not what it used to be."

"I see," she said politely.

"*O time!*" Villiers declaimed, "*thou must untangle this, not I.*"

"I assure you that there is nothing to untangle," Mia said, quite untruthfully, "though I applaud your Shakespearean fluency."

"Marriage has made me more intelligent," he said, looking almost friendly.

Mia quickly withdrew her hand. The last thing she wanted was to have these people think of her as a friend. She wasn't. She had done a loathsome thing to Vander, for her own purposes, and she would be out of their lives very soon.

After they left, Mia turned to her husband before she could lose all courage. "Your Grace, we have much to discuss," she said.

"The possibilities for conversation are endless," Vander drawled. "*Lear? Hamlet?*" Unsurprisingly, it seemed he hadn't enjoyed the literary conversation as much as she and Lady Xenobia had.

"I am serious," she insisted.

"I can spare you a short time. I want to take off these clothes and get out to the stables. I have a new horse that is having trouble settling in."

Mia decided on the spot that she was sorry for whoever ended up married to Vander.

The poor lady was going to have to steal minutes of conversation, given that horses were clearly more important than wives. Hopefully, the next duchess wouldn't have trouble settling in, because Vander would be in the stables coddling a horse.

"Ten minutes," she promised.

Chapter Nine

From the offices of Brandy, Bucknell & Bendal, Publishers
September 9, 1800

Dear Miss Carrington,

I eagerly await your response to mine of August 27, but in the meantime, I am including here a number of readers' letters. I have taken the liberty of opening them, given that unpleasant business last year with the gentleman who felt at a disadvantage compared to your heroes. I wish to bring to your particular attention the letter from Mrs. Petunia Stubbs.

With deep respect,
I remain,

William Bucknell, Esq.
Brandy, Bucknell & Bendal, Publishers

Mia walked to Vander's study, trying to ignore the way her heart quickened due to her husband walking beside her.

The worst part of this whole affair—other than the fact she hated herself for forcing Vander to marry her—was Mia's discovery that, even given all the despair and humiliation and the years that had passed since the poetry debacle, Vander was still able to make her feel . . . something.

It wasn't infatuation. Of course not.

It must be animal lust. She had read about that somewhere. It was a natural constituent of being a healthy animal, which she was.

Vander was the most healthy animal—or man—she'd ever known. In fact, he appeared to be virtually bursting with life, his legs thick with muscle, his skin darkened by the sun.

Her father had been handsome in a way that Vander was not. Her husband—what an odd word—looked more like a boxer than a gentleman. He would never coax his hair into a smooth wave, the way her father used to. And his fingernails were not shaped and polished to a sheen. Instead, his fingers were callused from holding reins.

They had entered the study, and Vander was saying something to her. She looked up at him, confused. In that moment, watching his lips move without comprehending what he was saying, she understood something very important: her husband had the ability to break her.

Even though she had decided to loathe him after he mocked her poem, he had been her first love.

The weakness of a foolish girl, Mia reminded herself. The wanton side of herself, if she wanted to call a spade a spade. She was a woman now and knew a muscled stature was far less important than a kindly heart.

No one could call Vander *kind*. It took her a moment before she realized that he was waiting impatiently for a response.

"I'm sorry," she said. "What did you say?"

"I asked when your belongings will arrive. I have an important race on the fifteenth, and I'd like to have you settled. I can send my men over to Carrington House to gather your possessions, if you haven't already made arrangements. Oh, and I gather they should collect your nephew. My solicitor informed me yesterday afternoon that I now have a ward."

The last was uttered in a jaundiced manner that suggested he'd also been informed that Sir Richard Magruder was likely to sue.

Mia swallowed a sigh and sat down. The time had come. "I am fairly certain that you did not read the letter summarizing my expectations for our marriage."

"I didn't bother," Vander said, dropping down opposite her. "You should know, Duchess, that a man is the master of his household. If I decided that you should sleep in the attic, the butler would have a bed up there before nightfall."

"There is no need to go to such extremes; the bed in the attic can wait for your next wife. We only need be married for six months, at which point Mr. Plummer, my solicitor, will arrange for annulment of our union." The details tumbled through her head in perfect order, rather like one of her own plots. This was the cue for Vander to rejoice.

"*What?*"

"Mr. Plummer is a conservative man by nature, but he is hopeful that he will be able to end this marriage by early next year. I have asked him to pay a call on you tomorrow so he can explain the details."

Vander leaned forward, eyes glittering. "What are

you talking about? You forced me to marry you. You corralled me as deftly as I've ever broken a horse."

He's like one of the great Norse gods, Mia thought with a literary flourish. Acting as if he might whip out a lightning bolt and cleave her in two. She wouldn't be surprised to hear a clap of thunder in the distance.

She pulled her attention back to the subject at hand. "We needn't turn this into a Cheltenham tragedy. We can simply go our own ways. Divorce is allowed only in cases of infidelity or abandon—"

He cut her off. "You are *planning* to be unfaithful, before we've been married one day?"

When Vander set his jaw, he looked like a prize-fighter about to take on an opponent. His gaze seared her, but Mia didn't let herself be intimidated by his anger. She knew instinctively that his fists might curl, but he would never be violent.

"Of course not, Vander. I thought we could request an annulment."

"*Vander?*"

His voice lashed her. This was awful, just awful. She had momentarily forgotten that while she thought of him by the nickname his friends gave him, he scarcely remembered who she was.

"I apologize," she gasped. "Would you prefer Your Grace? Of course you'd prefer Your Grace. You are a Your Grace." She was babbling, but she couldn't seem to stop. "My mother died years ago and I have no idea how married couples address each other in private. Not that we're truly married. I just . . . I'm sorry."

A moment of ominous silence followed before he shoved a hand through his hair. "It is I who should apologize. You caught me by surprise. No one addresses me by that name other than my intimate friends."

"Of course," Mia said, forcing a smile. "You needn't

apologize. And as I said, my solicitor is fairly sure that he can have the marriage dissolved in a mere six months. There's no need for us to become intimate in any fashion at all." She drew out a folded sheet of paper from her reticule. "I drew up another explanation once I concluded that you hadn't read the letter I initially wrote you."

He took the sheet from her and skimmed it. "You want to marry me for six months, after which the marriage will end. And you expect no financial support either during or after the marriage."

"Yes, that's it," she said, making her tone bright. Now that he understood, he could stop being angry. His eyes would probably fill with joy.

Instead, his mouth tightened, and slowly, methodically, he ripped her letter into pieces and dropped them on the floor.

"What are you doing?" Mia gasped.

"I plan to go through that farce we endured in the chapel only once in my life."

"Why would you—what are you talking about?"

"Marriage. A mechanism by which two people are forced to remain in proximity for a lifetime. The truth is that your proposal made me see that a love match is the last thing in the world I'd want."

"But—"

"As we have discussed, you are not who I would have chosen for myself," he continued, his gaze drifting from her face to her shabby dress. "But there was always the chance that I would have made my father's mistake, and married a beautiful woman who would collect lovers the way squirrels gather nuts."

Mia could feel her face growing hot. There was part of her, the part that wrote love stories, that wanted to believe that not every man found her unlovely. The shallow, naïve side of her.

She raised her chin a notch. "Be that as it may, I don't wish to remain married to you. You may not dream of a loving marriage, but I do hope for that someday. Your Grace." The last two words were spoken with a touch of asperity.

He gave a crack of laughter. "You should have thought of that before you blackmailed me into marriage, Duchess. It seems your scheme has turned against you. I believe that is often the case."

She stared at him, trying to find words. He was serious. He meant to keep her in the marriage. "Please," she said, beginning to feel genuinely fearful. "I can see that you're angry at me, and I know I deserve it. But mightn't we be reasonable about this? I will happily offer proof of adultery, leaving both of us free to forget this marriage happened."

"My mother spent the latter part of her life jaunting around the country with another man, incidentally, your father." He leaned forward, his words clipped and furious. "I am neither mad nor incapacitated. My wife will live under my roof. She will *never* commit adultery."

Mia took a deep breath. "But I don't wish to live with you," she explained. "I don't consider us truly married."

A grim smile touched his lips. "The vicar who just married us would not agree."

Her heart was beating so quickly that she thought she might faint. "You don't even want me around you. This is supposed to be a temporary arrangement!"

"But it isn't."

"You can't mean that," she said desperately. "I'm sure that in time you will meet another woman, one whom you will love. Remember? You told me that it was likely to happen, and you're right."

"What difference will our marriage make?"

The cruelty in his voice lashed her again. She could hardly claim to be insulted that her new husband would take lovers, considering she'd blackmailed him into making his vows.

"Do you have a mistress now?" she whispered.

His eyes couldn't have been colder. "That is none of your business, and it never will be. You made your way into my bed, but not into my confidence." His lips curled, but only a fiend would call it a smile. "Four nights a year, Duchess. That's what you got from me, in return for my father's letter. You agreed to that. What you seem to have overlooked is the fact that those four nights will happen annually—for the rest of our lives."

Mia could hear her blood pounding in her ears. This had all gone terribly, horribly wrong. "A marriage, a real marriage, between us would never work," she said, her voice rasping with the shock of it.

In a flash he was standing in front of her, pulling her upright, his hands gripping her upper arms so tightly they would be bruised. "You've made your bed and you must lie in it four nights a year, with me. I think that's enough to ensure we end up with an heir, don't you? My parents didn't bother with a spare, but in view of your brother's demise, perhaps we should keep trying after our first child. Heroically, you know. For the good of the name."

She told herself not to panic. "You can't mean—"

He cut her off again. "You are my *wife*. My only wife, Mia. You may have married me on a six-month lease, but I married you for life."

"We're in a marriage of convenience!"

"No, we're not. It's inconvenient, for both of us."

A wave of horror crashed over her. She *couldn't* be married to Vander. Not forever. Not . . . not living in the same house.

No.

He must have sensed what she was thinking. "You will live here, at Rutherford Park. Your nephew will also live with me. And"—he leaned forward and there was a distinct flare in his eyes—"you will sleep with no one but me."

"You don't understand!"

"Oh, but I do understand. I understand madness all too well, and I suspect you have more than a touch of it. I'd say that we have even odds on whether our children will be as cracked as a broken egg. Another reason we ought to have spares: the eldest might have to be put away before he reaches majority."

The sob that she had held in check broke and she tried to twist free. "Let me go!" He released her immediately and she dashed sideways, putting a heavy chair between them.

"You really thought I wouldn't mind having a temporary duchess?" Vander asked incredulously.

"I imagined that we would live separately for the few months that we would be married," she said, rubbing her arms where she could still feel the pressure of his fingers. "I planned—*plan*— to travel to Bavaria with Charlie."

"I gather you didn't picture yourself fulfilling your wifely duties. Presumably you would lure some unwary Bavarian into giving you evidence of adultery if annulment didn't work?"

"No! I'm sure I could bribe someone. With my own money. I would be writing," she explained. "You can't know it, but I—"

"If you *ever* write another one of those deplorable poems that could be construed in any way to address me or a body part of mine," Vander said flatly, "I cannot be responsible for the consequences."

Anger flashed up Mia's spine and she drew herself

as tall as she could be. "My poem was not deplorable," she retorted. "If you think that I would write a line about *you* again, you are sadly mistaken." She added, "Besides, I don't write poetry anymore."

With a violent shove, Vander pushed aside the chair that stood between them and took a step toward her.

"Stay there!" she cried. "If you—if you try to hurt me in any way, I shall *shoot* you!"

That caught his attention and he gave a rough bark of laughter. She hated that his face still affected her, even knowing how arrogant he was. It was just that he was very beautiful, with his tousled hair and deep bottom lip.

"Allow me to tell you something important, Duchess. My wife lives with me."

"No." She managed to make the word firm but polite.

"No?"

You'd think no one had ever refused him in his life.

"No," she echoed, feeling like a parrot. "No, Your Grace, I will not live with you, dine with you—or sleep with you, even for four nights."

Chapter Ten

NOTES ON FREDERIC

- Florida wakes knowing her heart is in Frederic's keeping, he of the angelic eyes and . . . something.
- "I will love none other than him he," she announces to Mr. Mortimer's solicitor.
- His request she give up her bequest appeals to Flora's sacrificial side. "Filthy dross means aught to me; I would live in a Hovel with my beloved."
- Mortimer's solicitor notes Frederic has palazzo in Italy. (would that make his name Frederico?) Frederic has palazzo somewhere in Bavaria. Or a castle? Ugh.

Frederic draws her into his arms, kisses her passionately. Flora feels her head swim ('Flora feels'?), and her slender body sways in his, overcome by the Force of Pure Sentiment. Recalled to herself by a whisper from an Angel on High (her dead mother), her slender delicate hand strikes his cheek. "How dare you forget yourself, Count! My Circumstances have been difficult but my Soul is that of a lady!"

*V*ander was in the grip of shock. No one—not even Thorn—gainsaid him. Not that he issued orders to Thorn.

But where he did command, he was used to unquestioning obedience.

He was a *duke*.

His wife didn't seem to appreciate what that meant. Every inch of Mia's small body was rigid with defiance. A sense of profound surprise rocked Vander to the core. For once, it seemed he truly had made a mistake. That he had both underestimated and misunderstood his opponent.

"Why in the hell did you want a temporary marriage?" he demanded. "If you are so infatuated with me, why didn't you bid for more time?"

"You truly believe that I would blackmail you into making me your wife because I was still in love with you—after over ten years in which I hadn't even seen your face?"

Vander's eyes narrowed and his body stiffened. Put that way, his assumption had indeed been illogical.

Mia's voice took on a distinctly derisive edge. "And the 'four nights' proviso? I suppose that was meant to corral my adulation. Did you come up with that, or was it your solicitor's addition?"

"Mine," he bit out.

"My father thought a great deal of himself, but I don't think even he believed himself quite as irresistible as you apparently do!"

Vander cursed, more or less under his breath. "It seems I misunderstood the motive behind your marriage proposal," he said.

The mockery in her eyes vanished. "It wasn't a proposal," she admitted. "I blackmailed you into marriage, which is an ugly business. I would never have done it if I hadn't been desperate. No decent woman would have." One side of her mouth quirked up. "Even so, I must confess myself surprised by the arrogance of your thinking I would commit a felony in order to buy myself four nights in your bed!"

A moment of silence in the room made the air sizzle.

Vander drew a hand through his hair and said, "I must be losing my bleeding mind. None of this makes sense. You didn't marry for ambition, for money, or for love. Why the hell did you blackmail me?"

"It's a long story."

"I have time," he said grimly.

"I was jilted," Mia blurted out. "At the altar in St. Ninian's. Well, not quite at the altar, because I was waiting in the vestibule, but everyone else was in the church."

That was unexpected. "When did this happen?"

"Around a month ago. I *had* to marry, you see. I'm—well, I'm a mother." She stopped.

Vander froze. No wonder Mia's bosom was lush. She was *carrying a child*. Hell, India looked like that too—now that she was carrying Thorn's child.

Her eyes widened. "Not that sort of mother!"

"Do you count me a fool, Duchess?" Vander demanded. "I can see your shape well enough. What will you say to me in four months, when your waist-line expands? Even more than it already has," he added, knowing it was unkind but unable to control his tongue.

Mia's mouth trembled, and he felt a stab of guilt. "I am not carrying a child," she repeated. "Yet in every way that matters, I am my nephew's mother and have been since his birth. Charles Wallace Carrington, my nephew, is the child your solicitor mentioned. My brother's will specified that I would remain his guardian only if I were married to a man of worth within a year of the will being proved. I was be-trothed when John died, so it didn't appear to pose a problem. We waited until I was out of mourning—but he fled the country rather than marry me."

Vander frowned at that. "I gather the guardian-ship reverted to Sir Richard Magruder if you did not marry?"

She nodded. "Unfortunately, Sir Richard made it clear that I would no longer be welcome in the house, and I would have had to leave Charles Wallace—Charlie—behind." Mia's voice trembled for the first time. "I could not allow that to happen. Moreover, Sir Richard is recklessly litigious and will lay waste to my nephew's inheritance. In the last year, he has launched three separate court cases on behalf of the estate."

Bloody hell. It all made sense now. Jilted and des-perate, Mia used the only tool that came to hand: his father's treasonous letter. Vander choked back an-other curse. "So you came to me with a proposition to marry for six months, which I promptly chucked into the fire."

"My solicitor thought if you knew all the details beforehand—the fact that Sir Richard will almost cer-tainly sue you—you would be even more disinclined to make me a duchess, temporary or otherwise."

Somewhere in the back of Vander's mind, in his very blood, a pulse pounded, and he knew what it was. His wife had been betrothed to marry.

To another man.

He took a moment to consider the emotion rationally. It wasn't possessiveness. Hell, a few days ago he'd scarcely known Mia existed. That wasn't entirely true: he had clear memories of her from years before, but he certainly wouldn't have turned a hair if he had heard she'd married.

Not possessiveness. He was feeling lust, that was all. He lusted after his little wife, with her tempting curves and rumpled golden hair.

It must be something to do with the fact that she had just become his wife. That changed things. He'd seen perfectly sound men go mad when they thought that their wives were unfaithful.

Satisfied, Vander relegated that feeling to its proper compartment. Someday he would take Mia, whether it was for four nights or longer.

He simply had to convince her that he had no intention of enduring the charade that would be necessary to find a second wife, particularly considering divorce would further blacken his reputation and make the process more difficult. Mia was good enough, and he'd be damned if he would allow her to leave him on the grounds of adultery, and saddle his family name with yet another scandal.

Now he knew her weakness, he was not above exploiting it. "It seems that I am now Charles Wallace's guardian," he pointed out.

"That doesn't mean we have to live together!"

He smiled at her. "Charles Wallace will live with me."

He watched as the reality of it sank in. The battle was won. Over.

"In exchange," he continued, "I will counter Sir Richard in court when he sues me for theft of the estate and whatever other charges he trumps up. I will raise your nephew as if he were my own son. I will endeavor to make the Carrington estate double in value by the time Charles Wallace is of age."

"I would make a terrible duchess," she cried. "Look how I dress."

He shrugged. "Not exactly *à la mode*, but I don't care."

"Society will care!"

"I don't go into society."

Panic was settling into Mia's bones, making her cold from the inside out. Vander meant it. She was caught in a trap of her own making.

He rose and moved toward her in a lazy stroll. "All I need is an heir, and I'll take that from your body."

"No, you won't!" Mia snapped, unnerved by that grotesquely vulgar statement. "I'm not your wife, not really."

"Yes, you are."

She knew what he had in mind. He was going to kiss her. Once, Edward had kissed her for long minutes, and afterward Mia had felt flushed all over, and had a happily muddled feeling low in her stomach. He had laughed, and put her away, and said, "You'll be the death of me before I get you to the altar."

The memory sent a pang through her.

Stupid Edward and his stupid promises.

Sure enough, Vander bent his head and forced his way into her mouth—or perhaps surprise made her part her lips. His kiss was hungry and disrespectful and raw.

She should struggle. She should hit him. She should stamp on his foot, or bite his lip.

Any of those things.

All of them.

But instead her mouth opened and her head tilted. Her arms went around his neck while his hands tightened on her hips. He brought their bodies together with a jolt.

Mia felt an ache move through her, slow as honey and twice as sweet.

Vander's hands slid down, rounding her bottom. He pulled her closer, and ground his hips against hers. Her breath caught in her throat.

When he drew back, she blinked up at him and found his face completely unmoved. "My instincts are always good when it comes to women," he told her, sounding as triumphant as a farmer who got a bargain on two piglets.

"Wh—what?"

"I like the way you wiggled against my cock."

Mia's mouth fell open and every bit of sultry warmth drained from her. "Did you just say that to me?"

"I did." Vander held her gaze. "Why the hell not? The good thing about us is that we don't have to bother with the stupid rigmarole of polite conversation. We can be honest. There was no surprise in your body when I rubbed against you."

Heat crept up Mia's cheeks again.

He shrugged. "In case you're wondering, I'm no virgin."

Mia couldn't even speak.

Vander, on the other hand, was becoming visibly more cheerful by the second. He leaned in and whispered in her ear, "I can't wait to remove that ugly gown."

"You think my stomach is large and my breasts

are cabbages and I'm a charity case!" she retorted. He opened his mouth and she gave him a look that closed it. "You don't want me. Don't start lying now. You just said that we would be truthful with each other."

"I do want you," Vander repeated, sounding annoyed. Before she could stop him, he pulled her in again and encircled her with his arms and his scent and his strength.

The problem was that when he was kissing her, her mind dimmed like the sun fading at twilight. She stopped thinking, because he was tasting her . . . or the other way around.

One of his hands closed on her bottom in an entirely inappropriate manner that made her long to push closer. The other held her head so that his tongue could do as it wished. Her brain shut down and it became nighttime, dim and dark in her head.

His arm hitched her higher and he was grinding against her again. She whimpered, and it was only that sound coming from her own lips that brought her back to sanity. She pulled away and brought a trembling hand to her mouth.

"This is the best possible marriage," Vander stated. "And you can't complain that I don't want you, because the evidence is clear."

He didn't sound calm anymore; his voice was rough. His silk breeches stretched in the front, just the way they had when he—the first time. The sight made her heart thump at an even faster rate.

"I don't want to be married to you," she said once again, her voice coming out cracked, like a shard of glass.

"That's no longer your prerogative," Vander replied. He shifted his position and winced, and before she could stop herself she looked *there* again. He was adjusting himself.

It was the most erotic thing she'd ever seen. Not that she'd seen much. Or anything, really.

Mia fell back a step, and then another. She had to get away.

"Do you believe that I want you?" he inquired.

"What I believe," she said, blurting out the truth, "is that you're one of those men who desires any woman within reach. You think that I will remain faithful to you for the whole of our lives."

Something savage and primitive crossed his eyes. "You damn well better."

"But you will go around London and bed whomever you wish, is that right? I merely wish to understand the arrangement clearly. You may take lovers and do whatever you please."

He folded his arms over his chest. "If I feel so inclined."

"While I spend my entire life with someone who finds me fat and mousy." She made herself meet his eyes. "Maybe if I were really in love with you, I would count myself grateful. Or if I had any ambition to be a duchess. But do you know, Vander? I don't feel grateful. I don't feel fortunate."

His mouth tightened.

"I think there might be someone out there who doesn't think those things about me. My fiancé, Edward, *liked* me."

A big sob rose up, but she forced it back down.

"But now I will never find someone who will love me for myself, because you're so angry that you want to punish me."

He began to speak, but she shook her head. "Don't bother to deny it. You're happy to be punishing me; I can see it in your face. But I don't deserve this . . . I don't."

"I am *not* punishing you," he said impatiently.

"Bloody hell, I'd think you had ample evidence that I desire you. Are you always this dramatic?"

"No," she said shakily. "Only when I find myself being punished for the sins of my father."

His face froze.

Mia didn't even feel triumphant at the evidence she was right. "You can see to it that *I* never have a chance to fall in love," she cried. "You can take that from me. But you will never know whether I am unfaithful to you. Never!"

Vander's response was blasphemous.

"You'd better enjoy those four nights with your mousy duchess while you still have me," she added, "because one day I will find a man who—who respects me."

"Respects you?" His eyes raked her body. "Does that mean that you'll never tell him *why* I married you and *how* we married? Because he won't respect you after he knows that, Duchess."

The sob pressed so hard that Mia could no longer suppress it. He was right. "I'm going to my room," she managed, running for the door, blinded by tears.

He caught her just as she reached it, spun her around.

"No!" she said with a little scream. "Get away from me."

"I respect you," he said in a grim voice. "You did what you had to for your nephew, and any decent person would respect that."

"Get away," she gasped. "Let me go." Tears were pouring down her face, and it wasn't decorous weeping. It was the kind of sobbing that tears a woman apart. The kind that comes after she's reminded that she's not beautiful, and not loved, and not even respected.

She shoved him again, and this time he backed

away, a helpless look on his face, the same look that her father got every time she had a female problem. For example, when her father had ruined her debut year by sharing her poem.

Without another word, Mia wrenched open the door and ran up the stairs, ignoring Vander's butler. Tears were salty in her mouth and she needed a handkerchief . . . ten handkerchiefs.

A moment later she was on her bed, two pillows over her head, sobbing as hard as she had when her brother and father died. Since she'd learned the terms of that bloody will.

"I hate you," she croaked to her brother, John. "How could you . . . how could you?"

Talking to John sometimes made things easier, but not this time. She didn't want to hate John. She had loved her brother. She loved his memory, even though he was irritating, with his conviction that a man had to head every household.

He wasn't there to defend himself.

And yet: "I do hate you," she said again, her voice cracking.

Her husband had been smug about his ability to get his tool stiff, given the fact he thought she was plump enough to be carrying a child.

When she whispered "I hate you" into her pillow this time, she was aware of two things: the first was that she was no longer addressing her dead brother.

And the second was that she was lying.

She hated Vander. But she didn't hate those greedy kisses, and the way they made her feel sensual and treasured.

She was a fool.

An idiot to fall under his spell once again.

She hated herself.

That was true.

Chapter Eleven

NOTES ON BEQUEST SCENE

Miss Flora Percival listened with disbelief to the solicitor as he informed her that she had just inherited a fortune with disbelief.

"Sir," she said, "I am but a poor maiden and ... (something)"

"Miss Percival, you are now one of the richest young ladies in all England," the solicitor said, ~~wiping his forehead~~. "But I must caution you: under the terms of this bequest, you are not allowed to give the money to anyone. You must spend it on yourself."

"That is a most perplexing stipulation," Flora replied, knitting her fair brow.

"My client watched you from afar for many months.

He had determined to leave his money to a young woman of Excellent Character, with a Noble Mien and Aristocratic Bearing."

"My grandfather was an earl," Flora admitted. "The family disowned my mother when she fell in love with an impoverished violinist."

The solicitor nodded. "Your breeding heritage is reflected in your bearing. I have taken the liberty of buying a furnished townhouse in Mayfair. I have also ordered a carriage enameled in gold, to be drawn by four white steeds."

(Does gold enamel exist ~ Painted in gold? Gilt?)

Vander leaned his head against the door of Mia's bedchamber. She was sobbing as if her heart was broken.

The hell, she wasn't still in love with him. Obviously she was. He'd never kissed a woman who exploded in his arms like a swift flame that singed and consumed. It had taken every bit of self-control he had not to push her onto the settee and rip that ugly gown from her.

Even now, hearing her sob on the other side of the door, blood was pounding through the lower half of his body.

He could make her feel better.

No, he was being the self-righteous idiot that she believed him to be. Had he really said that she was mousy? He couldn't remember saying that. In the depths of fury, he tended to say things he didn't mean, as when he had glanced down to see her thick gown bunched under her breasts and said she was plump. He'd never cared much what shape a woman had. He just liked their bodies.

Hell.

He had to adjust himself again. Their kisses had started a wildfire in his loins. Round breasts, curved hips, warm skin, sweet mouth, wet . . . he hoped she was wet.

The involuntary groan that came to his lips was like a splash of cold water. What in the hell was he doing? He straightened and returned downstairs.

In the entry, he informed Nottle that he was leaving for Carrington House in order to collect his wife's nephew, and told him to instruct the housekeeper to have the nursery in order by evening.

To his surprise, his butler's face curdled. The change was slight, but distinct. Vander raised a questioning eyebrow.

"The boy is deformed, as I understand it," Nottle said, lowering his voice. "I've heard some around the village say as how he turns the stomach. One leg is more like a flipper than a leg. Amphibious." He shuddered visibly.

Vander considered this new information as he waited for his carriage to draw around. It certainly clarified Mia's desperation. He was fairly certain that she would fight to protect any child, not merely an unsettlingly incomplete one. But the boy's deformity likely increased her panic.

·What's more, it provided something of an excuse for the absent fiancé. He found it unlikely that a man who had seen through Mia's ugly clothing and reserved demeanor would jilt her. But now there was the possibility that the blackguard hadn't been able to face the responsibility of raising a crippled child.

He swung into the vehicle, feeling a bit disturbed. There had been a boy at school who was missing two fingers; other boys had been cruel to him. Vander and Thorn had never joined in, and in fact they had pummeled a couple of fourth-form boys who were being particularly vicious.

But he couldn't lie to himself and claim he and Thorn were high-minded about the matter. The boy couldn't wield a cricket bat properly, and so they left him alone.

When Vander arrived at Carrington House, Mia's butler emerged from the house to greet him. "My name, Your Grace, is Mr. Gaunt." He paused as if waiting for a response, likely to do with the fact that he was round as a plum pudding.

Vander nodded and handed over his coat. He didn't care to bandy words with the man about the incongruity of his name any more than he would comment on his nose, which had obviously been broken in the past. Gaunt didn't look like a butler in a lord's household, but that wasn't his concern.

"May I convey the household's congratulations on your marriage?" the butler asked.

"Thank you," Vander said. "I'd like to speak to Sir Richard."

Sir Richard Magruder turned out to be a slim fellow with a beard trimmed to a stiletto point, a style that hadn't been fashionable for two centuries. Vander took an instant dislike to everything about him: the shrewd look in his eyes, the way his hair had been coaxed to a curl, the gleaming surface of his boots.

"Your Grace, it is a pleasure to welcome you to Carrington House," the man said, coming out from behind a large desk with a hospitable air that failed to acknowledge that the desk now belonged to Vander.

Vander bowed, and watched as Sir Richard dipped and stayed down, making a few extra flourishes with his right hand while bent over that, along with his Elizabethan beard, seemed to indicate that he fancied himself living in the past. A servant to the queen, in short.

He'd barely straightened before Vander strode to a chair and dropped into it. "As you know, Miss Carrington is now my duchess."

Sir Richard seated himself neatly and pressed his knees together. "I offer you my heartiest congratulations," he said, his face positively wreathed with happiness, quite as if he wasn't on the verge of filing a lawsuit. Vander's solicitor didn't seem to know precisely what the lawsuit would assert, but Sir Richard was famous for using the court to conduct personal feuds. He'd already sued Vander over a horse he bought from the Pindar Stables, though the suit had never made it farther than their respective solicitors' offices.

After a moment, Sir Richard said, "Look here, Duke, you aren't still chaffing about that lawsuit a few years ago, are you? I was misled by my stable master, who insisted that the horse's droop ears meant he couldn't possibly be the product of Matador. He was incorrect, and I fully accepted the evidence submitted by your stables."

Vander didn't bother to answer. Sir Richard had claimed that a horse from the Pindar Stables had come with falsified papers, an allegation that Vander's solicitors had promptly squashed.

Now Sir Richard began to go on and on about droop ears and thoroughbreds, doing nothing more than proving himself an ass.

"Your lawsuit was frivolous," Vander finally said, cutting him off, "and cost me more than fifty pounds to counter."

Sir Richard blathered about the prevalence of unfair practices and a man's entitlement to breach of warranty.

Vander cut him off again. "My solicitor tells me that you are likely considering another lawsuit, resulting from my marriage to Miss Carrington and ensuing guardianship of young Lord Carrington."

Sir Richard's face cracked into a smile. "Your Grace, it is clear to both of us, I'm sure, that your eleventh-hour marriage to Miss Carrington—scarcely a month after she was jilted by another man—was cobbled together to enable you to absorb my ward's estate, which not coincidentally runs alongside your own."

"In fact, that was not part of my reasoning," Vander said.

Sir Richard scoffed. "Shall we be honest between ourselves, Duke? You married the woman to get your hands on the unentailed estate, and I do not blame you for it. However, you understand that there will have to be compensation. I had the expectation of living in this house and enjoying the lands for at least ten years and quite likely longer, given the frail health of my ward. As it happens, my lands also adjoin the estate, to the east of here."

Vander knew he was rough around the edges for a duke. He had a darkness that came straight from his childhood, bred from an instinct that had warned him that his father's mind was not just chaotic, but dangerous.

That instinct was urging him to squash Sir Richard like a maggot. He stretched his legs, contemplating the situation, allowing the silence in the room to grow. There was no way in hell that Vander would pay him off.

The real question was whether he should thrash Sir Richard now or wait to see whether the ass carried through with his implicit threat of a lawsuit.

Better to wait, he decided, eyeing Sir Richard's fastidiously groomed face. The man seemed unafraid, which was interesting. Perhaps he knew enough about fighting to offer a proper challenge.

More likely, his lordship was under the illusion that the spring dagger concealed in his pretty walking stick would protect him.

"I will pay you nothing," Vander stated. He added a silent self-congratulation; he had managed to keep his tone even.

Sir Richard had groomed his eyebrows to a point, hence surprise—feigned or otherwise—made him resemble a pet rat Vander had once had as a child. "Are you quite certain, Your Grace? I will bring a suit of law against you, as I'm sure you are aware, in Berkshire, where I am not unknown." He paused just long enough to make it clear that the justice of the peace was in his pocket.

If Vander remembered correctly, the Honorable Mr. Roach had been justice of the peace for some fifteen years. The beast inside Vander growled softly, thinking of the many people who had likely been abusively treated in that period.

Sir Richard wasn't just a man with a feeling that the world owed him, paired with a reckless disrespect for the law.

He was a villain, the sort who would slip a dagger between a man's ribs and continue on to the opera, completely unperturbed.

Vander nodded, as if he were actually considering Sir Richard's threat. He could kill him, of course, but that was messy, unproductive, and might lead to trouble. Even dukes were not encouraged to make themselves judge, jury and, especially, executioner.

And his conscience occasionally reminded him that he had no right to play those three roles.

"We both know it would be best to avoid the courts," Sir Richard added, his voice oily with confidence. "It might be different if Mia were a great beauty; you could claim to have been stricken with Cupid's arrow at first sight." He chuckled quietly. "But given her limited charms and your parents' scandals . . ."

That did it. Vander was going to kill him. It was just a matter of when. He leaned forward, wielding his body's leashed power as a weapon. "If my wife's name passes your lips again, I will become extremely angry, Sir Richard."

One of those absurdly pointed eyebrows rose again. "I applaud your loyalty. It's such a rare quality in your family."

The man had a death wish. .

And Vander was damned sick of being black-mailed. "I want you out of this house today." It was good to realize that he was in complete control of his temper. There were a few moments with Mia when he almost started bellowing like a madman, but here he was, confronted by a veritable weasel, and he was in no danger of going off like a half-cocked pistol.

"I shall bring suit against you today," Sir Richard hissed. "I shall make your name a byword, not that it isn't already. After all, isn't your marriage incestu-ous? Oh, wait, your mother wasn't married to your bride's father."

"Will you remove yourself on your own feet, Sir Richard, or shall some of my men assist?"

Sir Richard rose and went to the fireplace, silent for a moment. When he turned about, as trim as a china figure on a music box, he said with an appeal-ing catch in his voice, "I feel that we have got off on the wrong footing, Your Grace."

"Do you?"

"I merely wish to be compensated for the losses

that you inflict upon me by a marriage calculated to disinherit me."

"As I said, my marriage was not contracted with the Carrington estate in mind," Vander reminded him.

"Are you saying you're in love?"

"It's none of your damn business why or who I marry, any more than it's the business of the courts." Vander rose.

"It's my business now." Sir Richard's face darkened. He lost the air of an Elizabethan and looked like the rodent he was. "You are stealing my estate. Did you really think I wouldn't fight back? That I would simply hand over the keys with a smile?"

"I can do without the smile." Vander prowled forward, noting the way that Sir Richard was fingering his cane. If only he would pull out a blade, Vander would be perfectly justified in beating the living daylights out of him.

But Sir Richard had to strike first; Vander had given up on fisticuffs except as a matter of self-defense.

"Everyone will know!" Sir Richard was growing shrill. "Do you think that anyone in polite society will acknowledge your homely wife, given the disgraceful relations between your parents?"

Vander's fist tightened and gladness unfurled in his chest. If there was ever a man who deserved a beating, it was Sir Richard.

The man fell back a step and, sure enough, he pulled out his tinsel-dagger. "Don't touch me!" he shrilled. "I'll sue you for assault and battery. And I'll tell the world that you attacked me merely because I was brave enough to speak the truth: you married a fat wallflower in order to steal an estate from an orphan."

A second later the tinsel-dagger was in Vander's hand and poised at its owner's throat.

"You have just said a great many things that displeased me," Vander remarked.

"My servants know you're here," Sir Richard gasped. "You can't kill me."

"I don't plan to. Unless you neglect to offer a groveling apology, that is. My wife is a lovely, intelligent woman. She has the kind of curves that a man longs to find in his bed. I may not have been the first to wish to marry her, but I am the one who succeeded." To his total astonishment, he discovered that he meant every word.

Sir Richard's eyes narrowed. The wretch was dredging up some sort of nasty and irrelevant retort. Vander thought about perforating him with his own dagger just to shut him up, but daggers were for cowards. He threw it across the room and it pierced the door and stuck there, quivering.

Sir Richard fell like a sack of flour after a single blow to the jaw, a disappointingly quick finish. Vander prodded him with his boot. The man's head rolled to one side; he was alive, but insensible. Satisfied, Vander walked to the servants' bell and rang for assistance.

Gaunt materialized within moments. He took in the situation with one swift look, and said, "Dear me. Sir Richard seems to have fallen and injured his head."

Vander shrugged. "Something like that. Have a footman load him in the carriage. He can recover in his own home."

"Would you prefer he be sent to his country estate or to his townhouse?"

"Where is his estate?"

"It runs just to the east of here."

"That's right," Vander said, remembering what Sir Richard had said. "What happened to Squire Bevington? His family's been on that land for generations."

"I believe that Sir Richard took Squire Bevington's estate as partial payment for an action he brought for assault and battery against the squire." Gaunt put his toe in Sir Richard's ribs none too gently. "He appears to be devoid of consciousness."

Vander boxed regularly in Gentleman Jackson's salon. When he struck someone squarely on the jaw, the bout was over.

"Assault?"

"Squire Bevington was under the impression that Sir Richard had interfered with his daughter," the butler said, his face expressionless. "Unfortunately, it was proved in court that the young lady was an impudent young baggage who had made advances to Sir Richard herself, thereby rendering her father's attack an unjustified action of battery. The Bevingtons have since emigrated to Canada."

"Christ." All this had happened under his watch. He damn well should have known about it. Hell, the Dukes of Pindar may be responsible for appointing the justices of the peace in Berkshire, though in view of his father's condition, Lord only knew how the Honorable Mr. Roach had been appointed. "Pack Sir Richard off to Bevington's house for the time being, Gaunt."

The butler summoned a pair of footmen, whose faces revealed a mixture of glee and pure hatred as they hauled Sir Richard from the room.

"Send his things after him within the hour," Vander said. "He is unmarried, is he not?"

"To the best of my knowledge. His valet can pack his clothing. It's a matter of a trunk or two."

"You'd best lay on more men to patrol the grounds.

I wouldn't be surprised if Sir Richard attempted revenge."

Gaunt's face lit up for all the world like a jolly—albeit murderous—elf. "Let him try, Your Grace. Just let him try."

Sir Richard, it seemed, had not made friends among the servants. "The duchess will want her ward to live with her, so I will reduce this household to a necessary few," Vander said. "We'll find employment for people in my other houses; there's always room for more. Was there anyone you know of wrongfully dismissed after Sir Richard moved in?"

"I shall make you a list," Gaunt said, beaming.

A list. Bloody hell.

Vander turned to leave. But something nagged at him, and he paused to look back at the butler. "Gaunt, I take it you were acquainted with my duchess' former intended?"

The butler inclined his head. "Indeed."

"Send a couple of footmen—or hire a Bow Street Runner—but I'd like you to make absolutely certain that the man still lives. It strikes me as exceptionally convenient that she was jilted. He referred to '*my* estate.'"

Gaunt's eyes widened. Clearly, the idea had never occurred to him.

Vander was a great deal more cynical; a life spent in and around the stables had taught him that men like Sir Richard Magruder felt that they had a right to effect change wherever they wished, and the devil (and the law) could take the hindmost.

Quite likely, Mia's fiancé had actually fled the responsibility of a wife and child. A vision of Mia came into his head, lips rosy after his kisses, breast heaving.

Or not.

Chapter Twelve

NOTES ON PLOT

1. Flora left a 100,000£ by the ancient but kindly Mr. Mortimer. Proviso she spend it on herself (a struggle, bec. of sweetness of her nature). Torn between Count Frederic, who wants none of the money & Mr. Wolfington.
2. Gives up bequest; Count Frederic jilts her.
3. She ends up nearly dead in countryside, rescued by the evil Lord Plum, who has designs on her virtue.
4. Although Lord Plum offers her a castle, she cannot forget her first love. Bec. he is wild and reckless and has a devil's heart (and an angel's form).
5. Escapes from castle. Lord Plum wld. rather she die than marry another. No: Boring.

6. *Evil Lord Plum has a <u>pet tiger</u>! Trained to attack.*
   <u>Excellent!</u>

"*I*'ll take my ward home with me to Rutherford Park," Vander told Gaunt, after Sir Richard had been dispatched. "Have my carriage brought back around in thirty minutes. You can send over all personal belongings at leisure."

At that, Gaunt took on the air of a stern yet attentive grandfather. "Is Her Grace aware that you are fetching Master Charles Wallace?"

Vander was not accustomed to being questioned by servants. He gave Gaunt a look. "Show me to the nursery, if you please, or must I find it on my own?"

The butler didn't even twitch at this set-down, but began pacing up the stairs, keeping Vander behind him by dint of walking in the middle of each step. "The young master has faced challenges in his short life," he said, pausing on a stair as if to catch his breath. "Yet he has all of his father's courage and forbearance. He is a Carrington to the bone."

"Good to hear it," Vander said. The disquisition was irritating, but he admired the butler's loyalty. It was good that the amphibious child had supporters.

When they reached the nursery door, Gaunt gave him yet another inappropriate look, saying without words that he had better be kind or else.

It seemed to Vander that everyone he'd met in recent days was challenging the hierarchy that underlay all society. It was unsettling. "I'll introduce myself, Gaunt," he said.

With obvious reluctance, the butler bowed and retreated down the stairs.

At first, the nursery seemed empty. It was a large chamber, bright and cheerful, though it could use repainting. Its walls were covered with lumpy-looking paintings on foolscap, which he assumed must be the artistic efforts of young Master Charles.

Vander had never seen anything like it. His nanny hadn't allowed paints, and if she had, his crude efforts would surely not have been displayed.

From the corner of his eye he caught a movement. A young boy had put a thick tome aside and was rising from a chair, pushing himself up awkwardly. Vander had no experience with children; his new ward looked around five or six.

As he watched, Charles Wallace picked up a small crutch, hitched it under his armpit, and stood. The problem seemed to be his right leg, though Vander didn't see anything particularly deformed about it.

"Good afternoon," the boy stated. "May I inquire who you are?"

Not five. Older. His voice was clear, composed, and—unexpectedly—authoritative.

Vander approached, but not so close that he threatened the boy in any way. "I am the Duke of Pindar, your new guardian. And you must be Charlie."

A moment of silence ensued before the boy said, "If you will forgive the impertinence, Your Grace, I am Master Charles Wallace to those who know me, and Lord Carrington to those who do not."

Vander felt a flare of amusement and it took everything he had to suppress a smile. Instead, he swept into the bow he had been trained to give to royalty. "Lord Carrington."

On straightening, he was disconcerted to discover that the gray eyes opposite his showed distinct signs of disapproval.

"If you are expecting me to bow in return," the boy said, "I shall disappoint you. As you can see, my right leg does not function as well as it might."

Vander had never had much to do with children, though he was extremely fond of Thorn's young ward, Rose. India had told him once that it was best not to deceive children. They saw through you.

"My bow acknowledged your rank," he said. "In the event that a gentleman is unable to bow with a bended leg, whether through illness or injury, he bows from the waist."

"I might topple," Charles Wallace countered.

His eyes were light gray and surrounded by an extraordinary fringe of dark lashes. His hair was curly and thick, and stuck out from his head; his chin was pointed and his cheekbones were sharp. He wasn't beautiful, by any stretch of the imagination.

Still, the worst thing Vander could do was to coddle him. Mia had probably pampered him, albeit with the best intentions in mind. Kept him around the house splashing paint onto sheets of paper even though any idiot could see the boy had no talent.

He shrugged. "Give it a try."

Charles Wallace gave him a narrow-eyed glance, bent at the waist and—as he'd predicted, toppled. He rolled smoothly as he met the floor.

Vander took a few steps closer. "Nice form in the roll," he observed coolly. "Would you like a hand up?"

"No," Charles Wallace said. He turned onto his side and pushed himself up.

"I think your crutch may be a bit short for you."

"Are you Aunt Mia's new husband?"

"You call your aunt by her first name? Just don't do it in public."

"I do not go in public," Charlie stated, with all the hauteur of a young emperor.

"Why not?"

He didn't answer, but his eyes silently informed Vander that he shouldn't ask stupid questions.

"I believe I'll sit down," Vander said. "Why don't you join me?" He moved to an ancient sofa and sat, deliberately refraining from looking back to check Charlie's progress.

The boy showed up after a moment and seated himself at the other end of the sofa.

"Haven't you a tutor or someone of that nature?"

The boy shrugged his thin shoulders. "Sir Richard declared my tutor a toadying idiot, and dismissed him. The curate is drilling me in Latin and Mr. Gaunt is teaching me chess."

"Why didn't Sir Richard find another tutor?"

"He says it's absurd for a cripple to study as if he were capable of going to school." Thankfully, Charlie sounded unperturbed by his former guardian's insult.

"How are you meant to run your estate, if you remain uneducated?"

"Aunt Mia has asked him that. He said that there would be time enough to consider it if I survive to my majority."

It occurred to Vander that, had he not entered the scene, there was a distinct possibility that Charlie might have suffered from "an unfortunate accident" sometime in the next few years. "You look quite healthy to me. Have you anything wrong with you other than your leg?"

"No."

"And what is wrong with it? Oddly shaped, unable to move, too short?" He kept the question direct, but asked it without any special emphasis.

"It isn't shaped properly below the knee." Charlie's mouth tightened. "The villagers all think my foot is a flipper, but it isn't. It's a normal foot turned sideways."

"You have to look on the bright side: if your estate is lost one day you can hire yourself out to a traveling fair."

With this, he managed to break the defensive calm that surrounded Charlie like a suit of armor. A flush rose in his sallow cheeks. "That isn't a nice thing to say."

"Boys don't say nice things to each other," Vander told him.

"You're not a boy. You're a duke. You ought to be more polite!"

Vander grinned at him. "You're my ward now. I don't feel like being polite. What's the matter? You don't like traveling fairs?"

"I don't know; I've never seen one."

"Why not? The fair comes through the village twice a year."

Charlie shrugged and his eyes went flat again.

"You're afraid to be seen in public."

"No!"

That was good. He had backbone and fight in him.

"Since you won't let me call you Charlie, perhaps I'll call you Crip instead."

"For cripple?" Charlie's jaw set. "No! You wouldn't wish to be called Crip, if you were me."

"When I was at school," Vander said, stretching out his legs in front of him and looking at his boots, "I was called Horny. And sometimes Vulcan."

"Vulcan, like the Roman god? Why? And why Horny?"

"They were references to the fact that my mother, the duchess, was blatantly adulterous. Do you know what that means?"

"No."

"She was intimate friends with a man who wasn't her husband."

"Oh, the way that Venus took lovers and Vulcan didn't like it," Charlie said. "Did your father get angry, the way Vulcan did, when he found out? Vulcan used to make a mountain explode every time Venus took a new lover." Charlie's voice was bright and interested now.

"My father never learned about my mother's friendship. Horny is a reference to a cuckold's horns, a nasty way of identifying a man whose wife's affections are otherwise engaged."

"Oh."

"Most of the boys would make this gesture whenever they saw me, particularly in the first year I was in school."

He showed Charlie how to make horns with his thumb and little finger. Like any boy, Charlie started making horns left and right.

"I could either get on with it, and realize that people were going to call me names because of my mother's behavior, or I could fight every boy in the school."

"That's what I would have done," Charlie said, showing a sudden bloodthirsty side. "If I were you, I mean, and I had two normal legs."

"I tried that in my first year," Vander said meditatively. "I pummeled quite a few of them. Smashed their faces in the dirt and made them swear never to call me Horny again. I didn't mind Vulcan as much."

"Did they stop making horns?"

"No. Some people will call you Limpy or Crip and names like that behind your back your whole life."

The corner of Charlie's mouth twitched.

"A great many people will be watching me to see whether your aunt falls in love with another man," Vander continued. "They will be curious about whether the men in my family have some sort of deficit. They think that the Dukes of Pindar aren't unable to satisfy their wives."

Charlie had been tucked into his corner of the sofa, but he leaned forward and patted Vander's knee with a thin white hand. "You needn't worry about that," he said comfortingly. "My aunt will never fall in love again. She told me so. That means that she'll never leave you the way Venus left her husband."

Vander felt a sudden stillness. "So she was in love with her betrothed? What was his name?" he added casually.

"Mr. Edward Reeve," Charlie replied. "He is the son of the Earl of Gryffyn."

An icy sensation swept over Vander. It was that possessive instinct, of course. Nothing but that. No man liked to hear about his wife's affection for another man.

"In the end, he couldn't face the responsibility of raising me. That's what he said in his note." Charlie's eyes slid off to the empty fireplace.

"He was a selfish fool," Vander said, his voice harsh. "How did you learn what was in his note?"

"Sir Richard read it aloud." Charlie's voice trembled a bit. "He shouldn't have done that. Aunt Mia shouted at him afterward."

Vander's response was blasphemous.

Charlie brightened instantly and asked what two of his words meant.

So Vander defined them, with the proviso that he not share his expanded vocabulary with his aunt.

"The worst of it was that Sir Richard had Mr. Reeve's note in his pocket, but he waited until the church was full. Then he pretended to remember it had been delivered earlier that morning."

"Sir Richard should be horsewhipped."

"Aunt Mia called him a bastard," Charlie said with relish. "That's someone whose parents weren't married. Mr. Reeve was a bastard, too, because his parents weren't married *and* he left my aunt in the church."

The image of his wife waiting in the church for some numbskull while Sir Richard played vicious games was enough to make Vander's gut burn. "I'll make him pay."

The corner of Charlie's mouth quirked up. "So violence is the solution now?"

"There are times when it is the only thing that satisfies."

Charlie's brows furrowed.

Vander guessed what he was thinking. "We're going to put you on a horse. Build up your muscles. And we'll find a way for you to defend yourself when you're on your own feet."

"Anyone can shove me over."

"Not if you had a dagger or a rapier," Vander said, giving him a wolfish grin.

"A *rapier*?" Charlie's face lit up. And fell just as quickly. "How would I hold a rapier? I'm always carrying my crutch."

"We could put a concealed danger in your crutch. They do it with walking sticks all the time. Not that you want to stab anyone, but a man needs a weapon."

"You should stab Sir Richard with a rapier!"

"It's best to avoid manslaughter except when absolutely necessary," Vander said, the thought crossing his mind that perhaps he wasn't the best model for a boy. He was hardly peaceable in his temperament.

Neither, it seemed, was Charlie. "You should kill

Mr. Reeve as well. Aunt Mia says that sometimes men are not as courageous as one would hope, but I think he was horrid to leave her like that."

"I'll consider it," Vander promised. "Your aunt's fiancé is definitely a scoundrel. He blamed his inadequacies on you, which is a shameful thing to do." He leaned over and poked Charlie in the stomach. "Don't you agree with me, Crip?"

Color washed Charlie's thin cheeks again and he lurched to his feet, his crutch thumping the wooden floor. "I don't wish to be called that name!"

Reeve's loss was his gain. Vander genuinely liked this boy. He rose and then crouched down in front of Charlie so their eyes were on a level. "All right, I won't."

"Never?"

"No. Can I call you Gammy?"

"No!"

"Peg-leg?"

"No."

"I must address you as Lord Carrington?"

Silence. Then, "I suppose you can call me Charlie."

"Does that make me Uncle Vander, in private at least?"

A tiny smile played on Charlie's mouth, the first Vander had seen. "I think I'll call you Vulcan in private."

Vander snorted. "You call me Vulcan and I'll call you Crip. That way you won't give a toss by the time you get to school."

Charlie blinked. "*School*! I can't go to school."

"Why not?"

"I'm a cripple. You don't understand. It's like going to the fair. I might be pushed over."

"So what? You've shown me that you know how to

roll. You can't stay in this room like a fairy-tale princess asleep behind her briars."

"I'm not a princess," Charlie said, scowling.

"Then let's go downstairs and fetch some food from the kitchens, and after that we'll set out for my house. There's an art to raiding the larder, Crip, and every young lord needs to know it."

They made their way to the top of the stairs, and stood for a moment looking down the rounded sweep.

"Is this one of the reasons you spend so much time in the nursery?" Vander asked.

The boy nodded. "It takes me too long to get down. I have to cling to the rail and I feel as if the footmen are laughing behind my back. Mr. Gaunt used to carry me down, but I'm too big for that now."

"I agree." Vander put Charlie's hand on the magnificent mahogany banister. "Do you feel how smooth this is? It is meant for sliding down. I'll take your crutch this time, but next time you can tuck it under your arm."

Charlie's eyes grew round. "Aunt Mia would *kill* me."

Vander pretended to look around. "Aunt? Any aunts here?" He grinned at Charlie. "I'll catch you at the bottom. Turn around and slide on your stomach."

Charlie was clearly apprehensive, but he was a brave fellow. When Vander reached the bottom and shouted, "On you go, Crip," he clambered awkwardly onto the banister.

"Let go!" Vander hollered.

He did, with just a little squeak.

Vander watched as the small body slid toward him, black hair flying. He caught Charlie easily before the newel post could inflict damage. "At my house we'll post a footman at the foot of the stairs and tell him it's his job to catch you. When you've had more practice, you'll be able to stop yourself."

Charlie's cheeks were red and his eyes shone. "That was terrific!"

"Good," Vander said, grinning at him.

"Aunt Mia will hate it." Charlie's smile was reckless and delighted.

"Mothers, and aunts, are generally vexed when their children discover speed. Wait until she sees you galloping."

"She won't permit it," Charlie breathed.

"A man can't let himself be governed by a woman, can he?"

The boy's thin chest swelled. "No."

"Right. Time for bread and cheese. I'm tired of calling you Crip. What do you think of Peg-Legged Pete?"

"I don't like it," Charlie said happily.

"Hop-Along Harry?"

"No!"

Chapter Thirteen

From Miss Carrington to Mssrs. Brandy, Bucknell & Bendal, Publishers
September 9, 1800

Dear Mr. Bucknell,

I expect you have seen this in the <u>Morning Post</u>, but you should learn of it directly from me as well: since our last exchange, I have become married to the Duke of Pindar through a series of misunderstandings that could enliven the pages of one of Lucibella's novels. It is but a temporary arrangement; we shall soon have all this bother unraveled, but it does make it even more imperative that no one discover my identity as a novelist. There may be those who would find the Pindar legacy tarnished by Lucibella's literary efforts.

*I assure you I am working diligently on the novel, and not
in the least distracted by my new circumstances. I am sending
this missive with one of the duke's grooms, who will be happy
to wait for your response. I would be grateful to receive the
Quiplet novels as well.*

~~Miss Carrington.~~ *Her Grace, the Duchess of Pindar*

Mia spent the afternoon fuming over her husband's
presumptuous ways. She would rather have introduced Charles Wallace to Vander herself.

And what was taking this long? It was a mere
hour's coach ride between their houses, and after
three hours turned to four, she began to fret. Perhaps
Charlie had objected to leaving home with a stranger.

In an effort to distract herself, she began to write
notes toward her novel, working on the little desk in
her bedchamber. An hour or so later, she took her writing materials down to the drawing room and, after
clearing away a herd of glass rabbits, set herself to
writing at a table that faced the courtyard.

Poor Flora was being excoriated by the unpleasant
owner of a lace-making establishment when she finally heard the rumble of carriage wheels coming up
the drive.

Nottle and two footmen were loitering in the entry
when she dashed out of the drawing room. "Open
the door, if you please," she said.

"I shall fetch your pelisse, Your Grace," he said,
managing to convey just what he thought of a duchess with ink-stained fingers and—she glanced
down—ink stains on her cuffs as well.

"The door, Nottle," she said, between clenched
teeth.

A groom in splendid livery was just opening the door of the carriage. Vander descended, then he stuck his head back into the carriage and stepped back. Before she could dash down the steps, Charlie appeared in the carriage door, crutch under his arm, and hopped down.

Mia didn't make a sound, though a scream was caught somewhere in her chest. Of course, it wasn't a great distance from the carriage to the gravel. But she had always been careful to have a footman place a handy step and hold Charlie's elbow.

At any rate, Charlie was swinging toward her, his eyes shining. She caught him up when he reached her, swinging him in a circle so that his hair flew into the air. "Charlie, my love!" He tolerated three kisses, but then he struggled away and turned to look up at the ducal mansion.

His mouth fell open. "Is this where we're going to live?" Vander had caught up with them, and Charlie turned. "Is this your house?"

"Never show astonishment, Crip," Vander said. "But yes, this is Rutherford Manor."

Mia frowned. "What did you call Charlie?"

"I told you she wouldn't like it," Charlie said to Vander.

"Charlie and I are trying out nicknames to decide which one he likes the best," Vander said. "So far he's rejected Hop-Along Harry and Peg-Legged Pete, but I have high hopes that he'll get used to Crip."

"That is *not* acceptable," Mia said, low and fierce. She glanced down to see if Charlie was scarred by this calloused treatment, but he had tipped his head back to see Vander's face and there was an unmistakable look of hero-worship in his eyes.

Vander shrugged.

Mia opened her mouth to elaborate, but Nottle

was standing in the doorway, and Charlie had three marble steps to climb, as well as the sweeping round of stairs leading upstairs. "Let's investigate the nursery," she said instead, making up her mind to discuss the subject with Vander when they were alone.

Vander squatted down and said, "Charlie, old man, it's been a long day, and I think you should take a ride upstairs. Give your crutch to your aunt."

"Charlie hates to—" Mia began.

"On your back?" Charlie said eagerly, passing her his crutch.

"Yup. The same way we came up from the kitchen."

As she watched, dumbfounded, Vander turned about, and Charlie wound his thin arms around Vander's neck and his legs around his waist.

Vander's embroidered coat probably cost more than a cottager made in three seasons. But he showed no signs of worry about damage from Charlie's boots.

It took time to settle Charlie into the new nursery, and all the while Mia was awash in contradictory feelings. Part of her was still incredulous about Vander's demand that they remain married. Another part was fearful. A third was grieving for the husband she had hoped to have someday.

And the marriage she'd hoped to have too: a partnership with a rational, honorable man who would love, cherish, and respect her.

She only had herself to blame. *She* hadn't been honorable so, of course, a merciless fate had handed her Vander as a husband. It was like something out of the great myths, the ones in which an awful blunder led to a catastrophic end.

With a proverb at the finish, something about deceitful women, no doubt, and dishonorable men. Not that Vander was dishonorable. So it went:

around and around in a vicious, maddening circle, all afternoon and into the evening until Mia was so desperate that she promptly downed a glass of sherry on entering the drawing room.

Vander was already there, looking none the worse for wear for having engaged in a round of fisticuffs with Sir Richard. Susan had told her the details as Mia dressed for supper, and reported as well that the downstairs was galvanized by a sense of vicarious triumph.

Mia heartily approved. Frankly, if she had been strong enough to pummel Sir Richard, she would have done so long ago—perhaps the first time that he assured her that Charlie had little chance of living more than a few years.

There was no sign of Chuffy in the drawing room, which gave Mia a prickling feeling of unease. Nottle had taken himself away to supervise preparations for the evening meal, and she and Vander were alone.

Vander had changed into a plain black coat. His hair tumbled around his ears in a style that bore no resemblance to the latest fashions but was fifty times more sensual for that. His cravat—well, it was tied. That was about all you could say for it.

Still, she was uncomfortably aware that she couldn't take her eyes from him. It was preposterous: she was a civilized young lady of the brand-new century, and yet an errant part of her soul was thrilled by his rough edges and brutishness. According to Susan's account, he had knocked out Sir Richard with one blow.

"More wine?" Vander asked, eyeing her empty glass.

"I shouldn't," Mia answered. "I become tipsy very quickly."

"Chuffy has the monopoly on that particular sin," Vander said, taking a drink of brandy that smelled far better than the bitter sherry Nottle had handed her. Without asking what she'd prefer, she might add.

She wandered over to say hello to the glass menagerie on the mantel. "If you dislike the animals, have you thought of boxing them up?"

"They will soon perish as clothing flies through the air." There was something about the way he drawled that which made her pause. What on earth did he mean?

She turned. "Do you often disrobe in the drawing room?" she inquired.

"Only when driven to do so." His eyes had a truly wicked glint. "I have high hopes for marriage."

Mia choked. "That sounds like a man who thinks four nights with him are worth a king's ransom."

"I suppose that disrobing in a public room is akin to bedding: I shall do so only if my wife implores me."

"Your valet will be happy to know that I have no plans to disturb his labors," Mia said, taking a deep breath of the mixture of horse and sunshine that hung about her husband. It made her long to fly into his arms and simply breathe him in. Absurd.

"I am curious to know more about the fiancé who preceded me," Vander said, just as Chuffy wandered into the room.

"Oh, had you a fiancé?" Chuffy asked genially. He was already equipped with a glass of brandy.

Mia smiled at him, relieved that he had joined them. "Good evening, Sir Cuthbert. Indeed, I did have a fiancé before His Grace was kind enough to come to my aid."

"Don't beat about the bush, gal," Chuffy advised. "Vander didn't come to your aid as much as you forced him to marry you. I like the turn on an old story. Why, if this got out, it would gladden the hearts of maidens everywhere. Like one of my novels."

"Your novels?" Mia's heart bounded. She had never met another novelist, let alone formed a friendship with one, for obvious reasons.

"Chuffy has a weakness for gothic novels," Vander said. "He reads every one he can get his hands on. The more disreputable, the better, isn't that right, Chuffy?"

"My taste is not entirely respectable," Chuffy confided. "I imagine you've never read anything so paltry. I say, do you mind if I call you Emilia? I find 'Your Gracing' right and left to be taxing. Hard to remember. You'd better start calling me Chuffy now, because I'm getting on in years. In no time I won't remember my own title."

"I would be honored, if you called me Mia. But truly, as I have been trying to persuade the duke, our marriage is one of convenience only, designed to safeguard my nephew's inheritance. I shan't be here in five years."

"Convenience!" Chuffy's eyes rounded. "My favorite plot device! Tell me, my dear, have you read any of Miss Julia Quiplet's novels?"

"I have read one," Mia said. "I liked it very much, and—"

Chuffy interrupted her. "There's another novelist who's just as good. Though I can't seem to remember her name at the moment."

Despite herself, Mia stiffened. It would be disappointing if Chuffy was referring to Mrs. Scudgell's novels; in Mia's opinion, those books were hurt by their reliance on implausible situations. Not that her own plots were particularly credible, but at least in her novels it never snowed in July simply because the heroine's tears affected Mother Nature.

"I have all her novels bound in calfskin editions tooled with gold, with silk inserts and marbled end-papers," Chuffy said. "Dang it, I cannot believe I forgot her name! In my favorite, the heroine is almost guillotined."

"Given the fact that you have told me the plot of each and every book you buy," Vander put in, "I would venture to say that you are speaking of Miss Lucibella Delicosa." He turned to Mia. "The travails of Miss Delicosa's fictional heroines are generally our primary subject of conversation for at least a week after a new novel arrives."

"I only wish it happened more frequently," Chuffy lamented. "My favorite authors are horribly lazy. I'm sure they could write more quickly if they truly applied themselves. At any rate, Vander is right. Miss Delicosa is my favorite novelist, so I order her novels in special bindings. They cost a pretty penny, but they're worth it."

Mia felt herself grinning. She knew to the penny how much her publisher charged for those special editions, because she had authorized production of the three-volume editions at two guineas and five pence, a veritable fortune in the world of publishing.

"I gather you have read those novels," Vander said.

In that moment, it struck Mia that she had an inspired way to convince Vander that she was not duchess material. "I have a secret identity," she announced.

"Are you a French spy?" Chuffy asked, his face lighting up.

"Don't be absurd," Vander said, scowling at his uncle, and then at Mia. "What in the bloody hell are you talking about?"

"I write novels."

"You do?" Chuffy was clearly delighted. "My dear,

I couldn't be happier to hear that. I adore novels. Live for them. I can be your muse!"

"*You* a literary muse, Uncle?" Vander was obviously on the verge of laughter.

"You don't understand my point," Mia said, nettled by his amusement. "Novels are scandalous, and duchesses definitely can't author books of that nature. Some of my fellow novelists have quite irregular lives."

"Really?" Chuffy cried. "Do tell me everything you know! What about Miss Quiplet? I imagine that she is a young lady of great refinement, but of course I have no real idea."

"I know nothing of her personal circumstances," Mia said, "but I can tell you that the author of *Ellen, Countess of Castle Howel*—"

"I adored that novel," Chuffy said eagerly. "It was one of the first I ever read, over five years ago now."

"Lives in irregular circumstances with a vice-admiral," Mia finished.

"Goodness me," Chuffy exclaimed, clearly delighted. "How do you know? Have you met her?"

"Irregular circumstances covers so many possibilities," Vander drawled. "Could you be more explicit so that we can better judge the moral fiber of all living novelists by the vice-admiral's mistress?"

Mia scowled at him. "You may jest, but I assure you that the greater part of Britain considers female novelists to be little better than concubines."

Vander looked even more amused. "Concubine is such a delightfully biblical word, isn't it? Are you saying that the reason I have not yet met a concubine is because I'm not part of a literary set?"

"You are entirely too dismal about the reputation of novelists," Chuffy said, ignoring Vander's nonsense. "Miss Fanny Burney was a member of Queen

Charlotte's circle, at least until she married General Alexandre D'Arblay and left the court."

"That's very good to know," Vander said. "I have recently realized that I need a connection at court. All dukes should have them, as my solicitor informed me after the debacle of my father's letter. We'll forward your manuscript to Her Majesty immediately."

"Novelists are *scandalous*," Mia told him, marshalling her patience. "My father was appalled."

"I have to say, Lord Carrington showed a great deal of nerve in expressing distaste over fictional exploits," Vander observed. "According to Sir Richard, our marriage is practically incestuous, given our parents' love affair."

"Nothing of the sort," Chuffy said indignantly. "Why, my poor brother wasn't confined to an asylum—and the late duchess didn't meet Lord Carrington—until you were well out of short pants, Nevvy."

"Nevertheless, my point stands," Vander said, tossing back his drink. "Many in polite society will be so scandalized to learn of our union that they might faint upon encountering one of us unaware. Nothing you can do on the literary front will top what my parents did for the ducal reputation— which we have exacerbated by our marriage."

"He tends to look on the dark side of things," Chuffy told Mia. "You must forgive him."

"I think you are underestimating how frightful it would be if my other identity were discovered," Mia said. She was feeling perversely irritated, because Vander not only wasn't shocked; he didn't even turn a hair at the revelation she had a secret identity.

"Vander is right, my dear," Chuffy said. "My brother and his wife exposed the family to intense scrutiny; your marriage has increased that; frankly, even if you publish a novel one day, it will merely be grist to the mill."

"In fact, I think you should publish," Vander said. "Why not? I like the idea that the Duchess of Pindar might be excoriated for something other than adultery. It would throw a luster on the family name that we haven't managed to this point."

"Why do you assume that I haven't published a novel?" Mia inquired.

Vander raised an eyebrow.

"*Have* you published a novel?" Chuffy cried. "Because I assure you that I shall order bindings for your novel that will put Lucibella Delicosa's to shame! Jewels—or no, velvet with embroidery!"

"I have published several novels," Mia said, enjoying herself. "Six, to be precise."

"You are a *published* novelist?" Vander asked.

There was a touch of disbelief in his voice that Mia didn't like. "Not only am I published," she stated, "but I am Lucibella herself."

Chuffy gasped audibly and put a hand to his chest.

"So I cannot possibly remain the Duchess of Pindar," Mia said, trying to study Vander's expression out of the corner of her eye. Did he look alarmed? Or did he think she was fibbing? It was hard to tell.

He definitely didn't look outraged, the way her father had been when she told him that her first novel had been published (she had decided it was better to ask for forgiveness than permission).

Given that her audience seemed struck dumb, she added, "It is only a matter of time before one of my readers discovers the truth about Lucibella's true identity."

"You refer to yourself in the third person?" Vander asked.

At the same moment, Chuffy seized one of her hands and cried, "You are a treasure! A national treasure! Your books mean the earth to me, and I never thought to meet you."

"I'm very glad that you enjoy my novels," she said sincerely.

"*Enjoy* them? They have saved my sanity, such as it is. Truly, my dear, in the darkness of the last year, when I lost my beloved sister-in-law and my brother shortly thereafter, your books became my refuge."

"Oh," Mia said, startled by the fervor in his eyes. Readers did tend to confide that sort of thing in their letters, but insofar as she'd always had to conceal her real identity, she'd never before met one.

"My refuge," Chuffy was saying, "and my joy. Where, my dear lady, is *An Angel's Form and a Devil's Heart*? I've already ordered it in the matching binding. I've been waiting for months!"

Mia withdrew her hand. "I'm afraid the book is yet unfinished," she told Chuffy, turning to Vander. "You must see how impossible it is that I continue as Duchess of Pindar."

"As long as you don't take to publishing odes to members of my household, I can't see that it matters."

"'Matters?'" Mia echoed. "Certainly it matters! I don't write solemn epic poems or—or historical dramas or great literature. Do you know what *Grapple's Ladies' Magazine* said of my last novel?"

"It doesn't matter what they said," Chuffy said instantly. "Your work is genius, my dear, pure genius."

"They said that it was a mystery that any human being could try to read the book without committing suicide, that's what they said. They called it a 'compound of vulgar depravity and unnatural horrors.'"

"Now that's just unkind," Chuffy said. "I'm quite certain that the reviewer had a depraved home life herself. That's why she couldn't recognize the true goodness of a Lucibella heroine!"

"My books are *depraved*," Mia told her husband, who still did not seem to be registering the import of what she was saying.

"I haven't read many novels," Vander said, pouring some brandy into her empty glass and handing it to her, "but I might start. They sound quite informative. Even inspiring."

"You've never read a single novel," Chuffy corrected.

"That's unfair," his nephew replied, unperturbed. "One could make an argument that *The Sporting Magazine* is akin to a novel: luridly untrue, and fond of recounting unnatural horrors."

"I shall sully the Pindar name," Mia insisted. The brandy was quite good, though she had the vague sense that it was supposed to be drunk only after a meal. Her father had never allowed her to drink spirits, on the grounds she was a lady. She took a hearty swallow, in his honor.

"Vander couldn't divorce you, even if he wanted to," Chuffy said. "It's impossible to get rid of a wife. There's many a British peer who has tried, believe me."

"I'll have to read your so-called depravity to judge for myself," Vander said. "Perhaps I can help you act out scenes for future books."

She glared at him.

"Just so that you can better visualize them," he added.

"There's no escaping marriage, my dear," Chuffy said, ignoring Vander's nonsense. "Your bed is made, so lie in it!"

Vander's eyes had taken on that wicked glint

again, and a shock of heat went through Mia. He was just so—beautiful: raw and masculine and proud, even though she'd supposedly defeated him with her blackmailing letter.

No one could defeat Vander.

He cocked an eyebrow, as if he could read her mind.

"Never mind this foolish talk of divorce," Chuffy said, topping up his glass. "I want to know what's happened to your new book."

"I haven't written it yet," Mia confessed. "That is, I've written bits and scraps of dialogue, but I have a few plot points to resolve."

"Tell me everything!" Chuffy cried. "I'll be your muse, your guardian, your mentor, Jonson to your Shakespeare!"

Mia managed a weak smile. "I would rather not discuss it just yet. I have some delicate aspects left to work out." She managed to stop herself from adding, *"around three hundred pages' worth."*

"At least tell us what happens to the heroine." Chuffy turned to Vander. "A Lucibella heroine is always in peril. I shiver in terror from the first pages, knowing what's in store for her. Just give me one hint about the plot," he implored.

"Her name is Flora, and she is jilted at the altar," Mia stated.

At that, surprise crossed Vander's face. "As you were yourself?"

"The circumstances are entirely different."

"A Lucibella heroine is nothing like our Mia," Chuffy chimed in.

Mia winced. If she had ever managed to think well of her figure—not that she had—having near and dear relatives like Vander and Chuffy would clearly knock her down to size. So to speak.

"That is true," she admitted.

"In what way?" Vander asked.

"Oh, my heroines are invariably and incomparably beautiful," she explained. "Slender, blue-eyed, all the usual. The genre demands it."

"You are beautiful," Vander said flatly. Mia blinked at her husband, but he didn't appear to be mocking her.

"I generally don't pay much attention to those parts of the book," Chuffy said, "but now I think of it, Lucibella heroines aren't precisely beautiful. They're always emaciated owing to their poverty. Sometimes when I finish a book I take a moment to imagine how happy they will be to have all the food they want."

"My heroines aren't emaciated!"

"Starving," Chuffy said. "Why, one of the heroines floated downstream simply because of all the air in her ribs."

"The air in her ribs?" Vander repeated, seemingly quite struck.

"I don't mean ribs. In her stomach, of course! Why, the poor lady had nothing but air in her so she popped to the surface like a bubble. Until a duke towed her to shore, of course."

"Naturally," Vander said, taking another swallow of brandy. "I would hope that any man of my rank would do as much."

"He risked his own life," Chuffy said. "The adventuresome bits are my favorites. When the duke saw his beloved bobbing downstream like a cork, he dove straight into the river. The icy water closed over his head more than once, but he got her to shore."

"I would do the same," Vander said, grinning widely. "Trained for it from the cradle."

"My novels have nothing to do with real life," Mia

insisted. "The fact my heroine is jilted is purely coincidental."

"There's nothing wrong with spinning your novels from real life," Chuffy said. "Your life is easily as interesting as those of your heroines."

"Only in the last few weeks, I assure you," Mia said.

"Are all your heroes dukes?" Vander inquired in a way that suggested she may have modeled her heroes on him.

Which she had.

"No!" Mia exclaimed. "Of course not. My current hero is a count. At any rate, a title is merely a way of conveying a man of worth and substance."

"Mia's love scenes are famous," Chuffy said. "I expect that's why that perishing magazine got a little tetchy. Her characters go on and on about how much they adore each other."

"Would you say they are lyrical?" Vander asked, oh so innocently.

Mia felt helpless, as if she were one of her own heroines, bobbing in a river that was carrying her somewhere beyond her control. Vander was eyeing her in a way that suggested he knew that she had spun him into the heroes of six novels. The only words coming to her mind were profane.

"You must have really loved that fiancé of yours," Chuffy said. "Here, have some more brandy. I hope you don't begin writing tragedies now that you've been disappointed in love. He was unworthy of you, my dear. You're better off with Vander, for all he smells of the stables."

Mia grabbed onto that lifeline as if it had descended from heaven itself. "That's why I've been unable to finish my current book. A broken heart . . ." She let her voice trail off.

Vander stopped laughing and his eyes went steely.
Good. She had suffered all the insults that she could
take for one day. Although he *did* say she was beautiful. She stored that compliment away to think about
later.

He set down his glass with a sharp click. "Have you
any idea as to your former fiancé's whereabouts?"

"No," she said wearily. "He wrote that he planned
to travel to India."

"I certainly hope your heroine—Flora, isn't it?—
won't return to her jilter, any more than you did the
blackguard who treated you so rudely," Chuffy cried.

"Actually, she will," Mia said. "She loves the count
so much that she forgives him."

"I think you're damned lucky that Mia was between fiancés when she thought of you," Chuffy said,
turning to Vander. "You never would have found a
woman on your own. You're too wrapped up in
those horses of yours, and last time I checked, there
ain't any ladies out in the stables. Damnation, that's
more good brandy I've spilled on my coat. I'd better
change."

He moved remarkably fast for someone in his
cups; he was gone from the room in a moment. Mia
was forming the distinct impression that Chuffy was
sometimes less inebriated than his consumption implied he should be.

"Your Charlie informed me that I replaced an earl's
son," Vander said, taking a swallow of his brandy.
"May I assume that your father did not wave a letter
in the man's direction to inspire a proposal?"

Mia set down her glass so abruptly that liquor
spilled over the rim. "I know that our marriage isn't
what you wish, but I would ask that you not mock
me because I was jilted." She paused and added, "Mr.
Reeve and I were very much in love, and had been

betrothed for months before we were due to wed. I can assure you that he wanted to marry me."

"Forgive me for pointing out the obvious, but his marital intentions are strongly in doubt, considering his absence at the altar." Vander's face had taken on that expressionless look again, a trick she suspected he used to mask strong emotion of one kind or another.

"That's true," Mia admitted. She was still coming to terms with the fact that Edward was not the man she had believed him to be. She seemed unable to find gentlemen as decent and honorable as those she invented; perhaps they existed only in the world of fiction.

Her readers often complained of the same lack in their letters.

"It wasn't that he didn't care about me," she added, coming belatedly to her own defense. "Edward could not face the responsibility of raising Charlie."

Vander's mouth was tight with disgust. It was a pity because she really liked his mouth. Very few men had that deep lower lip. He would hate the idea, but she thought it softened his face and gave him a deep sensuality.

Unbelievable.

She realized it too late. She'd fallen into the same trap again.

Vander tapped on her nose and she looked up to meet his eyes. "You escaped that marriage by the skin of your teeth. You see that now, don't you?"

"Yes," she said.

Vander stared down at his wife, wondering why he felt such a blistering sense of relief at the unmistakable ring of honesty in Mia's voice. Why would he care if she was still yearning for a man who wouldn't have her?

She was *his* wife.

A novelist? Who would have thought? He knew she was intelligent, but he wouldn't have dreamt that she had the talent to become a successful novelist. Frankly, that dreadful juvenile poem made it seem especially unlikely.

Contrary to what she thought, he didn't give a damn if she was writing depraved novels. Though he would like to read them.

There was just one aspect of her novels that he had to clarify, though. He moved closer. His hands itched to touch her, but he kept them to himself. "You'll have to teach me something about your work. I'll read one all the way through. And the depraved bits of the rest."

"I can't imagine why you would do so. My father and brother made no attempt to read them. And despite your uncle's enthusiasm, I am certain that most of my readers are females."

"I shall read one, or even more," Vander promised. "But I do have to tell you, Duchess, that you must give up the romantic dreams you have about marriage. I'll never do any of those other things you envision."

She put on a mock shocked face. "Your Grace, are you informing me that you will permit me to go bobbing down an icy river?"

Vander let out a crack of laughter. "I promise to throw you a rope."

"No need," she said, looking away. "I'd sink like a stone anyway."

The image of Mia floundering in an icy river was surprisingly unpleasant, so Vander barreled on. "I was referring to romantic gestures like the dukes in your novels probably make. Bringing you posies, writing poetry, showering you with jewels. Your father was constantly giving my mother litters of glass animals. I will never do anything of that nature."

"All right," she said readily.

"We won't have that marriage." He caught her eyes, because this was truly important. "We can have much more, Duchess. That romantic claptrap is for novels, not for life. For dreamers, like Chuffy. Like my mother, for that matter. She satisfied herself with glass steeds, when there were flesh-and-blood horses in the stables."

Mia gave a tight little nod.

Satisfied, he recognized that they had reached the point in a negotiation at which his opponent understood that there was no logical reason to continue arguing: Vander was going to win.

On all points.

She would capitulate now, and agree to live with him as his wife.

But she surprised him, raising that firm little chin in the air. "To be perfectly honest, even though you are forcing me to remain your wife, I do not intend to beg you for those four nights. *Ever.*"

That was a facer, not merely because his body was pulsing with desire to possess his bride, but because he did need an heir at some point. He let some of that desire show in his eyes. "What if *I* begged *you*?"

Her expression did not change an iota. "I will say no. This afternoon I came to understand that I cannot fight the fact you are using Charles Wallace to ensure that I acquiesce to our marriage. I made myself vulnerable through my own actions. But you placed yourself at *my* mercy when you wrote that contract specifying that we would be together only on the nights I implored you to join me."

A reluctant grin touched Vander's lips. He had just

come face to face with a negotiator who had adroitly circled around behind his defenses.

And bested him.

If he was honest with himself, in some twisted way he had been looking forward to the four nights with Mia.

Of course, that was when he had believed she adored him. When he believed that he would be doing her a favor. He had felt an errant pride that a woman—any woman—had loved him to the point at which she would go against her own moral code in order to bed him.

He hadn't been dreading the marriage bed. No, he had pictured himself looming over Mia, her curls spread across the pillow, eyes soft with desire and love, rounded body *his* and only his. She would be ecstatic because she was finally his.

Wrong.

This woman's mouth was set in a firm line and her eyes were fierce.

Very wrong.

"All I ask is that we revisit the issue in a year or so," he said. "At some point I must produce an heir. There is no particular urgency."

Mia frowned. "I suppose we could consider it once we are better acquainted. But Your Grace, I *beg* you to rethink your decision about this marriage."

Why the hell was she so reluctant? It must be the fiancé. Maybe he was one of those pretty men. Vander knew perfectly well that there was a brutal shape to his chin, and an energy about him that women either loved or loathed.

"You are my wife," he stated, "and you shall remain my wife. We should have a conversation about Sir Richard's litigious intentions, as well as about management of the Carrington estate." He saw exhaustion in her face, so he added, "but that can wait until tomorrow."

Her eyelashes flickered. "Will I be part of management of the estate?"

"Of course. Unless you'd rather not."

"My father did not believe that a woman could have a head for business."

"Given what I've paid for Chuffy's novels, I would venture a guess that your career is quite profitable."

A smile lit her eyes. "My father told me that I could keep my pennies."

"I always thought he was an ass."

"I would not say that. But we often did not agree about business matters."

"Are you really one of the most popular novelists in England?"

Pink came up in her cheeks. "Yes."

"Brava," he said sincerely. Suddenly his body was more aflame than he could remember being; something about Mia's combination of sensuality and intelligence was wildly arousing. Bedding her would be the key to turning their marriage into the comfortable arrangement he had envisioned. Only it would be even better than he had thought, because he now respected her reasons for forcing him to marry.

After spending the afternoon with Charlie, he knew already that he'd blackmail the king himself to ensure his new ward's safety.

Once he managed to seduce Mia, he would dispense with the four days proviso and give her access to his bed whenever she wanted.

Hell, maybe he would even let her sleep with him. He had never slept with a woman, but he was warming to the idea of reaching for Mia in the middle of the night.

Rolling over and sliding his hands between—

"If you'll excuse me, I will retire and have a light supper in my chamber," Mia said. "The brandy went to my head and besides, I have a letter to write."

"Of course," Vander said, thinking that perhaps they could eat together in his bedchamber. It would be a prelude to eating in bed.

Before he could put the idea into words, Mia withdrew, nipping out of the room. He almost started after her, but thought of the blue shadows under her eyes and stopped himself.

His wife would be his wife for years.

He thought he might like her to kiss him good-bye when she was leaving a room. Her lips were . . . delectable.

They could work on that later.

Chapter Fourteen

NOTES ON JILTING SCENE

Flora has to confront Frederic or seem a jelly-boned coward.

She should toss her prayer book to the side and tell the jilting faithless count exactly what she thinks of him, that sniveling, dribbling, dithering, palsied, pulse-less man.

Flora waited at the altar, her graceful hands clutching the prayer book that her dying moth—

Count Frederic walked into the church, and Flora knew instinctively, with just one look at his devilish black eyes, that he intended to humiliate her in the worst possible way, in front of the whole of the beau monde. She hurled her prayer book like a discus, knocking him to the ground.

~~Then she walked over his prone body on her way out the door.~~

This isn't working.

$\mathcal{M}$ia awoke the next morning feeling much better.

Few women would complain about being married to a wildly handsome duke. Though they might grumble about Vander's ready agreement to forego consummation of their marriage.

She would have put it down to dislike of her figure, but although Vander thought she was dumpy, he had kissed her that one time. Well, two times.

Men were like that, by all accounts. Merely being in the vicinity of a woman made a man eager to bed her. It was interesting to discover that her governess had been correct in that respect.

She rang the bell for Susan and walked into the bathing chamber, only then making an important discovery. A door on the opposite wall from the bathtub almost certainly opened into Vander's room. And Mia couldn't see a hook that would prevent him from walking straight into the chamber while she was bathing.

Naked and surrounded by all those mirrors.

That would absolutely not do. Hooks must be installed immediately. In the meantime, she made Susan stand guard before that door while she bathed.

Sometime later she made her way down to the breakfast room, finding it empty but for Nottle.

"Good morning, Your Grace," the butler said. "May I offer my felicitations on your wedding?"

The words dripped with insincerity, but Mia chose to ignore his tone. "Thank you, Nottle. On another note, I should like someone to install locks on the inside of the doors in my bathing chamber.

Both the doors leading to my bedchamber and to the duke's."

"To be quite certain that I understand Your Grace," Nottle said in a wooden voice. "You wish to have locks nailed onto both sides of the bathing room doors? Those doors were imported from Venice, where they graced a three-hundred-year-old palazzo."

"Precisely. Those doors," Mia confirmed.

When he didn't immediately agree, she asked, "Perhaps you would be happier if His Grace confirmed my request?" It appeared that Nottle felt that her rank was trumped by her sex.

"Of course not," he said, as if butter wouldn't melt in his mouth. Mia wasn't sure what that meant, but she disliked melted butter.

And Nottle.

She moved toward a chair to sit down, but the butler said, "If you will forgive me, Your Grace, I have an urgent domestic conundrum on which I would request your guidance."

"Oh," Mia said, turning back. "Of course, Nottle. What is it?"

"The late duchess' animals."

"All those glass ornaments," she said, understanding his problem. "They must be very tiresome to dust."

"I was referring not to the collection, but to her canines," he said, with a pained expression.

"Winky and Dobbie!" Mia exclaimed. "Of course I remember her dogs. Dobbie must be getting on in years. What became of them in the last year?"

"Generally speaking, they have been confined to the gardener's shed. And, on occasion, the potato cellar," he added.

Mia frowned. "Why on earth are they in a shed? They're used to having the run of the house."

"I would ask you to bend your eye to the carpet in this room."

Through a triumph of will, Mia did not roll her eyes, but instead looked down at her toes. "Yes?"

"Silk, woven in the mountains of the Kashmir," the butler said, his voice exhibiting signs of enthusiasm for the first time. "Not only are claws deleterious, but I regret to inform you that in the wake of the duchess' passing they developed a propensity for unconstrained urination."

Mia took a moment to work out what he was saying. "They were probably in shock! And no wonder, if you confined them to the potato cellar. Did the duke approve of this treatment?"

"I do not disturb His Grace with domestic arrangements," the butler said loftily.

"You didn't even ask him?"

Nottle's eyes shifted. "The duke has no interest in such trivial matters. However, as it has transpired, His Grace accompanied Lord Carrington to the kitchens for a late-night snack, and the dogs were discovered. I should be most grateful, Your Grace, if you could ensure that the animals are confined to the nursery at all times. I will have the carpet in that room taken up."

"Winky and Dobbie will not be confined to the nursery, any more than they should have been in a cellar," she told him. "Accidents will cease as they grow calmer."

If possible, the butler's long face grew even longer. "Am I to understand that the rugs are hostage to the emotional state of those animals? May I have your permission to keep them confined until they achieve a point of serenity, Your Grace?"

"One might almost think you were trying to be humorous, Nottle," Mia said. But it was clear he was not. She sighed. "The dogs will reside with Charlie; since he is unlikely to spend much time downstairs, the carpets will be protected."

Nottle inclined his head, apparently mollified. "Perhaps you can inform me, Your Grace, what sort of accommodations we should make for your ward, given his . . . condition."

Mia's eyes narrowed. Was that revulsion she detected? She gave him the benefit of the doubt. "My nephew is somewhat restricted in his movements, but he never causes trouble."

"I was wondering whether some of the chambermaids who do not have strong stomachs should be reassigned." There was a look in his eyes that confirmed he would prefer that Charlie live in the potato cellar to the nursery.

With this, Mia's previous doubt was erased. Her face must have conveyed a warning, because he added, "For the good of the young master, of course. No one would want him discomfited by the foolishness of a country girl."

" 'The foolishness of a country girl,' " Mia repeated. "What precisely do you mean by that?"

The butler looked down at her from his considerable height. "This household prides itself on overlooking disagreeable particulars whenever possible. It is the way of the Dukes of Pindar."

"I understand there have been more than enough to avoid," Mia said. "But I am the current Duchess of Pindar. Are you telling me that you foresee maids fainting at the mere sight of Charlie?"

"One would hope not," Nottle said. "But one must be awake to such possibilities, given the child's malformation."

Mia came to an abrupt decision.

"You are dismissed," she said, pulling herself up

as tall as she could, which unfortunately was only to his armpit. "I am letting you go. If the duke wishes to furnish you with a recommendation, that will be entirely up to him. But I would like you gone by noon."

Mia had dismissed only two servants before, in both cases for stealing. And in both cases, the servant in question had responded with every sign of guilt.

Nottle did not adhere to that pattern.

He too pulled himself upright until he towered over Mia—obviously using his height to try to intimidate her—and announced, "I have served the Dukes of Pindar since I was eighteen."

"In that case, His Grace must see virtues that I do not," Mia snapped. "He can enumerate them in his letter of recommendation. But no one in this household will retain his or her position if my nephew is treated with even the slightest sign of disrespect. You might wish to impart that to the household, Nottle, before you pack your belongings."

"We'll see what His Grace says to this," the butler said, his voice all the nastier for verging on a hiss.

A sound came from the open door behind him and Chuffy walked into the breakfast room, clapping his hands lightly. "Come, come, Nottle. You don't really think that a newlywed duke will countermand his wife's control in domestic matters, do you?"

"This is unconscionable," Nottle said, for the first time looking a trifle disconcerted.

"I shall not stand up for you," Chuffy advised. "I don't care for the way you look at me when I've had a drop more than is advisable."

"I'm sure that I have never offered you the least offense."

"Well, you'd be mistaken. I think you're often offensive when you believe you aren't," Chuffy retorted. "Come now, my dear, would you like a glass of Canary wine? It's just the thing to settle a morning stomach, I find."

Mia discovered that she was shaking. She wasn't used to this sort of confrontation. She retreated out the door Chuffy had just entered, followed—to her dismay—by both men.

"If you'll excuse me, I must return to my chamber for a moment," she said to Chuffy, ignoring Nottle. She walked back up the stairway, keeping her hands in front of her so that neither man could see they were trembling.

Upstairs, she darted back into the room, closed the door, and leaned against it. Susan looked up in surprise. She was unpacking the trunks that had arrived the night before, carefully putting Mia's gowns in the clothes press.

"Goodness, my lady," Susan asked, "whatever is the matter?"

"I've just dismissed Nottle."

"You did what?" her maid cried.

"I let him go," Mia said, sinking into a chair. "I told him to be gone by noon." Her heart was still racing. "It was dreadful, Susan. He initially refused to leave until he spoken to the duke, but mercifully, Sir Cuthbert was very supportive."

"Sir Cuthbert is a drunkard, but a sweet one, by all accounts," Susan said, dropping the gown she was holding onto the bed and coming over. Her face was alive with curiosity. "What on earth made you so angry at Mr. Nottle? Mind you, I don't care for him. He thinks entirely too much of himself. You'd think *he* was the duke."

"He was rude about Charlie," Mia said. "Beastly, really. He implied that the chambermaids would faint at the sight of his foot."

"That *is* beastly."

Mia's heart was beginning to slow. The dark, frumpy gowns lying on the shelves of the clothes press caught her eye and she made another lightning decision. "I need some new gowns, Susan, made from silk, in beautiful colors."

She'd be damned if the floors of Rutherford Park were better dressed than its mistress.

Susan beamed. "Now that Sir Richard isn't holding the purse strings, you can order whatever you wish. You're a duchess!"

"I suppose," Mia said. She had never really bothered about clothes before. Charlie didn't care what she looked like, and she hadn't wished to spill ink on expensive fabrics. Ever since the season in which she debuted—only to be roundly ignored by all eligible young men—she had lived quietly at home, occasionally attending local assemblies, but rarely venturing to London, and never into high society.

But she felt shaken by Nottle's contempt. She had a shrewd feeling that her wardrobe had something to do with his attitude, though her father's relationship with the late duchess likely lay at the heart of the problem.

Susan veered back to the topic of the butler. "It was terribly ill-bred of Mr. Nottle to oblige the grooms to talk about His Grace's fisticuffs with Sir Richard. Mr. Gaunt would never allow such gossip. Mind you, Mr. Gaunt had a way of making his feelings known: he never cared for the way Master Charles Wallace's mother used to shudder if she caught sight of him. But he wouldn't say anything aloud."

That particular memory confirmed Mia's impulsive decision to get rid of Nottle. Poor Charlie had put up with disdain from his mother; he needn't face the same from the butler.

"Last night Nottle said at the supper table that Master Charles had a flipper instead of a foot," Susan said, both hands on her hips now. "I said as how he was utterly wrong about that, and he told me to shut my mouth."

Mia felt as if there wasn't enough air in the room. It wasn't merely the confrontation with Nottle; it was all too overwhelming. "Susan," she said desperately, "I *cannot* stay married to the duke."

Her maid plopped down on the bed. "Why not? He's a fine figure of a man, and the household likes him. That says a good deal. And now you're a duchess."

"I don't want to be a duchess! I never did."

Susan scoffed at that. "That's like saying you hate diamonds. Only a witless woman would say that she doesn't want to be a duchess. You can have all the gowns you want."

Mia shrugged.

"All the *books* you want," Susan added. "And the young master can have a tutor again."

"His Grace thinks I'm dumpy," Mia said, coming out with the truth of it. "And fat."

Susan's brows drew together. "How do you know?"

"He thought I was carrying a child."

"*What?*"

"I was able to disabuse him of his error," Mia said miserably. "But I dislike the idea of being married to him. He's too handsome, Susan. There's a disbalance between us that cannot lead to a happy marriage."

"Were you wearing the blue merino when he said that? It does bunch up under the bosom. I've always said that Mrs. Rackerty down in the village should keep to her garden." She hesitated, and added, "I noticed that he didn't visit your bed last night, though it was your wedding night."

Of course she'd noticed. Servants saw everything. "We've decided to put the business of making an heir off for a good period of time. Years, most likely."

"You are not fat," Susan stated firmly. "You have lovely curves. We shall have to prove him wrong."

"*Dumpy* is another word for short. I'll be known as the Dumpy Duchess."

"It's a possibility."

"You think so?" Mia was actually a little hurt. Susan had been her maid—and, in practical terms, her only female friend—for three years.

Susan pulled Mia until she was standing before the glass. "Your dress goes up to your collarbone," she pointed out.

Mia nodded. "I like it that way."

"And these extra ruffles at the shoulders do you no good."

"I need them."

"Why?"

"To balance my breasts. They're too large."

Susan's eyebrow shot up. "Is that why you always want ruffles?"

"So would you if you were short and had cabbages in front. You're a full head taller than I am, Susan, and you have no idea what it's like to be my size."

"I would love to be your size. Particularly in front." She plucked at her bodice. "Look at me. I have almost nothing here."

"Apple dumplings, not cabbages."

"What? Why are you talking about food?"

"I don't like to draw attention to my bosom. I'm too short for dresses that catch up under the breasts. They're made for ladies with long legs, while on me, they billow out and make it appear that I'm carrying a child."

"Your legs are nicely shaped," Susan said. "As are your ankles. I think we should order a scandalously short gown with almost no fabric in the bosom."

Mia rolled her eyes.

"You are married now. You have to dress like a duchess: à la mode, not behind by two years." She plucked at the ruffle. "Or ten."

"It will make no difference."

"Costly gowns make all the difference. We could leave for London tomorrow."

"Tomorrow?"

Susan nodded vigorously. "In order to visit a modiste. You know my sister Peg is in service with Lady Brandle. When I visited Peg last month, we discussed every modiste in the city of London, and I know precisely whom we should see."

"I can't. My novel—"

"Your husband neglected you on your wedding night," Susan said, her voice sharp. "No woman should stand for that. We'll transform you into a woman so exquisite that the duke will beg for entry to your chamber."

Mia liked the idea, though she didn't believe it possible. "I can't go to London. You know Charlie doesn't like to travel, and I am certainly not leaving him alone in a strange house while I gad about to buy some new ribbons."

"You need more than ribbons!" Susan cried.

"I thought I might go for a ride," Mia said, changing the subject. "Do you happen to know whether Lancelot was delivered last night? I'm not hungry for breakfast."

"Yes, he did," Susan confirmed, "which reminds me, you need a new riding habit as well."

Mia nodded, painfully aware that her habit had

apparently shrunk, as the fabric was straining at the brass buttons that ran down her front, which lent even more emphasis to that area.

"Now that you are no longer plain Miss Carrington," Susan said thoughtfully, "you might be able to summon a modiste to Rutherford Park."

"They would come here, to the country?"

"We shall offer double."

"Double?"

Susan put her hands on her hips. "My lady, your husband did not even attempt to join you in bed last night, did he?"

Mia frowned at her. "Must we go around and around on the same topic?"

"The right gown will make you irresistible," Susan promised.

In Mia's expert opinion—as a novelist who had crafted three Cinderella transformations—that was as improbable as snow in July. But she couldn't help it. A germ of hope sprang up in her heart.

Chapter Fifteen

MORE NOTES on Flora

- *Problem: Flora is boring. Too like a hearth rug. She should issue set-downs. "You flea-bitten fungus!"*
- *At least defend herself.*

The vapid Mrs. Dandylion (shrilly): "Don't count your chickens before they are hatched!"

Flora: "I am happy to say that I would not recognize a chicken, nor do I own any. Obviously our social spheres have been quite, quite different."

Readers might think she is overly tart?

She must be sweet.

Vander's stable was nothing like the simple enclosure at Carrington House. It was four times the size, with a wide, spotless central corridor and elegant stalls over which horses stretched their heads. Each stall had a brass plate engraved with the horse's name. And each horse was more graceful than the last.

"Watch that one, Your Grace," Vander's stable master, Mr. Mulberry, said, touching Mia's arm and nodding to their right. "He's new to the stables, and he's proven to have a terrible temper. He bit one of the stable hands in the arse, and the lad will have a scar to the day he dies."

The horse poked his head out to look at her. He was an amber chestnut color, with a black mane and a rather sweet tuft that fell over his eyes. Muscles rippled as his powerful neck curved over the door of his stall. His eye caught hers. It was dark brown, ferocious, wild.

Mia froze. "He's the size of a house," she breathed. She vastly preferred the size of her mount, Lancelot; he was as stubby as she was. She was terrified by large horses.

"Sixteen hands," Mulberry confirmed.

"What is his name?"

"Jafeer. That means 'the sound of the wind,' in the language of Arabia. His Grace imported him at great expense on the basis of his bloodlines, but no one can tame him. He's stopped eating. Doesn't like England is my guess."

"Oh, dear, that's terrible," Mia exclaimed. Luckily, that would never happen to her horse, because Lancelot liked eating more than anything in the world. She doubted he would even notice if he was moved to a different country, as long as they grew oats there.

"I put your mount in the stall beside Jafeer, as he seems unlikely to be riled by all the carryings-on next door."

"Nothing riles Lancelot," Mia confirmed.

Mulberry was trying to guide her past Jafeer's stall, but she halted. "If I approach him, what will he do?"

"Likely start kicking his stall," the stable master said. "*Please*, Your Grace, don't do that. I have twenty-four animals here, and they all grow upset when Jafeer tries to escape, which is all he's been doing for the last five days."

Mia nodded and edged past. Lancelot didn't look up as they approached; he was taking a nap, his head hanging.

"Could Lancelot have a brass nameplate too?" she inquired. "I know he's not of the quality of the rest."

"His Grace will undoubtedly procure a new mount for you without delay," Mulberry said.

"I don't want a new horse," Mia told him. Lancelot was just right for her. He resembled a sofa with legs. Short legs.

Sir Richard had sold all the horses belonging to her father and brother, claiming that Charlie had no need of them. He would have sold Mia's horse too, but for the fact no one thought Lancelot was worth more than a shilling.

"He and I have been together for years," she said, reaching out to tug on Lancelot's forelock.

Lancelot ignored her, keeping his eyes shut. He had a strong belief that inertia was better than movement.

"He's awake," she told Mulberry. "He doesn't want to leave the stables, but if you pull him out of his stall, he'll become livelier."

Mulberry looked dubious, but he opened the stall door and dragged Lancelot away.

Mia was about to follow when she noticed that Jafeer had moved to the closest side of his stall and was staring at her, his brown eyes bright and curious.

He didn't look wicked or wild anymore. He looked interested.

She took a step toward him and he bent his head and whickered. There were times when the only thing that would get Lancelot moving was a piece of apple, which meant Mia's pockets were full of them.

She held one out to him and he lipped it delicately from her palm. "Are you as fast as the wind?" she asked him.

He jerked his head up, almost as if he were answering her. "You are *not* the horse for me," she told him, because he had begun snuffling her hair, almost as if he were flirting. "You're taller than any horse should be. And you're as fast as the wind, remember? I don't even care to trot."

Mulberry reappeared at the far end of the aisle. Mia quickly backed up before she could be caught. Jafeer made a little sound in his throat, as if he were disappointed, which was ridiculous.

"I have to go," Mia said. She turned and began walking toward the open door. Immediately she heard the bellow of an infuriated horse. Whirling, she saw Jafeer rise up on his back legs, come back down and give the back of his stall a vicious kick.

Without thinking, she marched back and said, "You stop that immediately!"

He was rearing up; his front hooves thumped back to the floor and it seemed to her that he had a guilty look in his eye.

"You know better than to make trouble like that."

Jafeer arched his neck again, reaching over the door to snuffle her hair.

Mia patted his muscled neck tentatively. He was lipping her curls and threatening to make her hair fall from its pins, so she gave him another piece of apple.

He ate it enthusiastically, and then with a gusty blow of air from his nostrils his large head came down and rested on her shoulder.

Mia remained still, raising her hand to scratch around his ear. He moved his ears forward and back, and sighed once more, an unmistakably contented sound. After a moment, Mia stepped back and put both her hands on his face, looking into his eyes.

They stared back at her, liquid and sweet. "*You* are nothing more than a fraud," she said. "Aren't you? You aren't unmanageable at all."

"Your Grace," Mulberry said from just beyond her shoulder. "Please step away slowly. I warned you about that horse. He bites."

"Nonsense," she said, reaching up to scratch Jafeer above the eyes. "He's as sweet as Lancelot, just less sleepy."

Jafeer gave another gusty sigh and closed his eyes, letting her scratch his brow. His eyelashes were long and curled at the ends. "I think he's lonely."

"Lonely?"

"See? He just wanted someone to pay some attention to him."

"Your Grace, he has had attention," the stable master said in a stifled voice. "The horse cost hundreds of guineas, so he's not only had the attention of the duke, but all of us in turn have attempted to calm him."

"Perhaps you didn't try the right way?" Mia suggested. "Have you tried apples?" She reached in her pocket and took out another piece of apple. "Look, he loves them."

"Did we try apples?" Mulberry sounded stupefied. "Your Grace, we have tried every conceivable kind of vegetable and fruit, the best oats, specially made bran-and-mash. Do you see his ribs? That horse has been starving himself."

Mia let go of Jafeer and rose on her toes to look over his door. He instantly backed up to give her room.

Sure enough, his manger was full of oats. "Jafeer," Mia said, pointing to the box. "You must eat."

He made a funny noise, almost as if he were talking to her.

Mia leaned against the door. "I suppose I could stay here for a little time," she told him, "but I must go for a ride. Lancelot is waiting for me." Jafeer bent his head and began to lip up the oats.

"Well, damn my britches," Mulberry exclaimed, instantly adding, "Please excuse me, Your Grace."

Mia laughed. Jafeer had obviously remembered how delicious oats were; Mia patted his neck and he raised his head and whickered at her, but lowered his head again immediately.

After a few minutes, Mia made her way out to the paddock. Mulberry hoisted her onto Lancelot's broad back just as a groom emerged from the stable on his own mount. Mia's heart sank. She was desperate for escape, and the last thing she wanted was the quizzical gaze of a bored young groom as she and Lancelot meandered down the path, stopping now and then, which allowed Lancelot to fortify himself with some grass due to the unwonted exercise of carrying her.

"I have no need for an escort," she told Mulberry. "I'm sorry to have wasted your time," she added, nodding to the groom.

"Your Grace," Mulberry objected, "you cannot think to go for a ride without an escort."

"That's exactly what I intend," she said. When he started to protest, she drew herself upright. She might as well practice looking like a duchess. "I shall ride alone," she stated. "I shall return in an hour or thereabouts. Good afternoon, Mulberry."

With that, she pointed Lancelot toward the open gate. He ambled through it, resigned to the fact that she was forcing him to take her for a ride.

Mia leaned forward and patted his neck. "Good boy, Lancelot." Behind her she heard Jafeer's infuriated bellow and the pounding of hooves. He must have realized that she had left while he was eating.

She followed a path that wound from behind the stables, skirted the edge of the lawns and wandered off into the woods. The moment she was out of sight of the looming house Mia felt as if she were finally able to breathe. It was as if she'd been swept up in a whirlwind, only to find there was no air in the middle of the storm.

A short time ago, she'd been in the local church, waiting to become Mrs. Edward Reeve, when Sir Richard had announced that Edward had fled, and she had instantly plunged into a panic from which she had yet to emerge.

In the last weeks, her every muscle had remained taut with fear. Now she could relax. Whatever happened to her, Charlie would be secure, financially as well as physically. Vander would prudently administer the estate, not like Sir Richard, who would have wasted Charlie's patrimony in frivolous lawsuits.

Vander would never do that, and Edward wouldn't have either. For the first time she let herself really think about the fact that her fiancé had left the country rather than marry her.

Her throat tightened. It felt terrible.

Edward had kissed her as if he meant it. After their first kiss, he had pulled back, laughing. And yet he looked at her in such a way . . .

Obviously, desire was not enough to ensure loyalty. She had believed Edward loved her, but in hindsight, he had been temporarily lustful. Like Vander.

For a moment she wobbled in the saddle, struck by the realization that someday Vander would take a mistress, a beautiful sylphlike woman, someone he might love the way Thorn Dautry loved his wife.

Tears began to slide down Mia's cheeks. There was a reason she wrote Lucibella novels: she longed to be loved, and to fall in love.

Her father hadn't been adept at paternal duties. But he had loved the late Duchess of Pindar. He was happiest dancing with Her Grace. Mia had seen him circling the dance floor a hundred times, his hair gilt-bright in the light thrown from chandeliers, proud to be holding his love in his arms.

The memory made the tears come even faster. She had hoped—dreamed—that someday she would love someone with the same passion, but within the bonds of marriage. She hadn't felt overly ardent with Edward, but she had genuinely liked him and she had been certain they would grow to love each other with time.

Now, if Mia were ever to experience love, it would have to be adulterous. Her love would be tarnished like her father's, hemmed in by shame.

She closed her eyes and let Lancelot go where he would as an occasional sob wracked her chest. She came back to herself only when they stopped moving.

The first thing she saw, blurrily, when she opened her eyes was a large hand holding Lancelot's reins. She looked slowly from the hand past an expanse of fine wool, a strong jaw, blue eyes. Angry blue eyes.

"What in the hell do you think you're doing?" Vander barked. He had maneuvered his horse beside

Lancelot's side in order to grab the reins. His leg was touching hers.

There was no point whatsoever in trying to pretend otherwise. "Crying."

"I've never seen anyone riding with closed eyes," he said. "Your horse could have tripped on a mole hole. Though he's so stubby that you likely wouldn't have suffered injury. I must get you a decent mount."

"Lancelot is a perfect horse for me," Mia managed, blotting her tears with a damp handkerchief.

"As long as you attempt nothing faster than a walk," he said in a jaundiced tone. Men tended to be unkind to Lancelot. Mia had never succeeded in convincing her brother that she had no need to trot, and that therefore Lancelot's sluggishness was irrelevant.

"Here." Vander thrust a large white handkerchief toward her.

Mia took it, glancing sideways. He was as exquisite as ever, whereas she was tear-stained and disheveled.

"Thank you." She defiantly blew her nose as no lady would do in a gentleman's presence, and tucked away his handkerchief to give to Susan. "I apologize for causing you concern, Duke."

He frowned at her. "What made you cry?"

To reveal to him that she was grieving for the love affair she would never have was out of the question. "I was thinking of my father." Vander was staring at her chest, or possibly her middle, so she straightened her back, rather than sit in the saddle like a bag of flour.

"Your father was a cicisbeo with nothing better to do with his time than dance attendance on my mother in her bedchamber, adulterously, I might add."

"My father loved your mother! It might not have been right, but that's . . . that's the way it was."

"She was his mistress," Vander said, his voice cold. "She lent him consequence while they cuckolded my father."

"That's a very vulgar way of putting it," Mia said, jerking herself straight again.

"It's the truth," he retorted.

"I think I'll return to the stables," she said. She pulled at her reins, but Vander didn't let go.

His leg brushed hers again as his mount shifted uneasily. "I gather you terminated Nottle's employment this morning."

"Yes, I did," Mia said. "He was very unkind while speaking about Charlie."

"So Chuffy said. Nottle has been with the family for years, so I dispatched him to do his butlering at the townhouse. I'm rarely there, which will suit him fine. And I sent a groom over to ask your Mr. Gaunt to join us. He should do well."

"That's a brilliant solution," Mia said with relief. "Charlie will never go to London, and they needn't encounter each other."

Vander's brows drew together. "Why would you say that? Of course, Charlie will visit the townhouse. But believe me, Nottle will never say an untoward word about your nephew again, upstairs or downstairs. He knows full well that he will leave without a letter of recommendation if I hear a whisper."

"Excellent!" Mia said, giving him a beaming smile. "I try to surround Charlie with positive influences at all times. He can learn about the world's cruelties when he's older."

"'When he's older,'" Vander echoed. "How much older?"

"Twenty, perhaps? As long as I can possibly shield him. And now he has you as well!"

"No, he hasn't," Vander said flatly.

Mia's heart fell to her feet. Vander was forced into marriage; he was hardly likely to take on the role of guardian with any sort of enthusiasm. "Of course, I understand. If you'll excuse me, Duke, I shall return to the house."

"You haven't understood me."

"Yes, I have," she said. "Do you think that you're the first who found Charlie too much of a burden?"

"I only meant that I will not join you in coddling your nephew."

"Oh." She nodded. "I understand. I'll return to the house now." She had had all the marital conversation she could put up with. Besides, she could feel the heat of his leg through the skirts of her riding habit and it muddled her brain.

With one swift movement, Vander dropped both his and her reins, caught her around the waist, lifted her from her sidesaddle, and pulled her up and over until she was seated in front of him.

Mia gasped. "What do you think you're doing?"

He looked at her silently, and then his mouth came to hers, the kiss open-mouthed, as if they were speaking to each other. Her right side was plastered against Vander's chest and he had one of his hands tangled in her hair, and his tongue . . .

Feeling swept through her body, crashing into her like a thunderstorm.

The way two tongues met . . . it was *carnal*. She had clutched his coat, certain she was about to fall; now her fingers curled into thick, soft hair.

Another moment, and parts of her body were hotter than others. A sound like a growl came from Vander's throat. Mia responded as if a piece of silk were being drawn across her naked body.

She pressed even closer and Vander's grasp tightened. Mia melted against him as if she had no bones. As if he could do whatever he wished to her.

Then he stopped. "Any interest in requesting one of those allotted nights?" he asked, his eyes impenetrable.

It took her a moment but she croaked, "Request? Don't you mean that I should *beg* for a night? Never."

With one swift movement, he deposited her back in her saddle. It was lucky that Lancelot's back was broad, because she might have toppled straight off the other side. Her knees felt wobbly.

No matter how wonderfully Vander kissed, there was nothing particularly interesting about him.

If she told herself that enough times, she might come to believe it. She looked up at Vander again, and opened her mouth to say as much, but somehow everything had changed again.

When he had tossed her back onto Lancelot's back, her skirt had caught around her knees, and now her legs—clad in pale pink silk stockings—were exposed right up to her thighs, and creamy flesh above that. Vander's eyes were smoldering, as if he wanted not just to kiss her, but to do something truly scandalous. Heat surged up her middle as she pulled her skirts back down.

"Hello, hello!" A deep voice broke the moment as effectively as a rock might smash a window. "Who have we here? Well, if it isn't the newlyweds, having a little *tête-à-tête*."

"Hello, Chuffy," Mia said, managing a smile.

The muscle was working in Vander's jaw again. Mia felt a perverse stab of satisfaction.

"Good morning, my dear," Chuffy asked. "Shall I continue to the village by myself, Nevvy?"

"No, no, I'll be off," Mia said hastily.

Vander's eyes narrowed again. "I just realized . . . Where's your groom?"

"I chose to ride alone," Mia said. "Goodbye." She would have liked to gallop down the path, but she knew better than to try. There was silence behind her as she and Lancelot plodded away, which gave her time to wonder whether her bottom looked absurdly round in her tight habit.

Vander was probably watching her go and wondering if she even had a waist.

She couldn't turn to look. She mustn't.

She had almost reached the curve in the pathway when she heard the rumble of Chuffy's voice. "Gal has extraordinary hair. Took that from her father, I suppose."

She rounded the bend and brought Lancelot to a halt, dying to know what Vander would say in return. Chuffy continued, "I'm never certain of my gossip, but isn't she the one who was madly in love with you when you were only a lad? I couldn't remember for sure."

Mia froze. All she could hear was her own breath, choppy bursts of air; she missed Vander's response entirely.

"You're right about that, lad," Chuffy said. "Right about that. You're a duke, after all."

"It wasn't about the title."

Oh good. At least Vander recognized that she hadn't been—

"But yes, she used to be in love with me," he finished.

"Not pretty enough for you?"

Mia's heart thumped.

"She had a round face in those days, and I was fifteen," Vander said flatly. "I wasn't interested in young ladies of quality, any more than I cared for poetry."

Her fists clenched. That self-righteous, bumptious ass. *He* had yanked *her* onto his horse, for goodness' sake.

He had kissed her, round face and all, not the other way around.

Mia had heard enough. She loosed Lancelot's reins and the horse ambled on, swishing his tail. She didn't deserve this sort of treatment. She may not be the prettiest girl in the world, or even in the country, but no one except Vander had ever made her feel downright homely.

After the poetry incident, she had tried a thinning regime, but all it did was whittle her waist, which made her breasts seem even larger. In short, this was as alluring as she was ever going to get.

Damn it, she was crying again, so hard this time that she began hiccupping.

Marriage was awful.

She hated it . . . nearly as much as she hated her husband.

Chapter Sixteen

From the offices of Brandy, Bucknell & Bendal, Publishers
September 10, 1800

Your Grace,

I write to offer the most hearty congratulations of
myself and my partners on your recent nuptials. We are
honored to have you on the roster of our authors.

I was also most happy to learn of your excellent progress on
<u>An Angel's Form and a Devil's Heart</u>. If I might offer editing
suggestions on the first one hundred pages, rather than wait
for the full manuscript, I would be most happy to do so. I am
certain I could find lodging in the village, where I would be
readily available and better able to offer encouragement and
advice, as well as editing the pages as they come from your pen.

In more happy news, sale of the gold tooled set of your earlier novels has surpassed our expectations. We have alerted the printer that your new manuscript is imminent, and we will once again issue both a board binding with blue paper and a leather label on the spine, and a leather-bound, gold tooled volume on the same day, pleasing all your readers.

With deep respect, and in hopes of seeing you soon, I remain,

William Bucknell, Esq.

P.S. I include herewith not only Miss Julia Quiplet's works, but a new novel written by Mrs. Lisa Klampas, which I believe you will enjoy.

*V*ander dressed for the evening meal feeling unsettled. He'd left Chuffy in the alehouse surrounded by a ring of his cronies.

When he had returned to his stables, he had found Mulberry buzzing with excitement—about his wife. Jafeer was calmer in *Mia's* presence? Mia, who rode a horse that moved like an ancient turtle, stiff-legged and slow?

Moreover, he couldn't get their kiss out of his head. Most of his life, Vander had been attracted to tall, slender women. But now he was struck with raging desire for a woman who nestled into his shoulder. A woman who wasn't even tall enough to look him directly in the eye. Who could be plucked from her saddle and kissed until both of them were breathless.

When Mia was irritated, her eyes darkened to a

wintery green color that he'd never seen on another woman.

Suddenly Vander realized his valet was offering a waistcoat.

"Sorry. Do you know how my new ward fared in the nursery this afternoon?"

His man grinned. "From everything I hear, he's a character."

"I would agree."

"Mr. Gaunt is another one. He sat the household down and gave us all a good talking-to about how we're to treat Master Charles."

"Excellent," Vander said with satisfaction. "Was there rejoicing below stairs at the departure of Nottle?"

"Certainly not." But a momentary pause had told Vander exactly what he needed to know; he made a mental note to retire Nottle to a cottage on his Yorkshire estate.

He turned to shrug on his evening coat. "The duchess has summoned a modiste from London," his valet reported. "Her lady's maid is quite happy that Her Grace has decided to put aside her half-mourning."

It seems his wife had truly mourned the death of her father. Vander didn't like how much her tears had affected him. Mia's soft mouth had quivered, and he'd wanted to kiss her until she trembled all over for a different reason. The moment he'd realized she was crying, he had wanted to take her into his arms and kiss her until she cheered up.

Absurd. He never felt that sort of thing, and he'd be damned if he let himself be disturbed by a wife, let alone a wife whom he hadn't chosen for himself.

Not that he was complaining, he had to admit. Every time he saw Mia, his desire spiked higher.

That was useful, insofar as they would have to come together enough times to create an heir and a spare.

Perhaps even a daughter. For a moment he imagined a little girl with Mia's extraordinary hair and green eyes, and his heart skipped a beat.

Four nights . . .

He suppressed a bark of laughter.

It would take him more than four nights to get her out of his system.

A few minutes later he entered into the drawing room and was amused to find Mia in a high-necked, ruffled gown that resembled the garb of an elderly housekeeper. It didn't matter. He took one look at her, and his cock stood to attention.

She was wearing her hair tumbling down her back with a bandeau holding it off her face. It suited her. With those big eyes, heart-shaped face, fly-away eyebrows . . . and hell, those lips . . .

Interestingly enough, Mia seemed to have no idea how beautiful she was. He was used to women who were polished and pruned, ruthlessly displaying their best assets in the marketplace.

The mere act of watching Mia's throat ripple as she swallowed her wine excited him. Gaunt offered him a glass of claret. He took the glass and strolled toward his wife, adjusting his coat in order to conceal the situation below. "Good evening, Duchess," he said.

Mia did not meet his eyes. "Good evening, Duke," she murmured. Her nose had a perfect shape. It wasn't bulbous or too pointed, as many women's noses were.

"I have a question about your father," he said, deliberately bringing up a subject that would create some distance between them.

Sure enough, her brows furrowed. "I do not wish to discuss my father."

"Why did he give your poem to my mother?"

Mia finally looked at him. Her gaze felt like a hot poker that sent blood straight from his head to his toes, most of it pooling halfway between, if he were honest.

"He thought the poem was funny."

"I presume you didn't give him a copy."

"My father had idiosyncratic ideas about ownership. He was also irrepressibly curious. That is undoubtedly how he came into possession of the letter your father wrote."

"Do other letters of that nature exist?" he asked. "Have you a safe crammed with people's secrets?"

She shuddered almost imperceptibly. "No. The theft of the poem was partly my fault, because I titled it in such a way that you were identifiable. I should have known he would find it irresistible."

"I would have minded less if you had titled the poem to Evander. I've always hated my middle name."

The corner of her mouth curled slightly. "At the time, I found Septimus a far more romantic name than Evander."

She turned away and walked to a settee. Despite himself, Vander's eyes followed her bottom. She had the most luscious arse that he had ever seen. Round . . . perfect.

To go with her perfect nose.

He followed her and dropped into a chair opposite, taking another swallow of wine. "Does that mean you'd prefer Septimus to Vander?"

"No," she said thoughtfully. "I think you were right to request that we not address each other in such familiar terms. Whether or not our marriage survives—" She saw he was about to speak, and raised a hand. "My point is that neither of us wishes the other to develop an unwise affection."

Vander was suddenly quite convinced that he'd like his wife to develop just such an affection. "Do you think it's possible?"

A ripple of pain went through her eyes. It instantly disappeared, disguised by a veneer of well-bred courtesy.

"I gather you cannot imagine the situation in which you would fall in love with me," she said, chin high. "But what if I were to fall in love with you, Your Grace? *Again?* I think we can both agree that it would be better to avoid that unfortunate situation."

"I didn't mean to hurt your feelings," he said, the words coming out in a husky caress.

"You did not hurt my feelings," she answered readily. "I am well aware of the differences between us, Duke. You do me no harm by reminding me to keep them in mind."

He frowned. Differences? But before he could ask her to elaborate, Chuffy toddled in. His uncle wasn't three sheets in the wind, as the saying went: he was more like six sheets.

"Evening, love birds," he said, turning on his heel and looking behind him, for all the world like a puppy looking for its tail. "Have you seen that new butler of ours? He was here just a moment ago."

Vander reached over and pulled the cord. "His name is Gaunt, Chuffy."

"I know that," his uncle said. "You'd never know it by his stomach these days, but he used to be the boxing champion for this county, Nevvy, as you'd know if you weren't all-fired up over stables, stables and nothing but stables."

Mia was smiling, so presumably she already knew the origins of her butler's crooked nose.

Damn it, one glance at her, and lust slashed through him again.

She was his wife. She was *his*.

She would love him.

Again.

Chapter Seventeen

MORE NOTES on the Jilting

- Perhaps Frederic is inebriated and forgets to come to church?
  "Frederic keenly felt the impropriety of his conduct. 'Now
  I am myself again, no longer under the Dangerous
  Influence of Spirituous liquors . . . my affections
  suppressed by Demon Rum, I forgot the most precious
  gift that Life had given me.'" No. (Readers wouldn't
  like it.)
- Perhaps he accidentally tips Flora over a waterfall. Puts her
  in Mortal Peril and permanently lames her. He jilts her
  from guilt. (They wouldn't like that either.)
- or he's Jealous! A deceitful friend tells him that Flora is
  naught but a wanton deceiver. Yes, this works!

*Very Shakespearean – wasn't that <u>Much Ado about</u>
<u>Nothing?</u> Or <u>Measure for Measure?</u>*

Mia was beginning to feel that she would deserve
a medal if she survived the meal. There wasn't much
conversation; Sir Chuffy was humming to himself,
and Vander was eating a beef steak in the devotional
way that men eat large slabs of meat.

She couldn't stop worrying about the question of
intimacy—and she didn't mean first names. When
she and Vander did consummate their marriage,
which was bound to occur at some point, she would
insist that all the lamps be extinguished first. No can-
dles either. Sheets pulled up to their chins.

Was it permissible to insist that a man not touch
his wife above the waist? She had a feeling it wasn't,
though she didn't really know. Not having known
her mother, she had only foggy ideas about the finer
points of conjugal intimacy.

Enough! They had to talk about *something*.

"I met Jafeer today," she said brightly.

Vander looked up from his plate. "So Mulberry
informed me. Don't go near that horse. He's far too
high-strung."

"I gather Jafeer is a new addition to your stables?"

"Yes, he arrived a few days ago," Vander said,
taking another forkful of beef.

"You did tell me that you had a race upcoming, did
you not? Will he take part?"

"I hadn't thought to enter him because he has been
unsettled. He won races in his native country as a
yearling, and I'd like to have a sense of what he's like
on the track. But perhaps I shall . . . now I know that
the way to his heart is a duchess with a pocketful of
apples."

Mia knew she was beaming, but it felt wonderful to triumph where Vander's stable master had failed.

"Good for you, m'dear," Chuffy said, leaning back with an expansive wave of his glass. He nearly tumbled but caught himself. "You've deduced the way to your husband's heart."

Vander's eyes narrowed. He probably thought she was trying to trap him into unwanted emotion by befriending Jafeer—when she'd had nothing like that in mind. "There's no need to go to such lengths, Duchess," he remarked. "I'm bought and paid for."

Mia froze, unable to speak. Chuffy, on the other hand, made a sharp gesture and barked, "Nevvy, I—"

His chair toppled backward with a crash, and a hard thump indicated that Chuffy's head had hit the floor. Mia sprang to her feet with a squeak of distress, but Vander merely leaned forward far enough to peer down at his uncle and got up in a leisurely way.

Mia rushed around the table to where Chuffy was lying on the floor. To her relief, he was blinking up at the ceiling, looking surprised rather than injured.

"Here I am, on the damn floor again," he observed.

Vander hoisted Chuffy to his feet and deposited him back in his chair. "Having second thoughts about our marriage?" he asked Mia in a mocking tone, as he walked back to the head of the table. "This household does not fit the mold of the *beau monde*."

"I need a restorative," Chuffy said, hauling on the cord to summon Gaunt.

"If I had dreams of a life in the *beau monde*," Mia managed, "I gave them up long ago. If you would both please excuse me, I shall retire for the night." She stood up and nipped out the door as Gaunt entered, running up the stairs to the nursery.

The ducal nursery was three times larger than that in Carrington House. It was bright and airy, with a rocking chair with metal mounts and red velvet cushions. A sofa was positioned in front of the fireplace, which was fronted with an elaborate grate guard.

In the corner was a child-sized iron cot; next to it was a child-sized wash table and basin. Charlie was in bed, but when she tiptoed into the room, she could tell that he was awake. She sat down on his bed, leaning over to kiss his forehead. "Why aren't you asleep, Barley Charlie?"

"I'm too excited," he whispered. He sat up. "Uncle Vander is going to teach me how to ride, Aunt Mia! He's going to teach me to ride a horse. And he showed me how to go downstairs all by myself."

"What?"

Charlie grabbed her hand and put it against the inside of his thin knee. "Do you feel this?"

He pushed against her hand, and she nodded.

"That means I can ride a horse!" he said triumphantly.

Mia's heart sank. "Honey, riders use these things called stirrups—"

"A true rider needn't use them," Charlie said fiercely. "You can ride a horse with your knees. The duke says that is the best way to ride. You don't need feet; you only need strong legs."

Mia opened her mouth and shut it again. She was hardly someone who knew the finer points of horsemanship. "I suppose you could ride Lancelot."

Charlie shook his head. "I shall ride proper horses, starting with a pony named Ginger, and after her, the biggest horses in the duke's stables. I shall ride them *all*."

"Oh, no," Mia moaned. She knew that look. She'd

seen it on her own face, when she'd realized that if she wrote novels and published them under an alias, she could keep writing about love without risking humiliation.

Charlie's face was small, but all of a sudden she saw that it was no longer delicate. His chin was square and his eyes were fierce.

"You're growing up, aren't you?" she asked, unable to keep a smile from her lips.

"Of course I'm growing up," Charlie told her. "All boys grow up. I shall go away to school soon. It's going to be an adventure."

"No, you won't!" she cried, the denial coming straight from her heart. "Who told you such a thing? Did the duke say that?"

Charlie snuggled back into his covers. "Yes, he did. He's going to send me to his school. It's called something funny . . . like Eating. I think that's it. He's sending me to Eating." His eyes were growing slumberous.

"Eton," Mia mumbled, shocked down to her toes. Her baby would never go away to school, where cruel boys like that dreadful Oakenrott would taunt and bully him.

She would throw herself in front of the carriage first. Had she done this? By marrying Vander, she had ensured that Charlie would endure agonies of humiliation, not just once, but every day, for years?

No.

Charlie's eyes opened again. "You can't keep me a baby, Aunt Mia," he whispered. "I have to grow up."

Her heart was thudding in her throat. Her marriage wasn't consummated. Charlie might be better off with Sir Richard. At least Sir Richard would keep him in the house, rather than throwing him onto the back of a horse or sending him away to school.

No. She had been right to get Charlie away from Sir Richard, no matter what.

Charlie had fallen asleep, so she reached out and smoothed the hair that tumbled over his brow and tiptoed from the room. She had to think, but Susan was straightening her bedchamber. She needed a place where she was unlikely to be disturbed.

Suddenly she remembered Jafeer. He was as distressed and lonely as she was. It took her a while to find a side door, but finally she slipped into the night. It was warm outside, and the sky was full of stars, like shining cherries in a bowl.

She walked the path to the stables, letting the evening air wrap around her shoulders. Weren't lamps dangerous in a stable? Yet the building was illuminated inside as if by daylight, and as she approached, she heard a shout.

Followed by the high whinny of an enraged horse.

"Oh for goodness' sake," she said, under her breath.

Still, she felt better. Someone needed her. Vander didn't care to have her around, for obvious reasons, and Charlie was growing up.

A couple of grooms came running toward her, down the corridor away from Jafeer's stall. They tried to stop her, but she brushed past them.

A moment later she stood in front of the stall. The stallion's eyes were wild, rolling, both ears flat back, his hide blackened with sweat. Mia put her hands on her hips. When he was two years old, Charlie had gone through a spell when he would lie on the nursery floor and scream.

Jafeer, she decided, was having a tantrum. Just as she had with Charlie, Mia waited until she caught Jafeer's eyes. Instantly, the wild loneliness drained out of his expression, and he brought his front legs to the floor with a thud.

The groom who had been hauling on his reins, trying in vain to control the horse, let out a string of thankful curses, turned, saw her, and started.

"Your—Your Grace!"

"Jafeer," Mia said, "just what do you think you're doing?"

The horse blew air and shook his head. He wasn't going to throw in the towel immediately. It was all her fault, apparently.

Mia stepped forward. "Come here," she said, reaching toward him.

He held out for another moment, letting her know that she shouldn't have abandoned him in a strange place where men shouted at him. With a huge sigh he lowered his head to her.

Mia reached her arms around his neck. "You mustn't behave this way," she told him. "It's not as if I can sleep in the stables with you."

As if he could understand her, Jafeer gave a little snort and lipped at her hair. Susan had left it down in a style that she swore was all the mode, but Mia thought was merely untidy.

She drew away. "There's entirely too much light here," she said, turning to address the stable hand. "Oh, Mulberry, there you are! Wouldn't it be better to extinguish the lamps? Look at poor Lancelot. He wants to go to sleep."

In fact, Lancelot was asleep. It would take more than a terrified, homesick horse in the stall next door to keep him awake.

"If I'd known that stallion needed a duchess to make him happy," Mulberry said, "I never would have recommended we buy him."

"It's probably just a woman's touch," Mia said, even though she didn't like that idea. Jafeer was *hers*.

Mulberry shook his head. "No, Your Grace. Since

you were here this morning, we tried all the scullery maids, the downstairs maid, and one of the dairymaids. I tried to lure the cook, but she wouldn't come."

Mia ran Jafeer's velvety ear through her fingers. "I can't remain in the stables with you all night, silly boy. Mulberry, if you would be kind enough to extinguish all but one of the lamps, perhaps I can quiet him enough to sleep." She turned her face and dropped a kiss on the horse's whiskery nose. "You're sleepy, aren't you?" The Arabian's eyes drooped. It couldn't be easy having a daylong tantrum.

Charlie used to drop to sleep like a stone after his fits, back when he was two years old.

One by one the lamps were turned down and the stable descended into near-darkness. The men all left, with Mulberry the last to go.

Finally it was just the two of them. Well, the two of them and two dozen other animals, slowly breathing in a warm darkness that smelled like horses and clean straw.

Mia unlatched the door to Jafeer's stall and entered. The moment she was next to his head, he folded up his long legs and collapsed like a house of cards.

"You're going to sleep," Mia said, in a calm low voice. She sat on the floor next to him and leaned against his shoulder. He curved his neck around her, and she stroked his cheek. "Pretty soon I shall have to leave, and you will sleep through the night. I'll visit you in the morning, and perhaps again in the evening."

Jafeer's head slid off her shoulder to the straw as he fell asleep.

Mia just sat, hand on his neck, thinking about her life. She had sacrificed everything for Charlie—her self-esteem, her self-respect, her chance at a happy marriage. But it had been the right thing to do; even thinking about his shining eyes made her smile. He wanted to learn to ride, so she'd have to allow it.

Ever since the moment when she'd realized that her newborn nephew might die due to his mother's extravagant use of opium during birth, and the doctor had chosen not to rouse the baby because of his deformity, she had taken responsibility. It began when she upended a pitcher of water on the baby's head and woke him up from an opium-induced daze.

As Mia saw it, there were times when only one possible road lay ahead, and so she had snatched Charlie from the arms of the nurse. And eight years later, she had faced a similar conundrum, and married Vander.

She leaned back against Jafeer, pushing the subject of Vander out of her mind.

Perhaps the count jilted Flora because he was an inveterate inebriate, along Chuffy's lines? But there seemed to be so much pain behind Chuffy's drinking . . . she couldn't manage it if Frederic was in that sort of emotional state.

Novels weren't like real life.

The darkest problems were like syphilis and lice. She couldn't touch them, not in the pages of her books.

Chapter Eighteen

DRAFT: Wedding

Having grown up in an orphanage, Flora's knowledge of the marital state is near to non-existent. The image of a gentleman on his knees knocked together in her head with a vision of herself in a silk gown, being served by ~~a liveried butler~~ footmen in livery.

Flora had long dreamed of a man in an exquisite coat who would sit beside her, vowing eternal adoration.

She had never imagined this . . . this agony.

~~With trembling fingers she unwrapped the screw of paper the priest handed her, his face riddled with compassion.~~

("Riddled" sounds as if he has pox, which no man of the cloth should have.)

*With trembling fingers, she opened the sheet of paper. The
words danced before her eyes. ~~Black dots swam before her eyes.~~
Frederic had changed his mind.*

$\mathcal{V}$ander stared at the dining room door as it closed
behind his wife, and felt a leaden sense of guilt settle
in his gut. For a moment, before Mia smiled insin-
cerely and bade them goodnight, he had seen misery
in her eyes.

Misery.

He had done that.

"You're a horse's ass," Chuffy confirmed. He had
taken up his fork again and spoke through a mouthful
of beef. "I know she blackmailed you and all the rest
of it, but your bed is made, lad. What are you going
to do, spend your whole marriage sniping at her? She
doesn't even fight back. It's hardly a fair fight."

Mia hadn't fought back. A wooden look had slid
over her face that he didn't like. Not at all.

"I'll have to give you some lessons in how to deal
with women," Chuffy said, waving his fork. "God
knows, your mama was unusual, which is probably
why you don't understand 'em."

"Unusual?" Vander said, bristling. "I don't think
she was unusual."

Chuffy frowned at him. "What's your meaning?"

"She was unfaithful to your brother," Vander said.
"She took a lover and cuckolded him in plain sight of
all society. There's nothing unusual about that."

Chuffy put his fork down. "That's taking the ugli-
est possible look at it."

"What other way is there?" Bitterness swelled in
Vander's heart. "I watched her, Chuffy. I saw my
mother swan around ballrooms on that man's arm.
He would stay for months, sitting in my father's place

at the table. Even when I was still in the nursery, I knew it was wrong."

Whenever his father was to be released from the private asylum, Lord Carrington would vanish back to his own estate. Vander had never spoken to his father about what happened during his confinements.

If the duke had known that every time he fell too deeply into melancholia to bathe himself, after he was banished to the asylum again, Lord Carrington would stride back into the house, a shock of golden-gilt hair waving above his forehead . . . It would have been terrible.

So Vander had unwillingly become a party to deceiving his father. A party to adultery.

"It was complicated," Chuffy said, interrupting his thoughts. "I suppose we should have discussed this earlier."

"There's nothing to discuss," Vander stated.

Chuffy rose and went to the sideboard, retrieved the bottle of wine, and poured it into the glass he'd carried with him.

"You're supposed to summon Gaunt to pour," Vander snapped.

"Are you really going to try to turn your house into a ducal establishment?" Chuffy asked. "Bit late for that."

That was true. Vander liked to work in the stables all day. He didn't care to change for the evening meal, though he'd done it today. He had married a woman who dressed like an elderly housekeeper. His uncle was drunk most of the time.

"I suppose not."

"I loved my brother," Chuffy said, leaning back against the sideboard and sipping his wine. "When we were young, he was like a god to me: always telling stories, getting into trouble and talking his way out, dragging me along even though I was much younger."

Vander nodded. "Thank you for that." He stood. "If you'll excuse me—"

Chuffy cut him off. "I will not."

Vander instantly froze. Before this damned marriage, no one—ever—told him what to do. He was not only a duke; he had made thousands of pounds training, racing, and betting on his horses. He commanded, rather than the other way around.

"Nephew," Chuffy said.

"Of course," he said, sitting down again. "I apologize. I'm at your service." He could do this. He hated more than anything to discuss his parents, but he owed this courtesy to his uncle.

"Your father's illness came on when he was fifteen, though we didn't understand it at the time," Chuffy said, rolling his glass between his hands. "He started staying up all night, telling mad stories that would go on for days. At first, I stayed up with him. But I couldn't . . ." He was silent for a moment. "I couldn't keep up with him. He would take a horse and ride all night long. When we were in the house in Wales during the summer, he would dive from cliffs and swim back around to the village. You know how long a swim that is, lad."

"He could easily have died," Vander said, frowning. "He must have been mad already. Of course, he was mad."

"Yes." Chuffy took a gulp of wine and started turning, turning his glass again. "He began to grow angry, flaring up between one word and the next. It wasn't him, not really. He was never like that as a boy. He was always at my shoulder, defending me."

Vander nodded. "He lost his temper with you?"

"At first, I thought it was my fault," Chuffy said. "That if I could somehow be a better brother, more quiet, more helpful . . . he wouldn't grow enraged. But he always did. The anger, the blows, would come out of nowhere."

Vander stood again. He didn't know what to do or what to say. He wasn't the sort of man who knew how to console another.

Damn it, a tear was sliding down his uncle's cheek. "I was relieved when he married and moved out of the house," Chuffy whispered. "My own brother."

"Anyone would understand," Vander said, moving around the table to put a hand on his shoulder. "My father was out of his mind. Cracked."

"He turned from me to your mother," Chuffy said, his watery eyes meeting Vander's.

Vander suddenly went cold all over.

"I was so grateful for my release . . . but it just meant that he turned that anger against her. Didn't you ever wonder why you never had a sibling? Or why your mother never conceived a child with Lord Carrington, since they were together more than twenty years?"

Vander's jaw tightened. He didn't like where this conversation was heading.

"After you were born, she couldn't have any more children, because your father—my brother—took that away from her." Chuffy's voice was low, tortured.

Vander turned away instinctively, stumbling as he did.

"With his fists," Chuffy added, taking a deep gulp of wine.

Vander's gut convulsed and, unable to help himself, he threw up on the floor.

"Hell," Chuffy muttered. "I shouldn't have told you." He grabbed a cloth from the sideboard and tossed it over the vomit.

"I should have known." Vander took a glass of water from the table. "How could I not have seen it?"

"He didn't mean it," his uncle said urgently. "It wasn't his fault, lad. The madness would take over . . ."

"Let's get the hell out of here." Vander put down the empty glass and strode to the door. In the corridor, he paused and said, "Gaunt, I was sick on the floor. Please convey my apologies to whomever cleans it up."

"The fish soup!" the butler exclaimed.

"No, no, the soup was excellent."

Chuffy followed him to his study, clutching the bottle of claret in his hand. "You always had that trick of throwing up at bad news," he said, leaning against the doorframe.

Vander frowned. He had no particular memories of vomiting.

"You were a bellwether for my brother's madness," his uncle said. "When the mania came on, I knew you would lose your meal. I think it saved your life a time or two."

"Surely not," Vander said, his voice rasping.

"Everyone tried to protect you, of course, but you were small, and children are terribly fragile, aren't they? My brother insisted on going into the nursery, no matter how many footmen were stationed at the door. Mind you, he didn't mean it. He had delusions, you see. Sometimes he thought it was his duty to kill you."

Vander searched his memory. "I remember he once mistook me for a burglar . . ."

"That's what we told you." Chuffy's voice was so sad that Vander could hear the tears. "Yet he loved you, and your mother, and me as well."

Vander cleared his throat. "That's not enough." He met Chuffy's eyes. "He may have loved us, but he didn't protect us. He didn't make certain that we were safe. Quite the opposite, it seems."

The corner of Chuffy's mouth twitched. Regret and shame were battling in his uncle's face.

"I'm glad you told me," Vander added.

That was a lie.

Chuffy nodded and upended the bottle.

"I'll be in the stables," Vander said, and escaped past him into the entry, then out the front door into the shadowy darkness.

Chapter Nineteen

NOTES ON FREDERIC'S REPENTANCE

- day after Frederic cruelly leaves Flora at the altar, his deceitful friend breaks down and confesses that Flora had never kissed him. It had all been a lie.
- Frederic realizes All Too Late the plight that his terrible jealousy has led him to. Loss of the Woman of his Heart, etc.
- Rushes to her house, only to discover it repossessed by Mr. Mortimer's solicitor, and a new (formerly impoverished) maiden established there.
- Horrified, he realizes that Flora's clothes and jewels were delivered to his house before the wedding.
- She has naught but the gown she had worn for the ceremony.

- *Agony of Repentance. Ha!*
- *In a frenzy, Frederic vows to give up his fortune/horses/ servants until such time as he recovers his Beloved. Sets out on foot, following stories of a Divinely Beautiful woman in tattered wedding dress, begging for bread.*

*V*ander headed down to the one place in his world where everything made sense, only to be met on the way by Mulberry. A moment later he was running down the path toward the stable. What in the hell was Mia doing, going near that horse again?

He'd made a mistake in buying Jafeer. The animal had clearly been part of a herd, and some horses never recovered after being separated from their family. It was rare, but it happened.

He pushed open the door and ran toward Jafeer's stall. He didn't see Mia, and his imagination presented him with an image of his wife crumpled under the horse's hooves. The double flip his heart took startled him, but there she was.

His duchess was curled up against the shoulder of the most unpredictable stallion that his stables had ever housed. She was fast asleep, as was Jafeer, looking more peaceful than he had since his arrival in England.

In the wan light of a single lamp, Mia's skin against her dark-colored gown was as white as porcelain but warmer, silkier. Golden hair had fallen all around her shoulders, curling like the wood shavings the grooms shoveled into horse's stalls.

She probably wouldn't like that idea, but it was true. Shavings were gold and amber and even buttercup yellow, and her hair had all those colors as well.

But what really caught him was how small she was. Curled up like that, her brave, independent eyes closed, she looked fragile. Which made a rush of protectiveness go through him like a streak of lightning.

"Mia," he whispered. He had to get her out of the stall. She didn't stir, so he walked in quietly, bent down, and collected her into his arms.

She weighed about as much as a chicken. Maybe a newborn foal. And she felt good in his arms. She must be exhausted, because she didn't wake. Her cheek fell against his chest and she nestled in as if he'd been carrying her around for years.

He backed out of the stall and carefully maneuvered the gate shut with his knee, quietly enough that neither horse nor lady woke. Then he set off toward the house.

Granted, he knew nothing about flowers, but he was reasonably certain that she smelled like honeysuckle. Honeysuckle with a dash of vanilla.

Halfway up the house, she stirred, and her brows drew together as if, in her dream, she was scolding him. Her eyes flew open and she gasped, "What are you doing?"

"Carrying you back to the house," Vander said. His hands tightened around the soft, fragrant bundle in his arms.

He didn't want to think about Chuffy's revelations. He'd rather think about the fact that for the first time in his life, he had someone who was *his* and his alone, inadvertently or not.

Mia.

"Please put me down immediately," his wife said. Her body had gone tense, which wasn't as nice as when she had cuddled into his arms.

"I enjoy carrying you," he told her.

"I'd rather walk."

"I neglected to carry you over the threshold yesterday," he told her, enjoying the stern tone in her voice, "so I might as well do it now."

She attempted to twist free. "I'm not a toy, Duke."

Her jaw set. Damn, but she had the prettiest face he'd ever seen. It wasn't angular and stern the way some women's were. At the same time, he could see strength in every contour.

"I don't understand why you are acting this way," she said in a chilly voice.

"Carrying you?"

They were coming up to the wall of the house now. It had been constructed of blocks hewn by some distant ancestor (or, more likely, his serfs); just looking at the stonework was calming.

His father and mother were gone, and with them, all the pain and turmoil of their lives. He was married to the pocket Venus he had in his arms, and some day they would have babies, one of whom would be his heir.

Given the way Mia calmed Jafeer, their children would have the same tingle in their hands and bones that he had: a tingle that told him a particular yearling would race to win, whereas another colt was innately indolent and would do better pulling a dog cart.

He pushed open the swinging door to the deserted kitchens and walked in, belatedly realizing that Mia was still talking and that her voice was rising. "I'll put you down as soon as we are upstairs," he told her. For the first time in days, Vander felt happy.

He liked Mia's softness, her curves, her perfume . . . everything about her. He backed through the door to his bedchamber, which fortunately was empty.

Mia was getting red in the face and thrashing

about, so he finally put her down. She whipped around, hands on her hips.

"Just what do you think you're doing, manhandling me like that?" she demanded.

Vander grinned. "Carrying my wife up the stairs." He moved nearer to her, wondering how a disheveled woman wearing a grain sack with a ruffled neck could make his entire body taut with lust. "I think we should pretend this is our wedding night."

She backed away. "Our marriage will remain unconsummated until *I* beg for one of my allotted nights, don't you remember? *You* decreed that. And you made me sign a contract to that effect."

"I've decided to break the contract," he said, entirely at ease with the decision. He had Mia, and he was going to keep her. That asinine rule about four nights had to go.

"That is not in your purview. I am not requesting a night. In fact, I will *never* beg for a night with you." She darted to the door leading to their shared bathing chamber. "If you'll excuse me." She tugged on it in vain.

Vander strolled over. "It must be hooked from the inside."

"That's absurd!"

"So is the idea of keeping your husband out of the chamber when you're in the bath." If he hadn't already had an erection, he would at the thought of Mia's creamy skin slick with water.

She apparently decided there was no point to further discussion, because she headed for the door to the corridor.

Vander caught her by the waist and spun her about until their bodies were aligned. Instantly she stilled, her eyes caught by his. A deep certainty swelled in his chest, even as his body throbbed with desire. It was a certainty that felt as right as spring rain, as momentous as when the first horse he trained won a race.

They were married, and Mia was his, and that was significant. It wasn't just a matter of papers and negotiation.

There was something about it. Chuffy's song tumbled through his head: *Then come kiss me, sweet and twenty . . . Youth's a stuff will not endure.*

Vander brought his mouth down to hers, and it was just like the last time they kissed: passion flared so high and fast that it felt tangible. Actually, it was tangible, in the hard length that pressed against her softness.

His mouth demanded . . . hers opened. Threaded into the rough, sensual joy of it was his hunger and desire.

His hands slid down her back and pulled her closer. He was shaking with lust, but he had enough sense to realize that Mia was no longer trying to escape, or caviling about those four nights. She was kissing him back, her tongue curling around his in a way that sent fire through his blood.

Voluptuous curves melted again his body. His hands slid further down her body and he hoisted her up, swinging around until her back was against the wall, supporting her weight so he could ravage her mouth without bending his head.

She made a soft sound. He felt like a madman, overwhelmed by desire. Her eyes opened . . . they were heavy-lidded, sensual, desirous. A shudder went through him.

"Will you please request one of those nights?" he whispered. Before she could answer, he bent his head to kiss her neck. He wanted to lick her all over, drive her to writhe under him, make her gasp and call his name.

The thought of her open lips as cries broke from her throat drove him an inch further toward insanity. "Every time I touch you, I feel like a madman," he muttered. Had there ever been such a beautiful pair of eyes? They were the color of green water. They made a man imagine that her eyes saw things no one else did.

"Did you really stop writing poetry?" he asked.

"Yes," she replied, the first word she'd uttered since they began kissing. Her husky voice ignited his body and he took her mouth again, silently commanding her to ask for him. To ask for his services. To demand that he service her . . .

However she wanted to put it.

He would do anything, especially when her fingers curled in his hair and she pressed close to him. He would throw her on the bed and devour her, and the hell with promises and contracts, four nights or three hundred nights. Three hundred and sixty nights might not be enough.

"God, I want you." The words jumped from his mouth, as brutal and simple a sentence as a dockworker might say to a streetwalker.

"I think it would be better—" Mia said, with a gasp, stopping because he took her mouth before she could finish. Her sentence wasn't going in the right direction.

Without allowing her to speak, he pivoted, walked to his bed, and laid her there, his heavy body following hers.

It occurred to him that for the first time, he wasn't entirely sure that he could wait for a woman's permission. Shocked, he reared back and rolled to the side.

"Mia," he murmured, putting a finger on her

plump lips. Should he demand a night? Hell, she was his wife. She was—

"All right," she whispered, pink coming up in her cheeks. "If you . . . if you really want to."

Vander stared at her with incredulity. " 'If I really want to?' " His cock was against her leg, so he rolled forward slightly. "Does that feel as if I'm of two minds on the issue?"

Mia blinked and looked down at his breeches. They were strained over an erection so ferocious that his smalls had given up the fight and slipped down. Which was damned uncomfortable, by the way.

There was one question he should ask, though he already knew the answer. Mia's response to him spoke for itself. She had surely slept with that imbecile of a fiancé.

"Have you ever been with a man?" he asked, schooling his tone to be neutral.

He knew instantly that he'd made a mistake. "I haven't had that opportunity," she replied, her voice stilted. Before he could stop her, she sat up and slid toward the edge of the bed. "This has been remarkably educational, Your Grace, but I think we shouldn't . . . shouldn't overtax our ability to spend time in the same room."

He sat up and caught her waist just as she got to her feet. "Stay with me."

"I would prefer not to."

"I had to ask that question."

She turned her head and looked at him. "Why? Because I am a blackmailer, you think I am generous with my favors?"

"No! It had nothing to do with that. A man treats a woman differently if she has experience, that's all. Many a couple anticipates their vows."

Mia's lips tightened. "Edward and I did not," she stated.

The feeling sweeping Vander's chest was primitive and uncivilized . . . powerful. "I'm glad," he said, before he could catch the words.

"If you will forgive me, Your Grace, I'd like to retire to my chamber. I think that clearer minds should prevail."

"No." He tightened his fingers, holding her in place. "We must talk, Mia. We can't keep snapping things at each other. We're married now. We share responsibility for Charlie."

"You have no responsibility for Charlie," she said instantly.

"Yes, I have," he said. "There are few people who could meet Charlie and not be both charmed by him and happy to take responsibility for him. You know that."

Her mouth wobbled. "You think so? Really?"

"All the same, you've been coddling him. He needs to leave the house, get on a horse, figure out how to carry himself around other boys."

"You have no idea how cruel children can be. It might break his spirit."

"I do have an idea, and it won't break him."

"How would you know? Once, when he was five, I left him alone for just a few minutes in the village and when I returned, they had him in tears."

"There will be more tears," Vander said calmly. "There will be difficult moments. But if we are at his shoulder, he'll be fine. He must do it, Mia. He has to grow up to be a man, not an invalid."

She was grinding her teeth, which made him grin. Marriage to Mia would never be boring.

He settled his arm more firmly around her waist,

drawing her closer. "I want to change the terms of our arrangement. Of our marriage."

"I see no reason for that," she replied, not looking at him, but somewhere around his right ear. "Four nights a year is more than enough to produce an heir. If four nights prove insufficient for that purpose, we might reconsider after a year has passed." She tried to leave, but he reeled her back against his chest as easily as a dappled trout caught in summertime.

"I want you," he said again, his voice dark with lust. He nipped her ear. She jerked, but she didn't struggle free, and he felt her pulse quickening against his arm.

"So let me tell you how this shall be," he said, when she remained silent. "We shall consummate our marriage tonight, because that's what newly married couples do. They go to bed together and they don't stand upright again for hours."

"We do not have a normal marriage," she tried.

Her voice was tight, which Vander didn't like. "Turn your head so I can kiss you," he said against her sweet-smelling hair.

She shook her head. "This is inadvisable." His wife was stubborn. Hell, if he looked up the word in a dictionary, he'd probably find the name *Mia* printed there. "We're not really married," she insisted.

"Yes, we are. You're my wife, and you're staying my wife. And if you think we're not going to sleep together, after you kissed me like that, you are wrong."

"Kissed you . . ." She cleared her throat and turned her head just enough to frown at him. "You kissed me, not the other way around."

"No."

"Yes!"

Desire boiled in his gut, urging him to topple her backward again. But he'd already pushed his wife enough. If he pressed open those strawberry lips, he could seduce her.

But that wasn't enough. He suspected that bedding Mia would be like learning the art of making love all over again.

You can't do that alone.

"That kiss was a long, slow ride into oblivion, and it took two of us," he whispered, his lips brushing her cheek. "You opened that sweet little mouth of yours, and tangled tongues with me as if you wanted me just as much as I wanted you."

Chapter Twenty

NOTES ON CHURCH & JILTING

- *Shocked gasps from the assembled audience. guests in the cathedral. Westminster Abbey (only for royalty?) St. Paul's.*
- *ancient priest pats Flora's shaking hand.*
- *Chin high, she picks up the hem of her wedding gown.*
- *Is she blinded by tears? "Slubbered with tears, she——" Don't know about "slubbered." Not sure what it means.*
- *She runs out the (side door—Nave?) unable to meet the curious eyes/Frederic's parents? All the way from Germany?*
- *Bursts through the back door of church into a sunlit day. Veil floats behind.*

> *- Runs like wounded animal: only idea to hide.*
> *- kindly man on cart takes her as far as . . . (somewhere outside*
>   *London) and drops her off with two a crust of bread.*

Mia could feel red patches breaking out on her neck from pure embarrassment. Her husband had hardly glanced at her, and the walls she'd built up to hide her love had cracked open. "I did not kiss you," she said stoutly.

The laughter in Vander's eyes made her at once irritated and aroused.

"The man whom you kiss would forget he's ever been kissed by another woman," he said, cupping her face in his hands and tilting her head until he had her just where he wanted her.

This was dangerous. All Mia's childhood yearnings flooded back into her heart as if they had never left. As if Vander was the only man she had ever loved or desired.

He bent his head again, at the same time one of his hands slid down over her collarbone.

She pulled away. "What are you doing?"

"Nothing," he said innocently.

"You are touching my—" she faltered, then cleared her throat. If they were to consummate the marriage—and she wasn't foolish enough to delude herself about that—some basic rules of conduct had to be established.

She might be destroyed by her marriage, broken into shards. But at least she could avoid the sort of humiliation that had scarred her after her poetry—and her chest—had been mocked.

He could have her body. But not that part. Not the part she abhorred. "You may not touch me there."

"What?"

"I prefer not to be touched there," she repeated.

His voice came out fast and low. "Did someone grope you against your will?"

"No!" Mia cried, startled. "No one has ever—and no one shall, and that includes you."

His face relaxed, but his eyes had lost the heated sweetness they had before. She regretted it, but it was essential that she made herself understood. She'd gathered from other women that men liked to feel women's breasts.

"Why not?" he asked.

She tried to explain. "We all have parts of our body that we are less than happy with."

An eyebrow shot up. "We have?"

Men, it seemed, liked everything about themselves. That didn't surprise her in the least. "Women have, at any rate. Some women don't like their knees, or their feet, or their hair."

"Your bosom is exquisite. And your hair. I can't speak of your knees or feet, but if given the chance, I can reassure you on those points as well."

Mia could hardly believe that Evander Septimus Brody, the most handsome duke in all England, was gazing at plain Emilia Carrington with desire in his eyes.

But he was.

Lust, even. Lust for someone like her? A quiet voice reminded her that men were like tomcats; they lusted indiscriminately.

But another part of her thought that his eyes had changed color since kissing her. That was for her.

Not for just any woman.

For her.

"Mia?" He leaned forward and kissed her, swift and hard. "Can we agree about your hair and move to points farther south?"

"I thought you hated my hair."

"Why on earth would you think that?"

"You said it was like my father's. Actually, you referred to him as my 'blasted father,' " she clarified.

Vander brought a handful of her hair forward, his strong brown fingers entangled in it. "I will never be fond of your father. But . . . Chuffy revealed a few things tonight that I—at any rate, I must give it some thought. Your hair is like sunshine. And your breasts are truly stupendous."

She stiffened. "I don't wish to talk about them." Back when Oakenrott had labeled them cabbages, they had been large for her age, but now they were larger still. Stupendous was one word for them.

But he persisted, asking again, "Why not?"

"I just don't. I think we should wait," she said, babbling a bit. "A bride should . . . A bride should look entirely different when . . . when intimacies . . ." Her voice died away because Vander's lips were sliding across her cheek, coming ever closer to her mouth.

"Go on," he said, "tell me more about what you think should happen." Rather than wait for a reply, though, he kissed her again. His kiss was rough and sweet, and his urgency made her melt against him helplessly.

Sometime later she opened her eyes. They were lying down again, and Vander's hands were sliding up her legs. His eyes were on hers, waiting to see if she approved. "You make me so fucking hungry," he growled.

Mia had overheard that word shouted by street sweepers and once, memorably, growled by her father, but no one had ever said it *to* her. "Did you say that word?"

"I did."

"You—you can't say things like that!"

"Why not?"

"Because you're a duke and I'm—"

"You're my duchess." His hand went higher, skimming over her thigh. She shivered under his touch. Her legs fell open because that part of her was burning.

He made a groaning noise. "I'm not much of a duke, Mia. You should know that by now. My mother was known as a whore the length and breadth of England by the time I got to Eton. I had to fight my way through school. My only friend was a bastard."

Mia froze, horrified. "The boys *spoke* to you about your mother's behavior?"

He grinned as if she had asked the silliest question imaginable. "They generally didn't speak; they just called me names. And I answered them with my fists."

"Oakenrott," she said with disgust. "That loathsome little toad."

"How did you—" He stopped. "I forgot that you know precisely what Rotter is like."

His hand had reached the roundest part of Mia's thighs and she was fighting an impulse to moan. Anything that would encourage him to move his hand higher, to the place between her legs that was waiting for his touch.

He smiled as if he knew what she was thinking, and his fingers slid right between her legs. Mia squeezed her eyes shut and concentrated on the aching darkness behind her eyelids, and the fact that her hands clutched arms hard with muscles.

She wondered for a second if this touch was permissible between a lady and gentleman, and pushed the thought away. She had no one to ask. And she didn't want him to stop.

In fact, she thought of allowing her legs fall open

and pulling his large body on top of her. That image was so shocking that she stayed absolutely still, not moving a muscle.

"I love touching you, Mia," Vander growled, his voice low, guttural but sweet. "I intend to kiss you there too."

Her eyes flew open. "No, you will not!"

He laughed, and his fingers swirled and pressed. Mia's head fell back again and she let out a sound that no lady would allow to pass her lips.

Vander rolled on top of her, all his delicious weight holding her down. He began kissing her so fiercely that his hunger soaked into her body, taking all her restraints, taking away her claim to be a lady.

Before she knew it, she was shuddering all over, her hands clenched tight around his forearms, begging without words.

And then begging *with* words, because she was bursting into flames and he was the only person who could help her.

But he stopped. Why had he stopped? She whimpered, looking at him through eyes dazed with desire. She was wound tighter than a spool of wire, vibrating like a note so high that it barely struck the ear. "Mia," he growled, "ask me for one of your four nights."

"Wh—what?"

His hand took up that rough caress again.

"Don't stop," she whispered.

"Is this to be one of your four nights?"

Something unraveled in her heart, destroying the last of her defenses, the final shard of sanity she possessed. "Yes! It is, it is."

What he said in response . . . what he did . . . was blasphemous. Miraculous. She felt like a river, liquid, rushing to a destination outside her control. She clung to him, crying out, her body clenching around his probing fingers as his thumb dragged over her soft flesh, setting it on fire.

The only thing that mattered was the stark lust that shimmered in the air around both of them. Vander was driving her to a pleasure greater than she could have imagined.

She hadn't quite got there when he bundled her skirts around her waist and, as if he were her maid preparing her for bed, began swiftly undressing her. As she would to her maid, Mia mindlessly obeyed his requests, her breath coming in little pants, her brain muddled by desire. *Raise your arms, Turn on your side, Twist the other way.*

Her corset was tossed to the floor. It was only when he tried to remove her chemise that she came back to herself and clamped her arms across her chest.

"No." She'd used the word thousands of times, but never under these circumstances. It came out with a kind of sultry intimacy that she'd never heard from her own lips. Or anyone else's, either.

In response, Vander stood and pulled his shirt over his head. She pushed up on her elbows, openly staring. When she was a girl, she used to sit on the fence and watch him working with horses, surreptitiously feasting her eyes on his chest. He hadn't even been fifteen years old.

It was all different now.

What had been a youth's sinewy leanness had filled out into a grown-up male beauty that made her tremble. His face was set in ferocious lines of need and his eyes roamed over her body without the slightest distaste. He bent down and pulled off his breeches, standing squarely before her, flaunting himself.

Her eyes widened. This was entirely different than seeing him in his smalls, when she proposed marriage.

Vander grinned at her with a purely male pride. "Is it the first time you've seen a man in the flesh?" he purred. He came down on all fours over her. This was truly happening.

Vander was about to make love to her.

She had the vague sense that she was expected to exhibit virginal apprehension, but she felt none. She wanted to touch him all over, wind his thick hair around her fingers, pull his mouth down to hers.

Of course she couldn't behave like that. She had to rein in this unfamiliar wantonness. So she reached up to him, but in a ladylike way, putting her hands delicately, loosely around his neck, sliding them to his shoulders with the hope that caress was appropriate. "Shouldn't we douse the lamp?"

Warm muscles slid beneath her fingers as he shrugged. "Why?"

Because darkness was more modest, she thought. But what part did modesty play in bedding, when a man put his fingers in such private places, and teased those pleading sounds from a woman's mouth?

Who could be modest after that?

It was too late.

Mia abruptly decided to abandon her plans for ladylike restraint. She surrendered to curiosity and slid her hand down his chest to reach the part of him that strained toward her.

He stifled a groan as she ran a finger down his length and, with a quick glance at him for approval, curved her hand around him. He was thick, hot and silky.

A curse, dark and guttural, wrenched from his throat. Likely every man thought he possessed the largest tool a woman had ever seen. And because society demanded that a lady never admit to intimacies of any sort, these delusions of grandeur were never dispelled.

Still, she could hardly imagine anyone larger than Vander. It would be impossible. It was impossible now.

The thought brought a chill down her spine and she felt a pang of fear. "What do we do now?" she asked, bringing her hands back to his shoulders. She was on her back, legs together, and he had a knee on either side of her hips.

The whole situation was embarrassing, and the lovely warmth she had in her stomach began to drain away.

"Is the rule about not touching your breasts still in place?"

Mia withdrew her arms from around his neck and crossed them over her breasts. Maybe she would start to wear her corset under her chemise to hold them in a bit. Glancing down showed that her breasts looked even larger from this perspective. She felt a lurch of disgust in her stomach.

He sighed. "I've never made love to a woman wearing clothing before."

Her turn to raise an eyebrow. "Really? I thought that gentlemen were always taking women into back alleys and tupping them against the wall?" She meant her tone to be sardonic, but somehow it came out a little intrigued.

"I have not had that particular pleasure," he said, after a telling moment of silence. "But I'd be delighted to experiment, Duchess."

"No!" she spluttered.

He lowered his head and his lips drifted across hers. "Fair warning: in lieu of a back alley, I propose to make you scream my name. I'm tired of being Your Grace'd."

Mia felt another chilly bolt of panic as Vander pulled her legs apart. He lowered his head, and dropped a kiss on her inner thigh. "That's inappropriate!" she whispered urgently.

He lifted his head, eyes devilish. "How do you know?"

"I . . ." His lips caressed skin, closer to the heart of her.

This was *too* intimate. It was one thing if he put that part of himself inside her. She could turn her head, or—or something. But she had a terrible feeling that if he kissed her there, she would lose what remained of her self-control.

It would be worse than when he touched her. She wouldn't be herself; she would be turned inside out by desire, ravished, begging him . . .

She was not wrong.

Without warning, he lapped at her and she screamed. His mouth was wet and ravenous, and set Mia on fire like a spark landing on a pile of dry kindling.

She couldn't think. She could do nothing but twine her fingers in his hair. Even his warm breath against her flesh made her shudder. She let go of Vander's hair because her fingers curled, and her toes curled. Everything in her was tightening, launching her like a boat to some distant shore.

And then it was happening; she slammed out into deep water, sensation rushing over her. Vander was urging her on, his voice smoky. She heard him dimly, realizing only later what he was saying.

And she . . . that wave brought her back to where she'd been years ago: in love. In love with Evander Septimus Brody.

So mad with love that she had written him a poem, had dreamt of him entering her moonlit room.

He was rising over her, pushing her legs further apart, whispering something . . . an apology? Pushing into her.

It was a possession her body welcomed, even though it was uncomfortable. Perhaps more than uncomfortable. Abruptly her mind slammed back into clarity and she stopped him with both hands to his chest. "No!"

Alarm had replaced every other emotion. Something was wrong. He was too large, like a cork that didn't fit a bottle.

His words were strangled. "Duchess, you can't stop me now."

"It doesn't fit," she said, choosing her words carefully. "We are not compatible. You'll have to—" She shoved at his shoulders. "Take yourself off. It's not working."

He took a breath, didn't move.

Mia felt a primitive surge of fear: "Get off me," she cried. "Didn't you hear me? It doesn't fit."

To her utter fury, a flash of amusement went through his eyes. "Are you certain?" he asked silkily. "Because it feels damned perfect to me."

"Don't swear!" she cried, beside herself. Then she realized what he was doing, rocking slightly as he spoke, slipping in further. And further. "Stop that," she said, between clenched teeth.

He was braced on his arms, over her. She smelled something heady: a man's sweat, combined with an elusive touch of leather and fresh air. Vander's eyes were intense blue slits, and she grasped that he was exerting tremendous self-control not to push forward.

Mia cleared her throat. "Let's try again at a later date," she suggested. *Such as never*, her mind supplied.

He nudged forward again. "Is it painful?" he asked, his eyes intent on hers.

It felt intrusive. Too much. Too wide. Too fast. "It isn't painful, exactly, but it's just not right. We're not compatible. You're too large and too *close*."

"May I move a bit more?" he whispered back. "You're driving me mad, Mia. I've never felt anything like it." He nudged forward again and as she watched, his pupils dilated and his head dipped so that strands of hair brushed her face.

Just like that all the heat bubbled up in her again. And just like that, he no longer seemed intrusive and too large, but like a part of her body that had been missing until now. He was both foreign and intrinsic to her.

Tentatively, she tilted her hips, and though he hadn't moved, the thick length of him came into her a bit more. Breath came harshly between his lips. "You," he whispered. "It's up to you, Mia."

A dark undertow of desire pulled her down, teasing her, taunting. She braced her knees, and slowly, slowly pressed upward. Her body shook, but it had nothing to do with pain.

Her body and his . . .

They were two halves of the same whole.

Vander made that inarticulate noise again, and she caught sight of his face: beautiful, voracious, raw. It fired her blood, dragged her under. With a wild cry, she pushed up, pulling him down at the same moment, seating him fully in the softness of her body.

His response was carnal, as his body surged into motion. Mia gasped, trying to learn the rhythm of the dance, an urgent, hard, pounding dance. She barely mastered it and she was shooting down that same river again, clinging to him, arms around his neck, legs curving around his hips, head back, being pulled faster and faster . . .

She finally let go with a scream, surrendering to the deep pleasure that washed over her, her fingernails digging into the thick muscles of his shoulders.

Dimly, she heard a harsh noise come from his lips and he pumped again, once, twice more, pressed into her so far that there was no place where he stopped and she started.

Chapter Twenty-one

From Miss Lucibella Delicosa to Mrs. Petunia Stubbs
September 11, 1800

Dear Mrs. Stubbs,

I write in response to your letter of June 17, informing me that you plan to name your unborn daughter—if she is a daughter—after one of my heroines. I am truly honored to think that you have read <u>Esmeralda, or Memoirs of an Heiress</u> over twenty times. And I am deeply moved to know that my books helped you overcome the tragedy of your mother's death.

I generally hesitate to offer advice, but since you express the fervent wish that your future daughter resemble my heroine in every particular, I do want to point out that Esmeralda's appearance might lead one to think that the hero loves her for that reason. It is not so: he loves Esmeralda for her loving spirit, kind heart, and courageous disposition.

It is my hope that your daughter will have those attributes of Esmeralda, as they will give her a much happier life than if she resembles my heroine's appearance.

I wish you and Esmeralda all the best in life,

Miss Lucibella Delicosa

Mia woke suddenly, the way she used to jerk awake when Charlie was a baby and she heard a wail from the nursery.

Vander lay on his back, his face turned away from her, the sheet barely covering his hips. Dawn was creeping into the room, just enough that it clung to the contours of his body, as if the glow originated within him. Bands of muscle marched across his belly in perfect order.

If she dared, she would have traced each band with her fingers, investigating how they knit to his back and shoulders, linking to burly arms stained brown by the sun.

His body was the opposite of hers. There wasn't a bit of fat on him; his body was like stored motion, shaped to conquer men and pleasure women. Her fingers itched to caress him, feel all that untamed strength under her hands . . . lying still at her command. She imagined him quivering as she drove him to make the unguarded, rough sound that had come from his throat the night before.

She snatched her hand back just in time. She had already made a fool of herself. It would be different if they were better matched.

The dissimilarities between them couldn't be more

obvious. It was unnecessary to glance down: Her knees were plump and her thighs were plumper. There must be muscle somewhere in her legs, because she managed to stand and sit and walk, but they certainly weren't visible to the naked eye.

Thank goodness, he hadn't argued with her about her chemise, though it didn't hide very much in the growing light of morning. She could see her nipples and the curve of her belly through the cloth.

Lower, where her chemise was still hitched up around her hips, she saw rusty stains on her leg. And on the sheets, she saw with some dismay. Susan—and the rest of the household—would have no doubts about what had happened the night before.

She wiggled backward cautiously, reaching her toe down to touch the floor, eyes on Vander. He breathed slowly, his arms flung out, as if he hadn't a care in the world. He slept like a man who owned the world, a duke whom everyone desired. It was another dissimilarity between them: she always slept in a ball, tightly coiled.

Once in the bathing room, and with the door to Vander's bedchamber firmly latched, she stared at herself in all those mirrors. Last night he had spread her out like a feast and done things to her with his mouth and hands . . . things that made her whimper and cry and generally act like a fool.

The four nights rule was a good one. She knew instinctively that it would hurt to do this more than once every few months. Oh, not hurt in a physical sense, but in her heart.

Making love could too easily become a habit, like some sort of honey dream leading her to believe that her husband adored her, the way Frederic adored Flora in the novel she was writing.

Except Vander was nothing whatsoever like Frederic. She was probably lucky that he remembered her name in the midst of passion. In fact, now she thought of it, Vander might not remember her name, since he always called her "Duchess."

Whereas for her . . . she stared blankly at herself, acknowledging the truth of it. She was fifty times more in love with him now than she had been as a young girl. Even thinking about him made her heart flutter in her chest.

If she didn't protect that heart, it would crack into a hundred pieces when he lost interest. Last night was like playing a game, the best game ever invented. She had to keep in mind that it was only a game, and one at which Vander excelled.

At least the four nights were at her discretion. As her husband, he could have demanded marital intimacies whenever he wanted, even if he came straight from another woman's bed. The thought made her feel ill.

For a moment, a gaping emptiness opened up before her, the conviction that she wouldn't survive this marriage. Men craved variety; she knew that even with her limited understanding of society and its relations. How could she join him in bed, once she knew that he had turned to another woman?

Ruthlessness took over.

She could. She would.

She wasn't the first woman to have fallen in love with a beautiful man. Besides, everything might change in a few months. Vander might wake up and realize that he wanted a wife like the one his friend Thorn had: a perfect, exquisite, noblewoman.

They would divorce . . . unless she was with child.

For a moment she lapsed into fear, her mind scurrying in circles. But her brother, John, had been married to Pansy for years, and they had but one child. Vander was an only child.

She had a vague understanding that it took repeated attempts over a long time.

The four nights rule would save her from that.

Chapter Twenty-two

NOTES ON FLORA'S EXILE

- Flora believes Frederic jilted her, made her forfeit the inheritance, from pure malice. (That's good!)
- Having spent her last 2d. on a crust of bread, she wanders along the lanes of England, tattered, cold, hungry. Near death? Yes. Faints in a field of ~~bluebells~~ poppies.

"Dear Mother, take me to thy Breast and save me from the Cruel Indignities of this ~~Cruel~~ World," she breathed, as a single tear slid down her porcelain cheek.

- ghost of mother? "The dear face hovered above her, just out of reach of her trembling fingers. 'The Goodness of

> *Heaven will guard you, my Dearest Child, & keep you from the heartless intimacy of a Loveless Marriage.'*

~ *More than hunger, thirst, and cold, the spur to her flagging life death was the understanding that the man who should most constitute her Earthly Happiness—he whose love ought to fill her heart and mind—had proved himself an infidel.*

~ *Infidel? Maybe not.*

~ *Ruffian. Rake. Roué.*

~ *Scoundrel?*

~ *"He whom she had long worshipped had proved himself naught but a Worthless Idol. It was that cruelty that broke the soft heart of this creature, the spirit, the joy of her family and friends. Now fallen lower than the lowest of tavern wenches . . ."*

~ *Tavern wenches?*

Mia bathed, dressed, and escaped her bedchamber without hearing a peep from her husband.

"Aunt Mia!" Charlie shouted when she opened the door to the nursery. "Look what Dobbie is doing now!"

He stood braced against the back of the settee, holding a crust of bread in the air while a shaggy pillow pawed his legs. "I'm teaching Dobbie to roll. Just look at this." He looked down at the dog at his feet and commanded, "Roll, Dobbie, roll!"

Dobbie sat down and looked up at him, panting with willingness.

Mia waited, but nothing happened. "You'll get it, old fellow," Charlie reassured the dog, dropping the bread into his open mouth.

"How did Dobbie and Winky sleep last night?" Mia inquired.

"They love being with me," Charlie boasted. "They used to be the duke's mother's dogs, and His Grace says they've been lonely. I let them both sleep on the bed with me, and they weren't lonely at all."

And neither was Charlie, apparently.

Mia went over and dropped a kiss on the top of his head. She remembered the duchess' exquisitely groomed and scented dogs, always tricked out in bright ribbons. A year after her death, the animals were considerably shaggier, with no ribbons in sight.

Winky trotted over to her so she crouched down and scratched his ears. He had thin legs, like the brown cigars that the grooms smoked when they weren't on duty. Age had brought touches of white here and there, but his eyes were still bright and cheerful.

"Do sit down, sweetheart," she said to Charlie. "You might fall, especially if Dobbie starts pawing your legs again."

"I'm trying to stay on my feet as much as possible. It will make me stronger. The duke says so."

Mia sat down and Winky hopped up, curling into a ball in her lap.

"Perhaps I'll sit down now," Charlie allowed.

She patted the sofa beside her and he picked up Dobbie and made his way around and sat.

"Mr. Gaunt thinks it best that they be kept out of the drawing room, but they can go everywhere else with me. Just think: that old butler made them sleep in the garden shed the whole last year," Charlie said, stroking Dobbie's ears.

"That wasn't very nice," Mia agreed. "I gather you rescued them from the potato cellar."

Charlie nodded. "The duke and I went to the kitchens night before last, because that's what we always do. We fetched something to eat, because I'm growing."

"What you *always* do?" Mia echoed. "You've known His Grace for only two days, Charlie!"

"Well, perhaps not every day. But we did it at home, in Carrington House, and last night too." He paused. "I suppose this is our home now, Aunt Mia?"

Mia cleared her throat. "For now," she said weakly.

"The duke said Dobbie and Winky look like hairy eggs." He held Dobbie up by his front paws and leaned forward to rub noses. "You're not a hairy egg, are you, old fellow?" Dobbie obligingly licked him, giving a little bark.

"Try not to let him lick your mouth," Mia said. She pulled her feet up beneath her and shifted Winky to the crook of her left arm. "These dogs are smaller than you were when you were born."

"Really?" Charlie was trying to avoid Dobbie's enthusiastic licks and giggling madly.

"You had a plump tummy. The duke is right: if Winky didn't have all this fur, he wouldn't be much bigger than an egg. Of course, it would have to be a large egg."

"Perhaps an ostrich egg," Charlie said. "I have just been reading about them. An ostrich is an enormous bird that can't fly. It has the biggest eggs of any bird."

"Where does one find an ostrich?"

"I don't remember. Not in Berkshire. Was my mother there when I was born?"

Mia opened her mouth and shut it again. Was Charlie still at the age where babies were found under cabbage leaves?

"Do you want to see how I can make Dobbie dance?" Charlie said, already having forgotten his question. "Look at this!"

Winky had gone to sleep, so Mia stopped stroking him. "I think I'll pay a brief visit to the stables, Charlie. Perhaps you should work on your essay for the vicar?"

"No, I want to come to the stables with you," Charlie said, dropping Dobbie's legs. "I want to see the wild Arabian horse who loves only you. Mary—she's the maid assigned to the nursery—told me all about him. His name means storm, or something like that. I shall ride him. Someday."

Mia's head spun. Charlie was thinking of riding Jafeer? Not while she had breath in her body.

He hopped up and put his crutch under his arm. "Let's go! Winky and Dobbie can come as well."

"Winky is having a nap," Mia said, moving the little curl of dog onto the sofa cushion as she rose.

"That's because he's older," Charlie reported. "Winky could be a grandfather. The duke says his mother bought Dobbie to be Winky's friend."

"Why don't you three wait here, and I'll ask a footman to carry you downstairs," Mia suggested.

"I can get down the stairs *myself*," Charlie said, marching to the door and pulling it open. "Come on, Aunt Mia!"

Mia's heart sank. He would hang onto the railing and make his way down backward, a step at a time, and agonizingly slowly; it could take an hour to reach the bottom. She was longing for a cup of tea and breakfast. "Have you eaten?" she asked Charlie.

"Not yet," he said, clumping his way along the corridor.

The stairs curved in a gracious semicircle. "Are you certain you don't want me to fetch a footman, Charlie? It would be the work of a moment for one of those young men to carry you down."

Charlie shook his head. "I'm too old for that. His Grace said so."

"His Grace said so?" What hadn't His Grace said?

"You may wait for me at the bottom," Charlie ordered, sounding for all the world like a duke himself.

He was growing up. That was natural, Mia told herself. Charlie issued another order. "Dobbie, you go with Aunt Mia." The dog frisked around Charlie's feet, paying no attention.

Mia picked up Dobbie and started down the stairs with a sigh. She would have to discuss this with Vander. He was treating Charlie with cavalier indifference, as if her nephew were a typical boy.

As she neared the stairs' midpoint, where the steps curved, Mia looked back to check on Charlie's progress and discovered he was still at the top, waving to a footman in the entry below.

"That's Roberts," Charlie shouted. "Hurry up, Aunt Mia, or I shall beat you!"

Before Mia could respond, he tucked his crutch under an arm, threw a leg over the railing, and whizzed past her.

Mia let out a shriek and dropped Dobbie. Mercifully, the animal landed on his feet, barking madly, and bounced down the stairs, ears flapping. For her part, Mia stopped breathing, heart pounding, until she saw Roberts deftly catch Charlie.

She sagged down onto a step, her hand pressed to her heart. Below, Charlie was hopping around the black-and-white marble floor as if he hadn't been close to bashing his head. Or losing his life.

"You mustn't worry," a deep voice said behind her.

Mia looked up, her throat too tight to speak. Vander put a hand under her arm, and helped her to her feet. "Children always hang on tighter than their parents believe they will. Shall we join him?"

She couldn't respond. She had to have a stern talk with Charlie. From this moment on, he was not allowed to touch the banister. If he did that again, she'd do something . . . something serious. Lock him in the nursery.

Even as the idea came to her, she recoiled from it. Charlie spent too much time indoors already; his skin was porcelain white.

She realized that Vander still held her arm. Shuddering alarm was replaced by a sense of warmth radiating from his touch. "I'm sorry," she said hoarsely. "I was terrified by that . . . by Charlie, and I didn't hear what you just said."

"I merely said that your nephew is a brave fellow. I'm proud of him."

"You're—you're proud of him."

They reached the bottom of the stairs. Charlie had already made his way through the front door that Gaunt held open, and was waiting for them at the top of three stone steps leading to the drive.

He turned, gave them an impish grin, and shouted, "Look at me!" Then, before she could take a breath, he dropped his crutch and jumped.

She screamed again, freezing in place. When Charlie landed, his right foot couldn't hold his weight and he collapsed, plunging forward and hitting his face on the cobblestones.

"Oh dear God," Mia cried, and ran down the steps toward him. Vander preceded her, and was already crouching over Charlie and gently turning him over. A bloody scrape discolored Charlie's brow and his eyes were closed.

Mia felt a dagger of fear when his eyes didn't instantly open.

"Charlie," Vander said. "You're frightening your aunt. Open your eyes."

Mia sank to her knees. "Darling?"

"That hurt," Charlie said, his eyelids flying open.

Her heart began beating again. That was the voice her child used when he bruised something, stubbed his toe, sprained a wrist breaking his fall. He had been falling since he could stand—but she'd never once seen him do anything deliberately dangerous the way he had today.

Twice today.

The timbre of Vander's voice was dark and commanding. "Look at me, Charles Wallace."

Charlie turned his head and looked up at him.

"That was exceedingly foolish. You had no way of knowing whether your leg would be able to support you, and it was possible that you could concuss yourself on the stones, or stab yourself with your crutch. And to try such a thing while your aunt watched showed callous disregard for her. I am disappointed."

"It wouldn't have made any difference if I hadn't seen it," Mia said, her voice wavering. "You must promise *never* to do something so dangerous ever again, Charlie. Never!"

Charlie sat up, rubbing his weak leg. "I won't get strong if I don't test myself." He sounded sulky.

"That's true," Vander said, "but you must go about it intelligently. Your leg has to be strong enough to bear your weight first. Remember when you told me that if you bowed, you would topple?"

Charlie nodded, his bottom lip jutting out in a way that made a pang of pure love go through Mia. When he was two years old, he had that expression almost every day, every hour, as he fought to walk. The doctors said he would never manage it, but they had been wrong.

"You knew how to fall and roll. That's how confident you have to be before you take a risk of any kind." He hoisted Charlie to his feet. "Do you think you can walk?"

"Yes!" Charlie said stoutly, leaning against Vander.

Mia blotted the scrape on his forehead with a handkerchief. Then she scooped up Charlie's crutch and handed it to him.

Tears were pressing on the back of her throat, and she longed to give him a tight hug, but instinct told her to keep silent. Charlie needed advice from a grown male, and no one was more male than Vander. The duke crouched again and ran his hand along Charlie's leg.

Mia straightened and turned away. Seeing Vander lean intently toward Charlie, without the faintest sign that he considered her nephew lame or deformed in some way . . . This was as dangerous to her heart as making love.

In fact, it tore at her defenses as nothing else could have. She decided to return to the house.

A large hand curled around her wrist. "Where are you going?"

Charlie plunked his crutch in place and leaned on it, testing his leg. "You said we're going to the stables, Aunt Mia. You mustn't go inside now."

"You frightened me," Mia said, the words coming out against her will.

Vander said quietly, "Apologize, Charlie. You are lucky to have someone who loves you as much as your aunt does. One of a man's duties in life is to try not to frighten the people who love him."

Charlie thought about it for a moment, before he said, "I'm sorry, Aunt Mia." He dropped his crutch, took a hop, and wound his arms around her waist.

A tear rolled down Mia's cheek. She met Vander's eyes over his head and smiled shakily.

"Hello, hello!" Chuffy charged out of the front door and down the steps. This morning he was wearing a black coat with a waistcoat of gaudy purple visible beneath. He carried a purple stick with a large stone in the top, and he was swinging it like a man without a care.

Or a headache from imbibing a vat of brandy, which, frankly, Mia thought was miraculous.

"This must be Master Charlie!" he bellowed.

Charlie pulled back from Mia and stared, awestruck.

"Just look at that," Chuffy exclaimed. "We're both in need of an extra leg." He waved his elegant stick.

"That's not a crutch," Charlie pointed out loftily.

Chuffy spun it in the air. "No, because I can do this with it. Can you do that with yours?" He spun it again.

Charlie laughed, a boy's high laugh. Clinging to Mia's sleeve with one hand, he retrieved his crutch, and tried to twirl it. To no one's surprise, it clattered to the ground.

A minute later, Chuffy had Charlie in fits of laughter, promising to teach him how to spin his crutch on the palm of his hand.

"The boys at school will love it," Chuffy said. "We'll have to get you a crutch with proper balance, of course. Not to worry; I know all the cane-makers in London. You've found your way into the right family, son!"

"Shall we go to the stables?" Vander asked.

"Pay no attention to him," Chuffy said, winking at Charlie. "He's my nevvy, but people have given him entirely too much attention since he became a duke. Poisoned his brain. So do you think you can beat me to the stables? They're right around the turn of the path."

"Of course I can!" Charlie cried. "You have to let me start first, though, because I'm younger."

"Don't you think I should get an advantage because I'm fatter?"

"No," Charlie said. "I also deserve more time because I have a bad leg."

"I have a bad body," Chuffy countered ruthlessly. "I can't drink nearly as much as I used to be able to. No advantage on that front."

"Well, then," Charlie said triumphantly. "I'm an orphan!"

"So am I!" Chuffy exclaimed, wagging his bushy eyebrows. "Oh go on, I'll give you a bit of a lead, purely from the kindness of my heart."

Charlie grinned and took off, swinging as fast as he could. Dobbie followed, barking madly.

"A fine lad!" Chuffy said, patting Mia's arm. He waited until Charlie was halfway up the path, and then took out after him.

"Did I correctly understand that you were escorting your nephew to the stables in order to introduce him to Jafeer, the most violent horse I own?"

"Jafeer is not violent," Mia said, trying not to think about how much she wanted Vander to drop her arm and kiss her. Kiss her the way he had last night.

He glanced down at her, eyebrow raised. "He's not the first horse I'd choose for Charlie to ride."

"Ride? Absolutely not! I must speak to you about that. I've never even put Charlie on Lancelot. He could never ride a proper horse: perhaps a pony, a very small pony." She gestured to a level near her waist.

"There are no ponies that size; you're talking about a large dog."

She heard the amusement in his voice and frowned. "In that case he must learn to ride on Lancelot. I'm entirely serious."

"As am I. Charlie has to go to school, and I mean to ensure that he'll be the best rider at Eton by the time he gets there. We'll send a thoroughbred along with him, so all the boys can see his prowess."

Mia inhaled sharply. "That's another thing. Charlie can't go to school, certainly not boarding school!"

"Of course he can."

Vander simply didn't understand. He hadn't watched as Charlie grew up, or seen how cruel other people—including the boy's own mother—had been to him. She glanced ahead and saw that Chuffy and Charlie had disappeared around the bend leading to the stables.

"Charlie cannot—" she began.

But she broke off when she met Vander's eyes. They were heavy-lidded, a devastating knowledge gleaming in their depths. A knowledge of *her*, of what they did the night before, of what she felt like, and tasted like, and sounded like.

The cool control in his eyes was gone, swallowed by an erotic abandon that she had scarcely learned, although her body responded instantly.

"Charlie will enjoy Eton." He placed his hands on her arms and drew her to him. "You left my bedchamber without saying good morning."

"You were sleeping," Mia said.

"Next time, wake me." His expression made her weak at the knees. "As I see it, this is still part of my night."

"*Your* night?"

"My first night."

Chapter Twenty-three

NOTES ON Near-death Scene

- *Flora lies dying amongst the poppies, her yellow hair & etc. Trembling, pale, her tuneful voice reduced to a prayerful murmur. Has eaten naught but an egg in the last day. Raw? Ugh. Dove's egg? It's splattering rain, Angel's Tears.*
- *Frederic has searched every lane throughout England. Too much to say that he would not long survive her death? Probably.*
- *he gives up only a few paces from her form: White and lean, sorrow concealed, his easy graceful movements reduced to—to something.*
- *Sinks to his knees only a few steps from her prostrate form and prays that the Almighty will give him the Dearest*

*Hope of his heart: his Flora. "I was made bewildered
and impatient by the strength of my feelings. Like a base
~~Indian~~ fool, I threw away a pearl worth more than all
my ~~tribe~~ possessions." (Another touch of Shakespeare!)*

~ *"If you restore her to me, Lord, I will become a humble
attendant to her daily Lesson of Love. No matter what
affections Flora awakens in the breasts of her admirers, I
will respect and honor her faithful love."*

"**Y**ou don't understand," Mia said, trying to ignore
the coaxing honey in Vander's voice. She desperately tried to remember the important issues she had
thought to discuss with him.

When her husband looked at her with that expression, all she wanted to do was answer his craving
with a kiss. Hurl herself into his arms and pull his
face down to hers.

Last night, she had felt sensuous, desirable . . .
almost beautiful—and she hadn't felt that way since
she was labeled a "charity case" at fifteen years old.

"We mustn't do this," she whispered, but he pulled
her close.

"A mere kiss," he whispered back. At first he didn't
even touch his lips to hers. Instead he opened his
mouth against her neck, licking her in a way that sent
her mind reeling.

She meant to turn away. She meant to say no, to
break free.

Instead she wrapped her arms around his neck
and tipped her head back, delighting in the way he
held her up, as if she weighed nothing, as if she were
as delicate as a flower.

Suddenly panic bloomed in her stomach. She was
behaving like a wanton in front of the house, where

anyone could see. The servants. Gaunt. "Stop," she gasped. "I must go to the stables. Charlie will be waiting."

"Very well," Vander said easily, his hands slipping away. "If you must go to the stables, I'll go with you." He took her arm and they began to walk. "And if you come," he added, "I'll come."

It took a moment, but when she grasped his double entendre Mia felt color flood into her face. "You can't mean what you just said!"

"Perhaps not in the front drive." His smile acknowledged the desire between them with a frankness she could never have imagined.

Just looking at his lips made her want another kiss. She craved more than a kiss. She wanted the bliss of last night, the way their limbs had slid over each other like water, the way his fingers had stroked her into a mindlessness where she needn't worry about her figure or her breasts. Or anything else.

She could just *be*.

They reached the first of the stables, but rather than enter, Vander steered her around the back. "Where are you taking me?" Mia asked.

When they were around the corner, out of sight of the house, he picked her up, braced her against the wall, and took her mouth. A craving, toe-curling hunger vibrated between them.

Vander pulled back just enough to lick her lips, his tongue flickering against hers, driving her into a low moan.

The sound startled her into sanity. "No!"

"No one can hear," he said thickly. "This building is not used as it's too old and unsafe."

She succumbed. They spoke without words, just murmurs of hunger, an emotion as primitive as greed.

As love.

Mia scarcely noticed that Vander was hauling up her skirts; all she could hear was her own harsh breath and the way her body felt empty, waiting for him. Every touch of his hands on her legs kindled the fire in her higher until she couldn't think straight.

The flimsy skirts of her morning gown were no barrier. Vander pulled back, just enough to meet her eyes. One hand was curled under her bottom, but he had jerked her legs wide, around his hips.

Mia was stunned into silence by the scalding ache between her legs. Vander was fumbling at his breeches with his other hand, but it didn't occur to her to demur. Instead she waited, her heart beating quickly, yearning for him.

His eyes were fixed on her mouth. "I must have you," he said, his voice low and hoarse. "I need you again."

His face wasn't beautiful now; it was savage, demanding, almost cruel. His fingers stroked her and Mia gave a little cry.

And then he was there.

What had been discomfort the night before was pain now . . . but exquisite pain. She gave a little gasp, her hands closing on his shoulders. He stopped instantly, his breath harsh, forehead against hers.

"I'm sorry," he growled. "Is it too soon?"

Irrationally, the only thing Mia thought was that she didn't want him in control so that he could think, could talk, could leave her. She leaned forward and let her tongue slide between his lips as if she'd done it a hundred times.

At the same time, she curled her legs around his hips and forced his rigid thick length into her body. A cry burst from her throat and was swallowed by him . . . he was kissing her, but she hardly knew it.

His weight pushed her legs so wide that as he pressed forward and withdrew, it sent exquisite sensations through her thighs, a fiery sensation gathering in her limbs.

She broke the kiss when she threw back her head.

"That's right." His words were more a groan than a growl, the bass note to the pumping of his hips against her. He was sliding easily now, driving her higher and higher into incoherence.

She bucked against him when she came, a cry wrenched from her chest and swallowed by Vander's mouth on hers. Her fingers tightened until she was clinging to him as if he were a raft in the heart of a storm, her body jerking uncontrollably, guttural ecstasy escaping her lips.

Vander gasped something in reply, a curse, a blessing, and he began thrusting even faster, grunting with as little elegance as she had shown.

Mia could feel him deep and hard inside her, but more than that, she knew instinctively that he was lost to himself, lost to the pleasure she was giving him. He was holding her as if he would never let her go. The thought made her legs clamp around his hips and push back toward him.

A word fell from his lips but she wasn't listening. Their eyes met and like that, the fire burst up her legs again. She writhed against the wall, twisting in his fierce grip, her moans fracturing in the air. The only thing in the world was the fierce weight of his body.

The hand Vander had braced on the wall over her head came down and he pulled her head toward him, taking her mouth with a hot, wet kiss, his body jerking so hard that her backbone struck the wall.

She'd have a bruise, but she didn't care.

She cared about nothing but the heat searing her

body, the mouth slammed down on hers, the grunt as he pressed home one last time.

Mia opened her eyes, finally, to discover that she was staring up at the ancient eaves of the roof above her head. Her mind tried to put pieces of herself, her inner self, back together.

She felt as if the two of them had cracked and flown apart, broken by pleasure. Last night had been wonderful, but in retrospect, it had been civilized. This was *mating*: sweaty, grunting, incomprehensible.

At least she hadn't been alone. She risked a look at Vander's face and saw he was stunned as she was. He withdrew slowly and lowered her to the ground; her skirts fell over legs so weak that she clung to him for fear she'd crumple.

Last night, he had been tender and desirous, soothing her when it stung, whispering reassurances in her ear.

Today, he had uttered only one word, a word she had scarcely registered in the instant. What was it he'd said?

Then it came to her: *greedy.*

That's what he'd said.

That was the word.

She glanced down, feeling as if she were in some sort of odd dream, and watched as he buttoned up his breeches.

Greedy. The word grew and grew until it occupied all the space in her head.

The tingling she felt now wasn't the pleasurable kind. "What did you mean by that?" she whispered, and then cleared her throat and elaborated, "By that word?"

His eyes moved slowly to hers. The good thing was that he looked as stupefied as she felt. Her hair had fallen down her back. His beard had scraped her face and her neck, and her legs ached because she had clung to him with all her strength. And other parts of her . . .

Ached too.

"What word?" Vander asked.

He was staring down at his wife, trying to work out what had just taken place between them. He had been with many women before; he'd sampled women as if he were at a banquet.

He regarded women the way he regarded food: necessary and sometimes delectable, but ultimately a distraction.

He had spent hours upon hours training a single horse. He would never spend hours on a woman. Hell, he'd never even had a mistress who lasted more than a few months. Either they wanted more, or he became bored—whichever came first.

But he had never had an experience like this one. A moment ago everything in him had turned inside out and poured into Mia. And he wasn't done, either. Even though he was still shaking, all he wanted was to scoop her up and head back to the house to start all over again.

A man could lose himself in a woman like this. He could find himself tied to her, so tightly that he would go mad if she strayed.

If she left him.

The way his father had broken.

"You said 'greedy.'" Mia's voice was hoarse.

Bloody hell, she was beautiful. All that bright hair had fallen around her shoulders, and her skin had turned rose where his stubble had scraped it. She had that perfect nose, and pointed chin, and her eyes were exquisite.

How had he ever thought he preferred blue eyes? He liked green eyes, dark green eyes like water tumbling in a Highland stream, reflecting pine trees.

There was nothing sunny and sweet about Mia. She was all hidden depths and passion. Her lips were plump and red, and looking at them made him start to harden, even though he'd just poured himself into her.

This was unacceptable.

The feeling lent itself to what he said, sharpened his voice though he didn't mean it that way.

"You're greedy for me," he said bluntly. "I had you pinned against the wall and you wanted more. Hell, if—"

He stopped. What was he doing, talking to a lady like that? Not just a lady, but his wife?

Mia's cheeks first turned red, and then pale. She swallowed so hard that he saw her throat ripple. She bent her head and hair fell across her face; when she looked back up a second later, her eyes were calm and her face empty.

She didn't look angry. Or hurt.

But she was.

Vander felt another stab of irritation about that, because he didn't like that he could read her face. He didn't care to wonder whether a woman was angry.

If she was angry, she was welcome to leave. If he disappointed her, she could leave. If he asked for too much, she could leave.

Or he could leave.

But he was *married* to Mia.

Neither of them could leave.

And even worse, he didn't want to go anywhere. It was as if her wedding ring strung a chain between them, because even now, after insulting her, he was hard and he wanted more than anything to take her back into his bed and fill her up.

That feeling sent a spasm of panic through him, and he didn't care that her face was no longer flushed and pretty and open to him, her eyes soft.

He didn't want a woman with an open face. Or softness in all the right places, including her eyes.

"Some women are greedy for a cock, and men love that," he said, stepping back and rearranging his breeches because commanding his tool to go down wasn't working. "It was a compliment."

"'A compliment,'" Mia repeated.

She gave her skirts a shake and pulled at her bodice, which stretched the fabric against her breasts.

He had to force his eyes away, because another streak of madness went through him. He had never made love to a woman—gone mad with lust—*without even touching her breasts.*

It had to be the novelty of marriage.

No ring would tie him to a woman, not even a woman who looked at him as if he could give her bliss. As if he had the only thing in the world she wanted—without meaning his title or money.

She looked at him as if he were a king.

"So, Duchess," he said. "Let's count that as part of last night, shall we? It needn't be the second of our four nights. It's morning, after all."

Her eyes weren't blank now; they were growing enraged. He welcomed it, because he could not resist her if she looked at him with aching hunger. If she looked at him that way again, as if she were greedy for him, he would follow her anywhere. Probably on his knees.

Shit.

"My treat," he added, and tapped her chin with his finger.

Her hand came up so quickly that he saw only a blur. She caught him hard across the cheek with her open hand. His head jerked back, but he welcomed the sting.

He deserved it, taking a lady against the stable wall with no more finesse than a man takes a cheap whore.

Gentlemen didn't treat their wives that way. They didn't behave like sailors on shore after a nine-month-long voyage. She had driven him mad. If she would allow it, he would have her against the wall again, her lush body cradled in his.

He'd never seen anything more erotic than the way Mia threw her head back, lips open, when she came. There was nothing feigned about it. She'd responded with her whole body.

Vander caught a hint of something . . . a delicious, heated hint of Mia, sweat and desire and honeysuckle. All of a sudden he was caught up in an erotic haze and took a step closer to her. Yet his words came out haltingly. "I apologize for my remarks. They were deeply inappropriate."

"Stop looking at me like that," she hissed.

He couldn't.

"*I am not a jam tart!*" The words came out in a scream.

What?

She was gone. Vander fell back against the stable wall, his knees weak, staring after his wife. His duchess.

A jam tart? Where in the hell had that come from? He'd no idea, though now he thought on it, she *was* like a jam tart. She was like sweet treacle and he'd like to eat her up.

Slowly his mind cleared. A memory came to him: Rotter calling Mia a jam tart years ago.

He had been appallingly rude, far more so than Rotter. He would likely have to grovel.

Of course he would grovel. He would make their excuses to Charlie and Chuffy, and follow her to the house.

Now Mia wasn't in front of him, he remembered that there were things he hadn't done with her . . . to her. Even though he'd just come, he was throbbing, damn it. Throbbing the way he had as a boy, on the verge of an unacceptable loss of control.

He wanted the jam tart. He wanted to eat his wife over and over, make her throw back her head like that until she was dizzy with it. Until he could rear up and pull her small body under his and pound into it.

He leaned against the stable wall, trying to force his mind elsewhere. The sky was pale blue and far away, and a hawk circled far above, below a single cloud. He rearranged his breeches again, trying to make room for a body part that no longer fit in his smalls.

He ached all over, his body telling him that there was only one thing he wanted.

Mia.

Thanks to his being an ass, he had exactly three nights in the rest of the year to enjoy her.

One would have to be tonight. Tonight . . . the promise of it sang in his blood. She was angry, but she would get over it.

He would tell her the truth: if she was greedy, he was as starving as a man who not only had been at sea for months on end, but at sea without food.

Surely she would understand. And they did have three nights left.

A slow smile curled his lips. That would be enough to take the edge off this frantic lust. He'd never slept with a woman for more than two nights in a row. He got bored.

Tonight should do it.

The second night would break the spell.

Chapter Twenty-four

NOTES on Castle Plum

- After Frederic continues on his fruitless quest, the Evil Lord Plum discovers Flora unconscious amongst the poppies and takes her to his castle.

"The dark air hovering around Castle Plum drew attention to the ravages of time, visible in some parts of the building. The massy gate of the castle was opened by a tall, dark-haired old man who screeched, 'Who goeth?'"

- Conscious of approaching death, Flora begs Plum to send her beloved Frederic a lock of her hair.
- Lord Plum keeps the hair and nurses her back to health

instructs his housekeeper to nurse her to health. Yes!
Very Bluebeard.
- Lord Plum: "How improbable that any man who had once
viewed the Ethereal Graces, the Matchless Beauty of this
maiden, should quit her side?" (Flora cheers up.)
- A ruse, because he has a wife in the attic. Or somewhere.
- Her youth and innocence not proof against the dangerous
combination of male beauty and sleek artifice. This is
good!

Mia made her way back to her bedchamber and
closed the door, which reminded her that locks had
been installed on the bathing chamber door, but not
on the door leading to the corridor. Vander would
follow her to apologize, and she would be unable to
keep him out.

She went straight into the bathing chamber, put
the hook on both doors, and looked about for a place
to sit. There were two alternatives: the bathtub or on
the floor. She chose the floor.

She sank down, so devastated that for some
seconds she didn't even breathe, let alone cry.

Their marriage was only two days old and already
a pattern was being established: Vander would blurt
out the truth about how he felt.

Afterward, he would apologize and pay her false
compliments . . . until the next time he let slip just
how little respect he had for her.

Even worse—and she hated this truth—he hadn't
been wrong: she *was* greedy for him.

She had written that poem all those years ago.
She had created the moonbeam, even if she hadn't
known what she was talking about. She had
dreamed he entered her bedchamber. Somehow, just

by being around him, that side of her sprang back to life.

She had allowed him to pull up her skirts and take her against a wall. It didn't matter that he was her husband. In a way, it was worse.

Real ladies were never treated that way. He had seduced her without a single compliment or an adoring glance, no matter how insincere. How could she blame him?

She had agreed, if tacitly, to being demeaned. She had opened her legs and let him do what he willed.

If at any point she had said "no," Vander would have stopped.

That was what hurt the most. She didn't want to be a woman like that. Words knocked around in her head, ugly words: *greedy, cock, pearls . . . jam tart.* They brought on tears that streamed down her face until she had her head on her knees, sobbing.

Sure enough, after a while, there was a knock on the door leading to Vander's bedchamber.

"No," she said, taking a shuddering breath. "Please go away."

A moment of silence, followed by the sound of retreating footsteps. Seconds later, the door to her bedchamber rattled.

"They are both locked," she said, choking. "Just leave me alone, *please.*"

"No."

It would seem that dukes expected to get their way all the time, even when their duchesses were desperate to be alone.

"Go away!"

"I want to talk to you. I must apologize."

Mia heard a floorboard squeak as Vander shifted his weight. She had known that apology was coming. Did she care to hear it? Not particularly.

He had already made clear what he thought. And he'd said it in the heat of passion, when a man couldn't lie if he tried. What he'd said was *real*. It was no great surprise he was now sorry he'd blurted that out. He was a decent man, and he didn't want to hurt her feelings.

But that didn't make it any less truthful.

She wrapped her arms around her knees. "I accept your apology," she said, clearing her throat and raising her voice. "I shall be out in an hour or so. Please give me some privacy."

She began pulling herself back together. After all, she wasn't sluttish all the time. Only around him. Her poem had been innocently desirous.

Not that she was innocent any longer. She had taken one look at his unbuttoned breeches, and she would have done anything to have him thrust inside her. Lie down on the ground, on the gravel, probably.

Another tear slid down her cheek.

Up against the stable wall.

She shuddered at the memory. If she could just get away from Vander, she could regain her self-respect. She wasn't like this with other men. She knew with absolute certainty that she would never have behaved like this with Edward.

They would have had an affectionate marital life, intimacies conducted under the bedcovers, with respect.

Love would have come in time. She had already loved him a bit. Or, at least, she had been tremendously fond of him.

"Duchess!" It seemed that her husband was growing annoyed. Her thoughts darkened. Vander ought to shoulder some blame as well. He had treated her like a hired harlot, even though she was his duchess.

The door rattled in its frame, more forcefully now. "Open this door!"

Did he really think that roaring at her would make any difference? He was far too used to getting his own way. Women had probably melted in front of him from the time he was . . . oh . . . fourteen. Thirteen, she thought, remembering what he looked like at that age.

The door rattled some more and he began ranting about something or other, but she had stopped listening.

Hadn't he said something about a race tomorrow or the next day? A pulse of relief went through her. He would be gone soon.

Suddenly she heard Susan's voice, and Vander ordering her to take herself downstairs, which he hadn't any right to do.

"She's *my* maid!" she shouted.

Susan abandoned her, of course; she could hardly refuse the duke's command.

There was a huge thump and the whole door vibrated.

"What are you doing?" Mia shrieked. "Nottle said that door was imported from Venice."

"So what?"

Another resounding thud.

"It probably cost as much as a thatched roof! Don't you dare break it."

"Then open the door. Now!"

"I want to be alone," she cried. "Is that so hard to understand? I want to think."

His voice quieted. "Don't think."

"How can you say that? Do you think that you can rule every moment of my day?"

"I know what you're thinking."

"No, you don't."

"You're thinking that I don't respect you."

"I am not." There was no point in dwelling on unpleasant truths.

The door rattled again. "Mia, if you don't open this door, I shall break it down."

"Oh, do go away, why don't you!" she snapped. "You don't care how I'm feeling. I'm the wife you loathe, remember?"

"I do not loathe you."

Her answer was a curse that she had never spoken aloud before. In fact, now she thought about it, he brought out all her worst tendencies.

"I do not loathe you," he repeated.

"You—you did that to me, and you said those things. A man only treats a woman he loathes in that manner." She kept her voice steady even though another tear ran down her cheek. "Or a woman he's paid for."

"That's it." Another thud, and the door bowed ominously inward for a long instant. With a shriek, the lock gave way and the entire hook and eye assembly flew across the chamber, smashing into one of the long mirrors.

She turned from gaping at the cracked glass to see Vander standing in the doorway, looking so stormy and beautiful that her heart temporarily lodged in her throat. "Look what you've done!"

"I hate these damned mirrors. In fact, I loathe everything about this room."

Mia wrapped her arms around her knees and put her head down again.

Edward would never have treated her like a harlot. He had kissed her with reverence. Once he even dropped a kiss on her forehead for no reason.

Vander hadn't kissed her when they wed, not even when the vicar bade him to. It was no wonder that his kisses were more like invasions than demonstrations of respectful affection. His kisses were just about lust, brute lust.

He stood over her now, as big and tall as a pine tree. Mia refused to look up. He could glower and bully her all he wanted.

Then Vander hunkered down before her. "I'm sorry, Duchess. I shouldn't have said those things. They were unconscionable."

"Yes, well," Mia said. "I'm sure you had your reasons. It hardly matters."

"Yes, it does matter, because I've hurt your feelings and I didn't mean to."

At that she raised her head. "Yes, you did mean to hurt my feelings. No man would speak in that manner unless he deliberately wished to hurt. But at least you were speaking the truth. I prefer the truth."

"What truth?" He sounded frustrated.

"You were correct. I—I bewhored myself." Her voice wavered a little. *Whore* was such an ugly word; she had never thought to apply it to herself. But she would never have thought that she could behave in such a manner either. "All the same, I saw in your eyes that you wanted to hurt my feelings, so don't try to insult me by pretending otherwise."

He sat beside her.

"I didn't deserve that from you," she said, steadying her voice. "You didn't say a single nice thing to me. Not even one. I may not have behaved like a lady, but neither were you a gentleman. I think they treat doxies with some respect."

"You did not behave like a doxy."

Mia's gut clenched. "Yes, I did. There's nothing you or I can do to change that. I have—I have a part of me that I loathe, but I will spend the rest of my life taking control of these disgusting urges. I vow it."

He flinched at her words; then his hands clamped on her arms and he lifted her straight into his lap.

Mia gave a startled yelp. "Let go of me! Just because I'm small doesn't mean you can keep moving me about like a doll."

It felt good to be in the circle of his arms, though.

"There was nothing disgusting about what we did." His voice was firm and unwavering. "And you are beautiful, not loathsome."

Mia would have snorted, but she remembered just in time that ladies don't snort.

"I behaved like an ass afterward," he said. "I just— I'm not used to feeling that way while bedding a woman."

"'Bedding!'" Her voice was bitter. "That would imply we got as far as a bed. I wasn't even worth a pair of sheets."

He gave her a gentle shake. "I was overcome. We both were. And Duchess, I've never been that mad for anyone. *Any* woman. Ever."

Mia's heart missed a beat.

"When it comes to refinement, I'm an ass," Vander said. "I didn't bother to learn ballroom etiquette and the rest of it. But I have never found myself so overcome by lust that I couldn't even get to a bed. You turn me into a madman. That's the truth, if you care to hear it."

An involuntary shudder ran through Mia. His arm tightened, pulling her head against his shoulder.

"I feel that way now," Vander told her, his voice low and gruff. "I just had you, and all I want is to take you again. I could do it on the floor or in that bathtub. I see you, and I want to get close. I smell you, and I want to taste. I taste you, and the only thing I want is to shove myself inside and ride you until you scream with pleasure."

Mia's entire body turned liquid at his words and she couldn't find an answer.

"If you think I have ever spoken to any woman the way I spoke to you," he continued, "you'd be mistaken. I may not prance around like a court dandy, but I'm a decent man. I have paid for my pleasures because I don't like adultery and I don't—I didn't—want to marry. But I have always been courteous. I've never behaved like a lunatic, not until I met you."

Mia closed her eyes. She didn't know what to think.

"Four nights won't be enough," he said, his voice rasping.

She struggled to keep up with what he was saying. "What?"

"This is some sort of erotic madness." He hesitated. "I think it will burn out. I don't want you to . . . I don't want you to fall in love with me again, because I'll end up hurting you."

"I won't," she said swiftly. "Do you think I could love anyone who would treat me this disrespectfully?" It was a lie. She loved him so much that she ached with it. But she couldn't let him know. She couldn't.

He would walk away, leaving her devastated. But at least if he didn't know how she felt, she could keep the humiliation to herself.

His hand stroked her arm. "I know it can be hard for women to keep their feelings separate when they're making love."

Was he feeling sorry for her? Again? Mia straightened and glared at him. "Vander, there is nothing that could get me to fall in love with you after what happened years ago at that musicale, let alone your coarse behavior this morning."

"That's good," he said immediately. Still, she could

tell that he believed he was so irresistible that she would fall for him anyway.

"I have been in love," she told him, keeping her gaze unwavering.

"I know that." His thumb rubbed across her lip. "You've been biting it again. Your bottom lip has turned the color of a ripe strawberry."

"Not with you. That was a silly infatuation, and I was only a girl. I hardly knew you."

His thumb stopped.

"My fiancé, Theodore Edward Braxton Reeve, courted me for a year and we were betrothed for another year. I knew him very well—and I fell in love with him." She wasn't precisely telling the whole truth, but it didn't matter.

A dark emotion flashed through his eyes. "You still love the man who jilted you?"

Mia ignored that question. It was none of his business, and he would like her answer too much. "Edward is brilliant, handsome, and very kind. He is a professor at Oxford, and he knows your friend Thorn. In fact, I believe Mr. Dautry bought a machine of some sort from him."

"The patent for a machine," Vander said slowly. "I remember now that Reeve was the man who designed a continuous paper-making machine. Thorn made a fortune on it."

"As did Edward," Mia said, a trace of pride appearing in her voice, even though the last thing she should do is feel pride for the man who had jilted her.

Vander's hand slid down to her throat, an indescribably soft caress. "I find it harder and harder to believe that he left you at the altar."

Was it worse to say cutting things to her, as Vander

did, or to leave her, as Edward had done? Mia cleared her throat. "My point is that you needn't worry that I will become infatuated with you, simply because you made love to me against the wall of the stable. If that is the right word for what we did."

"It is not." He leaned down and whispered a different word in her ear.

Mia felt herself turning bright red. "You mustn't use that word in my presence, let alone *to* me."

"It's part of the madness I fall into when you're around me," Vander said, his voice rasping. "I want you, Duchess. I want you so badly that I'm having trouble thinking even right now. You're telling me that you are still in love with that miserable son of a bitch you were betrothed to, and I'm sorry about that. All the same, the only thing I want to do is lie down and pull you on top of me."

On top? Mia gave that a second's thought before returning to the subject at hand. "You see my point, don't you? You needn't worry that I will fall in love with you."

"Because of Reeve."

"Edward broke my heart."

His thumb swept along her chin, and he said, "I hate to hear that, Duchess."

"Yes, well . . ." She suddenly realized exactly what she was feeling under her bottom.

"Has anyone ever told you that you have the most luscious arse in all Christendom?"

"No." She shifted her weight, just to see that flare of dark lust in his eyes.

"I'm starting to get the idea that you have no idea what effect you have on men."

Mia stopped wiggling. "I have no effect on men. And I don't want you to pay me compliments that you don't mean." She cleared her throat. "That—

what we did earlier—it wasn't ladylike. But on the other hand, it was real. It hurt to be characterized the way you did, but I can see that the truth is preferable to insincere flattery."

He frowned down at her. "I would have complimented you, but lust had such a grip on my throat that I couldn't do more than pant."

"Don't."

"Don't what?"

"Don't start making what's between us into some sort of romance. Or flattering me. I know what you think of me."

His arms tightened again. "How can you know what I think of you?"

Mia put his arm aside and pushed herself to her feet. She had to get this straight. It was bad enough when he lashed out, calling her greedy.

But it would be worse if he started whispering things he didn't mean. That would endanger her heart. She might begin to believe him.

"There's no need to fuss," she said, giving him a big smile. "See? I'm fine. I'm not crying. There's no need to flatter me."

He stood up. And up. He was so tall, compared to her. She folded her arms over her breasts and looked at him. "I shall see how Charlie is. After I wash my face and change my gown, that is."

"Perhaps we should retire to a bed and celebrate our newfound truce," Vander suggested.

Mia felt as if she had been torn apart that morning and clumsily put back together. Not just physically, either. She shook her head.

Vander paused, a frown on his face, as if he guessed how battered she felt. She summoned up another smile. "Perhaps, if you're very, very lucky, I'll request the second of your four nights soon."

He pulled her into his arms. "I'm amending the agreement."

"Oh?" Mia discovered that she was trembling all over. Being enveloped in Vander's arms, against his hard chest, was enough to make her want to moan.

"Four nights a month," he said, leaning down and biting her earlobe.

"What?"

"Or, hell, four nights a week."

"You cannot just change the contract whenever you please."

"I set the rules," he reminded her. "You agreed to whatever I decreed. As far as you were concerned, my letter could have said you had to appear in my bed seven nights a week."

"It's too late to change a legal agreement," she managed.

His lips brushed her ear again and her knees turned liquid. "Maybe four nights a year, but also four afternoons a week. Starting today."

"I don't think—" Mia began.

But Vander cut her off. He hitched her up against his body in such a smooth motion that Mia could tell it was becoming second nature. He kissed her into silence, and when he raised his head, he said only, "Duchess." His voice was dark as black velvet, and that smooth.

She bit her lip.

"No?"

"I'm . . . somewhat tender," she confessed.

"I'm an animal," he said, pulling her tighter. "I'm sorry, Duchess."

Mia was beginning to enjoy the way he called her Duchess, even though she understood it was a way of avoiding intimacy. She wasn't one of his friends; he wouldn't call her Mia.

All the same, she loved being called Duchess. His duchess.

"I didn't mind that much," she whispered. She put out her tongue and very delicately touched the indent at the base of his throat.

He gave a strangled groan. "Right. Perhaps in a few days. I'm going to the stables."

"All right," she said, kissing the tiny patch of moistened skin on his neck. He tasted like sweat and desire.

"Do you think that we might renegotiate your ban on being touched here?" He put a finger on her collarbone and slid down.

"No," Mia said instantly. She shifted her weight and he let her slide down his body to stand on her feet.

"Why not?"

"I told you already."

Vander gave her a look that made heat shoot through her stomach. "You will have to tell me again."

She didn't want to talk about her bosom. It hadn't slowed him down last night or today; obviously it wasn't very important in the scheme of things.

The scheme of erotic things, that is.

Marital things.

"I'd rather not," she said, walking through the broken door to her room and pulling the cord summoning her maid. By the time Susan poked her head around the bedroom door, Mia had managed to pull off her morning gown. The back, she saw with dismay, was stained the color of decaying wood.

"That won't come clean," Susan said, with a saucy grin. "The fabric was already pilling. I'll give it to the housekeeper to make rags with. May I ask whether you had an accident, my lady?"

"Please don't ask," Mia said. "What should I put

on? I haven't any gowns that aren't black or gray. Though no one cares what I wear."

"Yes, they do," Susan said. "Believe me, they do. Everyone in this house thinks your husband is the next best thing to royalty." She had opened the clothes press and was poking about in the shelves. "This will do."

She brought out an amethyst gown that Mia had last worn two years ago. "It'll be large in the waist, but it will do until Madame duBois arrives tomorrow morning. She might even get here as early as this afternoon."

"A modiste?" Mia asked, unenthusiastically. Seamstresses promised miracles, but she always ended up looking like a stubby woman with large breasts.

"Madame duBois makes gowns for all the very best people." Susan lowered her voice. "And some who are not: she has made frocks for Maria Fitzherbert, and you know what they say about her."

"She has caught the prince's eye," Mia said. "But, Susan—"

"More to the point, Maria Fitzherbert is short. Tiny! Short as you are, if not shorter. I directed Madame to bring along any garments she might have partially constructed for petite clients. I promised her that the duke would pay three times her going rate for ready-sewn gowns."

Mia sighed. Poor Vander had been forced to marry; the least she could do was not cost him too much money.

"You must dress as befits your station," Susan stated.

If she was going to be a duchess for more than six months, then Susan was right. "Very well," Mia said, resigned.

Her maid's eyebrow rose. "Does that mean that

you'll agree to lower your bodice below your collar-bone?"

"Yes," Mia agreed. Adding, "If I must. Perhaps only in the evening."

"Unless you want to look like a maiden aunt who is pretending to be a young duchess, you must. I didn't argue when you were at Carrington House, because you rarely attended any sort of social event. But it will be different now."

"I don't want that sort of gown every day," Mia protested. "Only if I have to make an appearance as a duchess."

Susan crossed her arms. "Mr. Dautry and Lady Xenobia live less than two hours away, and His Grace's man told me that they visit often. Your appearance reflects on me, and I can't imagine what Lady Xenobia's maid would say of your wardrobe. I cannot face her if your clothing is not à la mode. In the evening and in the day."

Mia knew when she'd been beaten.

She'd probably end up with a wardrobe full of gowns whose necklines landed just above her waist. The gleam in Vander's eyes came back to her . . .

Presumably, he would enjoy them, even if she didn't.

Chapter Twenty-five

MORE NOTES on Castle Plum

- the evil Lord Plum has <u>deceitfully</u> confused Flora's affections by giving her lavish compliments and gifts. He rains insults on the man who jilted her.
- what if Frederic happens on the castle, and is invited to dinner to meet Lord Plum's fiancée: Flora!

Count Frederic was appalled to find that the lovely, modest, artless, bashful, yet warm-hearted girl he jilted at the altar has become a young woman of fashion, resplendent in jewels and displaying an Artful Fastidiousness in attiring herself.

- Pale face now too thin for true beauty.

Two days later

Charlie was proving to be a fine equestrian. He had a tendency to favor his weak leg, which affected the direction in which his horse turned, but in time he'd get over that. More importantly, he loved everything about horses, and he especially loved Jafeer.

And Jafeer seemed to be cautiously affectionate in return; Vander had the idea that his new stallion considered the boy to be Mia's colt. Anything the duchess liked, Jafeer liked.

At the moment Vander was standing on the side of the yard, watching Charlie go around on his wife's palfrey, Lancelot. He had a groom guiding the horse with a line.

His wife. *Wife.* Vander still couldn't get around that word. He'd been blackmailed into marriage, but somehow a fact that had enraged him mere days ago seemed irrelevant now.

Mia Carrington was his wife, no matter how it happened. Jafeer adored her. Hell, everyone adored her.

She was the sort of woman who made a person try his damnedest to get her attention. He caught himself performing like a boy, trying to come up with witticisms to bring out that throaty laugh of hers.

He couldn't even concentrate on his work, because he spent his time thinking about Mia and all the things he meant to do with her once she felt ready.

How long did it take a deflowered virgin to recover from said deflowering? It wasn't the sort of question men talked about. He felt an absurd sense of pride, knowing that he was the only man who'd ever touched Mia intimately, plunged into her.

He wanted more. And more still. His lust had become so overwhelming that he had taken care not to touch her at all in the last two days. He hadn't even brushed up against her on the stairs. He didn't trust himself.

In any case, she spent most of the time tucked away in her room working on her novel. She and Chuffy talked with great animation throughout the evening meals while Vander watched.

Mia's hands would wave in the air, describing the spacious and magnificent apartments of some castle in which her heroine was taking refuge. Hell, if she wanted a castle, he could buy her one.

Chuffy had her in fits of laughter every night, suggesting wilder and wilder plot twists. Vander had nothing to contribute but common sense.

"That girl—Flora, isn't it?—would be a fool to go back to the man who jilted her," Vander had pointed out the night before. "Frederic is as limp as a noodle. It's despicable that he is 'bathed in tears' after jilting Flora. She should find someone better."

"Frederic is the hero," Mia told him. "She can't simply 'find someone'! There can be only one hero in a novel."

In fact, Chuffy and Mia ignored most of his suggestions. Last night they had spent an hour discussing whether the castle should be haunted by the "moaning voice of some unquiet spirit."

What with the unquiet spirit, the milksop hero, and the evil Lord Plum, the castle sounded like a version of Dante's hell. Vander had jocosely suggested that the spirits of four slain princes, all heirs to the Crown, should haunt the castle ramparts—only to have his jest taken seriously and put into play with foolish Frederic.

When Mia wasn't writing—or conspiring with Chuffy—she was sequestered with a seamstress.

Making herself into a duchess, by all accounts. It was ridiculous. He didn't want her to change.

He loped across the yard to Charlie. "Three more times around. Don't forget to groom your mount."

Charlie nodded. His eyes shone and both his posture and his seat were good, considering he was a new rider. Vander reached over and tapped his weaker leg. "How's this feeling?"

"It's fine," Charlie said instantly.

Beginning to ache, Vander diagnosed, seeing faint smudges under the boy's eyes. Charlie was not a complainer. "Three more times," he repeated, and headed for the house.

To find his wife. Ridiculous though that sounded, he'd hardly seen her except at evening meals, when Chuffy was there, taking all her attention.

Not that he was jealous of his own uncle.

It was merely that his irrational fit of lust had turned her from a near stranger to the only person he cared to spend time with.

Nodding at Gaunt, he ran up the stairs into his bedchamber and straight through to the bathing chamber. The door leading to his wife's room had been repaired, he noticed. That broken latch had undoubtedly caused a storm of speculation downstairs.

He was devoutly hoping that he'd discover her in dishabille, perhaps naked to the waist while being fitted for a gown.

Alas, no such luck; her bedchamber was empty. He returned to the hallway, went to the top of the stairs, and bellowed down, "Where's my duchess?"

Nottle had not been the sort of butler who would deign to raise his voice, but Gaunt was not as rigidly formal. He shouted back, "Her Grace is in her study."

" 'Her study,' " Vander repeated, feeling like an idiot. "Where is that?"

He had no memory of her mentioning it at supper, and when else were they supposed to discuss things? He was out of the house all day working in the stables, and they weren't sleeping together.

"Her Grace is using the Queen's Bedchamber as her study," Gaunt replied, appearing at the bottom of the stairs. "The great bed remains, but we moved a desk from the library."

A moment later Vander pushed open the door to the Queen's Bedchamber, only to find this room, too, unoccupied. Sunlight poured through the west-facing windows; he'd forgotten how much light this side of the house received.

He walked over to her desk and picked up a sheet of paper. Mia's handwriting hadn't changed much from when she was a girl, writing that love poem. It was a strong hand, with a beautiful, high-flung curve on some of the letters. It hadn't a trace of the madness that clung to his father's hand, or the timidity that characterized his mother's.

After it became clear that he refused to be in the vicinity of Lord Carrington, the duchess began to write letters to him. Her words had been hedged in by excessive curlicues, ornamented with arabesques, and flourishes. He had read her letters impatiently and tossed them aside, condemning her for adultery, for selfishness.

Now his heart bumped at the memory of Chuffy's revelation about the truth of his parents' marriage. All those years he had felt burning resentment of his mother's betrayal of his father, but the situation had been far more complicated and far more tragic than he had known.

With an impatient shake of his head, he focused on

the page he had picked up, headed NOTES: Chapter Three.

"I cannot bear to think of it!" Lady Ryldon cried pettishly. "Maurice must marry her. It has come to the very last ebb with us. We shall all be ruined if he doesn't manage it."

"How on earth did she come to have such a dowry? I knew her mother, and she was a worthy woman, but their fortunes were sadly depleted."

"As I understand it, Lord Mortimer glimpsed her in the street and wrote her into his will. It sounds very curious to me; everyone is saying that she must be his natural daughter."

That startled her friend. "Absolutely not! I knew her mother well before she was disowned by her father, the earl."

A peal of silvery musical laughter interrupted them. "Here she comes!" Lady Ryldon said urgently. "Now, dear, you must make certain that the little fool marries my son. Our very lives—or at the very least our wine cellar—depend on it!"

Vander stared down at the page in some perplexity. It didn't seem to match the plot he'd heard discussed over the dining room table. Who was Lady Ryldon? The whole desk was covered with drifts of paper, each sheet containing a scrap of dialogue or a list of notes. He picked up another.

"In the meantime," said Count Frederic, with a polite bow, "may I not kiss you?"

"Indeed you may not!" Flora cried. She peeped at him over her shoulder, with a captivating giggle. "I do not like kisses."

"Let me change your mind." His countenance was not merry: instead, the very air trembled with a solemn—

Unfortunately, the text broke off just when it was getting interesting. Vander sifted through the mess on the desk, trying to locate the next page, but he couldn't find it. He picked up Mia's quill and struck through a half line or so, and scrawled a revision.

"My dear, do let me change your mind." He pushed her back on the table, ran a hand beneath her skirts, and bent to kiss her silken thigh.

She threw her arms around his neck and cried, "But, sir, do you intend to ravish me?"

"Only if you desire such a wanton course," he replied, quite untruthfully, because he intended to ravish her no matter what she had to say about it.

"Modesty forbids my answer," she gasped, clapping her legs around his waist.

"Excellent," he said, debauching her enthusiastically.

This was rather fun. Vander poked around until he found a couple of other scenes which, in his considered opinion, needed correction. Flora should never go back to Frederic, for example. He picked up the quill again.

Vander here: This is rubbish. He's a fool who jilted her. She should treat him like the idiot he is.

The door opened. He hastily put down the quill and turned around.

It was Mia, naturally, and she was frowning at him. "What are you doing?"

"I seem to have been reading your memoirs," he said, strolling toward her and doing his utmost to look innocent. "I had no idea your life had been so enthralling before marrying me."

"Oh hush," she cried, her face turning rosy. "It's horrid of you to look at my manuscript without asking me first."

"I think you should spice it up a bit."

"Spice it up?"

"Well, what sort of man would say 'may I not kiss you now'?"

"My hero, Frederic, is extremely courteous."

"He's an addlebrained dunce. Who would want to kiss a man like him? Clearly not your heroine, since she makes up that whopper about not liking kisses."

"Frederic is a complete gentleman," she said defensively.

"And I am not?" Vander grinned and changed the topic. "What on earth have you been doing? I looked all over the house for you."

"Reading," she said, a bit guiltily. "I haven't been able to put Miss Julia Quiplet's books down in the last two days, even though I *must* write my own novel. Was there something you wanted, Duke?"

"Duke?" Vander looked insulted. "Surely we are on intimate terms?"

Mia had a moment of extreme irritation.

How was she supposed to guess what Vander felt was the appropriate degree of intimacy at any given moment? He still addressed her as 'Duchess,' after all. She avoided the question altogether. "I thought you were in the stables. Is Charlie all right?"

"I set him to grooming horses. If it were up to him, he'd ride all day long, but I thought his leg had taken enough."

"Perhaps I should check on his progress," Mia said. Vander had a look in his eyes that she recognized, even after a few short days of marriage.

But it was daytime. Afternoon. Servants were about.

"Charlie will not miss you," he said. He took a long stride, bent his head, and pulled her into his arms. Mia had to admit that his kiss was pure bliss. She even dropped Miss Quiplet's novel.

In the last two days, she had done her best to ignore Vander at dinner, because every time she met his eyes, she felt herself turning pink. She stayed up late reading, but he never knocked on her door.

Only the raw lust in his eyes when they encountered each other about the house kept her from despair. She wasn't feeling these ground-swells of desire all on her own.

Now she kissed him with all the longing she'd kept in check, coming back to herself only when she realized that her husband was nudging her backward toward the enormous bed on which Queen Elizabeth herself had slept.

"We mustn't," Mia said, pulling away. "Not that . . . Not here."

"Why not?" His urgent, hungry look sent a throbbing pulse down her legs.

"We should restrict intimacies to appropriate times and places, to wit, our bedchamber at night."

"This room is not a stable. It's arguably the nicest bedchamber in the house."

"It's my study, and besides, it's daytime."

Vander's only response was to topple both of them onto the bed.

"I mean it," she protested. "This just isn't proper!"

Vander planted his hands on either side of her and dipped his head, running his tongue along her lips. "I don't give a damn."

She pushed at his shoulder. "Well, I do, because I don't want to be called 'greedy' again. Just to be clear,

I am *not* asking you for intimacies, which are supposed to happen only at night."

He scowled down at her, with a frown that he likely thought would shake her resolve since it had terrified horse thieves in the past.

"I don't want you to say any more unkind things to me," she told him. "If I don't behave like a doxy, I can't be labeled one. Please, Vander, let me sit up. I'm going to the stables to see Charlie."

"I will never say another unkind word to you," Vander said huskily, brushing his lips across hers once more.

She must have looked dubious, because he continued, "I said those things out of fear. I want you more than is good for my self-esteem. Hell, Mia, I'm turning into a man who would walk to London for one of your kisses."

"*My* self-esteem matters as well," she pointed out. "I have no wish to become the type of woman whose husband feels he can—can *tup* her whenever and wherever he wants."

"You're the type of woman whose husband wants to tup her in a bed made for Queen Elizabeth. For a queen, Mia!"

He slowly lowered his weight onto her, and it was so delicious that she let out a little moan. His eyes sparked in response, and a callused hand ran up her legs.

"I don't think—"

"Hush," Vander said, kissing her. His fingers were teasing their way up her inner thigh. When his lips wandered to her cheekbone, Mia discovered that she had relinquished control. Again.

His fingers slipped upward, and she instinctively rolled her hips toward his caress. Despite herself, her voice came out breathily, like a silly debutante being introduced to the queen. "It's not right. Might be seen. Not . . . Not married. I mean, it's still daytime."

"We *are* married," Vander corrected her, as his fingers sank into her slick warmth and took on a rhythm that made her body shake, bliss hovering just outside her reach. "Perhaps you truly don't wish to continue?" His fingers stilled.

"Don't stop." Her nails dug into his forearm.

"It's still daytime," Vander pointed out, his eyes devilish. He slipped a broad finger inside her.

She let out a gasp and arched against him, trying to force his finger deeper inside her.

"Mia," he said, voice rasping in her ear, "I want to make love to you."

"Yes," she gasped.

"I want to see you naked."

She froze.

"*All* of you," he clarified.

"No." Mia's head cleared. She would never enjoy herself under those circumstances. Especially in the daylight. She pushed his hand away and began to inch toward the edge of the bed.

"Where do you think you're going?" he growled.

"We can't behave like this."

He let her go and she sat up and rearranged her skirts. But her heart sank, looking at his face. His eyes were steady on hers and there was no mistaking his expression.

His wasn't the face of a man who had ever heard the word "no." Well, except when he was trying to refuse her marriage proposal. That was probably the first time in his life that he had been thwarted.

This would be the second. The idea of undressing in the broad daylight filled her with horror: Vander would see every curve and dimple.

If she had married an average-looking man, she

might consider it, but given the difference between them, it was inconceivable.

He was the embodiment of one of her fictional heroes—excepting the fact that he wasn't madly in love with her, nor was he quiet, gentle, or even civilized.

Mia raised her chin and told him the absolute truth. "I am not the sort of woman who likes to be unclothed."

"Why not?"

"Ladies are very private. Chaste," she added.

"You are not chaste."

She flinched, and he said hastily, "I didn't mean that the way it sounded."

"Stop. Just stop. I shall not change my mind."

"Duchess."

"Yes?"

His face was about as malleable as a block of marble. "I intend to see you without your clothes. And I intend to touch you without your clothes. I'm tired of pushing your skirts out of the way."

"You are far too accustomed to getting your own way," she blurted out. "Has no one ever denied you in the whole of your life?"

He didn't answer that, just stood up and announced, "I'm going to remove my clothing. Brace yourself."

"It would ruin everything for me if I had to get undressed," she explained awkwardly. "I am not at ease."

Vander frowned. "Do you have a scar, Duchess? I don't give a damn."

"No, I haven't. Might you postpone your plan to remove your clothes until tonight, in the privacy of your chamber?"

Vander wrenched off his coat, which was its own answer. Mia's heartbeat quickened. Next to go was his waistcoat. The performance reminded her of the day that he had demanded she inspect him carefully before she purchased him. How was it possible that it was less than a fortnight ago?

Late-afternoon sunlight streamed through the windows, casting shadows the color of dark copper across his skin. His shirt flew across the room. Bands of muscle corded his body, making her fingers itch to caress his hard stomach.

When he bent over to pull off his boots, panic welled up in Mia's stomach. If Vander forced her to unclothe, she would faint from pure humiliation. Taking advantage of the fact he was busy with his boots, she headed for the door.

He made it there before her.

"This is *not* a good idea," she said, panicked. "It is deeply improper and no one . . . no lady would tolerate it." She could smell a mixture of saddle leather and spice.

It weakened her knees, so she made her expression even more ferocious.

Vander leaned back against the door and grinned at her. He hitched his thumbs into the waistband of his breeches.

"No!" she cried.

Of course he ignored her. His breeches and smalls slid down over the thighs of a man used to leaping on a restless horse. Mia let out a shaky sigh. His taut abdomen had a little line of hair that led . . .

Well, down there.

No wonder she'd been sore.

His shaft was far too large.

He kicked away his breeches and smalls and simply stood there, relaxed, as if he often stood naked in a shaft of sunlight.

"Do my looks please you, Mia?" he asked, looking at her from under long eyelashes, as if he didn't know perfectly well that desire was pounding through her like a drum beat. Directing her to touch him, to squirm against him, to lure him to the bed . . .

She had to clear her throat. "You are presentable, as I'm sure you've been told every day since you were a boy."

"Does my moonbeam meet your expectations?" The grin on his face said that he knew perfectly well that he was magnificent.

"Aren't you ever going to forget about my stupid poem?"

"I doubt it," he said, his smile deepening. "I'm the only one of my friends who's had an ode written to his cock."

Mia groaned silently. There was no point in trying to school him in the art of literary metaphor.

"I can't wait to read your novels," he added.

"There is *nothing* about moonbeams in my work!"

He shrugged. "It's your turn to disrobe."

"As I made clear, I am not at ease undressing in the daylight." She stepped closer, her hand drifting down his chest to his waist. "Isn't this enough?"

"Not by half," he said. But he took her hand and put it on his hard length.

Her hand instinctively curled around his silky maleness. To her delight, he visibly shuddered, then cupped her face, and brushed his lips over hers.

She tightened her hand just a little. His eyes glazed over and a harsh sound came from between his lips. His hands slipped down to her jaw, guiding her face up to take her mouth.

In the back of her mind, Mia was losing her nerve. What if Vander no longer desired her, once her breasts had been freed from her corset? Even she felt distaste for her breasts, so why should he feel any different?

"I want to touch you," Vander growled into her mouth, his hands gripping her bottom and pulling her against him. "I want to hold those lush breasts of yours, bury my face in them, suck your pretty little nipples . . ."

Oh dear God.

She would have to let him do it. Either that, or she could call the Four Nights rule into effect.

"Please," she asked desperately, "*Please* might we wait until tonight, when our room is dark?"

He ground against her, a harsh noise breaking from his chest. "Does it feel to you as if I can bloody well wait until tonight?"

Mia felt dizzy, as if she might faint. Perhaps she should get it over with? If she didn't look at his face, she wouldn't know how he felt. Would not knowing be better than knowing?

Yes. Unquestionably.

His nimble fingers were unbuttoning her gown in back, but he lost patience and ripped open the last few buttons. Mia numbly let him lift the gown over her arms and head.

He fell back a step. "Duchess, the corset you wore the other evening was impressive, but I must say this one resembles nothing so much as a steel cage designed to contain wild tigers."

The corset employed a great deal of whale-bone to control her figure. It fell from her body and the laces' silver aglets tinkled as they hit the floor.

Then all that remained was her chemise.

Chapter Twenty-six

NOTES ON FLORA'S NEW WARDROBE

Flora mortified to find seamstress views her as bony. "The Fripperies of Outward Appearance are unimportant," she informed the lady.

"Pas pour les hommes," the Frenchwoman said grimly, pins in her mouth obscuring her comment.

Flora knew no man of worth would take such foolishness into account. Still . . . "Can you improve the bodice of this gown?" she implored. The gown was made of white pleated muslin and left no doubt that Flora had very little in the way of feminine endowments.

The modiste mumbled something about sow's ears.

- is this working? Probably not.

Interesting change, though.
Do men truly like bosoms?

𝐼t was taking all of Vander's control not to lunge at Mia, now that her corset had fallen away. His wife had turned white as a bleached stone and she was visibly trembling, but she undid the ribbon of her chemise. Closing her eyes momentarily, she pulled it down around her shoulders.

Vander restrained a groan. He felt desperate to touch her, like an animal in a duke's form.

The white chemise dropped away to reveal breasts that were more beautiful than he could have imagined: plump and smooth, with nipples like ripe cherries.

Mia gave a little wiggle and the chemise slid from her arms, was caught briefly on her hips, and fell to the floor. And there she was.

His wife.

His duchess.

"Bloody hell," Vander said hoarsely, words deserting him.

Mia rolled her eyes. "There's no need to offer me such extravagant compliments."

"You are beautiful, Duchess." He could see her thinking about that, but he was in the grip of an overpowering lust and could not wait for his compliment to soothe her fear. He picked her up and lay her on the bed, coming down on his side next to her. "May I touch?"

"*No*." She meant it.

He ran a hand up her leg and straight to her sweetest spot. She was drenched, and a moan broke from her throat the moment he touched her.

Beside himself with desire, he rolled on top of her, reared back, and thrust inside. No preliminaries, no tender coaxing caresses—just fast, sweaty motion that sent pleasure racing down his limbs, smoky and hot as burning grass.

He kept his hands away from her breasts because she hadn't given him permission, but somehow it was all the wilder for that.

Instead he braced his hands on the bed next to her shoulders and hung his head above her breasts. He could have sworn that her nipples puckered tighter every time he looked.

The bed board slammed into the wall. Over and over and over. And Mia was with him. She was caressing his body, her hands running down over his arse and curling around his thighs, urging him on.

He stilled. "May I touch your breasts now?"

"No!"

"You'll love it," he promised.

With a sudden movement, he rolled, and then she was on top of him.

Mia had been lost in delight, allowing Vander's hard body to pleasure her while she stroked and caressed and kissed what parts of him she could reach.

But as always when her breasts were involved, she snapped to cold attention. Glancing down, she saw that they were standing out from her torso like globes.

"Look at me," Vander commanded.

Reluctantly, she did so. His expression was delirious . . . ecstatic.

"Your breasts are perfect," he rasped. "Soft, giving, your nipples like strawberries waiting for my mouth. I'm not touching. But I mean to kiss them now."

Before she could stop him, Vander's mouth closed

over her nipple, and Mia went straight from somewhat ashamed apprehension to a storm of sensation so acute that she involuntarily pulsed around his cock, making him groan aloud.

His big hands gripped her hips and pulled her down as he thrust up. Her hair fell around his face. With every suck to her nipples, the desperate, hot sensation inside her increased, as if she were a boiling pot on the verge of explosion.

All the time Vander told her in a hoarse voice what he was doing, what he thought about her nipples, about her breasts.

She believed him. And when she gave everything to him, her body jerking over and over, his in every sense of the word, the rightness of it echoed down to her soul.

She loved him.

She had never stopped loving him.

The pleasant affection that she and Edward had shared was not love. This mad, wild, consumption of each other's bodies, sweaty and real: this was love.

"Vander," she cried, about to tell him.

But he wasn't listening. He rolled again, and his strength and muscle and weight came down on top of her. His thrusts grew even fiercer; as he came, he shouted, the abandoned mad pleasure in his voice sending her body into another spiral, until she convulsed around him.

In that space of white-hot joy, there was no Vander and no Mia: they were one, panting, crying out, moving together in a primal dance as old as the earth itself.

It was blissful and raw.

When Vander withdrew, neither of them said a

word. He pulled her close, and dazed, Mia tucked into his shoulder.

She had given him everything, ceded her body. And he had given his back to her.

They had consummated their marriage.

Chapter Twenty-seven

From the Duchess of Pindar to her Publishers, Mssrs. Brandy, Bucknell & Bendal
September 15, 1800

Dear Mr. Bucknell,

I have scarcely left my chamber for two days while reading Miss Julia Quiplet's three novels, and shall shortly begin Mrs. Lisa Klampas's novel.

I know this may sound as if my own writing has been neglected, ~~and it has been neglected,~~ but I assure you that the opposite is true. Miss Quiplet's books have been very inspiring, and even partly restored my faith in romance, and renewed my conviction that Love is the Secret Architecture of the world.

I will happily provide an endorsement of Miss Quiplet's next novel.

All best wishes,

Her Grace, the Duchess & etc.

Two days later

*V*ander woke when the blue light of dawn crept through the window. For a moment he didn't know where he was, as if he had been thrown into a kaleidoscope, shaken and tumbled.

His body felt different.

Slowly he turned his head. Mia was curled against him, satiny hair falling over his arm. She was smiling in her sleep.

It wasn't just his body that felt different: *he* felt different. He felt unbalanced. Vulnerable. Every night he became a madman, pounding into his wife, groaning, out of control.

Control had been the backbone of his life. A flicker of panic followed that thought. Perhaps his father lost his mind because of the fierce love he felt for the duchess, for the woman who cuckolded him.

No.

He could not forget what Chuffy had told him: His father had shown signs of madness even as a boy. And the former duke had abused his wife. What sort of love was that?

Gently he slid Mia's head from his shoulder and stood up. His blood had a slow thrum, as if he'd never experienced pleasure before. As if the only thing worth doing in the world was kissing the woman in his bed.

Of course, he'd felt this much pleasure before. At the moment he couldn't remember precisely an occasion, but there must have been other women who drove him into a frenzy of lust.

He pulled on clothing without bothering to bathe or to shave. Jafeer would make his debut appearance at the races in the afternoon, on a track only two hours from Rutherford Park, virtually next door to Starberry Court, Thorn's country house.

He had to retreat to the stables and recover whatever the hell it was he'd lost last night. Part of his heart, maybe.

That was unacceptable.

He strode down the stairs, waving away Gaunt, except the man wouldn't be brushed off and trotted after him as he burst out the front door.

"Your Grace!"

Vander turned around with a growl. "What is it?"

"You asked me to find out"—the butler bent over, gasping—"about Her Grace's fiancé; do you remember?"

Of course Vander remembered, though he'd never mentioned the request to Mia. Why worry her with the idea that Sir Richard may have killed her beloved Edward?

"He's alive," Gaunt said, holding his side. "Blimey, Your Grace, you walk faster than a sow in heat."

"Excellent," Vander said, dismissing the subject of Edward Reeve from his mind. "Glad to hear it."

"But he's been in prison!" Gaunt said, raising his voice.

Vander froze. "Prison? Where?"

"Old Tolbooth, Edinburgh! The Bow Street Runner only found him after the man organized a prison break."

"Trumped-up charges," Vander surmised. No man would voluntarily leave Mia. Somewhere in the back of his mind, he'd always known that.

Gaunt nodded. "Indeed, that is so, Your Grace. The Runner will stand Crown's evidence that Sir Richard Magruder had Mr. Reeve sent to prison on a fallacious charge, under another name, without due recourse of law. Mr. Reeve almost died due to a head wound he suffered while being captured, and the charge will include attempted murder."

Vander cursed under his breath.

"It seems that Mr. Reeve was transported to Old Tolbooth under a falsified order stating that he had been given a life sentence and that he was a recalcitrant, lawless criminal unsafe to keep in England." Gaunt sniffed. "As if Scottish prisons were any better than English ones. He was about to be transported to Botany Bay when he made his escape."

Naturally the man broke out of prison to return to Mia. To return to Charlie, too. Reeve had the right to both of them. Nausea broke over Vander, but he fought through it.

"Where is he now?" he asked Gaunt.

"Mr. Reeve is on his way here, Your Grace." Gaunt's face was agonized. "To see the duchess. Likely he'll arrive here tomorrow morning; the Runner sent a messenger ahead."

"Right," Vander said. A strange calm had descended on him. Vander had one more day with her. One more night. "Not a word to Her Grace."

Gaunt's brow creased.

"I will not have her disappointed again, if the man doesn't appear," Vander said grimly. "I will inform her myself, tomorrow morning."

He had felt like this before: at age nine, after his father supposedly mistook him for a burglar and knocked him into the scullery wall; again one year ago, when the High Constable arrived to report that his mother was dead. "Prepare a bedchamber but tell no one the identity of our possible visitor."

"You don't plan to inform her until tomorrow morning?" Gaunt asked.

If then.

The last thing Vander wanted to witness was the dawning joy on Mia's face when she learned that Reeve had never meant to jilt her or to abandon Charlie. That her beloved Edward adored them both, and had broken out of prison to return to them.

He himself would have broken out of the Tower of London to return to Mia.

"No," he replied, as the truth slammed into him: he was as enthralled by her as his father had been with his mother. The late duke had died within days of the news of his duchess' death, as if the mere fact she was no longer in the world made him defenseless to pneumonia.

And yet his mother had been in love with another man. His wife, the current duchess, was also in love with another.

In short, he had somehow managed to replicate the domestic ménage à trois that had sent him to Eton reeling with rage.

Right, then.

He had one day left. One night. Suddenly, the irony of it struck him. Tonight would be his fourth night with Mia.

Fourth and final.

"Please inform the household that I shall escort her and Charlie to the Nestleford Races to see Jafeer run his debut. We will depart in an hour or so."

The butler nodded.

"Gaunt," Vander warned, "I shall be extremely unhappy if even the slightest hint of this news were to reach Her Grace before tomorrow morning. Have I made myself clear?" He thought he detected pity in Gaunt's eyes, but he didn't give a damn.

"The duchess will hear nothing from me, Your Grace. I would note, however, that there is a chance that Mr. Reeve will waste no time. He may arrive earlier than tomorrow morning."

"We will not be here," Vander said. "We shall spend the night at Mr. Dautry's residence, Starberry Court, as it is close to the racecourse. As always, if guests arrive at Rutherford Park, make them comfortable until I return."

Gaunt nodded and Vander turned to go back upstairs. He wanted to prepare Jafeer, and a hundred other tasks awaited him in the stables as well.

But first, he wanted to wake Mia.

In his own way.

Chapter Twenty-eight

*T*he ducal household was not ready to leave for the races in an hour; at least, the duke and duchess were not, since they were still ensconced in their bedchamber and no one dared enter.

But a couple of hours later, the house and stables were bustling. Charlie was wild with excitement to see his first race. Dobbie's leash was tied to his crutch and the two of them were milling about in front of the house. Chuffy too had made it downstairs at an unwontedly early hour, resplendent in a gaudy saffron coat and fawn breeches.

Besides Jafeer, the Pindar Stables was running two geldings and a filly. Grooms ran hither and thither with arms full of the duke's colors; jockeys strode up and down, striking their thighs with their crops.

Mia could barely take it all in. Vander was the calm center of the storm: servants, grooms, jockeys swirled about him. For his part, Jafeer did some sidling and complaining, until Mia and Charlie joined him.

Mia leaned on his cart and Charlie actually climbed inside and sat back against the low wall to rest his leg. Jafeer settled down instantly and looked about with an alert, interested expression.

"He'll do," Mulberry said, stopping briefly. "If you'd told me a week ago, Your Grace, that Jafeer would tolerate a child near him, I'd have said you were daft, begging your pardon."

Charlie had brought a small notebook with him, and was writing down everything he overheard about horses and racing, because—as he had explained to Mia—he meant to train the finest racehorses in all England someday. "Just as the duke does!"

As if answering Mulberry, Jafeer leaned down and snuffled Charlie's hair.

"Jafeer has adopted my nephew," Mia said with some pride.

"That's right," Mulberry affirmed. "You and he are his herd." He leaned over and patted Jafeer's neck. "I wouldn't be surprised at all if he won his race this evening. He's got the heart for it now."

Jafeer's coat was shining and he looked like a king among horses, one who could race the wind.

Once they reached the Nestleford racecourse, Vander escorted Mia and Charlie to his special box— which had its own footman—and left them there. "Thorn and India will be along at some point," he told her.

Something was odd about Vander's manner, but Mia told herself it was probably nerves over the race. While he exhibited no obvious signs of apprehension, he had paid more for Jafeer than had ever been spent in England on a single horse. Of course he felt some tension.

Journalists from every newspaper in the kingdom including, of course, *The Sporting News*, were running up and down the racecourse. As far as she could tell, no one was speaking of anything but Jafeer. Chuffy and Charlie were leaning over the front of the box, eavesdropping enthusiastically on passersby.

Mia wore a new gown. Thankfully, her breasts were fairly well covered. She had a shawl as well, and between that and her strongest corset, she felt quite pretty.

Though, if she were honest, the gown was less responsible for her new-found confidence than were her husband's frank, heartfelt compliments over the past several days. Vander's remarks were nothing like the elegant phrases uttered by her hero, Frederic, but they had a raw sincerity to them.

She was smiling into her glass of champagne at one particularly vivid memory when the footman presented a calling card for Mr. Tobias Dautry. A moment later, he opened the door at the back of the box and announced—quite as if he were in a drawing room—"Mr. Dautry, Lady Xenobia India Dautry, Miss Dautry."

Mia put her glass down and rose to greet them. She had no idea that Thorn had a daughter, but sure enough he was ushering in a solemn-looking little girl with a book under one arm and a doll in the other.

Charlie turned, and she saw him flinch when he realized that another child had entered the box. The limited contact he'd had with children had invariably been unpleasant.

But he swung his way over and conducted himself with a courteousness that disguised his discomfort at meeting Rose. He even managed to bow without toppling, a skill that Vander must have taught him.

She hadn't seen Thorn or India since the wedding,

but it felt very different to greet them now. She was still the woman who had blackmailed Vander into marriage, but she didn't *feel* like that woman any longer.

How could she, when he made love to her so passionately, and woke her this morning with the admission that he had been on his way to the stables when he realized he had overlooked something? It turned out what he had forgotten was a kiss—and that kiss led to such tender, passionate intimacies that Mia had cried a little from pure joy afterward.

Thorn and Chuffy took themselves off: Chuffy, to place his bets; and Thorn, to find Vander and check on Jafeer, promising to return for Mia if it seemed "her" stallion needed calming. Charlie hopped back to the front of the box, and Rose put down her book but not her doll and followed him. Lady Xenobia and Mia sat down and embarked on an awkward conversation about the children.

It turned out that India—as she wished to be called—was as nervous as Mia was about putting the two children together. "Rose has had very few encounters with people her age," she explained. "She had an unusual upbringing."

"Charlie, too, has met very few children."

"Why is he taking notes?"

Mia smiled. "Vander suggested that Charlie could make himself useful by noting down any gossip he hears. Charlie has taken it more literally than Vander intended, perhaps, but it was a brilliant maneuver: Charlie hasn't been comfortable going into public, let alone in crowds, but he's forgotten about his wariness because he has been given a task."

"I gather from my husband that Charlie is the reason you needed to marry Vander?"

"Yes." Mia hesitated and said, "I suggested a temporary marriage, but the duke was reluctant to go through the bother of choosing another wife. So here I am."

India turned to her, eyebrow cocked. "His words?"

"Well, yes."

"Men are idiots," India said, sighing. "You do know that if Vander didn't wish to remain married to you, your marriage would be well on its way to dissolution, don't you? He wouldn't allow my husband to do anything to rescue him from your proposal, and believe me, Thorn would have found a way to stop the ceremony if Vander truly wished for him to do so."

"Vander didn't want to lose his dukedom," Mia explained. "Actually, I think he cares far more about losing his horses than his title."

"That is probably true. His decision to buy Jafeer came after months of poring over bloodlines and the like, and I was the silent, bored observer to many of those discussions. But Thorn would have bought Vander's stables an hour after you made your demand, if Vander had decided to refuse you. For one pound or a thousand pounds, only to sell it back afterward."

"I hadn't thought of that," Mia said.

"Vander rejected every idea Thorn had, including outright destruction of the letter. Since then, he has refused to divorce you, or annul the marriage. What does that tell you?"

"He's honorable." The opposite of her father, to be blunt.

India burst out laughing. "Believe that if you wish."

"I see no other explanation," Mia said primly. She decided to change the subject, and soon they were deep into talk of something far more interesting: India's talent for organizing and refurbishing households. After a few minutes, Mia couldn't resist, and found herself swearing India to silence and telling her all about Lucibella Delicosa.

It was an entirely satisfactory few hours, broken by a light luncheon with the children, who had become, if not fast friends, intrigued acquaintances. Mia had the feeling that on the way home they would both label the other "quite odd"—but in an admiring way.

When the starting time neared for Jafeer's debut, Thorn and Vander returned to the box, but only briefly. To Charlie's huge excitement, Vander hoisted him on a shoulder, crutch and all. "We'll see you all after the race," he said, turning to the door.

"We need to be close to the track," Charlie shouted, waving at Mia. His cheeks were rosy and his eyes shone.

"I should like to accompany them," a quiet voice said.

India began, "Oh, dearest, I'm afraid—"

But Thorn hoisted his daughter into the air. "You'll have to hang on tightly," he told her.

Off they went, two large beautiful men with children perched on their shoulders. It made Mia's heart clench to see them.

She and India moved to the front of the box in order to watch the race.

As it turned out, Mia missed seeing Jafeer sweep to an easy victory, because she was watching the man standing at the railing below her instead, and the boy leaning trustingly against his head as the two of them yelled and cheered.

By the time Vander and Thorn returned to the box with the children, Jafeer was well on his way to becoming the most notable stallion in England. Journalists had leapt into waiting carriages and were writing copy en route to London, describing in overheated prose the extraordinary purchase by the Duke of Pindar.

The stallion was already the favorite for the Derby. At this rate, he would earn back in purses the exorbitant amount His Grace had paid for him in no time. Vander's expression remained unchanged, but Mia could sense a deep satisfaction. For his part, Chuffy was downright exuberant: he had bet his entire allowance on Jafeer, despite the long odds, and he now had sufficient funds to back an archaeological expedition to the Andes Mountains.

"Think of the material for your next novel!" he crowed to Mia, waving his champagne in the air.

That evening at Starberry Court, they all drank a toast to the gamble Vander had taken in buying such a costly steed solely on the basis of his bloodlines. When they had drunk, Vander turned to Mia and raised his glass again.

"Without my wife's attention, Jafeer would be languishing in his stall, ribs showing. She is his family and his heart."

Mia smiled mistily at him.

After that, Vander broke all decorum, snatched her up from the table, and carried her upstairs. She did not protest, and their hosts only laughed.

Sometime later, Vander said, "This is our fourth night, Mia."

She had stopped thinking about contracts and nights, and the sentence struck fear in her heart. Her fingers curled to hold him more firmly to her. "Will you deny me if I beg for more?" she whispered, her voice hoarse from the pleasure he had coaxed and demanded from her.

He was silent a moment. "I could never deny you if you beg me, Mia. Never."

Chapter Twenty-nine

*L*ate the following morning, as the carriage neared Rutherford Park, Vander deliberately put aside all the passion of the night he and Mia shared.

That was over. His four nights were spent . . . used up.

As Mia's husband, he could demand more nights; he could refuse to let her see Edward Reeve. Some ferocious part of him that cared nothing for right or wrong wanted to lock her in his bedchamber. She was his, damn it.

But another part couldn't ignore that Mia had made it clear, repeatedly, that she loved Reeve and had been heartbroken when he'd left her at the altar. She had only requested a temporary marriage with him in a desperate bid to keep Charlie safe.

But Reeve hadn't jilted her after all. The man Mia loved had returned.

And Vander wasn't a man who could accept a woman who loved another.

By all rights, he should prepare Mia for the likelihood that her former fiancé would be waiting when they reached home. He should explain to her that Reeve had never left her at the altar, and, what's more, had risked his life to return to her.

But the ungovernable side of him—the side that never had been a gentleman—rejected the idea. Hell, maybe the man wouldn't arrive today. Maybe Vander would have another night with her.

They pulled up at the front entrance, footmen hurrying out to meet them. Leaving the carriage, he said merely, "I shall settle Jafeer and the other horses in the stable, Duchess, and I'll be in the house directly."

A smile teased the corners of Mia's mouth, a reminder of their evening activities. Heat rushed through him, settling low. He nearly reached out and pulled her into his arms.

Instead, he turned and strode away with a muttered curse.

Vander reached the stables to find that Reeve had indeed arrived, several hours before. When the horses were once again safely in Mulberry's hands, he headed back to the house. Despite everything he knew to be true, a faint hope was beating a rhythm in his chest.

But when Gaunt opened the drawing room door, Vander went cold at the sight of Mia sobbing in Edward Reeve's arms.

His wife's head was nestled against the man's chest, hands clenching his coat. Reeve's head was bent over Mia, and he was murmuring something, his arms tight, possessive, around her.

Every fiber in Vander rejected what he saw. Barely contained fury rode him hard; he scarcely controlled the impulse to kill the man touching his wife.

But there was the rub: she wasn't really his wife.

He was no more than a temporary husband. A means to an end.

If there had been any doubt as to how he should proceed, the scene made up his mind. He, more than any man, knew that it was impossible to keep a woman who loved another man. Mia had loved her fiancé. Still loved him, as was clear from their tender reunion.

Reeve had been haunting their marriage from the beginning. Now here he was, back from the dead, having fought his way out of prison to return to the woman he loved. It was a romantic twist worthy of Lucibella Delicosa.

Mia didn't notice when Vander entered the room, but Reeve's head came up and their eyes met. If Vander had bothered to imagine Mia's fiancé, he would have pictured a weedy academic, a spectacle-wearing professor stooped from too much reading and too little physical activity. A coward who had run from the reality of raising a disabled child.

Instead, Reeve was as large as Vander. His nose had recently been broken, which gave him the air of a boxer. Yet Thorn had described him as brilliant, and Reeve had the indefinable self-assurance of an Oxford professor, suggesting Thorn was right.

Reeve clearly caught the murderous look in Vander's eyes, and his own narrowed. They were the eyes of a man who had just broken out of a prison designed to hold the kingdom's most violent prisoners. This was a man who would fight to the death for his woman.

Hell, that was no surprise. Any man would fight for Mia.

She raised her head, putting one of her hands on Reeve's cheek. "I simply cannot bear to think how much torment you have suffered," she said, her voice wavering. "I feel terrible that I ever introduced you to Sir Richard! If it weren't for me, none of this would have happened."

Reeve murmured something inaudible, and Mia turned out of his arms, her hands falling to her sides. "Vander, you will not believe what has happened!" she cried. "This is Edward Reeve, who didn't jilt me after all. Charlie's despicable uncle threw him in prison on false charges, and he nearly lost his life." Another sob broke from her throat. "He almost died!"

Vander moved forward the last few paces and bowed. "Reeve," he said flatly.

"Your Grace." Reeve bowed after a calculated delay, just enough to turn his gesture into a challenge.

Mia seemed oblivious to the battle of wills vibrating in the air between the two men. Her face was anguished, eyes full of tears. "Vander, this is horrible: Edward escaped from prison just as he was about to be sent to Botany Bay." She swallowed hard and tears spilled again. "And it was all my fault!"

It was Reeve who stated the obvious. "The fault is Sir Richard's, not yours, Mia."

Use of her first name was, to Vander's mind, a naked declaration of war.

"You could have lost an eye!" Mia cried, reaching out to touch the black bruise that went down Reeve's face. "To think you might have died in prison, and no one would ever have known where you were." A sob escaped and she pressed a handkerchief to her mouth.

Watching her, Vander felt an icy calm move through his veins. He didn't want a wife who sobbed over another man's pain. She was his on paper, but her heart was Reeve's.

"I feel so awful that I didn't have faith in you!"

Mia gave Reeve a watery smile. "Yet the whole story is unbelievable. You must admit that it sounds like something from one of my novels."

"I fully expect to see my adventures in a bookstore one day," Reeve said. He turned to Vander. "My parents' Runners are still on their way to India, hoping to find me there. I gather you know that it was your Runner who learned the truth. He had tracked me to Scotland and was trying to decide how to proceed when I escaped from prison. I am indebted to both of you, as he was very helpful in dispersing the guards on my trail."

Vander saw Mia's brows draw together, and uttered a silent curse.

"*Vander's* Runner?" she said, her handkerchief falling to the floor. "What on earth are you saying, Edward?"

"I hired a Bow Street Runner to find your fiancé," Vander said. "I thought it unlikely that the man had voluntarily left you at the altar."

"You did?" She gaped at him. He saw pink coming back into her cheeks. "And you didn't tell me?" He could see horror dawning in her eyes. "Tell me you didn't know before today that Edward had escaped from prison. That he hadn't abandoned me at the altar!"

Judging from her brilliant eyes, her tension and grief had just transformed to a fury not unlike Vander's own. But before he could respond, Reeve took her shoulders and gently turned her to face him.

"It doesn't matter, darling," he said. "I am here. I didn't leave you stranded. I will do everything it takes to make this right."

He looked over Mia's head. "I knew, of course, about the provisions of John Carrington's will, and Mia has told me of the extreme measures she em-

ployed to force you to marry her. I owe you my gratitude." His jaw visibly clenched, and then he added,
"I have strong doubts about how long Charlie would
have survived in Sir Richard's care."

"I assume you intend to press charges against Sir
Richard," Vander stated.

Reeve smiled, and any remaining hint of a well-
polished professor evaporated. His hands dropped
from Mia's shoulders, and his face took on the ferocious anticipation of a lion closing in on a kill. "Of
course. I mean to pay him a visit. But Mia came first."
He took one of her hands in his.

It was a calculated gesture. The metaphorical
gauntlet hit the pavement with a clatter.

Mia looked down at the fingers encircling her hand
and then up at Reeve. Her lips parted.

Before she could speak, Reeve said, "We must ex-
peditiously unravel the unfortunate circumstances
that resulted from my abduction."

Vander watched, his jaw tight. But it wasn't his
wife that he saw: it was his mother, gazing at Lord
Carrington. That tableau put him in the position of
his father, seething with impotent rage.

"I am confident it can be dealt with quickly,"
Vander confirmed, not letting on by a flicker of an
eyelash that the only thing on his mind was murder.
He *refused* to become his father.

He felt Mia's eyes on him. "But we're married," she
whispered.

Vander looked at her and blessedly, felt nothing.
He had closed off that part of himself. "As you yourself have told me time and again, Duchess, a divorce
can be arranged within six months." He kept his tone
easy and reasonable.

"Especially in this situation, sweetheart," Reeve
added. "The king himself will dissolve the marriage,

if my father requests it. The earl is quite close to His Majesty."

Vander nodded. "In that case, I'll trust your connections to take care of this." He had had enough of the tender reunion. "I doubt that you are carrying a child," he said to Mia. "Barring that, I will raise no barrier to a dissolution."

Mia pushed away from Reeve, taking a step toward Vander. "That's all you have to say?" Her voice was rising.

"Yes," he said, his lips hardly moving. "The man you love has come back to you, Duchess. You were never jilted. You no longer have need of my protection or name."

She leapt forward, one of those small fists raised, and hit him squarely in the chest. "We are married! I. Am. Your. Duchess!"

He had walked into the room to find his duchess in the arms of another man. The similarity to his parents' marriage brought on another tidal wave of anger that threatened to pull him under. "By vows that you begged me to annul," he pointed out.

"Yes, but after that—"

"For God's sake, Duchess, you're getting what you wanted," he bit out. "I'm getting what I wanted. This was a mistake from the beginning, and you know it."

She fell back a step. "It will be a scandal."

If he had hoped there was any chance that she meant more by her declaration that she was his duchess, that sentence disabused him of that notion. No woman wanted a scandal, any more than his mother had, but his mother's fears had come second to being with the man she loved. Still, his mother managed to remain a duchess and keep her lover.

He tightened his hand into a fist, forcing himself to speak calmly. "It may take a few years, but the scandal will settle down. You'll have Reeve, and I'll find another duchess. I'm in no hurry."

She flinched. "I see," she said, her eyes searching his face.

"You've been together for only a few days," Reeve put in, "so it's hardly a marriage. It isn't as if you've shared much."

Mia gasped. Reeve's brow knitted at the sound, and Vander said nothing, just looked at him steadily. *That's right, you bastard,* he thought in some deep, primitive part of his brain. *I had her first. She sobbed my name. I took her up against the stable wall and she begged for more.*

But Vander's pulse of triumph evaporated like mist in the sun.

Reeve was taking everything that mattered. He had Mia's love. He had all her laughter and tenderness. All the courage that meant Mia had never feared him, as a duke or as a man. All the intelligence and creativity and passion that she poured into her novels. All the kindness that had made Chuffy and Jafeer fall promptly in love with her.

Vander bowed and turned to summon Gaunt. He felt like a dead man as he walked across the room.

"One more thing," Mia said, from behind him.

Vander stilled, halfway to the door.

"You already knew that Edward did not jilt me, but you said nothing." Her words broke the silence like the sharp crack of a pistol. "Why didn't you tell me as soon as you learned the truth?"

His mouth tightened before he forced himself to relax. He turned to face her. "I found out yesterday, but I wanted my fourth night, Duchess. I had paid for it."

"*You* paid for it?" she repeated slowly. "*I* paid for

those nights, or don't you remember your accusation?"

"Four nights was the charm."

"Four nights," she whispered. "That's all I was to you: four nights?"

"Don't make me into a hero, Duchess. You can have only one of those in a story, remember?"

This time, when he walked to the door, no one called his name.

Chapter Thirty

Perhaps all the tears Mia had shed in her short marriage had dried up the supply. Or perhaps there is a kind of grief too bitter for tears. She had been shredded by the world, torn into scraps, and tossed onto the toll road.

Mere scraps of humanity can't cry.

She departed Rutherford Park with her manuscript and a valise packed with Madame duBois's creations. She even left Charlie behind, reassuring him that she would send for him as soon as she possibly could. It would be different if she was traveling to Carrington House directly, but Edward didn't think it was advisable until Sir Richard was in custody. She couldn't confuse and upset Charlie by dragging him off to an inn with Edward, especially when Sir Richard was still a threat. Instead, she left Susan behind to take care of him.

For the first several minutes as their carriage

bowled down the road, Mia stared silently out the window, trying in vain to harden herself. Her treacherous heart was screaming, demanding that she stop the carriage and return to Vander. Plead with him to keep her, seduce him if she had to . . .

Had she *no* pride? The man had taken his four nights and turned his back. Grief and rage were battling, but misery was threatening to win and pull her under when Edward leaned forward and put a hand on her knee.

"I've been in prison, Mia, but there hasn't been one hour as painful as that conversation with the duke. I'm sorry it happened."

"Vander just handed me off." Her voice caught and she took a deep breath. "He didn't even argue. I was no more to him than a wrongly addressed parcel."

"Some men do not give wedding vows the same weight as do women," Edward said carefully.

Mia felt as if a hole had opened up inside her, a well of pain that went back to her father's dismissive attitude and her brother's refusal to even consider her as an appropriate guardian to Charlie.

At the same time, her whole body ached at the idea of never seeing or touching Vander again. It was inconceivable. Impossible. He couldn't have really given her away.

But he had.

"He never asked what I thought," she said, her voice strained with pain. She hated the pity in Edward's eyes, so she added, "We only married a week or so ago, and he was beastly to me most of the time. I'll recover." It wasn't true. She'd never recover.

"Yet he was the man for whom you wrote that poem. The poem you told me about."

"Yes."

"Were you glad when I didn't appear at the altar?" His voice was as steady and calm as always.

Guilt ripped through her again. "No! Of course I wasn't! I loved—I mean, I love you. It's just that—"

"The result was that you married him."

"I had no choice," she cried, wrapping her arms around herself and choking back her tears. But wasn't he right? Hadn't she run straight to Vander, the first chance she got? Somehow, she could have found a gentleman to marry her. If worst came to worst, she could have married a total stranger, and bribed Sir Richard not to sue her. "I'm so sorry that I was the reason you almost died," she added, shame tightening her throat. "I feel terrible about what Sir Richard did to you. And I feel even worse that I didn't have more faith in you."

Edward rose and moved across to sit next to her, wrapping an arm around her shoulders. "I find it surprising that the duke is willing to give you up."

His words made another tide of despair wash through her, but an errant part of her wanted to defend Vander. "Before I blackmailed him, he had never been forced to do anything against his will. He told me over and over that I didn't have the qualities he would choose in a wife."

Edward's arm tightened. "He's a fool. But you should know that the moment I make you mine, I will never give you up. I would never be so foolish as he."

She closed her eyes and drew a breath, letting his words wash over her. They should have made her relieved. But all they gave her was greater despair.

Finally, she forced back more tears and looked up. "The truth is that I love him," she said, choking out the words.

She felt Edward go rigid, but she hurried on. "So

it's more accurate to say that *I'm* the fool, because I knew what he thought about me. How he felt about me."

The truth was that a woman like her should never have looked at a rich and handsome duke.

The truth of it reeled through her mind. She wasn't violet-eyed and slender. She wasn't even very sweet, and no one had left her a secret inheritance.

None of this was Vander's fault. She had forced herself on him, and then she had made love to him— but he had merely had intercourse with her. Four night's worth.

And yet he had been so generous in bed. What other man would have pushed away his rage at being blackmailed, forgiven his wife for her criminal behavior, and consummated their marriage with such tenderness?

He was a good man, and he deserved far better than she. His next duchess might have violet eyes or not, but she should be as forgiving and generous as he was.

Mia drew in a shuddering breath. She would get through this pain. It felt as keen as when her brother died, but that was ridiculous.

There was one thing that she had to make clear, though. She would not continue to make mistakes, and Charlie was safe from Sir Richard now.

"I cannot marry you," she said, turning to face Edward. "I'm so sorry. I'm just . . . I'm sorry for everything. I didn't know that I still loved Vander when we were betrothed, but after living with him, and being his wife, it wouldn't be right to marry you. Someday you'll find a woman who is *much* better than I am."

"What do you mean by that?" he asked, frowning at her.

"A real lady," she explained, a shudder passing

through her at the memory of her behavior in the stables with Vander. She forced some enthusiasm into her voice. "Someone beautiful and far more suited to you!" Now she sounded like a barker trying to sell an undersized pig.

"I never could get you to look at yourself in a glass," he said, shaking his head.

Mia looked down. It had turned out that Madame duBois's idea of a bodice was little more than a corset with a covering of tulle.

"Not just your breasts," Edward said, in the detached tones of a scholar, "though those are damned beautiful. You are exquisite, Mia. Every part of you: your spirit, your laugh, your face, your body."

Mia found herself turning rosy. "You never said anything like that before."

"I had a lot of time to think in prison."

She flinched at the thought of where he'd been, and only managed a wobbly smile. Edward took both her hands in his and raised one of them to his lips. "You're well out of that marriage, Mia. Marry me, and we'll raise Charlie in a house full of books and children, and the kind of love that grows and deepens."

"That sounds lovely." She managed a wobbly smile. "Thank you. But I can't marry you. I do love you, but—but more like a brother, Edward."

His eyes darkened. "It may feel familial now, but I assure you that with time a different bond will grow between us."

Prison had changed Edward. He was more muscled, and he had a ferocious edge that she didn't remember. He used to look professorial. But even with a broken nose, he was a very good-looking man.

"Don't answer me now," he said, before she could reply. "This is no time to make decisions."

"Very well," she answered. She was beginning to

feel like a teakettle coming on to boil. It wasn't just tears bubbling up inside her. It was anger too.

Vander had said hurtful things during their marriage, but he had also said other things. He had made her feel beautiful. He had laughed at her jokes. He had not shown even the slightest distaste when he learned that she and Lucibella were one and the same; indeed, he had been fascinated in her writing.

Her father and brother had dismissed her novels. Edward had been supportive, but uninterested. Vander might have poked fun at her characters, but he had listened intently and made suggestions, though none of them were usable.

He had made her feel accomplished. Cherished.

But it was all a lie.

Edward leaned forward and brushed his lips over hers. Before she could stop him, the kiss deepened. Mia froze, letting it happen. She felt no reaction at all. None. Edward had broken out of prison, then returned to her—and ungrateful wretch that she was, she felt nothing for him other than affection.

Mia used to think that love could come after a wedding. But her love for Edward would never be like a wildfire that ravaged everything in its path. It would never strip Mia of all her illusions about herself and the world, and throw her naked onto the ground. Turn her into a woman aflame with desire.

That would never happen to her again.

That's when the tears came.

Chapter Thirty-one

After Edward Reeve drove away with his duchess, Vander sent a message to Thorn, informing him of the man's miraculous reappearance. Then he rooted Charlie out of the nursery for another riding lesson.

He called him "Gimpy" all afternoon, because his ward looked pale and shocked, though Charlie improved after Vander allowed him to trot Lancelot for the first time. Sometime later they groomed the horse together, and Vander showed him how to pick stones out of a horse's hoof.

One thing led to another, and they ended up in the blacksmith's shop on the estate. Charlie was not afraid of the pungent smoke or glowing coals, though Mia would have shrieked if she had seen her beloved boy's jacket smoldering from a flying spark.

Once Vander explained what he had in mind, the blacksmith took Charlie's crutch apart and inserted a small dagger while they watched. Mia probably wouldn't approve of that, either.

On the way back, Vander hoisted Charlie onto his shoulder and the boy slung a thin arm around Vander's neck and chattered about horses and smithies all the way back up the hill. Charlie had decided that he would like to be a blacksmith. Vander didn't point out that a hereditary title and its estate could not be renounced in favor of a smithy. He was living proof that a member of the peerage need not restrict himself to lounging about ballrooms.

"I could make crutches for people like me," Charlie told him.

"From steel? They'd make an awful racket on the cobblestones."

"But wood isn't as strong. You could swing a steel crutch and take someone's head off," Charlie said, with relish. He was a boy, through and through.

Even as Charlie happily nattered on, resolve was slowly growing in Vander's mind. Sir Richard Magruder had ruined his damned life, as surely as if he'd swung a steel crutch at his head. And Vander meant to pay him a visit that very night.

"Aunt Mia says we're moving back to Carrington House," Charlie said, out of the blue. He was clutching Vander's hair to keep his balance.

"Yes. But you'll pay me frequent visits, as often as every day, if you're not at school."

"I will?"

Vander gave the legs dangling against his chest a squeeze. "You're mine, Squinty."

"I don't squint!" Charlie squealed.

"I'm preparing for when you do," Vander told him. "Looking ahead."

Charlie gave his hair a tug. "I want to live here, with you. I want to go to the stables every day."

Vander reached up, lifted him over his head, and set him down. Then he crouched down so they were at eye level. "You have to go away to school, Charlie. You'll be going to Eton with other boys. But you'll be luckier than they are, because you'll have two fathers: Mr. Reeve and me."

Charlie's mouth twitched.

"He's a good man," Vander said, hating every word. "Your Aunt Mia will be his wife. But never forget that your estate runs alongside my lands. We will see each often, for the rest of our lives."

Charlie stepped forward and with the great simplicity of childhood, put his arms around Vander's neck. He didn't say anything.

And Vander didn't say anything either.

After a while, they continued on their way. They talked about how a blacksmith was the heart of a great estate. Charlie would need to know these things.

Vander had the feeling that professors didn't know how to run estates. Why should they? "A good smith will say that a 'job well done is a job never seen again,'" he told Charlie, keeping an eye out to see if the boy was starting to flag from overdoing it. But his leg was visibly stronger, just in the last week.

They returned to the stables and stayed there until Thorn showed up, walking from his carriage with that loose-limbed ferocity of his. He didn't say a word about what had happened. Instead, the three of them got grubby washing down Jafeer, and ate roughly cut ham sandwiches with the grooms while discussing training schedules and other important things.

When Charlie had been dispatched to the care of Susan, Vander jerked his head at Thorn. "Sir Richard had Mia's fiancé—Reeve—thrown in prison under false charges. He was about to be sent to Botany Bay when he escaped."

"Reeve? Edward Reeve who made that paper machine I told you about?"

Vander nodded.

"I never knew the name of your wife's betrothed."

"Not my wife for long," Vander said, striding into the house. "She will be Reeve's wife, which is the way it should be."

"Right." There was something guarded in Thorn's voice, but Vander ignored it.

"Sir Richard?" Thorn asked, following him into his bedchamber.

Vander nodded. The time had come. He stripped, then donned a black shirt and close-fitting trousers that went to his ankles.

"My breeches and coat are dark, but my shirt won't do. Have you another black shirt?" Thorn asked.

"This will be dangerous. Your wife is carrying a child."

Thorn's response to this was a curled lip, and after a moment Vander tossed him a shirt like the one he'd put on. Then Thorn left to collect his matched pistols, left in his carriage, and Vander took his own Bennett & Lacy pistols from the gun cabinet. They were overly embellished for his taste, with the ducal insignia picked out in silver, but their aim was true.

It would take approximately an hour to reach Sir Richard's estate, on the far side of the Carrington lands, if they went across country on swift horses. If there was one thing Vander's stables could supply, it was swift horses.

He had thought to take his usual mount, but as he walked down the central corridor of the stable, he heard a soft whicker. Jafeer's head appeared over his stall door. His eyes shone with lonely, surprised betrayal. Mia hadn't come to the stables before she left.

"Saddle up Jafeer," Vander instructed Mulberry. "And Ajax for Mr. Dautry."

"Are you certain about Jafeer, Your Grace?" Mulberry had clearly appraised Vander's attire and guessed that something was afoot, not much of a leap, given the pistols tucked into Vander's belt. "He still tends to shy at the slightest thing."

"He'll be fine." Vander could see it in Jafeer's eyes. The horse had known love back in Arabia and lost her; he had known love here in England and lost her. He had won his first race. Jafeer had grown up.

A half hour later they were flying straight across Pindar fields, and Jafeer was responding to every touch of Vander's knees and hands as if he had been born with a man on his back.

The moon was rising by the time Vander slowed Jafeer to a walk, Thorn pulling up Ajax behind him. The horses were breathing heavily, but Jafeer's ears were twitching with delight and the willingness to gallop through the night.

They had reached the border of Sir Richard's land. They picked their way quietly through the surrounding wood, finally stopping at the edge of a long, rolling lawn.

Vander dismounted, tied Jafeer to a tree, and told him to be quiet. Thorn followed suit, and they melted into a clump of ash trees.

He had a shrewd notion that Sir Richard kept men on guard all night. He likely had enemies of every stripe. Sure enough, as Vander came closer, he saw that there was a man standing beneath the front portico, his outline just visible when the moon came out from behind a cloud.

Thorn touched his arm and nodded toward the

shadow cast by a man leaning against the side of the house. There were likely at least two more guards inside the front door.

At that moment, the moon emerged fully from the clouds and Vander saw the cruel face of the man guarding the front door. He had the bone-chilling air of a man who would kill for a triviality, for a baked potato.

Vander gestured with his hand parallel to the ground, and Thorn nodded. Silently, slowly, they sank to a sitting position against a tree and waited for something to happen, something they could take advantage of.

For an hour or perhaps longer, the grounds were utterly silent. More clouds drifted by, causing the moon to be obscured more often than it shone. The man in front took a piss off the steps, but no one made a circuit of the house. In fact, neither man stirred, which Vander took to mean that Sir Richard wasn't worried about the house being broken into from the rear.

No, his threats entered straight through in the front door, likely because he defrauded men like Squire Bevington, an honorable gentlemen who had no idea how to contend with a perfidious villain.

Vander's mouth curled in faint amusement. He and Thorn didn't qualify.

Thorn had grown up on the streets, and he had taught Vander a great deal. Vander had had all too many opportunities to practice those skills in the rough world of horse-racing, where a desperate owner could hire any number of thugs to take out the opposition by stealth or outright violence.

He touched Thorn's arm, and they rose and made their way silently up to the back of the house. Sure enough, no one appeared to be stationed there at all. Just as they were about to cross to the kitchen window,

he saw an indistinct figure against the wall enclos-
ing the kitchen gardens. It seemed Sir Richard had a
guard in the rear of the house after all.

As he and Thorn watched, the moon emerged from
a cloud and shone directly—on Reeve's face. Vander
swore under his breath and they both stepped out of
the shadows and walked over to him.

Reeve was wearing a tattered shirt, so shabby
that Thorn guessed he'd had it in prison, and leather
breeches of the sort that blacksmiths wear.

A shiver went over Vander's skin, visceral hatred
for the man who had taken Mia. His wife.

Bloody hell.

Reeve showed no surprise at their presence. Instead, he jerked his head at the dim light one story
above their heads. Vander took the lead. He would
have doubted that a professor had experience in
breaking and entering, but Reeve slipped into the
shadow of the house like a man trained to robbery
from the cradle. Of course, this was child's play compared to breaking out of Scotland's most fortified
prison.

A kitchen window had been propped open to allow
the heat of the ovens to escape the house. Vander
pushed it farther open and put a leg over the sill. In a
moment he had a hand clapped over the shoeblack's
mouth.

Large eyes stared at him, more excited than afraid.
Vander grabbed a cloth from the table and tied it
around the boy's mouth.

For a brief moment they all stood silently, listening to the sounds of the great house breathing. There
was a restless flow to the air. The master of the house
was awake; Vander would bet on it. Likely Sir Richard had received word that Reeve had broken out of

prison. Likely, too, he was planning to flee; only a fool would imagine no revenge would be taken, and whatever else he was, Sir Richard was no fool.

Thorn and Reeve followed Vander, low and close, down the servants' corridor leading to the baize door, which in turn led to the entry. There would be guards in the entry, trained for combat, but they wouldn't be expecting men to attack them from behind.

The three of them came through the door as one. There was a ferocious crack as Vander knocked a man to his knees, a bitten-off cry as Reeve took out another, and the sound of a brief struggle until Thorn dealt a third man a clout from the butt of his pistol. They were tying them up when a foot scraped outside; the man on the porch had heard the disturbance.

As the guard pushed open the front door, a flood of moonlight illuminated his coarse features and slack, thin lips. Sir Richard wasn't a man to do dirty work himself, so it was unsurprising to find that he'd hired a man who looked capable of anything. Vander took him in a silent rush, knocking him out with one well-placed blow.

At first Vander thought Reeve crossed to his side in order to help in tying up the guard, but instead he heard the sudden sound of a dagger leaving its sheath.

"What in the devil are you doing?" Vander growled, seizing Reeve's wrist.

Reeve's jaw hardened but he didn't resist Vander's grasp. "He shot two of my grooms, knocked me senseless, and threw me in prison. He kept me from my own damn wedding."

"Let the authorities take care of him." Vander had occasionally taken the law in his own hands—no one involved in the horse racing could avoid it—but he had never watched a man being killed in cold blood and he didn't intend to now. "The price of murder is too high," he added.

Their eyes held a moment. Then Reeve snarled, "He gut-stabbed my thirteen-year-old post-boy. I was told last night that the boy lived a full day in excruciating agony before he died. He's a monster."

"In killing him, you risk becoming a monster yourself." When the truth of that had registered on Reeve's face, Vander let his arm go.

They drifted up the stairs as quietly as snowflakes, Vander thinking hard. He loathed Sir Richard Magruder, but Reeve was transported by rage, his body clearly burning with steely fire. Sir Richard's greed had cost Reeve the life of that boy, of his other servants, nearly cost Reeve his own life, not to mention his marriage.

That same greed had given Vander the best days of his life. It had given him Mia. Even though he'd had her only a short time, it had been worth it. He fell back, ceding the other man's right to revenge.

Whatever Reeve did to Sir Richard . . . he did.

By the time Vander reached the top stair, it was as if the shock of Reeve's return had evaporated. Instead, a new truth ploughed into him with a body-shuddering blow. For good or bad, despite the similarities with his father, he could not live without Mia.

She *was* his.

His woman, his wife.

He stood in the door of Sir Richard's study as Reeve swiftly and cold-bloodedly pummeled the man into submission.

Watching absent-mindedly, another fact hit Vander hard: something that had been there, but he hadn't allowed himself to look at. She was his life. In a few short days, she had worked her way into his soul, and for first time in his life, everything had felt clean and true.

The hell with his past, with his parents' relationship. He refused to let her go without fighting for her.

If that aligned him with the tragedy of his father's marriage, the hell with it. He didn't give a damn. He had been a fool to walk away.

Vander left without bothering to say a word to Magruder. He no longer gave a damn about the man.

Mia was exasperating and fiery. She would likely disagree with him on a daily basis. She would court scandals, and ride with her eyes closed, and write stories in which men fell on their knees at the drop of a hat.

He would go to bed every night of his life hungry for her. And rise from that bed every morning satisfied.

All he had to do was make her realize that she was meant to be with him. He had to take her back, take her away from Reeve.

Make it clear to her that she loved him, and *only* him.

Chapter Thirty-two

By the time the coach arrived at the Queen's Minion, the inn closest to Sir Richard's property, Mia had wept herself to a standstill. Her heart burned in her chest and her throat was sore, but she had no more tears.

She climbed the stairs to her bedchamber, questions pounding through her head. Why was she never good enough? Her father, her brother, now Vander . . . she had been a charity case for all three: easily dismissed, insignificant. Her father never had much love to spare for her daughter; he had spent it all in his adulterous pursuit of the late duchess. Her brother was fond of her, but didn't trust her with his most prized possession, his son.

And Vander . . .

Vander had genuinely enjoyed her company, especially in bed. But he hadn't fallen in love with her. She had been just a female body, obtained for a few nights, used, tossed aside.

Losing Vander wouldn't hurt so much if she hadn't believed—truly believed—that he was falling in love with her.

Though she might as well be honest, at least with herself.

It wouldn't hurt so much if she hadn't cast and recast Vander in the role of hero. In Lucibella Delicosa's books, *Vander* always rode to his lady's rescue, and *Vander* always married a seamstress of low birth after love triumphed over every accident of fate—and that would have included being short and round, had she created such a heroine.

A low, bitter laugh wrenched itself from her chest as she dropped into a chair.

The real Vander hadn't even tried to convince her to stay.

She was a fool, who had to stop nurturing a dream of romantic love that didn't exist in real life. Vander was right: her father and his mother had engaged in a tawdry, sordid *affaire* that had tarnished everyone in their vicinity.

There was nothing honorable or beautiful about it. At best, it was pitiful, and at worst, it was contemptible. The years she had spent, putting her love for Vander into poetry or fiction? Equally pitiful.

And contemptible.

The most ironic point was that *An Angel's Form* still needed to be written, no matter how hollow and withered her heart felt. She had to support herself and Charlie when they were jaunting around Bavaria.

She was washing her face when a footman delivered her valise and manuscript, along with a note from Edward apologizing because he would be unable to join Mia for supper.

Presumably he was planning some sort of offensive against Sir Richard. Mia couldn't bring herself to feel even a shred of concern for Charlie's uncle. Sir Richard deserved everything he got.

She ordered supper in her chamber and began reading through her manuscript as she ate, scratching out a line here or there. It was appalling to realize just how much her silly girlhood dreams formed the bedrock of the novel, never clearer than when Frederic—on his knees—vowed that he loved Flora because of her inner beauty.

For few minutes Mia toyed with the idea of throwing the pages—all her notes and chapters and fragments of dialogue—into the fire.

But no.

She may have lost faith in love, but readers needed her novels, especially when they were sick at heart, desperate, nearing death, or watching a loved one fade.

They needed to believe in the fairy tale that she no longer believed in herself.

After finishing her meal, she slapped the pages down on the desk in the corner of her bedchamber, trimmed the wick on the lamp, and got to work.

Frederic had to change. He was too mealy-mouthed, too passive. A few hours later the lamp guttered, and she rang for more oil. By then she had turned Frederic into a man who was big and strong and prone to telling Flora what to do—although he loved her to the bottom of her dainty toes.

Rather than roaming English byways in search for Flora, growing thin and wan from hunger, Frederic went galloping after her, his greatcoat whipping behind him as he crouched over his magnificent midnight black steed. Or should it be a stallion?

She wasn't certain what the distinction was. Something young ladies were not supposed to know, she thought. She began compiling a list of vulgar words that she wanted defined. *Stallion. Cock-pit. Lolpoop. Quim.* She had a pretty good idea of what the last word meant, but she wanted to be certain. *Love custard.*

Wasn't there a dictionary of the vulgar tongue put together by someone named Grose? Obviously, she needed a copy so that she could create realistic characters.

She was searching her memory for more words banned to young ladies, when a leg suddenly appeared over her windowsill. Before she could make a sound, the leg was followed by the rest of Vander.

Mia jumped to her feet, dropping her quill. "What are you doing here?" she demanded, low and fierce. He had thrown her out like yesterday's bathwater, and it was pure foolishness that the very sight of him set her heart thumping.

He didn't answer for a moment, his eyes fixed on her.

"What do you want?" she demanded again.

His gaze raked over her, heated, furious. "A nightdress for Reeve?" he growled, ignoring her question.

His words hit her with all the force of a slap. As if a passerby on the street had given her a blow to the chin or called her a whore. "The gown *was* for you, for my husband. I am not a woman who commits adultery." She meant to shout it, but her voice betrayed her, coming out ragged with distress.

She saw satisfaction flash in his eyes.

Madame duBois had made the nightgown from black silk, which clung to Mia's every curve. She usually wore white cotton trimmed with eyelet lace, so Vander did have a point.

"I shall give you the name of the modiste, and you can order one for your next duchess," she replied, in a voice as chilly as she could make it.

"There will be no 'next duchess,'" Vander said, finally dragging his eyes from her body and stepping closer. "You are my duchess, my only duchess."

Before she could grasp what he was saying, Mia caught sight of a darkening bruise on his cheek and realized that his linen shirt had been sliced open by a blade. She gasped and took a step forward before stopping herself. "Are you hurt?" He didn't appear injured; he was moving with the same graceful power that he always had. "You went to Sir Richard's house! What happened? Was Edward there?"

His eyes darkened ominously at the last question, but she had never quailed before him, and she wasn't about to start now.

"Yes, he was." Vander spoke through gritted teeth. "When I saw him last, Reeve was fine."

A sudden, horrific thought struck her. "Are you here because something has happened to Charlie?"

"No. Charlie rode all day and went to bed exhausted. I came to see you."

Mia took an unsteady breath. Right. Her panic drained away, replaced by a desperate wish to protect herself. She literally could not survive any more humiliation courtesy of the Duke of Pindar. "Then why are you here?" she managed.

Vander pushed tumbled locks, dark with sweat, from his forehead. "I won't give you up."

Mia's heart bounded. Stay with Vander . . . live with him. Sleep in his bed, make love to him night after night.

The image snapped her back to herself. Where was her self-respect? Even the fact his ripped shirt revealed his muscled chest made her long for his touch. Something about him was destructive to her.

It was pitiful, she reminded herself, to want a man who was not only disrespectful, but unkind. As pitiful as all those novels she'd written about one duke—Vander—though she'd given him six different names.

"Have you changed your mind so quickly?" She tried for flippant. "Will you change your mind again tomorrow? You never struck me as a fickle man."

His jaw tightened. "I am not fickle: in point of fact, I am Charlie's guardian and I don't intend to give him up."

Incredulity scorched down Mia's spine and she drew in a searing breath. "You want me to stay married to you because of Charlie?" The mortification cut like a blade: it seemed that even her eight-year-old nephew was more valuable than she was. She had never felt more unlovable.

"Not merely that," Vander bit out. Then something else flashed through his eyes. "Look, regardless of what my mother did, my father never stopped loving her, all those years, even when he was in the asylum."

Somewhat to her relief, Mia discovered that fury was allowing her to view the scene from a distance, as if she had walked into a play.

"I fail to see how that is pertinent to our marriage," she observed. "If our parents are to be the subject of conversation, I think it's far more relevant that when I described my father and your mother as loving one another, you countered with an assessment of my father as a bastard who seduced your mother, and morcover, you implied that I was more of the same. A bad apple from a bad tree."

Another moment of silence followed. "I didn't say that."

"In so many words, you did."

"That wasn't my intent."

"You said what you thought at that moment! You said things you believed!"

"Damn it!" The words burst out of him, as if the

thread of his control had finally broken. "My whole life, I believed my father was betrayed by my mother," Vander said, taking another step toward her. "But then I learned he had been beating her."

Mia flinched. "I had no idea. I'm—I'm so sorry."

"He injured her so badly that she was unable to have children after I was born." Something in Vander's voice told her that he had never said this aloud before, and might never say it again.

"That is terrible," Mia said carefully. She had been right about all those glass animals. She would have to send someone over to Vander's house to box up all the fragile little mothers and their crystal offspring.

"When Reeve arrived this morning, all I could think was that I had married a woman who loved another man, just as my mother did."

"I—"

He took a final step and curled his hands around her upper arms. His eyes searched hers. "I let you go. Bloody hell, I pushed you away because I was so convinced that you loved another man. But the minute your carriage was out of sight, it hit me. I was wrong. You don't love him, do you, Duchess? You love me."

Mia gasped and opened her mouth to hotly refute his statement—but he bent his head and kissed her so ferociously that heat spread like wildfire over her skin. Only a slender instinct for self-preservation gave her the strength to pull away.

"Unfortunate though your parents' history is, I'm afraid it doesn't change our situation." She blurted out everything she'd been thinking about all afternoon. "You and I are not a good match. We're too volatile and too—" She couldn't think of the word. "I did things with you that no lady should do, and when you lose your temper, you say things I can't forgive."

"I can change," Vander said, his eyes fierce.

Mia shook her head. "It's not just that. I lost my dignity when I blackmailed you into marriage, and I lost even more when . . . um . . . well, you know what I mean. If we remain married, over time I would lose what fragments of self-respect I have left."

Vander's rough-hewn features were set hard. "There is nothing, and I repeat nothing, in what we did together that you should be embarrassed about. What we did together was a gift, Duchess. And I will have no other duchess."

"You will not tell me how to feel! Nor can you discard me and then demand to have me back, like a piece of lost luggage. What we shared is not good enough to sustain a marriage." She stepped to one side and pointed to the window. "Please leave the way you came in."

Vander's eyes darkened and without answering, he pulled her back into his arms. Like a flash of lightning, that dangerous warmth spread through her again. When she opened her mouth to protest, he took possession.

Mia didn't regain sanity for long minutes, coming back to herself only to discover that she was shaking, clinging to her husband, her knees weak. Vander was swearing under his breath as his hands roamed over her body.

Once again she had succumbed to her basest impulses. She was shaming herself again. Ladies didn't act this way.

She pushed against his chest. "You must go," she said, her voice cracking. "I cannot do this. You cannot do this to me. I deserve a husband who respects me!"

"I respect you," Vander stated.

The look in his eyes made her body throb with need. But she managed to clear her head. "You *want* me, which is not the same. You don't respect me, not the way a gentleman should respect the woman he marries. The heroes in my books would never say the things that you have said to me. They would never even think them. But you have. A minute ago you asked me if I'd worn this nightdress for another man, even knowing our parents' history and the toll it took on both of us. You have repeatedly expressed your low opinion of me, no matter what you say now."

She stepped farther away from him, as though putting physical distance between them would somehow translate to loving him less. "The truth is that I am nothing more than the title to you—the title, and a body to go with it." Anger once again began to shore up her courage, putting a layer of thick ice between them. "Are you aware that in our short marriage, you have never once used my name? To you, I am always 'duchess'; at one point I wasn't sure you even remembered my name. The final proof? Yesterday you and Edward renegotiated our marriage without bothering to ask me about my feelings—though I stood between you in the room."

"You misunderstood. It wasn't like that."

"Neither of you even thought to inquire whether I would prefer to remain married to you, or marry Edward."

Vander couldn't bear the look in Mia's face: her expressive features were lifeless, all her joy and passion locked away so it didn't shine from her eyes.

His wife was standing before him, telling him to leave, but he would not leave. She was his. With that thought, he picked her up, ignoring her gasp, and carried her to the bed, following her down. The moment his body lay on hers, he felt an exquisite wave of relief.

"I'm at home when I'm with you," he muttered,

kissing her nose, then her cheekbone. Other words eluded him, so he took her mouth.

And her body. When he slipped his hands between Mia's legs, she was already wet. After a second her eyes glazed over and she pulled him to her, so he slid into her tight warmth, mating with her like an animal, mad with the taste and the smell of her.

It was raw and magnificent, not slow and gentle. But after she had come three times, and he rolled, breathless, to the side, she still wouldn't meet his eyes. And when she sat up, his heart sank.

"This isn't right," she said.

"Duchess—"

She turned like a flash. "You see? Even now, you don't use my name."

Vander hated her hard, frozen look. He sat up and took her face between his hands, as if he could warm her with his touch. "Mia, you *are* my duchess. It is the greatest gift I have to bestow. My name, my title, everything that's mine."

Mia closed her eyes, opened them again. "I need . . ." She trailed off and began again. "That isn't enough. I need respect, Vander. You can't know how much I need it. I have to respect myself, and be respected. It's the one thing my family couldn't give me, and you do not feel it either."

"That's not true," he said, tempering his voice, keeping calm.

She waited, but the right words didn't come to him. He could only think of crude words.

"To you, I'm not someone worth loving," she finally said, with a sigh. "Not that I can blame you. I wrote that appalling poem; I blackmailed you; I lose my head utterly when you touch me. I'd rather . . . In time, I'll lose myself."

She got up without looking at him and put on a wrapper. "Go now, Vander. Please."

Vander followed and swung her about, not gently. "Everything you're saying is wrong. It's rubbish."

She gave a crack of laughter. "I suppose you do think that." She broke free, her chin in the air. At least she didn't look empty and wooden: now every part of her blazed with fire and determination.

"My feelings are not rubbish, Duke. Just because you do not agree does not mean that my feelings are invalid. In fact, you just confirmed what I already told you: at the heart, you think my opinions, my feelings, are unimportant. And if we remained married, your opinion would always come out in one way or another."

The pain in her voice made each word feel like a needle piercing his skin. "I don't think that," he said, straining to explain to the fiery, rebellious woman whom he'd hurt that—that what? He had never had any use for eloquence; he had paid for his pleasures. But Mia deserved eloquence.

"Go. Just leave me alone. Please." Her face and her voice were empty again, the charm and strength that everyone from Chuffy to Jafeer had responded to gone.

He tried one more time. "I know your name, Mia, and I don't want to live without you. I love being married to you. You are *mine*, my wife."

"I am no man's possession!" she flashed. "I am my own person, Vander. Always. And I want a divorce."

He stared at her hard as he realized something. Mia was right.

He didn't respect her the way a storybook hero might. He didn't want to kneel and beg for her hand; he wanted to throw her on the bed again, and do all sorts of disrespectful things to her. He wanted to spend a lifetime arguing with her over anything and everything, giving up and kissing her until neither of them cared about their disagreement.

He wanted to possess her, eat her, fuck her, live with her, die with her. Put his seed into her and have children—not because he needed an heir, but so that they created a child together.

So that someone with her eyes and her intelligence and her deep sweetness would always live in England, on his estate. So that future Pindar dukes would have some of her blood to counter the madness in his.

With a sharp nod, he turned to go.

Only when he was back in his carriage, turning into the drive leading to Rutherford Park, did it occur to him, with a pulse of despair, that the saintly Frederic would never talk about "putting his seed" into Flora.

When it came to it, Frederic wouldn't want to fuck her either.

That wasn't romantic. That wasn't what Mia wanted.

There truly was no saving his marriage.

Chapter Thirty-three

The next morning, after a few short hours of sleep, Vander entered the breakfast room to find Thorn meditatively spreading preserves on a roll while reading a note from his wife. Thorn and India were constantly sending notes back and forth, via footman if Thorn was in his study and India in her sitting room a few paces away, or groom if he was in London and she in the country.

Vander contemplated sending a letter to Mia, but promptly discarded the idea. She was the writer, not he.

"India is not pleased," Thorn remarked, looking up from his note.

"Did you tell her about your cracked rib?"

He shook his head. "Only the black eye. We're supposed to go to a royal drawing room next Monday, and a battered look leaves me at 'bastard' without reaching 'gentleman.'" He said it with distinct satisfaction.

Thorn had grown up on the streets, and this morning, he looked as though he'd never left them.

"Why do you want to go to a royal drawing room? It'll be bloody boring."

"India is rehabilitating me."

Vander snorted.

"She thrives in polite society, and I love her."

Thorn said that easily: as if his love were a fact of nature. Yet the very word made Vander feel stranded, as if he were on a small island encircled by rough waters.

For most of his life, he would have insisted that his father loved him dearly. But the duke had tried to kill him, multiple times, according to Chuffy.

Still, that didn't mean *he* couldn't love. He had loved his mother, even though he had cut her from his life. He had loved his father too, despite the tempests and violence he had conveniently forgotten. He loved Thorn. Chuffy. Charlie.

Mia.

He loved Mia. In fact, the truth was that talking about fucking her was just a way of saying that he wanted to be *in* her. The feeling that she was his . . . it was the same. A crude way of saying he loved her. A way of insisting that she could never be taken away from him.

He had the irrational conviction that she had taken all the broken, blackened parts inside him and mended them.

"So I am entering polite society," Thorn was saying, unaware that Vander's entire world had just turned upside down.

"What does that mean?" Vander asked through stiff lips. How was he to convince Mia of his feelings?

"A knighthood. My father favors it, so I suspect it is inevitable."

Vander chewed a piece of ham that tasted like sawdust. He'd no doubt that Thorn's prediction would be born out: the Duke of Villiers always got whatever he wanted.

He had to return to Mia. Kneel down if he had to. Tell her in the right words. Avoid saying things about bedding and owning her.

"You look like hell," Thorn observed. "May I take it that your wife is not inclined to return?"

"I intend to make her change her mind."

"Wasn't it scarcely more than a week ago that you were incensed at being blackmailed?"

Vander didn't bother to respond. For a while, there was only the clicking of cutlery as they demolished a great number of eggs, endless slices of beef and ham, and a mountain of rolls.

He had learned long ago that fashionable breakfasts sustained only those who spent the day moving languidly between carriage and sofa. He ate like a man with a mission, because he had one—the most important one of his life.

"I hope I didn't resemble you before I married," Thorn said, putting down his fork. "Though I probably did. Are you certain that the duchess does not love Reeve?"

"Yes," Vander said, sure of that now. "But she says I don't respect her." He suspected that when Mia talked about respect, she really meant love. And when he talked of *his* duchess, he meant the same. Love.

"Can you point out to her that blackmail does not precisely—" Thorn broke off at Vander's scowl. "Oh, very well; I suppose commonsense is irrelevant. I'll take it as a given that you've made a royal hash of it. That means you'll have to make a truly grand gesture."

Vander thought that over. What did he value above all else, apart from Mia? "I could give her Jafeer," he suggested. "I began to receive offers for him even before his first race was over. At present, he's the most coveted horse in all England."

"She doesn't want a horse, you idiot."

Chuffy rolled into the room and fell into a chair, looking the worse for wear. His hair resembled a graying bird's nest.

"Lads," he said blearily. "Don't ever challenge the village baker to a game of darts. I didn't win a single game until an hour ago, and that was merely because I hold my ale better than he does."

"Vander must win back his wife," Thorn said, without greeting. "Have you any ideas?"

Chuffy's head slowly sank down onto the table. "Not sure it's possible."

Vander's heart thumped. "Mia hates me that much?"

"No. But you don't measure up to a Lucibella hero." Chuffy's voice was muffled by the tablecloth.

That wasn't news to Vander, but Thorn frowned, clearly confused. "Measure up to a what?"

"Mia is an immensely popular novelist who publishes under another name, Lucibella Delicosa," Vander explained. "My uncle has read every one of her books."

"Novels and Shakespeare. Not exactly your forte."

"I realize that," Vander said grimly.

"So how does he fall short of a fictional hero?" Thorn asked Chuffy.

"He hasn't a poetic soul."

That was exactly the conclusion that Vander had come to.

"Kinross swears that he wouldn't be married

except for some poem by John Donne," Thorn said. "You could always memorize a poem. Or"—he grimaced—"you could try to write one."

"Are you referring to the Scottish duke?" Vander asked. "I have a very difficult time imagining Kinross reciting poetry."

"He told me one night that he considers Donne responsible for the happiness in his marriage."

"Poetry would be a start," Chuffy put in, straightening up, though he had the distinct look of someone who might pass out in the butter at any moment. "But there's more to it than that. At the climax of a Lucibella novel, the hero always does something heroic. In the one Mia is writing now, Frederic saves Flora from mortal peril."

"Frederic is an unmitigated ass," Vander said grimly. But he asked the obvious question anyway: "How does Frederic do it?"

"Presumably he saves her from the burning orphanage or something along those lines," Thorn said.

"No, a wild tiger," Chuffy said, stumbling to his feet. At some point during the night he'd lost his cravat, and his waistcoat was both unbuttoned and inside out. "I have to go to bed," he muttered.

"The tiger comes in at the end of the novel?" Thorn asked.

"Flora is fleeing the ghost-infested castle, but the villainous Lord Plum is enraged by her rejection of his unsavory advances—even though he has a wife in the attic—so he looses the half-starved, man-eating tiger he keeps in a cage in the castle courtyard." Chuffy rattled off the plot without pausing for breath.

"What's the heroic part?" Vander asked.

"Frederic sees his beloved about to be eaten by the tiger, so he hurtles into the courtyard to distract the beast, and as the animal is racing toward him, the man draws out a bow and arrow and shoots it dead. I tried to convince Mia that a pistol would do better, but she thinks arrows are more romantic."

A moment of brief silence followed as Vander (and presumably Thorn) tried to imagine this singularly unlikely sequence of events.

Chuffy added defensively, "It sounds a bit melodramatic, but that's because the two of you don't understand the genre. I assure you that readers all over the kingdom will be shivering with terror during that scene."

"Unfortunately, there's a scarcity of tigers in Berkshire," Thorn said, "so Vander can't reproduce that thrilling denouement."

"In one of Mia's most popular books, *Esmeralda*, the villain leaps from a stallion onto the heroine's moving carriage, which ends up in the river," Chuffy said, looking more alert. "The hero—that would be you, Vander—dives into the black and icy waters in order to recover the heroine, reaching her at the very instant she starts to drown."

"Ridiculous," Vander said impatiently, coming to his feet.

"Write your own ending, Nevvy!" Chuffy exclaimed. He thrust out a trembling but declamatory hand. " 'The Duke, the Duchess, and the Orphan'! To be sold in fine leather with a gold-stamped binding."

"I think you should memorize some poetry," Thorn said, ignoring Chuffy. "Try for someone less quoted than John Donne and you might even be able to pass it off as your own."

"Can you really see me falling on my knees and reciting a poem?"

Thorn and Chuffy looked at him, and Vander knew exactly what they saw: a burly man with no resemblance to a duke. At best his smile was wolfish; at worst it was downright menacing.

He had never read a Lucibella novel, but he had spent years listening to Chuffy recite breathless summaries of the plots of his favorite books. An idea began to take shape.

It would need Charlie.

Chapter Thirty-four

$\mathcal{M}$ia rose at four in the morning and began writing, the words flowing out of her as if a river had been undammed. Flora was proving to have a surprisingly practical bent. After a few encounters with a spectral bride—who had been drifting about the castle weeping ever since being jilted in 1217—Flora had come around to the opinion that spending her life grieving for Frederic would be a waste.

By midday, Mia was missing Charlie so much that she decided to fetch him and move back to Carrington House, on the grounds that Sir Richard was surely no longer a threat. Once downstairs, the innkeeper informed her that Edward was waiting in their private dining room, where luncheon would be served in a few minutes.

"Good day," she said, walking in the door.

Edward immediately stood, bowed, and kissed her hand. "You will be happy to know that a somewhat battered Sir Richard is now in custody of the justice of the peace, awaiting the Assizes," he said, guiding her to a seat.

A Lucibella heroine would feel horror at the mention of Sir Richard's condition, but Mia rather liked the idea that punishment had been served. "I am glad to hear it," she admitted. "I hope that you didn't suffer any damage?"

"Luckily not."

"Given those circumstances, I shall fetch Charlie immediately. I'd like to re-establish us at Carrington House without delay."

A throb of misery shot through her at the very idea of walking in the door of Vander's house. But she had to be strong.

She was her own woman, she told herself for the hundreth time that morning. She was not just a title— "duchess" or "wife," or even "daughter" or "sister."

She was Mia, and Lucibella too. And Charlie's mother. That would have to suffice.

After the meal, Edward went to settle accounts with the innkeeper, and she took herself out into the courtyard, tying on her bonnet as she walked. The moment she cleared the doorway, she heard a familiar whinny.

"Oh, for goodness' sake!" she exclaimed, unable to stop herself from smiling as Jafeer pranced over to her. "What are you doing here?" He looked tremendously pleased with himself. Before she could stop him, he caught her bonnet in his teeth and danced backward, shaking it as if he were playing a game.

Although Jafeer was saddled, and his reins were draped around the pommel, there was no one in sight. "Where is Vander?" she asked him, almost expecting the horse to answer.

Jafeer dropped the bonnet and came over. She stroked his nose as she looked around. The inn yard was deserted but for a carriage that stood on the far side of the yard, attended only by a slumbering coachman. Where were all the post-boys and grooms who generally lounged about, waiting for something to do? She narrowed her eyes. That snoring coachman had a distinct resemblance to Mulberry.

"Vander!" she called.

Instead of her husband, she heard a peal of boyish laughter, and Charlie hopped from the open door of the carriage. Jafeer gave an approving whinny.

"Darling!" She held out her arms. "What are *you* doing here?"

Charlie swung himself across the cobblestones, his entire face alight. "We've come to fetch you home!" he shouted.

"'We?' Is the duke with you?" Mia asked, pushing back the thick curl that had fallen over Charlie's face and dropping a kiss on his forehead.

"I have to recite a poem," he said, giving her a tight hug. "His Grace and I wrote it together. I am going to declaim it, the way Roman orators used to do."

Mia's breath caught when she saw Vander step from the carriage; then she looked quickly back at Charlie. He hopped up on the granite slab before the open door of the inn, and turned back to the open yard. With all the majesty of a young lord about to say something to Romans and countryman, Charlie announced, *"Roses are red, violets are blue—"*

An arm suddenly emerged from the shadowed darkness behind Charlie and wound around his throat. Mia screamed as a bloodied, disheveled Sir Richard shoved Charlie forward.

He was holding her child tightly against him, a

knife against Charlie's throat. The cultivated Elizabethan air that Sir Richard was so proud of had stripped
clean away, leaving a predator with savage eyes.

From the corner of her eye she saw Vander take
a careful step toward them. Mulberry suddenly
showed himself to be wide awake and leapt from his
seat.

"Sir Richard, what are you doing?" she cried,
hoping to draw his attention away from the men.

"Oh, merely thinking about killing a little gutter
rat," he answered. Horribly, his voice still had the
same cultivated tenor, as if he were speaking of tea
and toast rather than murder.

Charlie's eyes were wide and fixed on her. "Aunt
Mia," he said faintly. Another scream bubbled up in
her chest, but she managed to choke it down.

"Surely murder is an extreme solution?" Vander
asked. He now stood at Mia's side. Mulberry was
silently circling the yard so he could approach from
the rear.

"He's responsible for all of it," Sir Richard snarled.
"I have to leave the bloody country and it's all the
fault of this crippled little dunce, who should have
been drowned at birth." He gave Charlie a vicious
shake and the knife came dangerously close to the
child's throat.

"No!" Mia stumbled forward. "I am responsible.
It's my fault. Please, let Charlie go."

In answer to her movement, Sir Richard wrenched
the child's head farther back, placing the shining
edge of the knife blade just under his chin. She heard
Charlie's crutch strike the cobblestones, though she
didn't dare take her eyes from Sir Richard's face.

There had been more behind Sir Richard's perpet-
ual, ferocious lawsuits than she had realized. He was
cracked, utterly mad.

"Why Charlie?" she croaked. "Please! He's your nephew! He doesn't deserve this."

"*Now*," Vander barked.

To Mia's utter shock, Charlie's right arm darted up and back, and he stuck a little dagger into Sir Richard's arm. He probably didn't manage to do more than prick him, but Sir Richard's knife wavered, which gave Vander the second he needed: he exploded forward and wrenched Charlie free, spinning him away.

Sir Richard let out an enraged bellow, and lunged after them, knocking Mia to the ground. Charlie was already safely behind Vander, whose air of a savage warrior, ready to protect his family by ripping an enemy limb from limb, caused Sir Richard to freeze in his tracks.

Then, just as Mulberry sprang forward, Sir Richard veered left, grabbed Jafeer's pommel, vaulted into the saddle, and sent the stallion galloping out of the inn yard. With a curse, Mulberry charged through the gate after him.

For an instant none of them moved or spoke. Then: "He stole Jafeer!" Charlie shouted indignantly.

"He won't have him long," Vander said calmly. With one huge stride, he reached Mia and pulled her up and into his arms.

She couldn't bring herself to speak; she just leaned against his chest, eyes closed.

"Don't worry about Jafeer," she heard Vander say above her head. Had he dropped a kiss on her hair? "Sir Richard will sell him when he reaches the coast, but I'll offer a reward that will have every man in England looking for him."

Boots sounded on the cobblestones, and a disgruntled voice growled, "I hope to hell that wasn't Sir Richard Magruder."

"Charlie is too young to hear that sort of language," Mia said, opening her eyes.

"I apologize." Edward was looking with narrowed eyes at Vander's arms around her.

"Sir Richard has the justice of the peace for Berkshire in his pocket," Vander said. "Although that does not explain why he knew we could be found here."

"I expect that he was looking for me," Edward said. "He made a number of threats against me last night. After he was in custody, I told the sheriff that I would be staying here in case I was needed to testify."

Mulberry came back into the yard. "He's taken the road toward Dover," he said, panting. "Trying to get to France, I expect."

Vander nodded and turned to Edward. "If you will forgive me, Mr. Reeve, I should like to take my wife for a short drive."

The courtyard was silent for a long second.

"Right," Edward said. His voice was expressionless, but his eyes were bleak. "Charlie, old man, why don't you come inside with me?"

"Did you see what I did?" Charlie demanded. "The way I stabbed Sir Richard?" He didn't seem in the least shaken by the experience.

Vander moved away from Mia, picking up Charlie's crutch, which had apparently fallen in two pieces. She watched numbly as he screwed a little dagger into the crutch, where there had been no dagger before.

"It sounds as if you saved yourself," Edward told Charlie.

"No," he replied cheerfully, "the duke saved me. But I stabbed Sir Richard!" He took his crutch from Vander, stuck it under his arm, and started toward the inn door. Then he turned back. "You are coming back, aren't you?" he asked, the faintest quaver in his voice.

"Within the hour," Vander promised. That seemed enough for the boy. He swung away with Edward, the story tumbling out all over again.

"Sir Richard was about to kill Charlie," Mia moaned, swaying where she stood. "No, he couldn't have meant it! He is Charlie's *uncle*, his own blood relative!"

Vander picked her up and strode across the court-yard toward his carriage. Mia should have struggled. In a few minutes, she would definitely assert herself and become her own woman as she had planned.

But right now she was trembling from head to foot, and it felt wonderful to be held by a man of strength, a warrior who had protected her and her child.

"Sir Richard is mad," Vander said, seating him-self in the corner of the carriage and pulling her onto his lap, "and he may well have meant his threat. Apparently, my father posed a danger to me. I have no memory of it, but Chuffy says the duke periodi-cally tried to reach the nursery, and they had to put footmen on the door day and night."

"That's awful!" Mia choked. "Thank goodness your father didn't manage to injure you! I'm sure it would have broken his heart." Something in his eyes made her add firmly, "And thank goodness you didn't inherit his condition."

"I inherited his temper," Vander said flatly, thump-ing the roof to tell Mulberry that they were ready. "I used to break furniture, but these days the worst I do is occasionally engage in fisticuffs with Thorn."

The image of two beautiful men grappling with each other came to Mia but she pushed it away. "You would never injure someone in a rage," she replied with utter certainty. She leaned her cheek against the crook of his shoulder, soaking in his strength.

"But I do say things that I don't mean. I've been a bastard to you, Mia," Vander said, pulling away just enough so that their eyes met. "You're the most beautiful, intelligent woman I've ever met, and I have hurt your feelings. I'm sorry." The words were gruff, with an edge of ferocity.

She knew instinctively that Vander had never spoken words like this before. Mia swallowed hard. How could she reject him? But she had to.

"After I make love to you," Vander said, bringing one of her palms to his lips, "the only thing in my head is the desire to be inside you again, any way I can."

This was the hardest thing she'd ever done. "I can't," she whispered. It was what she'd dreamed of—but not in the right way. The aching tone in her voice was humiliating, and he remained silent, so she kept talking to fill the charged air. "It's not enough." Tears pricked her eyes. "I can't just be a woman in your bed."

Vander's voice sounded like a rusty gate. "My love for you has nothing to do with my bed."

"What did you say?" Mia gasped.

"I haven't loved many people, and I'm not very good at it. I loved my father, but he tried to kill me several times. I loved my mother, but I was caught between my parents, so I always felt as if I was betraying my father by being civil to her."

He paused, his eyes searching hers. "I love Thorn. I love India. Chuffy, of course. Charlie. And *you*. You most of all, Mia."

Mia's mind reeled. "But you said things that hurt me." That sounded like a petulant child. "You always called me 'Duchess,' as if I were merely the role, not the person."

"When I call you my duchess, I meant that you were mine to love, to hold, to make love to. That means— That means everything to me." She could hear the deep truth in his words. "Do you love me, Mia? If you don't, I'll walk away and I won't bother you again. I promise you that."

Her heart pounded as indecision swept through her.

"But if you do love me," he said, his hands tightening on hers, "I'll never let you go. Not until the end of our lives. Not if Reeve writes you a hundred love poems and says all the things I can't. Not if that blasted Frederic himself shows up. Do you understand?" His eyes burned into hers.

Biting her lip, she looked away. "It's not just—"

His hand cupped her cheek and gently turned her back to him. "There's only one important question, Mia. Do you love me?"

The words were a demand, yes, but she heard a trace of vulnerability as well, as if she were seeing deep inside him, a part of him that he had rarely if ever shown anyone. She couldn't lie to him.

"Yes," she said huskily. "I do love you, Vander. I'm yours."

"Thank God," he said, low and rough, pulling her close and burying his face in her hair. "I've been such a fool. Tell me that you will never leave me." His voice was raw with emotion, as if the ferocious warrior had finally been brought to his knees.

"Never." The word felt as right as sunshine, as right as Charlie's smile. "I love you," Mia told him again. "Always." What had seemed shameful was now a simple fact. "In fact, I have loved you since we were both fifteen years old, if you want the truth of it. Perhaps even before that."

"I don't deserve you," Vander said, pulling back, under control once more. "But I have this." He reached into his coat pocket, and brought out a handful of yellowed and torn scraps of paper.

The handwriting on them wasn't elegant, but it was earnest.

It was her handwriting.

"I fancied you back then," Vander said, spilling the poem into her hands. "Mostly your breasts, but I liked your laugh, and the way you made me less angry even if your father was in the room."

"Oh," Mia breathed.

"One of the worst things that can happen to a boy is to be mocked. I had had so much of it in school that by fifteen I had a very thin skin. After Rotter came in the library that day, I couldn't think straight. He said he was going to tell everyone. You would have been ruined, so I said the only thing I could think of to make him stop. Of course, it made everything worse."

Mia stared down at the scraps of paper. "You kept my poem all these years?"

Vander nodded. "I'd be damned if I would let my poem—the only poem anyone would ever write for me—be swept up like rubbish. So I took it."

Mia's smile was so large that it felt as if her face might crack. "Where has it been, all this time?"

"I put it in a box, and there it stayed. Until Thorn said I should make a grand gesture, and write a poem. Charlie helped me, but we both knew our verse was a failure. Then I thought of this."

"How on earth did you come up with the idea of wooing me with poetry?" She couldn't help giggling. The smile in her heart couldn't be kept down.

"I was desperate," he said simply. "But I have another plan in reserve as well, in case verse isn't persuasive enough."

Of course he did. "What is it?" she asked.

"Here." He handed her a letter. It was stamped and sealed and looked entirely ducal.

Mia crooked an eyebrow at him, and then broke it open. She read it once. Three times. "You're *blackmailing* me?"

He nodded. "If you leave me, I will send that letter to *The Times*. The entire world will know Lucibella Delicosa's real name. Everyone from the king to the littlest scullery maid reading by the kitchen fire."

She laughed, and let the letter fall.

"Do you know what I want most?" she whispered.

"I will give you anything I own, Mia. Anything you desire."

He meant it.

"A kiss," she breathed.

Vander surged forward, taking her mouth as he pushed her backward onto the carriage seat. His body felt wonderful on hers, and her blood sang with the pleasure of it, so much so that tears came to her eyes. Her arms curled around Vander as if her life depended on it.

"I love you," he told her again, just as one of his hands slid down and cupped her breast. Madame duBois's bodice gave way and Mia's breast spilled into his hand.

Vander bent his head and took her right nipple in his mouth. It felt so good that Mia whimpered, and her body went liquid, boneless. One of his hands had pulled up her skirts and was roaming, leaving quaking trails of fire, coming closer to where she most wanted him to be.

"I want you," he bit out.

A moan broke from Mia's throat. "Take me, then," she whispered. "I'm yours, Vander."

He stilled. "Say that again."

His eyes had changed from tenderness to something infinitely wilder. Still, he hesitated. "I do want you, Mia, but mostly I love you."

"You can have me," she said, giddy with the joy of it.

"Forever?"

"Forever."

There in the carriage, on a too-narrow seat, Vander came to her in heat and love and laughter. He came to her with respect and adoration.

After a while, things had become hot and sweaty. Mia's tangled hair was spilling onto the dirty floor. She was sweating behind her knees and other places too. She was gasping because Vander kept taking her mouth again, as if he could never have enough of her.

"I can't—not again. I—" she pleaded.

"Come, Mia," his voice was raw again. "Come with me."

She did.

A POEM WRITTEN BY THE DUKE OF PINDAR,
WITH THE INVALUABLE AID OF MASTER
CHARLES WALLACE CARRINGTON

Roses are Red, Violets are Blue.
Your duke respects you, and he loves you too.

Epilogue

The following morning, Gaunt had a terrible shock when he opened the front door: Jafeer was grazing on the front lawn below Mia's bedchamber window, riderless, his reins trailing.

Later that day, the sheriff paid a visit, reporting that Sir Richard Magruder, who had been erroneously released from custody, had stolen a horse, and was a fugitive from justice, had been thrown into a ditch in the midst of his flight, and had died instantly of a broken neck.

Jafeer, it seemed, had not enjoyed having Sir Richard on his back.

In fact, he much preferred his own herd; as long as his family was near, Jafeer was the most amenable of animals. In the year that followed, he went on many a painfully slow walk, during which he pranced around Lancelot and Mia. Yet no matter how ardently Jafeer courted her, Mia adamantly refused to ride a horse that size.

The following spring Her Grace changed her story, announcing that she didn't want to risk her unborn babe by riding a mount more energetic than Lancelot.

Two years after that, she declared that Flora became very irritable if separated from her mother for long periods, and so she meant to bring her on her daily ride. No one would trust Flora—who had her father's tumbling black hair and her mother's laugh—to a horse other than Lancelot.

Flora was followed in rapid order by Cuthbert (named after a beloved great-uncle) and by Edward (named after a special friend of his mother's); thus the Duchess of Pindar successfully avoided being thrust onto a monstrously tall horse for a long time.

By that point, Jafeer had won every race there was to win in all Great Britain, and he'd retired to stand at stud, a task which he took to with great enthusiasm.

Then, early one morning as the duke and duchess were lying about in bed after behaving in a fashion that would have shocked their nearest and dearest, His Grace pointed out that Lancelot was growing elderly, and probably would be happiest remaining in the stable.

Since anyone in the world could tell that Lancelot would, indeed, be happy never to leave his stall again, the duchess offered no counter argument. His Grace added that Jafeer wasn't *terribly* tall, and besides, all three of their offspring were dashing around on horses twice the height of the duchess.

Mia was draped halfway across her husband, tracing circles on his chest with one finger. "I simply can't believe the children all turned out to be such giants," she said with a sigh. "They were tiny babies, and now look at them."

Vander kissed her forehead. "They have your beauty and my height."

"Do you know, I think Bertie might become a novelist? He told me a story about something that happened at Eton with a perfect sense of timing."

Later that morning, Vander helped his wife onto Jafeer's back, much to Mulberry's astonishment. Though Mia showed a lamentable tendency to cling to the pommel and close her eyes—and Vander felt very strongly that all riders should keep their eyes open—they finally ambled down the path that led through the wood.

After that, there was never another horse for Mia.

If Mia had spent a great deal of energy avoiding Arabians, the same could not be said for Charlie. Just as Vander had predicted, Charlie quickly became the finest equestrian in five counties. He was fearless on the back of a horse, and could handle the most intractable of stallions.

At Eton, he had special permission to miss classes for various races, which at first caused not a little envy. But once the other boys came to understand that as long as young Lord Carrington rode for the equestrian team, Eton would not lose the Steeplechase Cup—a silver goblet that had been traded back and forth between Eton and Harrow for years—well, after that, no one begrudged him the missed classes or ever dared to call his lordship "Limpy" or "Peg-Legged Pete."

In fact, as Mia confided to her editor, Mr. William Bucknell—who had ceased to be Mr. Bucknell and become simply "Will" a few years before—it was as if her nephew had taken one look at the duke and decided to become Vander.

"Charlie has grown so muscled wrestling half-trained horses that he even looks like my husband; no woman notices his limp," Mia said. "And he talks like Vander as well. By all accounts, Miss Alicia Gretly, who is pretty enough to be one of my own heroines, is pining away for love of my nephew. But when I mentioned it to him, Charlie winced and said that when he took a wife he planned to chase her, rather than the other way around." She wrinkled her nose. "Precisely what Vander would have said at that age!"

Will Bucknell couldn't help laughing. It was the first day of his annual monthly visit to Rutherford Park, during which he edited the duchess' latest manuscript; that month was invariably the happiest of his year. "If he follows His Grace's pattern, Lord Carrington has a good ten years in which to find the right woman," he pointed out.

"It seems like only yesterday that he was a tiny boy, hopping around with his crutch," the duchess said with a sigh, picking up her quill. "I suppose we ought to start working; we've been gossiping for at least an hour."

Before Will could reply, the duke poked his head in the door. "Might I lure my wife away for a brief consultation on a matter of grave importance?"

Will watched with some interest. In his opinion, one of the reasons why the duchess' novels were being compared, in some circles, with Miss Jane Austen's, was because she took the joy that was so evident in her private life and shared some of it with her readers.

But Her Grace was shaking her head. "Off with you," she told her husband, blowing him a kiss. "No *consultations* until Will and I have finished at least ten pages."

After the duke closed the door behind him, Her Grace turned back with a wide, impish smile. "Did you see how peaceably he left? If you can believe it, my husband used to think that he could always get his way. It took me at least a year of marriage to disabuse him of that notion."

Will couldn't think of an appropriate response, so

he tapped the pile of manuscript pages that lay before him. "I suggest that before we look closely at any given scene, we discuss the fact that your hero, Lord Xavier Hawtrey, loses his memory after being thrown from a horse and no longer remembers his own wife."

"My readers will love it," the duchess said instantly. And defensively.

"I have no doubt of it," Will said, pitching his voice to a soothing tone. "But will they accept the fact that Lord Xavier miraculously remembers his wife's face only once he believes his evil second cousin has murdered her? I think your readers would prefer that he at least attempt to save her life. From good will, if not because of the family connection."

Her Grace sighed, and pulled the manuscript pages toward her. "I suppose you have a point. But we'll have to figure out how to keep the scene in which he throws himself off the cliff in the throes of guilt. Chuffy adores that plunge, and you know that Chuffy is my best critic."

Will chose his words carefully. "I am somewhat concerned that Lord Xavier would be dead before he could . . ."

And so it went.

If truth be told, the annual month during which Will Bucknell joined their family, editing her latest manuscript and arguing with Chuffy, was one of Her Grace's favorites in the year as well.

Though a woman who loves so dearly, and is so dearly loved in return, can find joy in almost every moment. Certainly in every month.

And definitely during every *consultation* with her husband.

Romancing a Career, in 1800 and Thereafter

This novel owes a great deal to its sources, but even more to the readers who have celebrated my work, encouraging me to write an (astonishing to me) twenty-four novels to date. In creating a female author of romance novels around the turn of the nineteenth century, I wanted not only to depict how much fun it can be to plot and write romance, but also to honor the authors of the time. For the most part, the authors' work is no longer in print, though their novels were enormously popular at the time. Authors like Sarah Scudgell Wilkinson supported themselves writing adventuresome fiction such as *The Fugitive Countess* (1807). Anna Maria Bennett began her long bestselling career with *Anna* (1785), whose first printing sold out in one day. The novels could be extremely lucrative: in 1796, Fanny Burney was paid 2,000 pounds for her novel *Camilla*, including its copyright, which would be over 100,000 in today's pounds. That doesn't mean their work was universally celebrated, of course. The review that plagued Mia so much that she can recite it from memory was real; it was published in *Graham's Lady's Magazine* in 1848, and the novel exhibiting "vulgar depravity and unnatural horrors" was Emily Brontë's *Wuthering Heights*.

I invented the publishing firm of Brandy, Bucknell & Bendal, but in fact, the publisher of Lucibella's books would likely have been Minerva Press. William Lane established the press in 1790 and thereafter published a constant stream of fiction, as well as operating a circulating library. He specialized in gothic horror-romance novels and would have welcomed Lucibella's heroines-in-peril. While Lucibella's prose echoes novels at the time, I took the inheritance plot of *An Angel's Form and a Devil's Heart* (a real novel, written by Selina Davenport and published by Minerva in 1818) from a Dorothy Parker short story called "The Standard of Living."

To ensure they were accessible to the middle and working classes, novels of this type were typically bound in cardboard with leather labels on the spines. Jane Austen's *Emma* (1816), for example, first appeared with "plain gray boards" and a title label made from stamped morocco leather. But Chuffy's more luxurious bindings existed as well: the foremost bookbinder at the time was Roger Payne, who re-bound volumes in Russian leather with gold borders, embedded pearls, and even (on occasion) silk embroidery that reflected the book's contents.

If Mia's character was inspired by late eighteenth- and early nineteenth-century female novelists, Sir Cuthbert owes his appearance and cheerful nature to one of Shakespeare's great characters, Sir Toby Belch in *Twelfth Night*. Chuffy mischievously quotes from that play, as Mia recognizes, but my greater hope is that he brings with him the reckless joie de vivre of his predecessor. Talking of quotations, Mia's much maligned poetry borrows from some of Percy Bysshe Shelley's romantic poetry. Finally, young Master Charles Wallace possesses something of the preter-natural intelligence of Madeleine L'Engle's namesake character in *A Wrinkle in Time*, though arguably Char-lie owes more to Charles Dickens's earnest and capti-vating disabled child, Tiny Tim.

Seductive scoundrel Edward Reeve needs a wife: a lady whose perfect reputation will persuade society to overlook his questionable past. The moment he meets Lady Regina Cholmondeley-ffynche, he knows that she is the one he wants.

But Regina would never marry a man like Ward. As the author of a wildly popular etiquette column, she can't afford to risk society's disapproval . . . no matter how tempting she might find the notorious charmer's advances.

Determined to win the hand—and heart—of the spirited woman who has bewitched him, Ward will take any risk to convince Regina they were meant to be together.

He promises her heaven . . .
She gives him seven minutes.

Pre-order
Seven Minutes in Heaven
now!

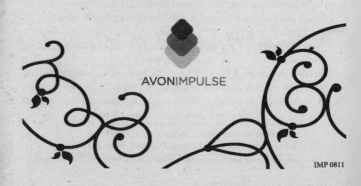